MW00617060

PRAISE FOR

BURYING THE PAWN

"*Burying the Pawn* serves up captivating characters and a riveting plot that spans the globe. But the novel does more than that: It performs a public service by delving into education reform, business ethics, and the role of humility in American society. Read this enjoyable and research-based novel to learn more about how school choice can help millions of disadvantaged Americans reach their full potential."

—**Mike Huckabee,** former governor of Arkansas
and host of *Huckabee*

"*Burying the Pawn* felt like it was written for me. Immigrating to America, the entrepreneurial experience, kids with learning disabilities, and college sports are things I've lived myself. Even so, I found the novel unpredictable. I loved how it took me around the world. What surprised me was how much I cared about the main characters. They were like good friends, especially Zeb and Leo. I see aspects of them in my own two sons. Beyond that, I learned a lot about education reform, economics, and life at a major Southern university. I was sad when the novel ended."

—**Luis Paz,** president of Inovexia Partners

"Reading *Burying the Pawn* was fascinating journey for me. Ostensibly, the novel highlights three bright and unique individuals, each one learning to compensate for his or her learning disabilities and mental health challenges. In reality, however, the novel is about their search for a meaningful life. . . .

I recommend reading this book, perhaps for one very simple reason: It provides hope to our society and, without embarrassment, shows that determination and faith in self are values found deep within each of us. We need only trust and believe in ourselves and our own self-worth."

—Rabbi Norman S. Lipson, founder and rabbi emeritus
of Temple Dor Dorim, Weston, FL

"*Burying the Pawn* is a wide-ranging novel that traces the intersecting lives of three disparate individuals who were challenged by learning disabilities and mental health issues during childhood: Zeb, a Jewish man from North Carolina; Kiara, the daughter of Black Caribbean immigrants; and Leo, who grew up with violence in Venezuela. Initially, their considerable strengths are overwhelmed by their disabilities and some bad decisions, but ultimately the novel is hopeful, as it illustrates, without preaching, how education reform can help special-needs people meet their potential. . . .

Highly recommended for anyone interested in education reform, adventure travel, and learning disabilities."

—Brian Harris, playwright and author
of *Monster Plays* and *Calling Mr. Beige*

BURYING
THE
PAWN

A NOVEL

BURYING THE PAWN

JONATHAN KAUFMAN

RIVER GROVE
BOOKS

This book is a work of fiction. Names, characters, businesses, organizations, places, events, and incidents are either a product of the author's imagination or are used fictitiously. Any resemblance to actual persons, living or dead, events, or locales is entirely coincidental.

Published by River Grove Books
Austin, TX
www.rivergrovebooks.com

Copyright © 2023 Jonathan A. Kaufman

All rights reserved.

Thank you for purchasing an authorized edition of this book and for complying with copyright law. No part of this book may be reproduced, stored in a retrieval system, or transmitted by any means, electronic, mechanical, photocopying, recording, or otherwise, without written permission from the copyright holder.

Distributed by River Grove Books

Design and composition by Greenleaf Book Group
Cover design by Greenleaf Book Group
Cover images: ©iStockphoto/Luchito Sangsoko

Publisher's Cataloging-in-Publication data is available.

Print ISBN: 978-1-63299-689-3

eBook ISBN: 978-1-63299-690-9

First Edition

To all those who learn differently: You have so much to offer this world and deserve every opportunity to fulfill your potential.

And to my wife and parents, who have enriched my life immeasurably and made so many things possible.

CONTENTS

1

AFLOAT

hapel Hill, North Carolina, 2016. Teresa sat at her desk at International Expeditions, looking down onto Franklin Street, frowning at the splendor. The red, orange, and gold leaves of the willow oak trees made the powder-blue sky look more intense. College students bounced along the sidewalks, past historic homes and quaint shops, their enthusiasm energizing the town. Most years she couldn't get enough. Not now: "Blue Heaven" had no business flaunting its magic—not when International Expeditions' prospects were so dire.

The familiar rhythm of Zeb's boots pounding up the staircase drew her attention away from the window. *About time*, she thought, glancing toward the entrance of the office. They both needed to be pedaling harder, especially after the dismal sales and pipeline numbers he'd recently shared. This wasn't just about the company or their clients. They had a larger responsibility—to the public, to America even. He'd taught her that.

The door burst open, and Zeb dashed to his office without a word or nod to her. *Sweet. The potted-plant treatment.* He'd always been passionate and frenetic—more so since the downturn—but he'd dialed up his intensity another couple of notches. She shrugged. Whatever the latest crisis, it was above her pay grade—at least until he beckoned.

"I'm here if you need me," Teresa called.

To push the doubts from her mind, Teresa forced herself to "come into the present," as her shrink had advised. Eyeballing a trip proposal, she unleashed a flurry of keystrokes, transposing the images of the Jain priest and Royal Bengal tiger. *Better!* No need to move Mount Everest or the hot-air ballooning. One of these days *she* would explore India and Nepal—not just play the hapless kid outside the candy store, forever looking in on other peoples' adventures. She moved to the pricing section and slapped 45 percent onto the net cost. No sweat—clients understood they were getting good value, even at these prices. How could they not? Tracking tigers from the back of an elephant, glacier trekking in Patagonia—the world was one big playpen. For some.

"Did you make it to Ye Olde?" she asked.

"What do you think?"

It *was* a dumb question. Still, Zeb's crankiness rankled, because she knew he'd surely been the picture of joviality earlier that day as he camped out with his buddies at Ye Olde Waffle Shoppe, feasting on a western omelet, hash browns, and too much iced tea. These Wednesday mornings were sacred, his one indulgence, no matter the circumstances. It was always the same. The guys would crack jokes, charm the waitress, and obsess over Tar Heel basketball, dissecting matchups with Duke and other ACC foes. Zeb would overtip the server and then schlep his overly caffeinated self to Torah study, where, according to what she'd heard, his enthusiasm, clarity of thought, and unique viewpoints enlivened the discussion of Bible passages. When class ended, Zeb's persona would morph. Probably mindful of his secular duties, he became hyperfocused, remaining that way until the end of the workday, after which he reverted to affability. *He's always been peculiar and probably won't change,* Teresa thought.

Zeb reappeared. He dropped a sealed envelope in front of her, grabbed the mail, and turned back toward his office.

"And a hearty good morning to you, too!" she needled. "How was Bible study?"

Zeb spun around. "Not Bible—*Torah*. That's T-O-R-A-H," he enunciated with mounting volume. "Jeez, I thought *I* was the one with a learning disability."

"Must have slipped my mind," she said. "I must say, Torah's doing wonders for your spirituality. Perspective, too." Being his lone, indispensable employee had its benefits.

"Perspective this: ARC revoked our license. I got the call on the way over."

"What the hell?!" she said, her eyes bulging. "Were our sales too low?"

"No, it was bureaucratic shit. Sales reports being late, not submitting a $60,000 bond."

She shook her head sympathetically. "Out of the blue, isn't it?"

"Yup, my reports are always late. And they jacked up my bond from $20,000. I can't afford it. I'm behind on rent as it is."

"Awesome—a tour operator who can't issue air tickets. That's like an ice cream vendor with no chocolate. What happened?"

"Someone must've put a bug in ARC's ear," he replied. "Probably some of the big boys."

"After the conference?" Teresa finished her coffee and put the mug down.

He nodded.

"Next time you tilt at windmills, be more diplomatic."

Zeb stared down at his feet, crestfallen. Sometimes Zeb looked a bit like Bruce Springsteen in the 1970s—wiry, doleful, as if he needed the music to stop more of his hair from turning gray.

"Let's not get sidetracked," he said. "What else is going on?"

Teresa massaged her temples. *Is he serious?* The saboteurs had played him, the regulators had pounced, and now they were on life support.

What had he expected? Poking industry giants in the eye publicly, without preparing for pushback, was classic Zeb. Did he *really* think the scoundrels would forfeit their gravy train and yield to a small-fry tour operator who hadn't marshaled support for his ideas?

"Not much," she managed. "Mrs. Nazarian called to thank you for the Armenian heritage itinerary. Said it was wonderfully crafted. They look forward to doing it in the future."

"In the future?"

"They're now looking for a more conventional tour—Budapest, Vienna, and Prague. For next month."

"Sonofabitch!" Zeb said. "She told me Armenia was ninety-nine percent definite, barring an act of God. All that time down the drain." He was pacing. "We should send Mrs. Nazarian to friggin' Turkey. If she wants plain vanilla, tell her to call AAA. I'm not wasting another second on that woman."

Teresa rose to her feet, wide-eyed. "You're seriously turning down *eighteen people*? We're talking luxury hotels for thirteen nights and business-class airfare. I need my paycheck, and I don't see any leads in the hopper."

"Then do it yourself," he said, zinging a rubber band into the wall. "I'm done with them."

"Can you take over Livingstone 1866? That one's a doozy."

"Yup."

"And, Zeb, that Turkey comment was beneath you. Your rabbi would be disappointed."

A sheepish smile tugged at his lips. "Jeez, I had to hire the one high school grad in America who's an expert on the Armenian genocide." His grin faded. "You're right, of course. I'm sorry. . . . Now, if that's enough contrition for you and the rabbi, I better go find an air consolidator."

"Good idea," she said gently. "By the way, don't forget, your tango lesson was canceled, and I'm leaving at four thirty. I promised Jim a home-cooked dinner—for once."

"Smart woman. Don't make the same mistake I did."

Zeb left the office, eyes downcast.

Teresa opened the sealed envelope he'd given her. Two tickets—his tickets—to the UNC–Virginia football game. She felt a lump in her throat.

The same mistake. Teresa rubbed the wedding band that was still on her finger. Years of commitment to International Expeditions had taken their toll. Was there enough to show for it?

Certainly their offerings were world-class. Zeb invested countless hours—not to mention his heart and brain—into every expedition. His creations were unique masterpieces of research and artistry. Leading historians and geographers had said as much. He was no more a "travel agent" than he was a sheepherder. What he had accomplished was extraordinary, starting with his upscale soft adventures and then, later, with his historical expeditions and genealogy tours. Not that she would feed his male ego by saying so.

Zeb also had vision, and it extended well beyond travel. Americans needed what he was fighting for, whether they knew it yet or not. Industry leaders and regulators were fools, all too shortsighted to see that *he* was their best chance for prospering long-term.

All of which made Zeb's obtuseness so tragic when it came to business. Obsessing over Mrs. Nazarian's change of plans—and *not* the lost ARC license—was exhibit A. Then there was the fact that he squandered market opportunities on a regular basis, even when spotting them first. He ignored signals, trusting only his own instincts on whether a product added enough value. How many times had he said it? "Whether a tour sells well or not means little compared to whether it enlightens the people who take it." His expeditions were meant to be continuing education, and, just as students couldn't be expected to formulate their own curriculums, travelers often had no clue what was best for them. They *weren't* always right.

As if that mindset weren't enough of a roadblock, Zeb went ballistic whenever he encountered unethical or discourteous behavior, apparently oblivious to his own crabbiness. He ignored administrative work to the point of gross negligence, a point that had been twice documented by the IRS and just now by the Airlines Reporting Corporation. He was allergic to making money, better suited for a think-tank job where he could analyze and create to his heart's content without the burden of financial solvency.

Yes, he was exasperating, but he needed a mother hen. *No one aside from my sweetheart son, Wylie, will ever need me as much.*

As for now—how to salvage the Nazarian booking?

Teresa turned onto Columbia Street, mindful of the pedestrians who always had the right-of-way. A placard in front of Ackland Art Museum touted a new Rembrandt exhibit. She made a mental note to visit it as she swerved to avoid a smartphone-engaged Greek crossing to Fraternity Court. She was approaching her favorite part of town. Visitors raved about Franklin, the gorgeous main drag, but for Teresa, the true heart of Chapel Hill lay here on Cameron Avenue.

The street was a feast for the eyes, lined with willow oak trees and ivy-covered brick buildings. It skirted the main quad of UNC and buzzed with activity. Backpack-toting students scurried to and from classes. Some took sun, read, or napped on the grassy expanses. Others played Frisbee, nabbing disks from frisky dogs set free by lecturing professors. Guitarists and harmonica players chilled out, practicing for evening gigs at Cat's Cradle. Megaphone-carrying activists strode toward the Pit, set to unleash their powers of persuasion. Professors held court on the lawn, shaded by magnolia, poplar, oak, and gum trees. Smartphones seemed somehow less ubiquitous.

Teresa paused at the Phillips Hall crosswalk. Memories of her own teenage years engulfed her as two coeds walked by. As a local high school student, she had dreamed of going to college here, with the goodies so tantalizingly close. What she hadn't witnessed firsthand she'd heard about from older friends who'd made it already. Beckoning her were the rollicking all-campus parties, where live bands played covers of the Police, U2, and REM, and where Miller Lite trucks dispensed free beer. She would sit courtside at Carmichael Auditorium, her face adorned with Tar Heel logos. She and the other student crazies would cheer for Michael Jordan, James Worthy, and Sam Perkins, and hurl abuse at Ralph Sampson and Danny Ferry—until Dean Smith told them to cut it out.

She would storm Franklin Street, along with 45,000 other fans, after another national championship. In winter she would attend a toga party at McIver or Alderman, cackling as a lover boy, wearing only sneakers and underwear, traipsed through the snow back to his own dorm, cussing out long-gone buddies. She would road-trip to Myrtle Beach, shag in the sand to "Miss Grace" and "My Girl," and watch dumbasses scale the walls at Crazy Zacks to avoid paying the two-dollar cover charge.

On football Saturdays she would throw on her favorite sweater and add-a-beads, feel the crisp fall air, attend tailgate parties, smuggle flasks of Jim Beam into Kenan Stadium, and watch the Tar Heels romp over conference foes. She would go to after-game parties at Fraternity Court and maybe meet a nice guy. She'd work part-time at Cat's Cradle and listen to the hottest new bands in the country for free. Late night she would devour grilled cheeses at Hector's and scarf down chicken-and-cheese biscuits at Time Out, picking on the scrappy "bones" if money was tight.

Alas, none of that was destined to be. As the Arboretum faded from view, Teresa sighed heavily. Ahead, dozens of culture freaks ambled toward Paul Green Theatre, as she should have been doing these past fifteen years. But her dreams of majoring in English and the dramatic arts and then becoming a playwright had all been extinguished. It still hurt her to see professors chatting with students over beers at Spanky's. What nuggets of wisdom had she missed?

Pulling into her driveway, Teresa expunged all negativity. She had salvaged a decent life for herself: She had an affectionate son, a doting husband, and a house in the "Southern Part of Heaven." Things could be much worse.

A friend of hers, a transplanted New Englander, had once said Chapel Hill's infamous heaven moniker was nauseating. It supposedly revealed how provincial and self-satisfied Carolinians were. "Maybe so, but heaven is heaven," she'd responded before marching off. Thousands of out-of-staters agreed, having voted with their feet. But for whatever reason, for Teresa personally, none of her life here worked without International Expeditions and her nutcase boss. They *needed* to stay afloat.

Teresa smirked. Surely, there was no harm in asking Zeb to cure her of her narrow-mindedness—a familiarization trip to Machu Picchu might just do the trick. "'Professional development' has such a nice ring to it," she said, before opening the door to a slobbering Labrador and a smiling husband.

2

THE RIDE

estern Venezuela, 2017. Two dozen ranchers rode westward from the cattle town of Machiques. They followed a looping trail that led to the Colombian border and back to town again. The sun was high in the sky, its rays scorching them, but they were used to it, and any further delay would mean missing the evening parade and festival.

The farmers appeared fit and strong. Unlike most Venezuelans, they produced their own meat and milk, and grew their own yucca and plantains. But their faces were wrinkled from constant exposure to weather and stress. As if to offset that, they donned stylish cowboy hats, western shirts and boots, and rode Paso Finos. As the group made their way up the trail, one rider, distinguishable from the rest by his blond hair, citified clothes, and youthful appearance, suddenly fell from his mount. Everyone came to a halt.

Leonardo lay sprawled sideways across the trail. Countless eyes gawked at him. This was not how he had envisioned his homecoming. But it was hardly a shock to him. Childhood memories flooded his mind. Those long-ago humiliations had dwarfed even this. Not that any of these ranchers had ever seen a sober man tumble from such a smooth-riding mare. Quite a feat, he had to admit.

Leonardo's back and ribs ached. Looking upward, he squinted and raised a bloodied hand to block the sun's rays and the incredulous glances of those around him, particularly Federico's.

"*Que mamita!*" Federico thundered, playfully contributing to his best friend's emasculation. "We haven't even downed our first beer, and our gringo-wannabe falls like a sack of arepas."

As a kid, Leo had been struck by how loudly his fellow *Maracuchos* chattered. Nearly all residents of Venezuela's second-largest city spoke at decibel levels that were off-putting to most outside the region. Profanity flowed freely. The joshing—though good-natured and comical—took getting used to, even for a returning expatriate. Folks from Machiques weren't normally so voluble, but Federico seemed carried away by the occasion.

Federico dismounted, pulled Leo to his feet, and gave him a bear hug, precipitating a cascade of whistles. *Sweet*, Leo thought. Some found returning home to be a source of comfort, but he didn't. He'd always felt out of sync. In America Leo had propelled himself to a different station, escaped the discomfiture of his youth. Here the past reasserted itself, this latest indignity puncturing his self-assurance. Without Federico the visit would have been unbearable.

Leonardo ambled to his horse and mounted it. Celebrating La Virgen del Carmen was serious business, and the ranchers were clearly hankering to leave. Why the patroness of seamen and fishermen held so much sway this far inland wasn't clear to Leo. Maybe they just needed to celebrate something, *anything*. Times were hard in Venezuela. But the way the riders were bantering with one another made it seem as if they weren't enduring the world's worst economy. Leo found himself howling with laughter at their inventive expressions. Humor seemed to be palliative, a kind of coping mechanism.

An elderly man riding a donkey sneered at one of the jokesters.

"You joke about everything," he said in Spanish. "Sixty percent of your countrymen are now skipping meals because they can't afford to eat. How about a little respect?"

The young man smirked. "Hey, the 'Maduro Diet' has benefits. Yesterday you were moaning about having no toilet paper. You don't *need* any if there's no food!"

Leo tuned out the politics. He hadn't escaped the concrete jungle to wallow in—or argue about—tragedies beyond his control. So he inhaled the fresh air, savored the green landscape, and relished the exercise.

"The *viejito's* got a point," Federico said to the young man. "If your *mamá* were here, you'd be singing a different tune."

Another smart-ass took up the mantle. "*Chavismo* is wonderful. It gives us options. We can choose between two meals a day or one meal plus toothpaste. On average we've only lost eleven kilos."

A female rider pulled even with them. "Yeah, 'from each according to his ability, to each according to his need!'" She grinned, apparently taken with her own erudition.

"Fools," the old man mumbled.

The young man cackled back. "Who's the bigger fool? Someone who believes Maduro will be booted out by rigged elections, corrupt generals, or the gringos? Or someone who sees the world as it is and goes riding and drinking with his pals while he still can? Rosaries are the real foolishness."

"No doubt," the woman said. "Religion is the opiate of the masses."

They traversed a hacienda that had been expropriated by the Chavez government, ostensibly because of underutilization. It remained idle. A rancher griped about the latest price controls on meat and milk, another about import restrictions that prevented him from getting machinery, spare parts, and livestock vaccines. Crime kept several ranchers from leaving their haciendas without hired guards; even then, they varied their driving routes and schedules to evade kidnappers and FARC guerrillas. One of the riders fretted about what would happen when the government carried out its firearms confiscation policy.

Sweat ran down Leo's spine, and his quadriceps were working overtime to keep him astride. If nothing else, he would stay in his damn saddle. The first watering hole couldn't be far off. There they would be joined by revelers arriving by vehicle. Everyone would toast La Virgen with ice-cold Polar and whiskey.

Federico approached. "Leo, what's your take on the gringos intervening? Any chance?"

Thanks, but no thanks, Leo thought. He would not be shedding his low profile. Speaking his mind had served him well in America; here he'd come across as a smarty-pants. Being a turncoat, a naturalized American, would only make matters worse. Yes, Venezuelans were traditionally pro-American, but dire circumstances and Chavista propaganda had strained those attitudes.

"I don't know," Leo said. "Your guess is as good as mine."

"Federico, it seems your favorite Yanqui is a lightweight in the brain, as well as in the saddle!" a big-hat rancher said. "Maybe he should—"

"It depends on what you mean by intervention," Leo interjected. "More economic sanctions and moral support, absolutely. Military intervention, no chance. That window passed when America became energy self-sufficient. Because of fracking, America has more shale oil and natural gas than they can consume. They're exporting tons."

Now can they just shut up and ride? Leo thought.

"It's always about the dollars," the big-hat man said. "What happens when oil supplies increase so much that prices drop, and fracking isn't economical? Supplies will drop, won't they?" He smirked.

The Venezuelan economy was so one-dimensional that many *Maracuchos* had become economically literate as a matter of necessity, Leo knew. This particular asshole clearly fancied himself Milton Friedman.

"Nope, not at all," Leonardo said. "The administration is opening up ninety percent of U.S. coastal waters to drilling—everywhere except Florida. That means way more land and shallow-water drilling, which are cheaper than fracking. The price cycle won't go away, but America will no longer rely on Venezuelan oil. Stick to milking cows, my friend."

"But don't American interests go beyond oil?" the woman asked. "You know, keeping the Russians and Chinese at bay, controlling the drug cartels."

"Absolutely," Leo said. *The brunette is way more attractive when she isn't quoting Marx.* "Americans still fear the spread of communism, especially in this hemisphere."

"And what about preventing a humanitarian disaster?" she pressed. "If America can give Haiti billions for an earthquake, why not help us? Don't they know if we're left to starve here it'll create a refugee crisis? What will happen then, when we're at their borders, begging to be let in?"

The ramshackle watering hole came into view, and a rancher roared, "*Cerveza!*" Leonardo exhaled deeply as the group's attention was diverted to lighter matters.

No sooner had the group tied up their horses and grabbed a few tables in the bar than the old beat-up pickups started to arrive, fitted with shiny speakers blasting reggaeton. Leo was tipping back bottles with Federico when the swarm descended. And to think this was all just the prelude to the parade—floats, Vallenato bands, dancing, to say nothing of the cattle and horse exhibition.

"And so?" came a voice from next to their table.

It was the eye-catching Marxist. She was nothing if not persistent.

"The truth is, starvation in Caracas doesn't get airplay in Richmond, Virginia," Leo told her, picking up their conversation from where they'd left it. "The plight of people here isn't a big deal for most Americans. There's sympathy but no *urgency*."

There was grumbling, so Leo felt forced to expand. "For politicians, the equation is different. It's no coincidence that Florida is the one state exempt from offshore drilling. It's a swing state in presidential elections. Whoever wins Florida has the inside track. Trump beat Clinton by only 113,000 votes in Florida. There are 225,000 Venezuelans living there, and that number's growing fast. Which means politicians all pay close attention to Venezuela if they want to win in Florida."

Federico set down his Polar. "*Coño*, our vice president hobnobs with Hezbollah and the Iranians. They've killed many Americans. Our narco-traffickers run wild. There's electoral fraud, censorship of the press. I expected a stronger response from los Estados Unidos."

Leo nodded. "Remember, America has a spotty history of intervening in Latin America. Diplomats are worried about damaging relations."

"The Colossus of the North—damned if they do, damned if they don't," the brainy brunette said, seemingly without sarcasm. She had lost her revolutionary veneer. "Their $20 trillion national debt can't help either."

A flurry of profanity made it clear that empathy for the superpower was in short supply.

"How about supporting the opposition?" Federico said.

"They're too splintered."

"Then it's up to the generals and colonels," the old man said. "After Barlovento, I pray they remember their duty. Besides, oil is down to fifty-five dollars a barrel. Maduro can't keep paying them off."

"Barlovento?" Leo said.

Federico caught his friend up, describing how Maduro's death squads had massacred forty-four political opponents from the Caracas slums—torturing them, chopping off their heads, and burying them in a mass grave.

A waiter approached and then backed away after seeing the patrons' horrified expressions. "It's grotesque, I know, to look for silver linings in such a thing," the woman said, "but the executions hurt Maduro's popularity with his base." She raised her Regional Light. "Here's to defections by the generals!" Bottles clinked.

"To them showing patriotism!"

"To them taking on the Cubans!"

The cute Marxist leaned over and whispered into Leo's ear, "And to you munching on as many *tequeños* as you wanted, no matter how many bathrooms you had left to clean."

Leo froze, staring at her wide-eyed. His mind traveled back decades to his teenage years, when he had toiled as a janitor at the country club. The unlikeliest of beauties had defended him one afternoon against an unassailable club member, her own boyfriend. Was this really her?

A young man burst into the bar. "Is Señor Bello here?" he asked breathlessly. Surveying the patrons, he approached the only blond man there. The ranchers fell silent. "I'm sorry to interrupt but—"

"It's okay," Leo replied swiftly, standing. Taking his elbow, Leo led the man to an empty corner of the bar. "What is it, Diego?"

"A Federal Express package arrived for you—from America," Diego replied. "They wanted me to find you in case it's urgent."

"I'm glad you did. Let's go." He headed toward the door, shrugging at Federico and the Marxist before following Diego out the door.

A simple day of fresh air and exercise, Leo thought. *Yeah, right.*

3

LAZY

hapel Hill, North Carolina, 2016. Two teams stalked each other through Duke Forest, treading lightly, listening intently, and taking cover behind trees. Occasionally they came into clearings or scampered around man-made barriers and obstacles. One team—a male Army ranger and an elite female athlete, Kiara—wore red jerseys, safety goggles, and body armor. She and her partner toted M16 paintball rifles as they approached to within sixty yards of the flag they coveted. The second team, two male Army rangers wearing blue jerseys, advanced toward the target from the left.

Kiara signaled to her partner, and just minutes later he splattered a blue jersey with paint. She leapt from the platform and hit the ground running, her thighs pumping like pistons. She was chewing up yards the way she'd done back in college. She stopped abruptly, ducking behind two barrels. Twenty yards of open terrain lay between her and the flag. She took off again along the flank, but a flurry of paintballs erupted in front of her. A secret sentry was there to defend against either team. *Sweet*, she thought. *That'll be one more feather in my cap*. Kiara zigged to the left, took four strides, and zagged right. Pivoting, she dropped to the ground and unleashed her own barrage of paintballs. Bull's-eye—just like a game-winning *golazo*!

Kiara dashed the final ten yards, leaped onto the base, and grabbed the flag. Hoisting it and yelling triumphantly, she pointed to her teammate to acknowledge the assist. Her Friday morning routine complete, she could now turn to her professional duties. Thankfully she hadn't lost, so there was no need to keep her patients waiting as she played another round.

On her way to the office, Kiara merged from Highway 15-501 onto Franklin Street. Smiling didn't come naturally to her, so it tickled her to know that she beamed every time she drove up this serpentine road—past the antebellum houses, under the canopy formed by magnificent oak trees, and onto the historic campus. Years ago she'd taken this very route in a taxi, and the experience led her to forgo the Ivies. The driver, a fellow African American, had sensed her mounting wonderment and pointed out all sorts of gems: flower ladies, street performers, Thai and Indian restaurants, the Intimate Bookshop, Carolina Coffee Shop, Cat's Cradle nightclub, Sutton's Drug Store, Morehead Planetarium, and the hilly UNC campus. All set amid trees, the ubiquitous trees. A South Florida girl, Kiara had soaked in everything like a child beholding Christmas presents. She wasn't the dreamy type, but there were times—even now—when Chapel Hill rendered her speechless.

Kiara entered her office through the back and, to her surprise, was approached by her assistant, Vicki. Normally, Vicki waited until late morning to talk to her; by that time she could be sure "the boss woman" had downed her second cup of java. This morning it seemed Vicki had noticed the sparse splotches of paint on Kiara's outfit, or maybe her look of satisfaction, and taken a calculated risk.

"I take it you won," Vicki said.

"We eviscerated them." Kiara sighed. "It was so invigorating."

"Said like a true healer. The staff will be relieved to know."

"Got any updates?"

"Yes. Patty's been working with Carmen Escobar, the first grader, since eight thirty. She's got two more tests to administer. You're meeting with the Murphys at ten thirty to go over Owen's results."

"Cool. I'll take a quick shower."

"Please, doc, not *too* quick." Vicki grinned. "That aroma isn't good for morale."

"The fragrance of victory." It was nice that Vicki could finally tease her without feeling disrespectful. As it should be.

Twenty minutes later, Vicki poked her head back into Kiara's office. "Mrs. Murphy has arrived."

"Alone?"

"Yes."

Kiara scowled and shook her head in disgust. "I'll be out in a minute." Massaging her temples, she tried to focus on what she loved about her job. Psycho-educational assessments allowed her to play detective—to find the root causes of kids' learning problems—and propose solutions. Interventional counseling gave her enough human interaction that she didn't feel like a radiologist but not so much that it drove her crazy. Researching Fragile X and other sexy genetic topics provided her with ample intellectual stimulation, but making nice with insufferable parents sucked, without a doubt. Winning Miss Congeniality had never been her goal. She was not here to make friends.

She escorted the fashionably dressed Mrs. Murphy to her office. "Please, make yourself comfortable."

"Thank you, Dr. Battle."

Kiara exhaled deeply and braced herself for the encounter. Owen had only avoided getting expelled from school because his parents had agreed to this evaluation. They had done so grudgingly, probably to preserve their social standing. At their first appointment the Murphys had set about taking charge, as they were evidently accustomed to doing. A federal prosecutor, Mr. Murphy had "done his research," latching onto the diagnosis du jour. She had pushed back, half joking and half fed up with his presumptions, "I'll have to charge you more if I have to change your mind."

Mrs. Murphy had insisted Owen be administered a particular test, to which she had responded, "There are few perks in my job, but one of them is *I* get to pick the tests." Fireworks had been averted for the moment, but tension lingered. Mr. Murphy had dispensed more nuggets on his way out: Owen "needed to buck up and get his act together," because he'd been "given everything on a silver platter."

"Your comments are duly noted," Kiara had responded, clenching her fists, "but let's see how the eval comes out. We'll talk in three weeks."

And now, of course, the big shot was MIA. Mrs. Murphy seemed out of sorts but determined to press on.

"Okay," Kiara began. "So we conducted a battery of tests on Owen, and we also collected questionnaires from you and his teachers. We've analyzed the results, and it seems—"

"Let me guess: Owen's a bright kid who's lazy as hell."

"You're partly right," Kiara replied patiently. "Owen *is* bright. But he's certainly not lazy."

Mrs. Murphy raised her eyebrows.

"There is no such thing as a lazy kid," Kiara said. "Some kids *seem* lazy. No one likes to be confronted with their own failures every single day. When someone tries and fails repeatedly at a task, they feel helpless. Eventually, they give up trying."

"That feel-good theory may apply to other kids but not Owen," the boy's mother responded. "He had decent grades through sixth grade, no Ds or Fs. He didn't suddenly turn stupid and then stop trying."

Kiara recoiled. The s-word stung since she had once been branded a slow learner herself. "As I said," she continued, composure in check. "Owen's cognitive abilities aren't below average. He excels in a number of—"

"Exactly! He's no dummy. He's just hanging around bad kids. The school has too many of them. I don't need to tell you how marijuana kills motivation. Same with video games. He's *addicted*."

Kiara rubbed her forehead. *I need to keep it civil.* The Psychology Board had already warned her once—next time she might not be so lucky. "With all due respect, Mrs. Murphy, I need you to hear me out. These are complicated issues and need to be examined in full. Or, if you prefer, you and Mr. Murphy can study the report at home and call me with any questions. It can be a powerful tool but *only* if there's buy-in from the family. Now, shall I continue?"

Mrs. Murphy nodded.

"Owen is bright. On higher-order thinking and abstract-spatial reasoning, he scores in the ninety-third percentile. He's gifted. But he also has severe learning challenges. He's in the fourth percentile for working memory and seventh percentile for auditory processing."

"Working memory?" Mrs. Murphy asked.

Kiara tried not to slip into lecture mode. "Working memory is basically holding things together in your mind at the same time as you use or think about them. If you forget what you're reading about *while* you are reading it, you have limited working memory. Another example would be losing your place in the middle of a long-division problem. Sound familiar?"

"Yes. And auditory processing?" Mrs. Murphy asked.

Kiara thought back to her own auditory challenges as a middle schooler and how the actions of one discerning teacher had transformed her learning trajectory. "Owen's hearing is fine, but he can't process, remember, and understand auditory information in the same way you might. It's worse when he's bombarded with new complex information. That's why he struggles with word problems and forgets material that's just been explained to him."

"Got it."

"Owen survived the earlier grades precisely because he's *not* lazy. He fought hard and found ways to compensate on his own. Considering the challenges that he's up against, getting Cs was impressive. He actually worked *harder* than his classmates"—Kiara's throat tightened with emotion—"just to be called 'lazy.'"

Mrs. Murphy winced. Maybe she wasn't impervious to feeling remorse after all.

Kiara continued, "How many kids would've battled as long as Owen did, if they were missing the lion's share of the information? In my experience, very few." Kiara could, of course, think of at least one. She and Owen were kindred spirits in this regard.

Mrs. Murphy's face was ashen. "What changed?"

Kiara's tone softened. "In the earlier grades, the demands on Owen's working memory and auditory processing were less intense. He got by on memorization. But things change in eighth grade. Students need to process lecture information, make associations with previously learned information, and send it to the right mental file for long-term storage. This was never going to happen with Owen."

"I guess he reached his limit. That would explain the marijuana. Who wouldn't want to escape that kind of reality?"

"Exactly," Kiara said, no longer yearning to pelt Mrs. Murphy with paintballs. "And the kids he's hanging out with—most are no worse than Owen. If we can help him succeed in the classroom, that'll kick-start his motivation."

"But how can someone who retains so little ever learn effectively, much less go to college?"

"Actually, Owen can retain almost everything if the material is taught in a way that matches his learning style. He can also pick up learning techniques and tools that capitalize on his strengths as a visual and kinesthetic learner. If everyone is committed—the family, his teachers, the guidance counselor—there's no reason he can't thrive."

"Dr. Battle, that's a whole bunch of 'ifs.' Seems pretty pie-in-the-sky to me."

Kiara pressed her lips together. "Look, it *will* be pie-in-the-sky if the three of you aren't committed—two won't do. Owen suffers from dual deficits, not one, and they're severe. If I had evaluated him five years ago—which is what *should* have happened—the situation would be different. I really need you and your husband to take this seriously, if Owen is going to have any hope of reaching his potential. Why don't we reconvene—"

Mrs. Murphy's face had been contorting as Kiara spoke, the vein along her neck throbbing until, it seemed, the agitated mother could take no more. She jumped to her feet and stormed out of Kiara's office.

Minutes later, a clearly browbeaten Vicki walked in, plopped in the chair, and sighed.

"I'm guessing you didn't ask her to complete our survey," Kiara said.

"It's not funny, doc. We should pray that's all she completes."

Kiara rolled her eyes. "Look, Mr. and Mrs. Murphy were lazy, self-indulgent, and negligent. God forbid they downsize their McMansion or sacrifice their Maui vacations so that Owen can go to a therapeutic school. She needed to hear the truth."

Vicki smirked. "I thought you didn't believe in lazy."

Kiara rummaged around under her desk. "Anyone see my paintball rifle?"

Kiara left the office with a pit in her stomach. Why she, a psychologist, should feel so upset made no sense. So much for compartmentalizing. She strolled toward Linda's Bar for a beer, comfort food, and a sympathetic ear. Reveling students wouldn't arrive until later.

Across the street protestors were again gathered around Silent Sam, a Confederate statue, pressing for its removal. Lest Kiara fall back into idealizing Chapel Hill, as she often did, the presence of these activists reminded her things weren't always so idyllic, not for her people. Still, Sam's sudden notoriety was surreal. She entered the tavern and, spotting Sarah in a booth, felt cheerier. Her best friend didn't visit often enough—even now, dinner would have to suffice. But, as always, Sarah's timing had been exquisite.

"My, my, don't you look hot," Sarah said, rising to hug her. "You're like some Fox News anchorwoman that men drool over."

"Yeah, right, not my team. But I can always throw on my paintball gear."

"Before you ask, White Zombies, cheesesteaks, and hush puppies are on the way. I gotta say, though, I feel a bit like Marie Antoinette"— Sarah gestured toward the crowd of protestors—"feasting amid the discontent."

"That's because you're rich, White, and from Duke. Don't offer anyone cake, and you'll be fine."

Sarah slapped her on the wrist. "Seriously, this is more of a hotbed than D.C. You never told me about all this."

"There was nothing to tell until a few months ago. The truth is, when I was a student, we never thought twice about Silent Sam, except for that old running joke. You know, that Sam would only fire his rifle when a virgin passed, and he'd yet to ever pull the trigger. The statue's history and symbolism weren't really part of the conversation back then, not even at the Black parties I went to."

The waiter delivered the food and beer.

"So what changed?" Sarah asked, taking a sip of her drink.

"Recent revelations made people rethink their indifference."

Kiara elaborated, as Sarah chewed thoughtfully on a hush puppy.

"Fascinating, but you know what?" Sarah laid her hand on Kiara's arm. "I'd rather know what's bothering *you*. You sounded down earlier."

Kiara detailed the morning unpleasantness without violating Mrs. Murphy's confidentiality. When she had finished, Kiara sat back and sipped her drink. It was such a luxury to have her confidant here in person.

Sarah sighed. "I totally get it. These parents ignore their child's problem for years, only coming to you when the school *forces* them to. Once you diagnose Junior's problem, they blame other kids, then Junior himself, until finally addressing the problem in a halfhearted way that's doomed to fail."

"It's infuriating."

"I'm sure it is," Sarah said, grabbing her cheesesteak. "But it's also what you signed up for."

Kiara frowned. *This was being supportive?* Annoyingly, Sarah did have a point.

"Besides," Sarah continued, "if the case were too easy, you wouldn't like it."

"When does your train leave?" Kiara asked with a smirk.

"Bottom line, girl, you better get a handle on your anger. Either that or find a different profession."

"So all I need is a personality transplant."

"Hey, you managed it once and didn't do so badly," Sarah said, digging up ancient history. "Three-time all-American, your number retired and everything."

Kiara's thoughts drifted back to her sophomore year in college. She had indeed found a way to relate better with her soccer teammates.

"Wish I could just sic Silent Sam on 'Mrs. Smith.'"

"Remember, she's not a virgin." They both laughed.

Way too soon, it was time to drive Sarah to Raleigh for her train to D.C. When Kiara got home, she popped three Tums and did calisthenics. Then she prayed for Owen before falling asleep.

4

THE CONTEST

Chapel Hill, North Carolina, 1981. Zeb's family sat at the breakfast table, grim-faced. Larry buried himself in the *New York Times*, having demolished his oatmeal. Ruth leafed through her agenda, updating entries. Zeb shoved a spoonful of Frosted Flakes into his mouth and stared blankly at Tony the Tiger. He saw no reason to speak if his parents wouldn't even acknowledge each other. The orange feline eyeballed him back. "They're Gr-r-reat!" said the caption. *Only the flakes*, Zeb thought.

Until now his parents had presented a united front whenever sensitive issues arose. They kept their differences private. Technically, this blowup had been behind closed doors, but their raised voices had eliminated all mystery. His mom's patience had run out.

Ruth locked eyes with Larry. "How about *you* be the one to tell Dean Gillespie I need to cancel my class at the last minute—that *you* won't take Zeb to the doctor, even though you have the entire morning off?"

"That's not fair, honey. It's not that simple."

"Simple? Ask Zeb how simple it is to go to class, year after year, and not absorb material because of a condition that can be remedied."

Larry shook his head. "Don't drag him into this."

"Maybe it's time he knows the options. It's his life."

"For chrissakes, he's a fifth grader!"

"Exactly," Ruth said, her exasperation matching his. "Old enough to tell us how *he* feels about all the useless therapies, the years of frustration, about doing what we should have done long ago."

Zeb rubbed his clammy palms against his jeans. It was hard to blame her. This had to be as tedious for her as it was for him. Here she was, a university professor, playing chauffeur to him because of her work schedule. Dad dealt with the doctors and teachers, coming up with "solutions" that were inevitably abandoned. Curing ADHD was a bitch, with no end in sight.

First it had been classical music therapy. Listening to that elevator music was supposed to fix all kinds of problems—impulsivity, concentration, language skills, and auditory processing. All it did was put him to sleep. His mom hadn't been impressed either, ultimately threatening to "buy her own damn Mozart tapes at a fraction of the price" so she could "start her own racket and retire early."

Next it had been the interactive metronome, which not only failed to improve his neurological timing but also almost turned him off video games for life.

Sessions with the social-skills group worked fine, until he broke the nose of a boy who called him a "dirty Jew." Told to take his socialization training elsewhere, his mom had responded, "I'll bring him back once he's a perfect human being—like the bigot you're harboring."

Jujitsu was supposed to have instilled discipline, but his sensei hadn't appreciated his proclivity for farting opportunistically and then blaming fellow students. He was booted from class after the instructor's own self-control wore thin. Zeb's mom had grounded him for a month.

Playing chess had made him feel smarter—he'd beaten everyone—but he still couldn't concentrate when he was in groups. Visual-planning charts and behavioral-reward systems helped some, but he was still disorganized and forgetful. His parents nagged him constantly.

Ruth looked at her son. "Dr. Gadea treats tons of kids with medicine. It helps them to concentrate and remember more of what they're taught. They have a better sense of time and do a better job planning, organizing, and prioritizing—everything that gives you trouble."

Larry grimaced. "Does that kind of one-sided reasoning work on your MBA students? Zeb's too smart to think that's all there is to it. Hell, we wouldn't be arguing, if things were so clear-cut."

"Sweetie," Ruth said, turning to her son, "there could be some side effects that come along with the medication."

"Like what?"

"It's hard to say," she said mildly. "Meds affect everyone differently. You might eat less and feel calmer."

"Tell it to him straight, Ruth," Larry said. He looked at Zeb. "'Calmer' really means 'depressed.' You wouldn't be your normal bubbly self. Also, you'd probably lose weight, and you already complain about being short and light."

Minutes passed in silence, and Ruth caressed Zeb's head in a way she rarely did. "A penny for your thoughts?"

"I don't know," Zeb said. "It's not up to me." This felt like a proxy war. He'd done enough damage. "You guys are the parents."

"We know that," Larry said. "But we value your opinion."

"Are the side effects permanent?"

"We can't be sure," Larry said quickly. "The findings are mixed. Better safe than sorry, though. What matters most is *your happiness*, not becoming the next Einstein. You're wonderful just the way you are." He sighed. "I'd rather see you compensate for your weaknesses and be happy than have to depend on risky meds and undergo a personality transplant."

"Now who's overstating their case?" Ruth asked. "Zeb, these drugs are approved by the FDA. Nothing is one hundred percent certain, but chances are that any negative side effects would stop once you stop taking the medication. You're a smart boy with lots of potential, and I refuse to lower my expectations for you. Dad talks about happiness, and he's right. But meeting your potential *is* the path to happiness."

Zeb stared down at his fidgeting hands. "I guess it's worth a try. I'm tired of being the weird kid—the one who can't sit still, who no one wants to hang out with. Right now I'm not on track to go to college. Maybe medicine can change that. If it hits me badly, maybe I can switch to one that doesn't?" He looked at the cartoon tiger. "If none of 'em work, then I can go back to being a dumbass with no future."

"You'll never be that, son," Larry said, his eyes welling up. "I'm so proud of your courage and smarts. I wish I'd been braver and smarter myself. I'm sorry for putting you through all this."

"No sweat."

His dad hugged him, squeezing hard. Zeb's throat tightened. His dad had fought hard to preserve what he thought was special in him. That battle was now lost, and it must have been scary. But, somehow, deep down, his dad also seemed comforted by making him happy.

"I'll drive him to Dr. Gadea," Larry said. He barely glanced at Ruth, whose mood had lifted.

Zeb shifted in his chair, trying to hide his own elation.

5

THE ACORN

Maracaibo, Venezuela, 1977. Leo hopped off the golf cart, unhooked the drag brush, and stored it in the club's tennis maintenance shed. The hackers on court six wouldn't be done anytime soon. Grabbing the line sweeper, he strode to the baseline of court one and got busy. The mechanics of his task were routine, so Leo let his thoughts wander.

The longtime head of security had commented on how much the Club de las Americas had changed over the years. Its location—bordering the northern end of Lake Maracaibo, just south of the Caribbean Sea—was the same but, otherwise, the club was unrecognizable. In the 1950s, when it was founded, it had catered to wealthy *Maracuchos* and foreigners, mostly American and Dutch oilmen who'd come as investors and technical advisors to help Venezuelans tap black gold. Through the early 1970s club members enjoyed waterskiing, boating, and swimming in the lake. By the time Leo's parents let him work at the club, the foreigners had disappeared, ushered out by Carlos Andrés Pérez's nationalization of the petroleum industry. The remaining members partook in land-based activities—tennis, fitness training, the pool—because Lake Maracaibo had become polluted.

Leo finished sweeping the fifth court and wiped his brow. He turned his attention to other pre–New Year's Eve urgencies: unclogging a toilet, replacing two lightbulbs, and changing the water filter at the bar. Court six could be swept in the morning when everyone else was sleeping.

Plunger in hand, Leo made a beeline for the men's locker room, skirting the pool deck. He averted his gaze from the clique of lounging teenagers. The intensity of their cackles signaled they'd been drinking. Most club members vacated before the big event, giving the staff a chance to prepare, but these angels—Venezuela's future leaders—had higher priorities. Who cared if the chef and waiter had to toil longer?

"What's up, *blondie*?" boomed an unmistakable voice.

Leo knew there was no avoiding them. His only friend, Federico, was relaxing by the pool with two guys and three girls. All sported stylish bathing suits, their bronzed bodies reflecting lives of leisure and fitness studios. A depleted bottle of Macallan 12 sat next to a platter of *tequeños* and an ice bucket filled to the brim, thanks to the overworked waiter. Leo began to sweat.

"Grab a seat," Federico said, pushing a chair his way. "The plunger can wait."

"Thanks, but it can't. The gala starts in two hours."

"*Coño!* As if you're the manager. Just grab a *tequeño*; no one will notice." Federico dipped a cheese stick into ketchup and handed it to him.

"Sorry," Leo said, his stomach instantly tightening. *Why can't I act like a normal person?* Federico had fraternized with him, "the help," risking a rebuke, and *this* was his reward? "I've got to work."

Federico nodded, betraying no bitterness.

Bernardo, a classmate who had never spoken to him before, said, "What a dumbass loser. Fix the damn toilet!" Leo laughed inside. The inability of the elite to find better adjectives or fashion better insults remained a mystery. As his mom had taught him to do, Leo visualized

a protective shield around himself, the slights bouncing off it like a
Nerf ball.

"Shut up, Bernardo," said a girl from class. She turned to Leo. "Will
you be going to Aquarena tonight?"

Leo rubbed the back of his neck. He couldn't say that nightclubs
repelled him almost as much as cigarette smoke. Or that he sucked at
dancing merengue, had never drunk whiskey, and hated talking baseball. That he had no interest in bragging about nonexistent sexual
exploits. That he hoped to go back to his room, read *Crime and
Punishment*, and crash at a respectable hour so he could sweep court
six in good time. "I'm not sure. It depends on whether my parents
give me the car," he said.

"You hear that—*the* car," Bernardo sneered. "They probably live like
guajiros."

"Well, if you make it, save me a dance," the girl said.

"You've got to be kidding, Clara!" Bernardo said. "Ken Doll here
is light in his loafers. He and Fede probably do book clubs together."

"Being good-looking and cultured doesn't mean he's gay," she
replied. "And if he is, so what?"

Leo flushed, his mind racing. There was no reason to feel buoyed
by her support. First, Clara talked a good game, but come midnight,
she'd be making out with the jackass. Rich braggers held court here.
Second, Federico had been humiliated after reaching out. Third,
questions had been raised about Leo's own sexuality. He couldn't
allow that to stand unchallenged.

"The only effeminate thing around here, Bernardo, is the way you
manicure your eyebrows," Leo said. "That and how you swing a tennis
racket."

"At least I don't look like a middle schooler," Bernardo retorted.
"Scram, jailbait!"

Leo took off and set about his tasks with maniacal intensity. How
a lowlife like Bernardo could live like a king made no sense. Actually,
it did. He had savvy parents who always knew which way the ball was

bouncing. They had figured out the shortcut to wealth—no great mystery. His own parents, by contrast, were among the few educated folks in Maracaibo to have missed the financial boat. In Zulia, where oil was as plentiful as gorgeous women, that took some doing. If they'd shown any ability to read the political winds and adjust their business strategy accordingly, he—not Bernardo—would be holding Clara's hand. Instead, he clasped a plunger.

I should've just eaten the damn tequeño. What had he expected after his oddball reaction? If his stomach was grumbling now, how would he feel after getting fired?

A vision came to him: an acorn falling. It landed right beside the tree. Leo shuddered.

6

THE RECOVERY

Sunrise, Florida, 1983. Seventh grade seemed to be more of the same—no different from sixth. Two boys, loners, stood in the shade, jabbing at their handheld electric-football games. The athletes and athlete-wannabes played soccer. The socialites chattered, looking trendy. Kiara's gaze fell on the popular squad. Two Black boys—the only other African Americans in her grade—held court, as several White boys vied for their attention.

Munching on her apple, she smiled. The minorities were on a roll. Well, some of them. Four days into the school year and she hadn't attracted the slightest interest. The downside of not being as dashing as Darren or Rodney. Still, watching the brothers was a trip, their flair and presumed athleticism assuring them a spot on Mount Olympus, socially speaking. The suburban White boys couldn't get enough. Poor fools had no way of knowing the truth: These dudes would get their asses kicked at any predominantly Black school for acting White. Here they had hit the jackpot. Soon they'd lay their rap on fawning White girls, never so much as glancing at her. *Whatever.*

Kiara trashed the apple core and, having forgotten to bring *A Wrinkle in Time* to school, ambled toward the soccer field. Two girls played among the boys. She cursed under her breath, wishing her old man had trained her even one hundredth as much as he had Brian. America wasn't Trinidad. She shouldn't have had to scream bloody murder to be included in their drills. Attending her brother's games—but never playing herself—had been torture.

"Play on that team," a boy said, pointing to the side that was getting pummeled.

Several teammates smiled as Kiara walked over. Apparently misery loved company. The center forward asked her to play defender. "All you have to do is cover this area," he said, pointing to a wide swath of field. "Keep your body between their striker and our goal." He was neither bossy nor condescending, so she nodded. Besides, he was the first student to utter more than five words to her.

A confident-looking winger brought the ball out of the opposing midfield. Dribbling with the outside of his foot, keeping his head up, he weaved past two of Kiara's teammates. As he sliced through her midfield, Kiara's adrenaline pumped. She recalled her father's exhortations to Brian: "Ready position, knees bent, five yards from the attacker. Take small steps. *Don't stab!*"

The dribbler came at her. Kiara readied herself, back-stepping quickly to keep him in front. She slipped and then steadied herself. He did a scissors move, faking to the left and nudging the ball rightward. She nearly fell for the fake—almost stabbed at the ball—but recovered and hung with him. He cut back instantly to the left. She lost her balance, faltering but staying upright. But she now was two steps behind. Kiara pumped her legs, working hard to catch up. The winger made a third move, a Cruyff turn, causing her to fall flat on her rear. Calmly he fired a left-footed rocket into the right upper 90. A spectacular goal.

Everyone, including her teammates, cheered. Scowling, Kiara popped up, fists clenched.

"That was amazing!" a scrawny girl said, slapping her on the back.

"No one's ever made Ralph use three moves—he usually blows by with one."

Ralph scored four more goals, but Kiara made him earn each one. When the bell rang for class, she pouted. Tomorrow, she would skip the people watching and eat her apple at lunch. She couldn't wait to see her dad.

Twenty minutes later, blood rushed to Kiara's head as her social studies teacher, Mrs. Foster, waited for a response. *What's the matter with me?* Kiara thought. *We just covered this stuff.* No fewer than eight hands were raised, most waving energetically. Somehow regurgitating information was beyond her capabilities. It didn't make sense. These kids weren't geniuses—no smarter than she was. Or maybe they were. Maybe that was why Mrs. Foster always asked them the hard questions. Kiara shook her head. "Sorry, I don't know." A classmate snickered.

"Not to worry," Mrs. Foster said. "Lisa, why don't you remind everyone of the First Amendment."

"Freedom of speech and religion."

"Would you care to elaborate?"

"People can say or believe anything they like."

"Are there limits?" Mrs. Foster said. "Is there speech that isn't protected?"

Lisa shrugged.

"Anyone?"

"We're not allowed to lie," one boy said, eliciting chuckles. Someone quipped they were studying the Constitution, not the Bible.

"Don't laugh," Mrs. Foster said crossly. "Brett's right, to a point. Americans aren't usually allowed to tell a lie that hurts someone's reputation—that's called defamation. Neither can we lie in a courtroom—that's perjury." She let that sink in. "Can you think of other limits to free speech?"

No one raised their hand, so Kiara raised hers. There wasn't much downside to guessing at this point. Besides, she needed to redeem herself. Clearly surprised, Mrs. Foster invited her to speak.

"We can't say anything that puts others in danger. Like yelling 'fire' in a crowded movie theater."

"Wow, excellent!" Mrs. Foster said, sounding astonished. "Can anyone think of another example?"

"I can," Kiara said quickly.

"Good, Kiara," the teacher said, winking. "We can all benefit by learning about hate crimes."

Kiara frowned. Mrs. Foster was trying to pigeonhole her, figuring she saw everything through the prism of race. This wasn't Black History Month, and, even if it were, she wasn't playing that game. "Okay, let's say some immigrants come to Miami from Cuba. They've lost everything and are willing to work for less money. Let's also say workers born in America start worrying about losing their jobs. If the long-time Americans say things to get people to attack the immigrants, that speech might be illegal."

"Well done, young lady! That wasn't what I was expecting, but you're right on target. Incitement to lawless action is a—" The bell rang. Mrs. Foster finished her point, announced the homework, and dismissed class.

Kiara zipped her backpack.

"Man, great recovery!" The familiar voice came from behind her. "That's twice today."

Turning, Kiara peered into the eyes of the scrawny girl. "What do you mean?"

"Well, you bounced back from that embarrassing flub. The First Amendment question."

"Thanks . . . I think."

"How in the world did you miss that question?"

Kiara didn't know whether to beat the girl's ass or not. Something in her manner suggested it wasn't spiteful. Probably, she had issues and needed remedial work on her social skills. "I don't know. It just happens to me sometimes."

"I see you decided not to be the spokesman for the entire Black race."

"Spokes*woman*. You might want to beef up on your grammar."

"Sheesh, nice social skills," the girl said, shaking her head.

"Well, birds of a feather . . . You said I recovered twice. When was the second time?"

"Recess, silly. You stayed on Ralph's ass, no matter what he threw at you."

Kiara snorted. "If you hadn't noticed, he scored five times."

"Gotta expect that. He plays club soccer."

They strolled through the building, the girl detailing the resumes of the better players.

As they reached math class, she stopped short, grabbing Kiara's forearm. "Hey! You want to train with me?"

Kiara grinned at her public display of eagerness. "In soccer?"

"No, tiddlywinks."

The girl was skinnier than a beanpole.

"Okay," Kiara said.

"I promise not to ask you about rappers, basketball, or fried chicken."

"And I promise not to ask how much you weigh or kick your butt if you don't stop talking."

The scrawny girl stuck out her hand. "Deal! Name's Sarah."

"Kiara."

"How could I not know, Miss First Amendment?"

7

NUMBER 23

Chapel Hill, North Carolina, 1981. Larry and Zeb sat at midcourt, six rows back at the Carmichael Auditorium. The Tar Heel basketball team and their lightly regarded opponents, UNC-Wilmington, were warming up. The preseason game was meaningless for most fans, but Zeb couldn't take his eyes off the Carolina players. Larry handed popcorn to his ten-year-old son.

"No thanks."

"Turning down popcorn, that's a first."

"Some things are more important. Gotta focus."

Larry smiled. "We'll dominate today, but don't get your hopes up. The preseason number-one ranking is a curse—and, frankly, insane after losing Al Wood."

Zeb glared at his father. "You remember where sportswriters had us ranked going into last season? Fourth in the conference. We wound up second in the country."

"I know, I know. Dean Smith is a genius."

"I can't believe you would forget that." Zeb shifted his gaze back to the court.

"I just hope Worthy stays healthy," Larry said. "What's the word on the freshmen?"

"Peterson was North Carolina Player of the Year and gets all the attention. But I like number 23, Mike Jordan. Look at his follow-through and the way he moves. Can't believe he didn't make varsity until his junior year."

"Neither could Dean, apparently."

The warm-up period ended, and the players left the court.

Zeb turned to his father. "Jimmy Black's going to have a great year."

"Really?" Larry asked, clearly surprised.

"He's on a mission. To help Coach win it all."

"Aren't they all?"

"For him it runs deeper. Coach was there for Jimmy when his mother died. And when he got into that accident. That'll motivate him." Zeb stuffed his mouth with popcorn.

"Speaking of motivation, your mother and I wish you'd pay more attention to your schoolwork."

"It's boring. Besides, basketball helps more."

"Helps what?"

"With people not making fun of me."

"I thought the meds were helping?"

"In some ways. They don't call me stupid anymore. Now, I'm just a stiff."

"I wish you had told us."

"No big deal," Zeb said nonchalantly. "I shut them up when I started answering Mr. Bell's sports trivia questions. And the Civil War questions. Keeps them off my back."

The teams trotted onto the court, cheered by fans. A Wilmington player shoved a Tar Heel unnecessarily.

Larry sighed. "Well, it looks like another battle is about to begin."

8

GENEALOGICAL FLUKE

Chapel Hill, North Carolina, 1983. "Move it," Larry said, nudging Zeb along the path to Hamilton Hall. "I can't be late for my own class."

Frowning, Zeb kicked a pebble forward and followed it. As if life wasn't already boring enough without having to sit through his dad's class. This was a far cry from firing off bottle rockets at home.

What had gotten into him? Normally, Dad was the reasonable one. Why had they conspired to ruin his afternoon?

Zeb booted the stone off the path. "Why can't I stay home?"

"Pyromaniacs don't make ideal house sitters."

"I won't do that anymore. I told Mom."

"Not until you've proven yourself."

"I'm twelve."

Larry nodded to a passing colleague. "Next time find another way to have fun. Now hurry up!"

The walkway ended at one of the few eyesores on campus. Zeb's mother had long complained that Hamilton Hall didn't do justice to the political science department. Maybe she had a point, but the lecture hall was three-quarters full when they entered. The Cold War and his dad's passion for teaching had obviously driven demand for Modern Russian History.

His dad led them to the front row and pointed to a vacant seat between two stern-looking Brunhilds.

"It's only forty-five minutes. I'll talk with Mom if you behave."

Why was his dad so uptight? Yeah, they had forgotten his meds, but he could sit still without them.

Stragglers settled into their seats as Larry began. He summarized events leading to the Soviet Union's entry into World War II, touching on the Molotov-Ribbentrop nonaggression pact and the agreed-on spheres of influence between the USSR and Germany. He discussed Hitler's anti-Bolshevism and the catalysts for Hitler's invasion—Stalin's occupation of the Baltic States and of lands near the Romanian oil fields on which the Nazi forces depended. Then he stopped.

"Mr. Berry, in 1941 what was the German strategy with respect to the Soviet Union?"

"Basically, to invade the country," the student replied.

"Can you elaborate?"

Berry shifted in his seat. "Hitler wanted living space in the east, a place for Germans to colonize and get more resources. He wanted to subjugate the Slavs. That was a core objective of Hitler's, along with eliminating the Jews."

"Quite right. That being the case, why did each side sign the nonaggression pact?"

"The pact bought time for Hitler so he could conquer the west before turning eastward. It gave the Soviets time to build their defenses."

"Correct."

Larry glanced at Zeb, exhaling deeply.

"Ms. Barrett, what part of Operation Barbarossa was most important?" Larry asked, his gaze finding another student.

"For me it was the strike force headed for St. Petersburg—well, Leningrad back then."

"Why?"

She twirled a pencil. "Leningrad was the former capital of Russia and the center of the Russian Revolution, so it had symbolic value. It was the base of the Baltic fleet and had weapons factories. The city accounted for ten percent of the economy. Destroying it was key."

"Good. Mr. Reilly, tell us about the northern campaign." Larry's attention had moved to another undergrad.

"The Nazis attacked Leningrad."

"A point made by Ms. Barrett. More specificity, please."

Blushing, Reilly shook his head and looked down.

Zeb jumped to his feet. "The Nazis surrounded Leningrad. They cut off its supply lines. They starved the people and then bombed the city. The siege lasted two and a half years. Four and a half million civilians died—way more than Dresden, Hiroshima, and Nagasaki put together."

Hands on hips, Larry stood with his mouth agape. Students cheered, even the humiliated Reilly. Zeb continued, "The Soviets finally won, but—"

"Enough, Zeb! Please sit down."

"C'mon, Professor, let him go. The kid knows his facts," one student yelled. Others seconded the notion.

"No, that's quite enough," Larry said.

After the commotion subsided, a student raised his hand. "Professor, you haven't quizzed us on today's most irrelevant historical fact."

"Sorry. I was distracted by World War II, among other things. But I do admire your thirst for knowledge."

Several students guffawed. Larry had introduced the query as a gimmick to bring fun to the classroom. The first correct responder earned extra credit. "Okay, why was the invasion of the Soviet Union called Operation Barbarossa?" No one knew it had been named after twelfth-century Holy Roman Emperor Frederick Barbarossa, who sought to establish German predominance in Europe.

When class was over, Larry took Zeb straight to the department chairman's office to apologize for the scene they'd made before it reached his ears. Larry promised to leave Zeb at home from now on. The chairman chortled, saying Larry was to be congratulated for raising a precocious historian. Larry insisted that Zeb's knowledge was a "genealogical fluke," but the chairman demurred. Zeb had obviously studied far more than family history, demonstrating his love of learning.

"Sorry, Larry," the chairman said, "but I agree with your students. I can't tell you what to do, but I fervently hope you keep bringing Zeb to class. He seems to energize the class."

That evening, Ruth hugged her son. "History beats bottle rockets any day of the week, but please don't ignore your other subjects."

Among the seventh graders at Culbreth Middle School, none was more visible than the boy from Amritsar, India. Asian American students were no longer a novelty in the Research Triangle but Ajit, a Sikh, stood out with his royal blue turban. Zeb had researched Sikhism in the *World Book Encyclopedia* and, although impressed, hadn't approached the kid, even though their lockers were nearby. Why compound his own social problems by befriending an outsider? And so, twirling the dial to his combination lock, Zeb pretended not to notice Ajit, who was looking in his direction.

The thud of books striking the ground provoked recognizable cackling. It was Scott Brochaw, the class bully. A classmate, Arnold, kneeled and, encumbered by a back brace, struggled to twist and grip an algebra textbook. Bystanders kept their distance.

Scott approached. "Gee, Arnie, you're having a tough time grasping math, here or in class. Here, let me help you." He booted the primer beyond Arnold's reach.

"Leave him alone!" a girl bellowed. "You're such a jerk."

"You sweet on weenie boy?" Scott asked, sneering and kicking two notebooks to the wall.

In a flash, Ajit rushed the bully, tackling him and ramming his head against a locker. When Ajit let go, Scott collapsed, his nose bleeding. "You can expect this anytime you pick on someone smaller than you," the Sikh said.

"Fuck you," Scott said, limping away to jeers.

Ajit righted his turban, collected Arnold's materials, and handed them to him.

"Thanks, man," Arnold said, rising slowly. "I owe you, big-time."

"Don't worry about it. I can help you with algebra. The best revenge is beating him on the next test."

Six weeks later, Maria Romero, Culbreth's seventh-grade homecoming queen, marched into the assembly hall, escorted by Ajit Kapoor, the homecoming king. For the first time ever, Zeb had voted for the class dignitaries. He clapped long and hard.

9

PAPÁ IS WORKING

Maracaibo, Venezuela, 1977. Leo drummed his fingers on the bleacher. Twenty-five minutes until sunset, and the ladies were still hacking away on an outer court at the Club de Las Americas. Two- and three-stroke rallies interrupted their continuous chatter about moisturizing creams, the best *hallacas* recipes, and the appalling decline of Aruban restaurants. Their drivel was almost as irritating as married men bragging about their girlfriends and Rolex watches.

But, deep down, Leo was tickled to be witnessing the sorry spectacle: It meant he still had a job—despite the New Year's Eve pool incident. In a Maracaibo ruled by Bernardo types, that was a minor miracle. The one-week suspension and formal apology had been a slap on the wrist. Federico had come through for him yet again.

Probably the ladies would finish after dark, shower, and collect their whiskey-swilling husbands from the bar. They would head to Mi Vaquita for succulent steaks while he would sweep the court and mop the locker room. If only he were allowed to read while waiting.

Instead, uncoordinated gossips would treat him to an unending stream of mishits.

Leo finished at eight thirty—later even than expected. Exiting the club, he strolled toward the dimly lit employee parking lot. Navigation lights on the drilling platforms made Lake Maracaibo lovely at night— nothing like the eyesore it was by day, thanks to the machinery and water discoloration. *This job is a piece of cake compared to toiling aboard a rig.*

As Leo approached his car, a man sprang out from behind it. Grabbed him by the shoulder. Pressed a gun against his temple. Leo stuttered. The smell of sweat and the lake. A second man yelled in his face. Leo held up his hands, surrendered the keys. Shoved into the back seat. Blindfolded. A prick in his arm. They drove off. Blackness.

Heading north along the lake, Ramiro fought the urge to speed. No sense getting pulled over and forfeiting profits. The regular police were no problem; they could be bought off for chicken feed, a few hundred U.S. dollars. The federal police, the CICPC, were a different story. They'd demand eight thousand dollars—enough to put him and Juan out of business. They might've survived that kind of hit before but not now. The country's economic collapse had put a damper on crime. The bolívar was worthless, fewer victims carried dollars, and bullets were expensive. Spare parts for getaway vehicles were hard to come by. Bottom line, no speeding. Which was why *he* was driving.

"Did you inject him?" Ramiro asked, checking the rearview mirror.

"Yes, he's in la-la land," Juan replied, patting Leo's cheek. The boy was out cold.

"He looks young."

"Probably just good genes."

"Check his credit cards. We'll tap them when we reach Santa Rita. He should be conscious by then. We'll call the father."

"Won't the stores be—"

"Hold on, I'm late for a call." Ramiro pulled over into a lot with a public telephone. He popped out of the car, his expression softening. "*Hola*, my princess. . . . Papá misses you too, but he's working tonight. . . . Don't worry, I'll be fine. See you tomorrow. . . . Okay, sweetie, I love you too. Don't forget to lock the door. A big kiss!"

As Ramiro reentered the vehicle, Juan blurted out, "Hold up! This kid isn't Domingo Florentino!"

"*Coño!* What the hell are you talking about?"

"I checked his ID," Juan said, shaking his head. "The guy's name is Leonardo Bello. No credit cards. Only twenty bolívares."

"Five dollars! No wonder we're driving a ten-year-old Corolla."

"What now?"

Ramiro pondered their options. "We might collect more than we think. If not, we'll pawn this piece of crap and learn our lesson." He drove east.

"This fuckup's on me," Juan said, shaking his head. "I should've done my legwork."

"No shit. We didn't quit the Invincibles gang to score a Corolla. When you cut corners, and don't surveil, our risk-return goes way up. The whole point is to hit singles and doubles, make money on volume. Not take risks for peanuts—that's stupid."

As they passed the U.S. Consulate, Ramiro recognized a Venezuelan policeman who was chatting with several Marines. The cop provided weapons for the Invincibles but had refused to supply Juan and him after their defection. Evidently protecting his gravy train—and his life.

"It won't happen again," Juan said.

"Better not."

Juan had always been a research guy. He'd surveil targets—see where they lived and shopped, who their family, friends, and business associates were. He needed to get back to that. No shortcuts.

The old model—kidnapping the super-rich, often for long periods—was a different animal. They needed a vast array of things: a fleet of vehicles, trained hostage takers who could prevail against heavily armed guards and armored cars, a secure place to stash hostages, a food budget, and people standing guard. Ransoms ranged from one to two million dollars. But the risks were proportionally greater because police had the time and incentive to pursue hostages. Express kidnappings, by contrast, lasted less than twenty-four hours. They targeted shopkeepers and restaurant owners who couldn't afford bodyguards, armored cars, or insurance. They pocketed ten to twenty thousand dollars on a regular basis, splitting it between three people. It worked better, if done right.

As they arrived in Santa Rita, Ramiro resolved to give Juan another chance. He would have to up his game, rededicate himself to his craft. And if not, well, business was business.

Leo awoke and got up from the floor, his head throbbing. The window-less cell looked like a storage room. He jiggled the door handle, but it wouldn't budge. His full bladder ached, so he walked to the far corner and urinated.

He peered through a crack in the wall. It appeared to be late after-noon. If so, something had gone wrong. Kidnappings never lasted this long, not for small fish. He should've been released already.

Probably they were mad as hornets, unable to monetize him. They'd have spoken to his dad and discovered just how badly the furniture business was faring. Neither were they able to load up on ATM cash and expensive watches. Pawning his piece-of-junk Toyota would be their last recourse.

Will they shoot me in a fit of rage? he wondered. Most kidnappers saw themselves as businessmen, not killers, but you never knew. How humiliating to be so unworthy of their efforts.

His parents must be stressing. The price of not having succeeded in all these years. For God's sake, not to be able to pay even a modest ransom! If they'd had any common sense . . . Instead, like sheep—no, like moral narcissists—they had followed every damn rule, both legal and moral. They got off on their own virtue. God forbid they should ever lobby, or pay to play with, the regime. How else could they secure import privileges or exemptions to foreign-exchange controls, or a government contract? No, that was beneath them. Never mind that businesses in every industry were playing the game. Failure to adapt meant extinction.

Sure, their obstinacy was admirable on some level, but righteousness only led to poverty. There was no greater good to be achieved—not here, not now. Their sacrifice had no upside. No one would follow their example, not even him.

He realized, then, that he was doubly trapped. Escaping this cell, he'd remain shackled by the system. Leo slumped to a squat.

10

DOUBLE TIME

eston, Florida, 1985. "Ready!" Corinda bellowed from the kitchen.

"Coming," Marcus said, not disturbed in the least.

Friends joked that it took Trinidadian delicacies to lure him from his beloved magazine without a frown. They were right. Some folks played chess, did crosswords, or read fiction to keep their brains nimble and have fun. For him, the *Economist* did that and more. It gave him confidence. Whenever he felt himself slipping—stagnating—he read several articles and, boom, he felt invigorated, no longer a drone. When a buddy had first recommended the magazine to him, he had thought it too highbrow. Now he never went anywhere without it. It was a stand-in for the soccer ball of his youth.

"Don't vex me now, Marcus. We're waiting."

Corinda hated it when he worked on the Lord's Day. This being April, he'd gone to the office to crank out another tax return, arriving home in time to read a nugget titled "Why Americans and Britons Work Such Long Hours." He would mine it for more gems tonight.

Marcus laid the *Economist* on his desk. "On my way."

He ambled to the dining room, beaming at the platters filled with his favorite Trini dishes—*pelau*, doubles, roti, *accra*, curry-stew chicken, and sugar cake. Kiara sat alongside Sarah, a de facto member of the family. Only the absence of Brian and his own parents kept the occasion from being perfect. Even so, it felt like Thanksgiving, as did every Sunday. They had been blessed.

Marcus took a seat. "Amazing, honey."

"Don't give me that sweet eye. You haven't even tried it yet." Corinda rose to fetch something from the kitchen.

"Kiara, help your mother." Both girls followed.

Sometimes he missed the carefree lifestyle of Trinidad. What stood out weren't the sensational experiences—swimming under waterfalls, playing Mas at Carnival, or snorkeling Buccoo Reef. Rather, it was the simple stuff he did as a kid. Going to the weekend fruit-and-veggie market with his mom. Helping fishermen pull in their boats and being rewarded with a kingfish bigger than himself. Going from house to house with *parang* musicians at Christmas, listening to them strum the *cuatro* and sing sweetly in Spanish—a language none of them understood—with everyone sipping *poncha crema* and munching on minced-meat *pasteles*. For him as a teen, it was dancing to soca, imbibing Puncheon Rum, and roasting an iguana or wild hog while camping.

But most of all he missed the people—their warmth and nobility. Who but Trinidadians would routinely leave their phone number on the dashboard of a parked car they had just dented—unnoticed? How often had he seen car-accident victims befriend the person who had hit them, with driver after driver stopping to help, and everyone partying on the side of the highway? He would always treasure his people and take pride in his roots. But immigrating to America had been the right decision.

Even if the first years had been brutal. They'd survived on Corinda's meager income as a nurse's assistant while he pursued an accounting degree at Broward College. No feasts then—only Honduran beef and chicken soups from Paisanos. Fortunately, he'd passed the CPA exam on his first try. Hanging out his shingle, he'd targeted the expat community of islanders. Lean years followed until an outlier client, a Venezuelan, sang his praises to countrymen who were by then moving to Broward County in droves. From that point on, Marcus's business thrived, allowing Corinda to enroll in nursing school. When she became an RN, he knew they'd be okay. He didn't love accounting, but they had financial breathing room and could finally afford kids.

The years had sure flown by. Brian, now a sophomore at UF, was on track to attend its highly regarded engineering school. The kid loved Gainesville, returning home only under duress. Yes, Brian had underperformed in soccer, but, as Corinda pointed out, he had been selfish to impose his sports passion on a son more enthralled with the Gators than Chelsea.

Meanwhile, Kiara seemed intent on proving that he had no eye for talent. Now attracting attention from college soccer scouts, Kiara locked horns regularly with her mother, who disapproved of the girl's immersion in sports. Corinda placed her faith in the Lord and academics, and she was by no means praying for a soccer scholarship for their daughter. She fretted about soccer's impact on Kiara's scoliosis, which was severe enough to require a full-time back brace. Corinda favored low-impact sports like swimming, which, of course, didn't interest Kiara in the least. At the same time, Corinda conceded that soccer had gotten Kiara into University School and that, without U School, Kiara never would have taken Learning Resources or figured out how to cope with her learning disability so quickly. She had blossomed academically, becoming an elite student. Soccer kept her fit, away from boys, malls, and drugs, and on track for an athletic scholarship, if she ever stopped racking up red cards.

As they joined hands, Marcus felt blessed. Aside from marrying Corinda, coming to America was the best decision he'd ever made. Even if the *Economist* editor thought Americans worked too hard.

The second Kiara finished saying grace, Sarah pounced. "Mr. Pinson, would you mind passing the doubles?"

Marcus frowned. The novelty of a White girl's craving Trini cuisine had long since faded. The timing and tone of Sarah's appeal—surely rehearsed—suggested that life itself depended on those curried chick-pea treats. She collected them as assiduously as she did fifty-fifty balls on the soccer pitch. And Corinda enabled her, chuckling and allowing Sarah to hoard doubles with impunity. All because she had befriended Kiara when no one else would.

Marcus passed the platter, not daring to serve himself first. Sarah pressed her advantage, tossing three doubles onto her plate. She would pay soon enough, he thought.

"Thanks, Coach!"

He grunted. "You sure you don't want five or six? How about passing them back this way."

"Marcus, behave yourself!" Corinda said. "Thank the Lord there's enough for all of us."

Sarah winked at Corinda. "Better belly buss than good food waste!"

Marcus rolled his eyes and smiled. *The darn girl should be arrested for impersonating a Trini.*

After the feast Marcus retired to his study. Grabbing some videocassettes from the shelf, he planted himself in front of the VCR. The cassettes were titled according to the player (Pele, Cruyft, Platini, Maradona, Beckenbauer) and featured skill (trapping, dribbling, shooting, passing, defense). He ordered them according to his training plan. By now the process required so little concentration that his thoughts reverted to his adopted homeland.

One thing nagged at him. Why did so many native-born Americans fail to see the opportunities in this country that he saw? Here government corruption wasn't endemic. Low tax rates, lenient regulations, and the world's richest domestic market made it easier to start a new business and succeed. Yes, the birth lottery and past discrimination gave White people an undeniable advantage, but poor people could move up the socioeconomic ladder if they worked hard, prayed to God, made responsible decisions, and had some ability. Hell, second-generation Black West Indians now earned more than the average American. Some of it was the creaming effect, many of the most talented islanders having emigrated to come here. But immigrants saw what natural-born citizens often missed: The American glass was 80 percent full, not 70 percent empty.

Racism persisted in America; that was true. Not the open, outspoken racism of segregation but a quieter, softer kind of bigotry. They had experienced it firsthand with Mrs. Foster. Initially Kiara's civics teacher had underestimated her, asking her only the simplest questions. Kiara had been humiliated, and her confidence eroded. Of course, Mrs. Foster had also identified Kiara's auditory-processing deficit and championed the school's purchase of a classroom FM system that enabled the girl to understand lectures. And when Kiara applied to University School, it had been Mrs. Foster who wrote the glowing letter of recommendation, describing Kiara as her "best student, a gifted thinker with tremendous analytical ability." Bigots could be won over. Rather than dwell on the negatives, it made more sense to capitalize on the ample opportunities.

Not only that. He had found that, despite their checkered history, Americans were, by and large, tolerant and generous. Pew was reporting that more than 90 percent of White Americans approved of interracial marriage and that marriages between White people and Black, Asian, and Hispanic people made up 17 percent of all American marriages—a statistic that was on the rise. Most years America took in more immigrants—of all stripes—than all other countries combined. Affirmative action and Great Society programs might never erase the pernicious impact of slavery and segregation, but, as several globetrotting Black friends of his had pointed out, no truly multicultural country treated minorities better than America did. America was far from perfect, yes, but it was clearly steadily improving, and it was a better place for his family than anywhere else on earth.

"Okay, ladies, I'm done," Marcus said.

"Coming, Pops."

"On the *double!*" Sarah said, snickering.

Marcus cherished this time with them. What a hoot Sarah had been, all those years ago, cornering him to verify that he had, in fact, played semipro soccer in Trini. She had detailed Kiara's soccer exploits at school and asked whether he was up to the challenge of training them. Wasting Kiara's talent would be a crying shame, as she could no doubt play college ball. All this before a single organized practice.

Sarah had explained that she was indispensable because drills required two players and, at his age and with his swollen knee, he didn't quite fit the bill. When he had protested, she had stared at him with undisguised skepticism and then quickly changed tack, confiding that she wanted nothing more in the world than to play club soccer. Would he please, please train her because her own dad could barely identify a soccer ball? And could he please let Kiara, her new best friend, try out for the same team? Kiara hadn't known about the ambush.

"I was gonna surprise her with the good news," Sarah had said.

Resistance had been futile.

Now as the girls stood before him, Kiara asked, "So what's the plan—learn more moves? I need to kick Ralph's butt."

"You'll see," Marcus said.

Sarah grinned mischievously. "Coach, how about you teach us the stop-red move?"

"Huh?"

"You know, where we *stop* yanking on ponytails, to avoid getting red cards?"

Marcus chuckled. Last season Kiara had warned a defender to stop stamping on her feet. Getting no sympathy from the referee, Kiara had warned the defender she would ram her cleat down the girl's throat if she persisted. The defender had paid no heed, so Kiara yanked the girl's ponytail, forcing her to her knees. The red card—her third of the season—got Kiara booted not only from the game but also from the team itself, which had dashed their hopes of making the playoffs. Enough time had lapsed to poke fun.

"Here's a better idea," Kiara said, glaring at Sarah. "How about we study tactics—learn how *smart* holding midfielders play defense, instead of acting like strikers and losing the game for us?"

Sarah's lips quivered as she was clearly remembering her crucial mistake from the previous match. No girl loved or studied the game as much as Sarah, and she typically made excellent tactical decisions. Kiara had found her underbelly.

Marcus shoved his index finger in Kiara's face. "That is flat-out wrong—on so many levels. You'll be running five extra sprints."

"Whatever," Kiara said, crossing her arms.

"Ten sprints!"

"Coach, I'm over it," Sarah said. "State Cup's coming up. Let's get to work."

But Marcus couldn't let it go. His eyes locked into Kiara's. "You're calling her stupid? Aren't you the one who's ignoring advice that would keep you from pissing away your dream?"

"I guess." Kiara looked down and shifted her feet.

"Name me one elite program that recruits players who were permanently kicked off their team."

"Can't."

"All right then. No more backchat."

Kiara nodded and turned to Sarah. "I hit back too hard. Sorry."

"No big deal."

Kiara wrapped her arms around Sarah and squeezed, eliciting a smile.

They moved to the sofa to view the images on the television screen opposite them.

Marcus adjusted the brightness and contrast. "Okay, first we'll go over advanced one-v-one moves. Simple moves won't work; defenders are too good. Afterward, you'll play one-v-one. Loser runs four laps."

A clip showed Pele, Kiara's idol, doing his patented runaround move. Kiara popped up to get a closer look, blocking their view.

"*Yuh fadder* is a glassmaker or what?" Sarah said in a Trini lilt. Marcus chuckled.

They studied Maradona's twister move and Platini's scissors and feint.

Kiara ditched her back brace, and they went out back to practice the new skills and play seven one-v-one games. As referee, Marcus was harder on Kiara. Periodically, he stopped the game to deliver tactical insights or correct their technique.

In the final game, with Kiara having already won five of six, Sarah juked Kiara and broke free, ready to slot in the winning goal. With a burst of speed, Kiara recovered but still trailed by two feet. Launching herself, Kiara caught Sarah from behind, cleats penetrating the exposed calves. Sarah went down with a scream.

"I didn't mean it, I swear!" Kiara screeched, kneeling by her victim. Kiara's eyes pooled with tears.

Marcus crouched over Sarah, eyes darting between her anguished face and bloodied legs. He laid his hand soothingly on her back. Abruptly, Sarah rolled over and jumped to her feet, grinning widely. Locating the ball, she booted it into the net. "I win!"

Kiara whooped and hollered as Marcus wiped his brow.

Kiara retrieved the first-aid kit from the car and painstakingly cleaned and bandaged Sarah's cuts. Sarah insisted on doing her "loser laps," and Kiara joined her. After a water break, Marcus assigned Sarah penalty sprints for having monopolized the doubles at lunch. "Nice try, Coach, but it's going to take more than running to put me off those goodies." Sarah cheerfully took her punishment, accompanied by Kiara.

Marcus whistled as he picked up the cones. Soccer was awesome. Designing drills. Researching workouts. Studying nutrition. Dissecting Barcelona games. Officiating one-v-one games. Teaching moves. Collecting VCR highlight videos. Fielding questions from college scouts.

One thing wasn't fun—disciplining. He took Kiara to the side. "You understand there will have to be some punishment?"

His daughter nodded.

11

ROOTS

*M*aracaibo, Venezuela, 1977. Leo surveyed the storage room that functioned as a cell and shook his head: one lousy table, not a single chair or bed. *It figures*, Leo thought. *Anyone stupid enough to kidnap me can't afford more.*

At least there was tons of space. Rubbing his glutes, Leo began pacing the perimeter. Might as well get the blood flowing and undo the effects of the drug.

Who are these guys? Rank amateurs probably. Unfortunately, there's no breaking out.

Most people in life, it seemed, had been trapped in one way or another. He was hardly the first, not even within his own family. All four of his grandparents had suffered. Hell, before emigrating from Spain, his father's father, Eduardo, had languished for a while on death row, the prisoner of General Franco. But none had been willing to settle—to be a pawn. They'd each taken a major leap. If he ever got out, he'd explore their stories more deeply.

The door burst open. A brawny clean-shaven man he'd never seen before entered. The man brandished a pistol in one hand, a bag in the other. Handcuffs dangled from the belt loop of his expensive trousers. He grinned disturbingly.

Leering at Leo, the man approached. "Your friends weren't happy with you."

"I understand, *amigo*." Why had he used the past tense?

"No, I'm sure you don't," the man said, still grinning. "You left them with no cash, credit card, ransom, or car to pawn."

"No car?"

"No working car. They didn't specify, and I couldn't care less."

The man's smile grew menacing. He stepped closer—too close. "Their misfortune, my gain. You're better than I expected." Pointing the pistol at Leo's chest, the thug handed him the handcuffs. "To the table."

Leo obeyed.

The man removed a plunger from the bag and, holding it aloft, cackled. "Compliments of Bernardo. We'll make very good use of it."

A poisonous snake ready to strike. Leo winced at remembering the confrontation at the tennis club. He turned his thoughts to Eduardo. *Abuelo, please, give me your strength. Help me.*

12

MAKING HISTORY

College Park, Maryland, 1985. Zeb's mind should not have been wandering—not when he was on his meds, listening to his favorite subject, and on deck as the next speaker. He had held it together for the first three presentations but couldn't help fidgeting during a talk on the Continental Army—its defeats and triumphs. Having Mom around would've come in handy. She kept him on edge. Edge was desirable when vying for the National History Day prize for eighth graders.

The Battle of Saratoga was in full swing while Zeb pondered his own turning point: going on ADHD meds. Before that, he had been scolded constantly, underperformed in school, and made few friends. Sure there were times when he had acted impulsively and had fun, unconstrained by disapproving adults, but they were brief, and usually when his mom was away on business. Mostly he felt like a hamster on a wheel. The Little Train That Couldn't. His habit of spontaneously saying hurtful truths hadn't endeared him to people. Neither had looking away when classmates spoke to him. "You have the attention span of a fly!" people told him.

Being Jewish hadn't helped matters. It wasn't an asset socially, not in the Bible Belt. "Christ killers," he had learned, weren't on the fast track to heaven. Not that a pill could change that.

But he had found ways to fit in. Two positive aspects of having ADHD—his focus and perseverance when motivated—offset the downsides. Most dudes were sports fans, so he had become an expert on the Tar Heels and the Redskins. And because true Southerners knew their history, he had soaked up as many Civil War details as possible, even of second-tier battles and generals.

There was no denying he had also downplayed his heritage. He never mentioned temple, Hanukkah, or Yom Kippur, and, instead of a conspicuous bar mitzvah bash, he had pressed for a family trip to the Caribbean. He let slip to schoolmates that bacon and pork chops were his favorite foods. He never disclosed his working knowledge of Hebrew. And, though he refused to acknowledge Jesus as Lord when saying grace or singing Christmas carols, his nonconformity went unnoticed. He knew he might one day consider these behaviors a betrayal, but, for now, being different was the greater concern.

Fitting in better didn't mean he didn't get in trouble. Once, after being sent to Dr. Blinder's office for cussing, the principal had invited him to sit. They chatted about *Planet of the Apes* before Dr. Blinder asked, "How badly do you want to make friends?" When Zeb admitted it meant everything, Dr. Blinder rubbed his chin. "Before you open your mouth to say anything, stop! Count to five under your breath, and then ask yourself three questions: Is what I'm about to say kind? Is it true? Is it necessary? If you can't answer yes to all three, don't speak. And ask your classmates tons of questions. People love talking about themselves." Zeb had followed the principal's advice and become a popular sixth grader.

Popular, yes, but not yet a good student. Everything had changed after taking the meds. School became a breeze; his mind transformed into a steel trap, and he retained details that had previously eluded him. For the first time he exceeded peoples' expectations. However, if he now avoided gaffes, he had also lost his carefree, chatty demeanor, leaving him at a standstill socially. But college beckoned, and his mom was delighted. His dad would come around eventually.

"Our next contestant is Zebulon Ackerman, eighth grader from Culbreth Middle School in Chapel Hill, North Carolina. He'll be speaking about genealogy."

Smiling, Zeb strode to the podium, his head held high. It was time to liven things up and breathe some life into history. Winning regionals had been child's play but also uninteresting.

"Hey, folks," he began. "Glad to be here. Let's do history!

"In 1978, thirty-three years after World War II, Irena Sendler was finally recognized for saving over 2,500 Warsaw children during the Holocaust. Before then, she was unknown. In 1969, the Navy overturned the unfair World War II court-martial of Captain Charles McVay, twenty-five years after the fact. In 1980, Edgar Killen was finally convicted of murdering three civil rights workers in Mississippi sixteen years earlier."

Zeb breathed deeply. So far, so good. "What do all three events have in common? They only occurred because of genealogy, the study of family history. Research done by winners of this very competition led to those events! In other words, the study of family history *changed history!*"

Zeb argued that the study of history—by revealing what organizational systems and priorities worked and didn't work—could do even more than science and technology to improve the human condition. Furthermore, genealogy was a vastly underutilized tool to examine history.

"Basically, history is the cumulative effect of billions of people acting over time. Genealogy looks at individuals and their families—the smallest units of history, sort of like cells in biology. Some people are giants—Alexander the Great, Winston Churchill—but most don't affect history that much. So why bother personalizing history, except in the case of the few great men and women? Because a bottom-up, microlevel approach teaches us a ton. Let me show you examples from my own family."

Zeb looked at the folks seated in the first row. *Not sleeping yet.*

He described the experience of his paternal grandmother during the Nazi siege of Leningrad. Millions died from starvation, bombardment, and hypothermia. Bubbe and her brother, the lone family survivors, ate tree bark, rats, cats, dogs, birds, sawdust, window putty, and boiled leather. After the war they emigrated to England, since America barred refugees. Bubbe eventually made it to New York, working as a seamstress in one of the few remaining clothing factories on the Lower East Side. She married Zeb's grandfather, a Yiddish-speaking watchmaker. They worked themselves to the bone, living frugally so their children could go to university. Both grandparents were Socialists.

"Studying their history raised larger questions for me: Why did the Nazis invade the Soviet Union in the first place? Did religion help my Bubbe survive, or did she lose her faith? Why didn't FDR help World War II refugees? Why did so many Jews, including my grandparents, become Socialists?"

Zeb shifted his hands on the podium. "What traits helped immigrants assimilate and succeed in America? What government services were critical to helping them, and how long did they need them? I could go on, but you get the idea. It's hard to learn about family history without learning a *ton* about history at large, even if your family weren't immigrants."

He sipped water. Only a few eyes were wandering. The rest were fixed on him, awaiting his next words.

Zeb moved on to his maternal grandparents, Sephardic Jews from Essaouira, Morocco. Historically, that city had welcomed Jews, but during the 1948 Arab-Israeli War forty-four Jews were killed during riots. Because his grandparents feared worse after Morocco gained its inevitable independence from France, they emigrated to Israel. They would help build the fledging state.

To their dismay, European immigrants to the Holy Land discriminated against Moroccans for their reputed hot tempers and unwillingness to work the land. After eight years working on a kibbutz—she as a doctor, he a planter—Zeb's grandparents left for America, settling in North Carolina. Zeb's grandmother earned little as a physician because she served poor patients and often waived her fees. His grandfather, a classical-music-loving tailor, dreamed of being a concert pianist but worked at Jos. A. Bank, where he was adored by the patrons. Their only child, Zeb's mother Ruth, taught marketing at UNC's Kenan-Flagler Graduate School of Business. She also consulted for corporations.

Again, Zeb spoke of the larger questions this story raised, how genealogy had brought him closer to family and made him more learned.

"Genealogy uncovers good and bad role models and promotes justice. Heroes aren't always recognized while they're alive, but history can fix that. Villains aren't always punished during their lifetimes, but history can take care of that also. If we're smart, we'll learn . . ."

Despite being the odds-on favorite after regionals, Zeb placed last. The National History Day judges appreciated his message but ruled that he hadn't advanced the body of knowledge. The guidelines had been clear, and Zeb had disregarded them. There would be no scholarship. But, regardless, Zeb knew his days of hiding his heritage were over.

13

DEBATABLE

eston, Florida, 1987. Kiara stared with glazed eyes toward the front of the classroom. If only she could read her book or lay her head down and snooze. No such luck. Two bozos were clutching the podiums with the earnestness of young politicians, debating the dangers of marijuana versus alcohol. Neither had yet made an interesting point. Maybe they should have indulged before going at it.

She really had no reason to bitch. Normally, her back brace bit into her thighs as she sat, cutting off circulation to her legs. Most days, her blouse stuck out irregularly, and she sweated into her undershirt, itching in places she couldn't scratch. Not today. Her indulgence was being free of the damn brace. The debates were a blessing, boredom a small price to pay.

Of course, if she had any sense, she'd be petrified. *Who in their right mind changes their debate topic at the last minute, without getting the teacher's approval?* Wasn't it enough that civics wasn't her bag, that 60 percent of her grade was based on this project? Or that her best friend was now set to trounce her?

This stuff was too touchy-feely, unscientific. The topics—legalization, gun violence—were so politicized that everyone always retreated into their intellectual shells, mindlessly repeating mantras and biased statistics, never giving an inch on any argument made by the other side, no matter how logical. Glorified mud wrestling—that was what this was. Not that she hadn't constantly challenged her long-suffering teacher, Mr. Generous. Her reward? Being paired with Sarah. Mr. Generous knew winning would be almost as upsetting to each as losing. Payback would be a bitch, he'd be laughing his ass off inside, and the class would learn a lot. The perfect trifecta.

Sarah looked relaxed. *And why wouldn't she be?* Kiara thought. *She* hadn't altered her debate topic. No trouble in store for her.

Sarah would also be sitting pretty at the showcase soccer tournament, without her. Talk about unfair. It was ridiculous, Dad pulling her from the event because of one dirty foul—in practice, no less. The college recruiters would all be watching Sarah, not her. Maybe it was time to kick her butt.

Easier said than done. Sarah was smart as a whip and annoyingly diligent, just like on the soccer pitch. She'd have done all her research—lined up every argument, anticipated counterarguments, and prepared rebuttals. Sarah hated to lose as much as she did.

"And by eliminating the black market," her classmate droned on, "legalization takes the risk and profit out of distribution. Violent crime will . . ."

Yeah, right. Kiara's thoughts drifted to what her dad's best buddy from Trini had said last night. That she was amazingly self-assured and accomplished. Her dad had snapped, "Why wouldn't a Black girl thrive at an elite school? Why shouldn't she be confident, even with a learning disability? There's no room for old thinking, my friend, especially among us."

But so much had gone right. Soccer had gotten her into University School tuition-free, though the admissions director insisted she enroll in Learning Resources. Joining what she then called the "Stupid Club" wasn't easy, when so many classmates were "gifted," as they and their status-seeking parents kept repeating. As if being a Black girl with a back brace wasn't bad enough.

But Learning Resources had helped her compensate for her auditory difficulties. She learned test-taking strategies, time management, how to repeat multistep instructions under her breath, and how to transform lecture notes into graphic organizers that brought meaning to concepts, boosting her long-term memory. When she reached tenth grade, she no longer needed extra time on tests. She discovered she was sharper than most gifted students. But this civics bullshit . . .

"All right, Kiara and Sarah, you're up," Mr. Generous said. "Our scholars will be debating gun control: Sarah in favor, Kiara opposing."

Kiara spoke up, "Actually, Mr. Generous, I changed my topic last night. I hope you don't mind."

"Actually, Kiara, I do mind." He shook his head. "What did you come up with?"

"What's the bigger danger to America, gun violence or narcissism? Sarah will stick with gun control—I'm the narcissism expert."

"Go ahead, but we'll discuss this later."

Sarah gave a brief history of gun violence in America. Presenting a slew of alarming statistics, she detailed the impact on society. Next, she outlined policy changes needed to address the crisis. She enumerated her points, punctuating them with examples. *Too bad Mr. Generous isn't this effective*, Kiara thought.

"Your turn, Kiara," Mr. Generous said.

"Look, we can all agree on two things. First, gun violence has reached crisis proportions and needs to be tackled. Second, Sarah's ideas are excellent because they're common sense and balanced."

Kiara peeked at Mr. Generous. His raised eyebrows tickled her.

"But rampant narcissism is an even bigger problem. Unless we address it, we'll never solve gun violence or, for that matter, any complex problem facing America."

She turned to Sarah. "Let's talk guns. Looking just at the politics, there's no alternative to pursuing an all-of-the-above approach that incorporates all your great ideas. Why? Because any strategy that focuses only on one aspect—for example, *only* banning certain firearms, *only* mental-health screenings, *only* improving security at schools, *only* improving intelligence and law enforcement—will alienate tons of voters. Any one-dimensional plan will push away most liberals or conservatives and never gain enough support in Congress.

"On the other hand, a comprehensive approach would be seen by most people as commonsense, fair, and more likely to fix the problem. It would stand a better chance of becoming law.

"I found numerous microfiche articles where experts were spouting off on gun violence—some liberal, some conservative. The common denominator? They all believed they had the only grasp on reality, that people who disagreed were stupid, uninformed, or evil. You see the problem? How can there be political compromise—a comprehensive solution—when so many Americans are narcissists?

"Gun violence *is* a vital issue. But so are the Cold War, poverty, drugs, and the environment. Like guns, these are complex problems that cry out for balanced solutions. That means drawing the best ideas from across the political spectrum. That'll only happen if we declare a war on narcissism."

The girls debated to a standoff and answered questions. Mr. Generous nitpicked two gun-control points, not bothering to address narcissism. Afterward, everyone applauded except him. Walking back to her seat, Kiara peeked at the notebook of a notorious doodler. *No scribbles!* And still free of the damned back brace. All in all, not a bad day.

14

BAD HAIR DAY

Maracaibo, Venezuela, 1977. Leo stormed out of the house and, no longer possessing a clunker, walked off aimlessly. Was there nowhere he could rest in peace, away from prying eyes and questions? At school his buddy, Federico, hounded him endlessly. At home, his sister, Carina, begged him to confide and unload some of the burden. Mamá burst into tears daily, frustrated at not being able to help.

No one could help. Actually, they all could—by shutting up. Some things had to be tackled privately. Eventually he'd been found—beaten and covered in blood—and gotten out of the cell. But now too many possibilities had surfaced, some unspeakable.

Leo wandered until the streets became unfamiliar. Just after sunset he entered a *barrio* notorious for assaults, but, at this point, what did he care? On and on he roamed until he stumbled upon the ritzy district where he used to work—until getting fired for not showing up for two straight weeks after the kidnapping. Across the street was a hair salon catering to members of the Club de Las Americas, including Bernardo's mother.

Leo paused. It was closing time, and the lone remaining employee, a young flamboyantly dressed man, was rolling down the shutters. The boss and clients were long gone, as was everyone else.

The hairdresser locked up the salon and sauntered along a side street, whistling a tune. With a mounting sense of rage and fear, Leo followed, his fists curling into balls. He overtook the hairdresser and, grabbing him by the shoulder, swung him around. The hairdresser's quizzical expression was met with a blow to the stomach. The man yelped and plopped to the pavement.

"*Por favor*, take my money," the hairdresser begged, shielding his head.

Leo would not be deterred from the rage that engulfed him. He fell to his knees and pummeled the man's nose. The hairdresser shrieked as blood spurted over both of them. Then, just as quickly, Leo jumped to his feet and kicked him once in the side.

"I won't stand for it!" Leo thundered. "You hear me? You're a disgrace."

Leo spat onto the street and strode off to the sounds of sobbing. His pace quickened, and just as his fury was transforming into something very different, he broke into a run. Oblivious to his surroundings, he somehow made it back home. Mercifully, his parents and sister, used to his late walkabouts, had retired for the night. Leo dashed to the bathroom, splashed water over his face, and, his hands shaking, dropped the bar of soap. He retrieved it and then scrubbed intensively, continuing long after the blood had disappeared. It wasn't enough. He jumped in the shower, scouring every inch of his body until it was raw.

Things weren't any better in bed. Leo lay sweating, unable to shake the images. The blow to the hairdresser's stomach. Bashing his face. The pain was so intense it felt like Leo had taken the beating himself.

What have I done?

And why did I do it?

And then, hours later, *Was I attacking myself?*

15

I GOT THIS, PROFESSOR

hapel Hill, North Carolina, 1989. Zeb smiled as he left Old East dorm and walked toward the periphery of campus. It was a sweet deal, living in the oldest public university building in America and popping over to his parents' house for laundry service and a tasty meal. He wondered what goodies were waiting for him. Fried chicken, creamed corn, and peach cobbler would really fit the bill. Updating his parents on his week was a small price to pay.

Minutes later Zeb sauntered through the front door of his home. Already, he was salivating. "*Shalom*, y'all!"

He dropped his bag in the laundry room, headed to the living room, and plopped onto the sofa. His father, ensconced Archie Bunker–like in his recliner, was immersed in *Crime and Punishment*. For the third time.

"Is dinner ready?" Zeb said. "I'm starving."

Larry peered above his spectacles. "Why, thank you, son. I'm doing just swell. Shall I press your shirts as well?"

Zeb grinned. "You're so weird." He gave his old man the obligatory hug.

"It's almost ready."

"Awesome. Where's Mom?"

"Finishing up paperwork. She'll be down soon."

"Cool."

"There's tons of admin in her new position." Larry set his book aside. "But she slogs through . . . Whoa, here comes the dean now."

His mom entered the room, radiating happiness. Whatever pressures she felt now paled in comparison with earlier years. Raising him had been no walk in the park. The day UNC accepted him, however, his parents' load lightened immeasurably. He was off in the right direction, not on cruise control but close enough. Yes, taking meds had cost him socially—turning him into a "stiff"—but it had been worth it. Family peace and good grades trumped fun.

"*Assistant* dean," Ruth said, hugging her son and motioning them toward the dining room. Soon they were reciting the *Hamotzi*, the blessing over bread, and savoring Larry's pot roast and scalloped potatoes, Zeb moaning in delight.

"So, how're things going for my budding tycoon?" she asked.

Zeb shook his head. Her fascination with his part-time job was unusual for an academic.

"She meant historian," Larry said playfully.

"Fine—tycoon of historic proportions. Did you figure out how to save Chapel Hill Travel?"

"Honey," Larry interjected, "that's above the pay grade of a college history major."

"I have some ideas," Zeb said, before lamenting how little pot roast remained.

"Don't be cryptic," Larry said. "Out with it."

"I'm thinking of developing multisport tours to Peru and Costa

Rica. We'll sell them to spring breakers from Carolina, Duke, Wake, and State."

"Multisport?"

Zeb smiled. "We'll offer as many different types of adventure as possible, give them tons of variety and excitement. In Peru, we're talking whitewater rafting and horseback riding in the Urubamba Valley, hiking the Inca Trail, biking and hot-air ballooning in the Sacred Valley, and jungle trekking and canoeing in the Amazon. You get the idea."

They did, having spent their honeymoon in Peru.

"And for people who hate camping?" Ruth asked.

"We'll offer a lodge-based option on the Inca Trail. Our motto will be 'Adventure by Day, Comfort by Night.'"

"Who's going to pay for these adventures?"

"Parents, of course." Zeb helped himself to the rest of the pot roast. "We'll win them over by keeping prices low and including a big educational component."

"Tell us about the cultural excursions," Ruth asked.

Zeb raised his eyebrows. His dad was usually the culture freak. "They can take a Peruvian cooking class or a dance lesson, meet an Andean mystical healer, learn to play an Andean instrument, paint a classroom, teach English, or enjoy lectures on Inca architecture or Amazonian flora and fauna."

"A far cry from doing beer bongs on the beach," Larry said, chortling. "How can you keep prices low with these customized itineraries?"

"With groups, fixed costs are spread over more people. As long as they agree on the same activities, we're fine. We'll use three-star lodges."

"What kind of margin can you make?" Larry asked, sipping Cabernet.

Zeb snickered. His father, the history professor, was sounding like a banker—like his mom. "Thirty percent. By offering so many options, the perceived value goes up. And the price is still affordable."

Ruth looked at him admiringly. "You sure you haven't been sneaking into my classes instead of your dad's?"

"What about the rainy season?" Larry persisted, his preoccupation with logistics completing their role reversal.

"Adventure travelers shouldn't be put off too much; everything will be greener and more photogenic."

Ruth handed Zeb a slice of key lime pie. "You're not worried students would rather go to Cancun, places like that?"

"I hear ya. Plenty would, but there's enough others to make it work. Remember, my generation is more focused on meaningful experiences than yours is."

"You don't say," Ruth said, guffawing. "You may be right but remember: The fastest way to bankruptcy is to ignore market signals for too long—to think you're smarter than thousands of consumers. But it's worth a try. I never see anyone in that place."

"Things aren't that bad."

"Just don't neglect your schoolwork, especially math." Ruth's expression turned serious. "You can't only work on what excites you."

"I won't, Mom."

When Zeb announced he needed to take off for his discussion group, Larry smirked. "I forgot: Small will be going over serious stuff."

"It's *Professor* Small, and you'd be surprised."

"I'm sure his doctorate is what lures you all. Tell him I said hi."

Zeb ducked into the alleyway leading to He's Not Here. His stride quickened as he spotted the tavern's logo—a hand pointing *away* from the establishment. He grinned. Bartenders here were reputed to respond, "He's not here," when fielding calls from significant others. These days the sanctuary bar was gender neutral—a refuge for everyone. For him personally, it offered a break from routine and his own personality.

The bouncer waved him on through to the grassy courtyard. Empty bottles of Bud lay on the stage where bands played on weekends. This being Thursday evening, Professor Small sat at the head of a picnic table, flanked by his half-dozen disciples. The unpretentious setting and cheap beer invited creative thinking.

The mostly depleted Carolina Cups were proof that he'd rambled on too long with his parents about travel. He'd probably missed some good scoop. He poured himself a beer and took a seat.

"But, Professor, I don't get it," a classmate said. "In your book, you said that before the European explorers arrived, there were twenty million Native Americans, not one million, like many sources claim?"

Whew. He was late but not *that* late.

"Absolutely, Adam," Professor Small said. Lanky and only beginning to gray, he seemed fitter than his students. "Tenochtitlán was one of the world's largest cities. And we're talking more than just the Aztecs and Inca. The Mississippi Valley had a sizable population supported by excellent farmland."

"And epidemic diseases in humans can only be supported by large populations, right?" Adam asked.

"Exactly. Within a short period, people either die from acute illness or recover completely. Those who recover develop immunity. Microbes need to find new hosts to survive. Unless a lot of new babies are born, which only happens with large populations, the epidemic dies out."

A medical school student jumped in: "Hold on, Professor. Many disease microbes can live in soil or animals. They don't need human hosts to survive."

"Good point." Professor Small refilled his cup with Bud. "There are a few infectious diseases—yellow fever is one—that can survive among small populations. It can be transmitted from humans to monkeys and come back to infect humans. But generally, the microbes that survive in animals or soil are associated with chronic diseases, not acute ones."

"So here's my question," Adam pressed. "European explorers infected Native Americans with Old World diseases. But if there were twenty million Native Americans, why didn't germs go in *both* directions? Why didn't the explorers get infected as well?"

"I got this, Professor," Zeb said, setting down his Carolina Cup. This was only the conversational appetizer, but his adrenaline was pumping.

"Go right ahead."

"You and Dr. Jared Diamond from UCLA gave three reasons. First, big cities developed later in the New World than in Europe and Asia. Second, Native American cities didn't trade internationally as much as the Romans did with North Africa, India, and China. So America never became the same type of breeding ground for germs. Third, Europeans and Asians domesticated many herd animals, but Americans didn't. Epidemic diseases came from their farm animals and pets."

Adam popped up. "Wait a second! Professor Small just said human epidemic diseases can't survive in animals."

"They can't, dude," Zeb said. "But herd animals are the *source* of most human epidemic diseases. Flu came from pigs. Measles, smallpox, and tuberculosis came from infected cattle."

"Why didn't New World people domesticate herd animals?" asked another classmate, Mary.

Professor Small gave Zeb the go-ahead to address her query. "Indigenous Americans did domesticate animals, but after the end of the last Ice Age, there were far fewer large mammals left than in Eurasia, partly because of hunting. Eurasia started out with far more animals and had much greater variety. Plus, New World animals—llamas, turkeys, ducks—didn't live in herds or flocks and weren't cuddly. So they weren't sources of epidemic diseases."

Tam flashed the time-out sign. "Enough, Zeb, my brain's hurting!" A stellar history student, Tam always determined when they'd met their quota of serious talk. "If we have to talk biology, let's figure out how to export flu to Durham."

Zeb chuckled. ACC basketball easily took precedence over the Pleistocene Age. The biological and environmental factors underlying human history fascinated them all, but they were hoops addicts and nothing Professor Small discovered in the research arena would ever rival his game-winning shots, as first man off the bench, during a particularly glorious stretch in the 1960s. This was the main event.

"Following in the noble tradition of Pizarro and Cortés, I see," Professor Small said, acceding to the conversational detour. "But, folks, there's no need to decimate the Duke Blue Devils before taking the court. The Heels will do fine."

"How can you say that, Professor?" Tam said. "With Laettner and Hurley, Duke could give an NBA team a run for their money."

"Sounds like Professor Small has some scoop," Zeb said. "Recruiting maybe?"

"Yeah, Professor," Adam said, grinning, "it's time to *earn* your beer!" Before tonight Professor Small had never allowed them to pay.

"No scoop, I'm afraid. Coach Smith usually gets a good crop, but we don't need a silver bullet. We've got him."

"The professor's right," Mary said, turning to Zeb. "Dean's a friggin' genius. Never mind all his innovations. You remember when we were trailing Duke by eight with seventeen seconds left and won—before the three-point shot? *Learn* from history."

Zeb winced. He'd never been accused of undervaluing history—or his idol. "I agree one hundred percent. I'm just saying their talent gives them more margin for error in case of injuries, bad calls, or unlucky bounces. Professor, what's the word on—"

"Sorry, Professor," the bartender interrupted. "There's a call for you." The students cracked up. Apparently, He's Not Here rules didn't apply to their mentor.

The group disbanded, and, having no Friday morning classes, Zeb joined Tam at Cat's Cradle, where a Seattle band was set to jam. Tam's roommate, a part-time bouncer, let them in free. They grabbed dollar Buds and hung to the side.

"To basketball and history," Zeb toasted. *And to offsetting my meds and feeling alive,* he thought.

"And girls," Tam said, clinking bottles.

They ogled chicks, talked hoops, and rocked out until a case of the munchies drove them to Time Out. Tam ordered a chicken-and-cheese biscuit while cash-poor Zeb ordered four "bones" for ten cents apiece, hoping the leftover chicken would salve his hunger. It didn't. They headed to campus and, still buzzed, sang "Deacon Blues" all the way down Cameron Street. A Carr dorm resident shouted out the window, "Shut up, you dumbfucks! It's three in the fucking morning!" So they cranked it up a notch, knowing campus police were minutes away. Obscenities escorted them to Old East, where Zeb bid farewell.

Collapsing in bed, Zeb cackled. He'd never had so much fun in his life. Something to remember when it came time for his next dose of meds.

16

WHATEVER

eston, Florida, 1987. Corinda stood at the kitchen sink, hands on hips, glaring at her daughter. "Explain to me, young lady, how you had an A going into the last week and ended up with a C-plus."

Kiara looked up from her bowl of oatmeal. "Arithmetic, Mom. The debate was sixty percent of my grade. He gave me a sixty-five."

"He *gave* you?"

"I earned it, whatever."

Corinda moved to the breakfast table. "What happened?"

"I ignored the topic." Kiara gulped orange juice.

"Why on earth would you do that?"

"Too narcissistic, I guess."

"You realize you killed your chances with the Ivies and UNC?"

"Whatever."

"Got it," Corinda said, her nostrils flaring. "Well, we're pulling you from varsity soccer."

"Yeah, right. You can't do that." Kiara bit her lip. "I already missed the showcase."

"Exactly. You should've learned."

"Damn!"

"One more word, and club soccer is next." Corinda shook her head. "Now rinse your bowl."

17

LAND OF
(BARBARA) EDEN

Canaima, Venezuela, 1977. Leo wiped the bar at the Lost World Lodge and peered at the last three gringos. The views of Angel Falls had faded more than an hour ago, and yet the tourists still sat overlooking the river, nursing the same cocktails. So much of life, it seemed, was spent waiting on others. The setting changed, but his role remained the same. At the club he had waited on Venezuelans and a smattering of foreigners. Here, gringos and Europeans predominated, with only a sprinkling of elite Venezuelans. Premium prices kept the riffraff out.

Gringos were cool. They tipped generously and didn't talk down to him. But it was already pushing midnight. He needed to restock the bar, replenish the stations, and then serve breakfast to German ornithologists at 5:30 a.m. Why couldn't those weirdos obsess over their checklists at a civilized hour?

Leo leaned against the counter, crossed his arms, and rested his head. For just a second . . .

Someone touched his elbow, and Leo recoiled as if a cockroach were scurrying up his arm. He looked up. It was the American with the Jimmy Buffett T-shirt and luminous smile. Embarrassed, Leo gathered himself. *This isn't Maracaibo; no one has abducted me.*

"Sorry, buddy. Didn't mean to startle you. Guess we kept you overtime."

"I am sorry, sir," Leo said, befuddled.

"I need to pay the *cuenta*, please."

"Of course, sir."

"I'm going to the bathroom. Be back in a minute." His companions had left.

Leo tallied the bill and then cleaned up. Nowadays, immersing himself in mundane tasks was just what the doctor ordered. Not that he'd seen any shrinks after the kidnapping, but had he done so, they surely would've approved.

He needed time to recover from his injuries. To ponder the damage he'd inflicted on others in the aftermath. To figure out how to prevent a repeat.

Señor Elio, his favorite club member, had anticipated his needs and lined up the job. The isolation would give him a chance to recover his humanity, not just run from problems.

But didn't humanity imply softness, the mindset that had led to the calamity in the first place?

Maybe he was overthinking. People got what they deserved, whether it was earning monster tips as a Lost World bartender or inviting degradation by being a pretty boy.

But the people I hurt didn't have it coming. They were innocents. How will I ever get over that?

The American returned and paid the bill.

"So where're you from?" the gringo said, fumbling in his pocket. "You look different than most folks around here."

"My home is Maracaibo."

"Ah, big-time oil country."

"You are right, sir."

"Your English is pretty good. Where'd you learn it?"

Leo smiled. "I watch much television from America—*I Dream of Jeannie* y *Get Smart.*"

The American chuckled. "I'd marry Barbara Eden at the drop of a hat. Did you study English in school?"

"Yes, sir, but classes was not good."

"You're doing just fine—much better than my *Español*," the American said, guffawing. "What are you doing here? I mean, Angel Falls is beautiful and all, but there's not much action for a single fella. Must be boring."

Leo's shoulders tightened. "In reality, city is bad place for me. I will never live there again."

"All cities or Maracaibo?"

"Maracaibo. Is not good for me. Bad things, bad people. Not like America."

"American cities have problems, too, but maybe one day you'll live there. You never know."

"My dream is live in North Carolina," Leo said, brightening.

The American chuckled. "How on earth did you choose North Carolina?"

"My father love baseball. We watch College World Series on TV. I see many pictures, beautiful! I do not like baseball, but I love North Carolina."

"That must've been Chapel Hill. Lots of trees?"

"Many."

"You would leave your country? Leave everything, everyone behind?"

"Yes, sir. I want study engineering in America, work there."

"Well, good for you. I admire that. Hope you make it one day. We certainly need more engineers."

"*Gracias.*"

"Can I give you a piece of advice, Leo?"

"Of course, sir."

"Don't let bad people keep you from chasing your goals. You'll bounce back. I'm sure of that."

"Thank you, sir."

The American signed the bill and returned to his room with the others. Leo pocketed the twenty-dollar tip.

18

THE FAKER AND
THE BRAGGER

hapel Hill, North Carolina, 1990. A line of third graders filed into a class taught by Zeb at the same religious school he'd once attended under duress. *Can this get any more surreal?* he wondered. They high-fived him upon entering. Unlike him when he'd been their age, the children smiled and chattered. They didn't grumble about being kept from more desirable pursuits.

Maybe Wednesday afternoons weren't as much of a sacrifice as the Sunday mornings he'd forgone as a kid—or just maybe Zeb was doing okay as a teacher. More likely still, these kids had better attitudes. People said they had special needs, but what they had were special hearts. They made his week, as unthinkable as that once was. And now the semester was ending.

It was too bad the temple scene overall didn't resonate. It had little of the allure that church seemed to hold for Christians, especially among African American communities. Their fervor was unmistakable. Television didn't lie. Rabbi Norman's sermons were wonderful, but how many times had he been given the evil eye for fidgeting as services dragged on? Mentoring kids was different.

In the corridor, Rabbi stopped to whisper and wink. "You'll miss them, won't you?"

"I sure will."

Rabbi had known all along: how not to push too hard, how these kids—once met—couldn't be dismissed, not even by a college sophomore. He would miss the little buggers.

I need to make today's class count. The lesson plan was crazy, but they deserved his best. That had little to do with Hebrew or key passages of the Torah. Thankfully, Rabbi gave him latitude.

Dropping to the carpeted floor, Zeb called, "All right, guys, gather around."

They drew together.

"Okay, now I've said this before but when I was your age, I was just like you guys."

"No way!" one kid said.

"Yes way, Tommy, and that's a *good* thing. Who remembers what my challenges were?"

"You couldn't sit still," a girl said as she got up to walk around.

"Exactly, Miriam. Here, sit next to me. What other challenges did I have?"

"You couldn't concentrate."

"That's right, David. I was easily distracted. What else?"

"You couldn't understand what you read," Tommy said.

"Absolutely. Anything else? Remember, I had a *ton* of challenges."

Miriam grinned. "You said things you shouldn't."

"Yes, I was impulsive. That means I blurted out things without first thinking *if* I should say them. You guys are great listeners, better than I was."

Cheers and applause.

"When I was your age, did I get good grades?" Zeb asked.

"No."

"Did people think I was smart?"

"No."

"Was I smart?"

"Yes!" they shouted in unison.

"Like all of you?"

"Yes!"

"I got great news today." They hushed each other to hear better. "You remember I work for a travel company?"

"Yes."

"Well, it was doing badly, so badly it was going bankrupt. But today my boss told me it's doing better than ever. You know why?"

Silence.

"It's doing well because of an idea I came up with. I'm not supposed to tell anyone, but I wanted to tell you. You know why?"

"Because you're a bragger?" Tommy said.

"Hopefully not."

Miriam leaned against him. "So we are proud of you?"

"That, too," Zeb said. "But mostly I want you to know that you can do great things too. Here's a secret"—they listened in rapt attention—"people like us are more creative than most people. We think of new ideas and new ways of doing things. *That* is what helped save the business. And when you guys grow up, you'll do your own great things."

Doubtful expressions surrounded him.

"Look, I know things are hard. You try and you try; you feel like all you do is screw up. But trust me, good things will happen. Just listen to your doctors, teachers, and tutors. Work hard and believe in yourself. Be patient. It'll take time, but whatever you do, *don't* give up."

Zeb waited for the message to sink in.

Tommy spoke first. "We won't give up, Zeb. We won't *ever* give up!" He stood and clapped, repeating the mantra. Others joined, and before long it was bedlam.

Rachel hugged Zeb as he fought back tears. With a lump in his throat, Zeb said, "Guys, settle down. Five-minute break. We'll start up at four fifteen sharp."

When they returned, Zeb said, "Okay, change of gears. How many of you know who Thomas Edison was?" Five hands shot up. "Tommy."

"He invented the lightbulb."

"Bingo! Edison was America's greatest inventor. He had over a thousand inventions—the telegraph, video camera, battery, and record player. He changed the way people lived. His inventions helped make America a world power."

"Wow!"

"Impressive, right? Do you think Edison was a good student?"

"Of course, he was," said David. "How could he invent everything if he wasn't?"

"Actually, Thomas was a bad student. He didn't learn to talk until he was four. He had terrible hearing, couldn't sit still in class. He was easily distracted. His writing and speech were poor. Teachers said he misbehaved."

"No way!"

"Thomas learned differently from most kids, but he was very smart. Teachers just didn't know how to teach him the right way. His mom gave him books on science, philosophy, English, and history—he loved to read them. When Thomas was eleven, he built his own laboratory. He didn't let his bad hearing discourage him. He focused on the positive. He was less distracted from his books and experiments.

"Now, who knows who Albert Einstein was?"

"He was a scientist," said Miriam.

"Bingo! Einstein was the greatest scientist who ever lived. Some think he was also the smartest person ever. People say 'Einstein' when they mean 'genius.' *Time* magazine named him the 'Person of the Century'!"

"Was he more important than Edison?" Miriam asked.

"Good question! They're both up there."

"What did he do?"

"To be honest, his work is too complicated for me to understand."

"Then how do we know he really did anything?" Tommy chimed in. "He might be faking."

"I promise you Einstein's achievements were real. Ask your science teacher about the theory of relativity, $E = MC^2$, and the wave theory of light. His work led to the development of television, lasers, the atomic bomb, tons of stuff."

"TV's good enough for me," Tommy said.

"I'm so glad," Zeb said. "So, tell me, was he a good student?"

"I'll bet he sucked, like Edison."

"Try a different word," Zeb encouraged.

"Stunk."

"Can't fool you. Albert had a ton of problems growing up. When do you think he learned to speak normally?"

"When he was four," David piped up.

"Try nine. Albert learned to read when he was *seven*, later than all of you. He was not a good student. He was kicked out of high school, and he failed the entrance exam to the Federal Institute of Technology in Switzerland. He was weak in every subject except math. He was disorganized and distracted."

"Did he do *anything* right?" David asked, seeming anxious.

"Well, he didn't give up easily," Zeb replied brightly. "Albert was curious about how the world worked. He played the violin. He mastered calculus when he was sixteen. But teachers overlooked his talents, like Edison. They had no clue how to teach him the right way. Even though he had ADHD and couldn't concentrate, speak, or read like others, he went on to win the Nobel Prize!"

"Maybe the *teachers* should go back to school," Tommy said, forcefully.

Zeb bit his tongue. "Luckily, teachers know a lot more nowadays, but that's a great point. Listen, I was also going to talk about Winston Churchill, my hero, but we need to review Hebrew and a chapter on Moses."

"I'd rather learn about Winston," David said. "That's got to be better than Hebrew. And we already know about Moses."

"David's right," Tommy agreed. "Winston! Winston!" Others chimed in, and, for the second time, pandemonium broke out.

Zeb glanced nervously at the door. "All right, Winston it is." He summarized Churchill's accomplishments as a soldier, inventor, writer, artist, journalist, and wartime leader.

"What were Winston's problems when he was a kid?" David asked.

"Remember: *challenges*, not problems," Zeb said carefully. "Winston had an unhappy childhood. He did badly in school, stuttered, talked with a lisp, and had attention problems. His dad, who was a brilliant scholar, thought he was a disappointment and ignored him. Winston was sent to boarding school when he was twelve and was the lowest-ranked student. But there he discovered his love for literature and writing. When he applied to the Royal Military Academy at Sandhurst, he failed the entrance exam twice, only passing on his third try. He applied for the cavalry instead of the infantry so he wouldn't have to study math, which he hated. But, as you just heard, Winston became the best orator and most impressive leader in the history of England. Not bad, is it?"

"Will we be as great as Edison, Einstein, and Churchill?" Miriam asked.

"Maybe so. What matters is, no matter what anyone else says, you have to believe in yourselves and work hard. If you guys are like me—and I know you are—you can accomplish a lot more than you think. Remember, my idea helped save a business. And I know I'll do more. So find your passion and stick with it. Learn from your therapists and tutors. Work hard. Most importantly . . ." He paused, waiting for their response.

"Don't ever give up!" the students shouted. They clapped, stomped their feet, and banged fists on their desks. Some had started screaming from the excitement in the room. One spun like a whirling dervish.

Zeb glanced outside. "Guys, guys! Your parents are waiting. Here's a handout; it's a list of important people who learned differently. Some names won't be familiar, so look them up or ask your parents; they'll be amazed. You guys have been awesome. See you in January!"

Many students hugged Zeb on their way out. When they'd all left, he perused the handout.

IMPORTANT PEOPLE WHO LEARNED DIFFERENTLY

American presidents: Abraham Lincoln, John F. Kennedy, Dwight Eisenhower, George Herbert Walker Bush, Woodrow Wilson

Political figures: Winston Churchill, Benjamin Franklin

Inventors: Thomas Edison, Alexander Graham Bell, Benjamin Franklin, the Wright Brothers

Scientists: Albert Einstein, Sir Isaac Newton, Louis Pasteur, Galileo

Athletes: Michael Jordan, Babe Ruth, Magic Johnson, Bruce Jenner, Greg Louganis

Actors and comedians: Robin Williams, Whoopi Goldberg, Dustin Hoffman, Will Smith, Suzanne Sommers

Architect: Frank Lloyd Wright

Composers and musicians: Mozart, Beethoven, Stevie Wonder, John Lennon

Authors: Agatha Christie, Emily Dickinson, Ernest Hemingway, Edgar Allan Poe, F. Scott Fitzgerald

Artists: Leonardo da Vinci, Pablo Picasso, Auguste Rodin, Salvador Dali, Vincent van Gogh

Military figures: Napoleon Bonaparte, General George Patton

Animator/cartoonist: Walt Disney

Movie producer: Steven Spielberg

Industrialists: Henry Ford, John D. Rockefeller

Historians were noticeably absent. Zeb sighed. *How will I make my mark?*

If special-needs kids needed a boost, so did special adults. Zeb bounded up the steps to Dey Hall and dashed to the peer tutoring lab, eight minutes late. Missing out on statistics problems was no big deal, but losing time with his gorgeous tutor was a bummer. Plan A—ditching his meds and snagging a seat next to her in Life Sciences—hadn't worked. He had tried to conjure up charisma and lay a rap on her but no dice. Nothing penetrated her armor of disinterest. Plan B—getting tutored by her—wasn't faring much better. She was an ice maiden, seemingly immune to his charms. But there was no way he was giving up.

"Sorry, I was tied up with my kids," Zeb said breathlessly, hoping that, like puppies, kids had transferable appeal.

Buried in a chemistry textbook, Kiara didn't move a muscle. Her legs, long and sculpted, vied for his attention along with her catlike eyes and wavy, butterscotch hair. Her smarts and athletic beauty were mesmerizing. He tried to ignore the bored, disapproving expression planted squarely across her high cheekbones and pursed lips. No doubt she was making a point about punctuality. Best not to gawk.

"If you're done checking out my ass, let's get started."

"It was your legs, actually. Couldn't scope the rest."

"Your frat brothers teach you that?" She shook her head. "Another smart-mouthed, preppie screwup."

"Hey, I'm not in a fraternity. Anyhow, don't you think that's a bit harsh?"

"Harsh is me wasting my time on someone who doesn't give a shit."

"What the . . . ?"

"As in showing up late after getting a sixty-eight."

Zeb recoiled. "You're joking."

"Do I look amused?" Kiara shoved a copy of the test in his face. "Your professor says you're able but not putting in the work."

"How would she know?"

Kiara's eyes narrowed. "Apparently, you went to her office hours after bombing the first test. You showed potential but apparently decided to squander it."

"You said 'apparently' twice."

"That's it, smart-ass. I'm outta here." Kiara gathered her materials. "I don't have time for this shit."

"Please, Kiara, wait. You're right to be ticked off. I'm sorry. The truth is I find it hard to concentrate on subjects I hate."

"Welcome to the real world."

"I'm not some superficial idiot."

"I don't care who you are, so long as you don't waste my time. And that's exactly what you're doing." She headed for the door.

"Hold up. Let me explain." Zeb rubbed his sweaty palms against his jeans. "My passion is history—European and Near Eastern history. I live and breathe the stuff. I plan to get my doctorate, do path-breaking research. But I'll never get there unless I pass statistics. That's why I need you."

"*Path-breaking* research? Yeah, right."

"Seriously. I want to build on existing research about why different regions of the world evolved at different rates. From the end of the Pleistocene on up to modern times. Why, for example, did Europe advance so much further than, say, Papua New Guinea?"

"Gee, I wonder what delightful conclusion that'll lead to." Kiara returned to her seat.

"You'd be surprised. There's a ton of evidence that none of the differences come from genetic, much less racial, differences." Her eyebrows rose. "Culture matters, but environmental factors are way more important. But there's tons more to examine."

"So maybe you're not a total flake," Kiara said. "But other tutors can help you. It's not going to work for me."

It was time to play the compassion card: "Even if I have a learning disability?"

"What?"

"I don't like telling people, especially women. Besides, like you said, I just need to try harder. I will from now on."

"You've had your come-to-Jesus moment?"

"I'm Jewish." He grinned.

"Zeb, no one likes a smart-ass," Kiara said, but her tone was softer now. "Seriously, I'm overextended. My dad's been on me to quit."

Time for a Hail Mary. "How's your soccer going?"

"What's that got to do with anything?"

"I go to all the games at Fetzer."

"And what?"

"Well, the team's doing great. But it's gotta be killing you that you're not starting and not playing much."

"What's your point?"

"Last year in high school you were a first-team all-American. You come to Carolina and dribble circles around every ACC player you go against. And from the practices I've seen, you also dominate your teammates. But you barely make it into the box score. Meanwhile, worse players are starting as freshmen."

"I said, what's your freaking point!" People were staring.

"I can help you."

"*You* help *me*?" Kiara's look of disbelief verged on disgust.

"Hey, I played high school soccer. I'm local, born and bred in Chapel Hill. I've been watching Carolina soccer since I was a kid, back when Bob Jeffreys only coached the men. He's old school, and I know what he wants. You may be the next April Heinrichs, with all the offensive potential in the world, but if you won't play reliable defense, you ain't gonna play, simple as that."

"Anything else?"

"Defense isn't just about effort and toughness; it's about using your mind. You're closing down well on attackers and forcing them to the side. But the coach wants you driving them to their weaker foot."

"I see," Kiara said, rolling her eyes.

"And you're falling for fakes too often. Keep your eye on the ball, not their feet, hips, or shoulders." Zeb got up to demonstrate. "Be patient, move backward, don't step in until they make a bad touch. Don't worry, we can fix these things."

"I'm so relieved."

"Look, you're the athlete—"

"You sure about that?"

"But I can use my knowledge to help you," Zeb continued. "Here's my plan: You keep tutoring me, and I'll develop defensive drills and a weight-training program to help you crack the starting lineup. Deal?"

Kiara dashed out of the lab, her fists clenched.

19

TURKISH DELIGHT

*I*zmir *Air Station, Turkey, 1979.* Leo flagged down a horse-drawn carriage for his quick jaunt to the coast. His midnight shift didn't start for six hours, so there was ample time to chow down, walk the esplanade, and have some fun. NCO Club food was tasty, but after two weeks in his new home, he was ready to venture out. He wanted tasty and atmospheric.

Twenty minutes later Leo was sitting in Cheap Charley's, a seaside restaurant popular with American airmen. He set aside the menu to gaze at the Aegean, the sweet smell of jasmine plants relaxing him. The fading light still showcased the beach, crystalline blue water, and craggy cliff. Palm trees swayed in the breeze. Lately, he'd been hitting the jackpot.

Never mind that he was the lowest ranking among some two thousand servicemen. None had been as fortunate as he. He'd have thanked God if he were still a believer. Instead, he'd be thanking Bill Walsh for the rest of his days.

The sequence of events still boggled his mind. Mr. Walsh, a total stranger, had formulated a plan to help him on his last night at Lost

World: He would serve in the U.S. military and hopefully become an American citizen. Bill had contacted his friend, an immigration lawyer and air force veteran, to arrange for him to train as an airplane mechanic, a job that dovetailed with his interest in engineering. They had asked if he would be willing to serve four years and risk being assigned to combat zones. He had never before considered military service—corrupt generals being his country's main output aside from oil—but this was a once-in-a-lifetime opportunity to escape Venezuela and make up for lost time.

International events had made his assignment to Turkey timely. After Turkey invaded Cyprus in1974, America had imposed an embargo on military aid that brought operations at Izmir Air Station to a halt. However, four years later, when it became clear that the embargo was undermining U.S.-Turkish relations and not helping Cyprus, Congress lifted the sanctions. By the time he enlisted, mechanics were urgently needed at Izmir to service the F-16s that flew on behalf of NATO.

Leo scanned the menu. Had Mr. Walsh known all this, or had he simply been lucky? Izmir was Turkey's best assignment, better even than Incirlik. Vacationers also flocked to Izmir, many lingering on the beach even at this late hour.

Spicy aromas made his mouth water. Sipping on tea, he stole glances at the delectable dishes on surrounding tables. He ordered kebabs with cumin, fish, *ekmek*, *gevrek simit*, *pide*, and *lamejun*. The server looked at him as if he were crazy. But Leo insisted. He was starving and had a twelve-hour shift to pull. Besides, the dollar was so strong he could afford to eat like a sultan. Leftovers could be given to a street kid.

Despite his good fortune, things weren't idyllic. Izmir was a different world from Sheppard Air Force Base in Texas or the bases in Germany, Japan, or South Korea. Regular power and water outages made the scorching summer unbearable. The heavy workload, earsplitting noise, and infernal heat made him dream of wading through the chilly waters of Kavak Gorge near Angel Falls.

Then there was the situation with the women. Unfortunately,

respectable Turkish women didn't speak with non-Muslim foreign men. Romance wasn't a priority to Leo, but he believed virility was a habit that needed to be reinforced—either that or he risked reliving the nightmare he'd experienced in Maracaibo. Unfortunately, Izmir offered few opportunities. The choices were to pay for sex, which wasn't his thing, or to thread the social needle perfectly, which was damn near impossible.

Hanging out with fellow airmen was no good—most smoked, drank, gambled, or chased prostitutes. Other than Thompson, the redneck who had taught him chess, Leo wasn't even sure how many had ever read a book for pleasure. Four years of their company, and he would lose all sense of what it took to be successful. No, instead of socializing, he'd take advantage of the base's library and bury himself in books until he mastered English. But he'd do so without reverting to being an overly refined choirboy. No sense tempting fate.

Leo ate voraciously, the food disappearing from his plate as quickly as sunbathers were leaving the beach. Before long, he'd devoured enough to astound the doubting Thomas. The waiter grudgingly fetched him a doggy bag, and soon Leo was retracing his earlier route. The bazaar's fruit-and-vegetable vendors had long since packed up. Spotting a painfully thin young girl on the street, Leo stopped the carriage to hand her the food. She beamed, and he bobbed his head before remounting.

They passed a string of carpet shops displaying alluring items he couldn't come close to affording. One day, he'd buy his mother a roomful of elegant rugs and tapestries. They stopped in front of a nightclub, and Leo handed the coachman a couple of bills. Getting off, he patted the horse and sauntered into the establishment.

Leo's eyes adjusted slowly to the dim lights. The retro-style speakeasy had a bar on one side and a dance floor on the other. "Here Comes My Girl" played, but the clientele were exclusively Turks. They seemed European rather than Asian, which improved his odds. What might work against him was the fact he was only twenty years old.

He found a table on the nightclub side and scanned the room.

Clusters of men stood within an arm's length of each other. Two guys came together in a half hug, gently touching the sides of their faces together. *Oh, shit*, Leo thought, preparing to bolt. A man called out to a woman seated at a booth full of ladies. She smiled; presumably she was his girlfriend. Leo exhaled deeply. Different country, different culture.

He ordered whiskey and scanned the scene. There had to be unattached ladies here, but no obvious candidates stood out. In Maracaibo, single women made things easy, shooting coy glances to advertise their status. In this place Leo's only opening appeared to be one booth that had three more women than hovering males. A brunette at that table began returning his not-so-subtle glances. He had finished his second whiskey when the woman's female companions left, taking the men with them. Grabbing the bottle, Leo made his way over to her.

"Hello. Do you speak English?" he asked.

"Of course," she said with a knowing smile, as if she were humoring a young admirer.

"I'm Leo. Can I top off your glass?"

"If you like. The service has improved."

"We aim to please," Leo said, leaning on the suave phrase he'd picked up from TV and hoping it would have transferable appeal with this lady. He added ice to two glasses, poured the whiskey, and sat beside her. She slid away.

"You're American—from the base?"

"I am," he said, not wanting to explain his status. His blondish hair fooled many. "I arrived two weeks ago. I work on F-16s. And you?"

"I'm Turkish."

Leo smiled. She wasn't going to make this easy. He'd been instructed to avoid politics, Turks being fiercely patriotic. History, culture, and sports were safer topics. "And a proud one, I'm sure. Land of the Ottomans, Mehmed the Conqueror, and Ataturk." He lifted his glass, and she raised her eyebrows. "I can't wait to see Istanbul, the Blue Mosque, and Hagia Sophia."

"They are indeed magnificent."

Indeed? Her English is better than mine. "Did you study in England, America?"

"England, for university."

"Oxford? Cambridge?"

"LSE."

"Awesome," he said, hoping his cluelessness didn't show. "Are you a Premier League fan?" It was a stupid question, but he'd exhausted his knowledge of Turkish history and culture.

"Yes. I went to some Chelsea games, but I prefer Turkish teams."

"Galatasaray?"

"Yes! I can't believe you know them." She motioned for him to replenish her whiskey. He did so eagerly.

"Sure I know them. They've done really well in the European Cup several times."

Improbable as it was, he'd hit a conversational sweet spot. She chattered about Turkish soccer the way Venezuelan men did about Major League Baseball. Midway through, she introduced herself as Azra, before resuming the conversation with undiminished enthusiasm. Whether whiskey or sports talk made her giddier, Leo didn't know, but it hardly mattered.

Leo inched closer until his thigh almost touched hers. When the soccer talk petered out, he foolishly mentioned the Kurds. To his astonishment, Azra spoke respectfully, insisting they weren't terrorists and didn't deserve to be repressed. Stunned by her comments—they could easily have landed her in jail—Leo agreed.

Azra's views said a lot about her attitudes. British educated, liberal, and sophisticated, she was exactly the type of woman he needed. Far too much time had passed since he had proven himself under the sheets. Suddenly, in his mind's eye, he was in the cell again, sitting in a pool of his own blood. He shuddered, forcing the image out. *I can't allow myself to get rusty. Ever.*

Leo gently placed his hand on her thigh. Instantly Azra stopped talking. She kicked out her leg. Sunk her fingernails into his hand.

Screaming, she jumped up and waved her arms frantically. Called for help. Leo recoiled, unsure what to do. A man dashed to the booth and launched himself at Leo. The Turk pummeled him with blows to the abdomen. Leo dropped to the floor. The man kicked him. Others appeared out of nowhere, rage in their eyes. They dragged Leo to the back office. The nightclub owner roared. Azra's fiancé and others slapped Leo around. There was nothing to do. He was helpless. He'd been here before. He protected his head, knowing that, as bad as this was, it really wasn't *that* bad.

This is nothing compared to Maracaibo, he thought. And that was why he'd had no choice but to act and why he would do it again.

20

TRANSCENDENT

C hapel Hill, North Carolina, 1990. Not since the seventh grade, when Kiara had stumbled to answer the simplest of Mrs. Foster's social studies questions, had Kiara felt her eyes twitching uncontrollably. Now as she walked to the McCaskill soccer center to meet with Coach Bob Jeffreys, she felt the same sense of helplessness and frustration. Strange because, for most of her first semester at the University of North Carolina, Kiara had viewed Bob's office as a sanctuary where she could stop by unannounced to confide, ask questions, or just shoot the breeze, and she did so frequently. But as her lapses on the soccer field mounted, meetings with Bob brought her face-to-face with her failures. Had this meeting not been scheduled and mandatory, she'd have stayed well clear of the building.

Kiara ambled into Bob's office and took the seat that was offered. The phone rang, and her coach grabbed the handset, shooting her an apologetic glance. Bob's patient responses did not signal that he had higher priorities, so the conversation dragged on.

Kiara took his measure. Disheveled hair, mismatched attire . . .

Coach was a piece of work. How could a dude who was so fastidious about some things—academics, conditioning, every touch of the ball—care so little about his appearance? *Is he color-blind?* He'd be very attractive if he worked on the packaging. Maybe he was a perfectionist about things he cared about and oblivious to everything else.

Whatever. It was clear Bob didn't get her either. At this point what was there to say? Resetting things now—just before summer—was unrealistic.

"Sorry about that," Bob said, setting aside the biography on Winston Churchill that he'd been reading during his brief lunch break. "So tell me, how'd your finals go? Aced them, I'll bet."

"Not sure about organic chemistry. I'll find out soon."

"I'm sure you did great. My money's on you—always is."

Kiara's poker face morphed into an expression of bewilderment.

"Listen, Kiara, it isn't complicated. Next fall, we'll go as far as you lead us."

Kiara sighed. Coaching phenom or not, the man needed to dial it down a notch, maybe lay off the Churchill speeches. ACC soccer wasn't the Battle of Britain. Still, something was up because Bob had never blown smoke up their asses. Brutal honesty was his hallmark, not cheap emotional ploys.

"Bob, are you sure you're not talking College Bowl? No offense, but every bench in the conference is engraved with the contours of my rear."

"Offense?" The coach shook his head. "I *want* you guys to be strong and vocal. More like my men."

"Well, okay, if bluntness is what you want . . ."

"Not bluntness, Kiara. I want you to find your voice. And that's just the start. It's about being hypercompetitive, taking risks, dominating mentally and physically."

"I've obviously checked none of those boxes."

"Not true, and you know it." He eyeballed her, obviously choosing his words carefully. "Kiara, I've found that the key to succeeding—in life, not just soccer—is finding the balance between being flexible and standing firm on core principles. Long ago I decided that fairness—holding everyone to the same rules—is nonnegotiable."

She nodded uneasily.

"Rarely, every fifteen years or so, we get a player with transcendent offensive ability. Usually it's some combination of speed, creative play-making, one-v-one ability, and a nose for the goal. Pardon my French, but I'd typically give my right nut for that type of talent. You with me?"

"It's not the most appetizing image, but, yes, I'm with you."

"Now transcendent players aren't usually grinders. They *in*spire more than perspire. They don't press tirelessly, track back on defense, make tough tackles, or take physical risks."

Bob leaned forward. "So the question becomes, what accommodations, if any, should be made for a phenom with these tendencies?"

Kiara's eyes resumed their twitching. Normally when her back was up against the wall, Kiara became aggressive. But she didn't have the urge. She knew where he was leading. Coach had a valid point.

"None," Kiara said firmly. "Chemistry trumps talent, especially in women's soccer. If you make special allowances, you'll destroy the team chemistry."

Bob's eyes sparkled. "Isn't losing a generational talent too high a price to pay?"

"Nope. If you play favorites, you lose the others."

"Now we're getting somewhere"—Coach Jeffreys beamed—"but we're not done. So how much room should there be for individuality?"

Kiara sighed. She'd always relied on her own instincts—so much so, her dad dubbed her "the female Sinatra." She'd gone against the advice of the college counselor, refusing extended time on the SAT. She'd taken a bunch of AP courses, again ignoring her advisor. When it came to her college applications, she had checked the box for "White/Caucasian"—and had been accepted to three Ivies. But this was different. She'd chosen a team sport, not skiing. And Bob was unquestionably the best coach in the country.

"Some room but within limits," Kiara said. "Give the special player a longer leash. Let her take more risks but hold her to the same standards."

"Bingo. You've always done things your own way, and I admire that. You certainly have national team potential, but you see my dilemma?"

"Yup."

"There's lots I can teach you." Bob's bottom lip pressed into his upper one. "But I sense your frustration and don't want to hold you back. If you want to transfer to Stanford or wherever, I'll grant you a release and recommend you highly. I'd be incredibly bummed, but I'll support you whatever you decide." Then he grinned. "Of course, if you do transfer, we'll kick your butt at College Cup."

Tears pooled in her eyes. *My God, he thinks I want to leave.*

"One more thing: You're not the only one who needs to improve. We should be playing way better than we are. That's on me. The things I do with my men aren't working with you guys. I'm too intense. I need to connect with you all better than I do. The key, my wife says, is to tap into my humanity"—he smirked—"to the degree it exists. My point is, we can all do better."

Kiara's throat tightened. Her selfishness had driven a genius to question himself. There was no holding back. "I'll be back, Bob, and I'll be your best defender. You can take that to the bank."

Kiara marched out before her weakness could show. After boarding her jalopy, she headed for Durham.

Two hours later, as she exited Duke University, Kiara glanced at the strange bird sitting beside her. Sarah's calloused feet rested on the dashboard as she fiddled with the radio dial and munched on a microwaved cheese dog.

"Please make yourself at home," Kiara said.

"Don't mind if I do." Sarah grabbed Kiara's chocolate milk from the center console and took a swig.

"I can't believe no one called security on me, driving up in this clunker."

"Nah, you're safe as long as you don't dent my classmates' BMWs."

"Easier said than done," Kiara said, merging onto I-40. "They're like locusts."

"You, *plagued* by self-doubt?"

"I'm plagued by your notoriously unfunny jokes."

Kiara smiled, recalling her first-ever soccer tryout. She'd been too shy to even step onto the pitch. Hoping to embarrass her into action, her dad had trotted out himself, alongside the girls and their bewildered coach. Sarah had run up, grabbed her by the arm, and explained to Marcus she had things very well in hand, thank you. Kiara's insecurity faded, and they had become inseparable, taking ice baths together, braiding each other's hair at youth tournaments, and now joshing each other as college rivals.

Sarah settled on WRDU Classic Rock. "How'd your meeting with Bob go? You tell him you'll be joining me and his other rejects?"

"It went okay," Kiara said, veering into the fast lane. "I need to improve defensively."

"You don't say?" Sarah had been telling her that since eighth grade. "That it?"

"I need to be less selfish. The rules apply to me as well."

"Whoa, now there's something new. Coming from your lips, I mean."

Kiara karate-chopped Sarah's thigh.

"Ouch!" Sarah rubbed the spot. "So how exactly are you being selfish?"

"I need to support our nonroster players more than I do. Show up for their recitals, academic awards—shit like that."

"Interesting."

"And Bob has this book club that teaches us about life. I should take it more seriously."

"Why?" Sarah asked innocently.

"Because even a sage like me can learn a thing or two. It builds chemistry when teammates share their vulnerabilities and invest in each other."

"You're sounding like a friggin' shrink! I can't speak to the other stuff, but I do know defense. It's about effort and conditioning, which depend on attitude. Your mindset does seem better."

"Maybe. Talk is cheap."

"So, what's your plan?"

"To get in the best shape of my life and learn how to slide tackle properly, which is where you come in. I'll do tons of defensive drills and scrimmage against men."

"How about a summer job?" Sarah said.

"I'm lining one up."

"Doesn't leave much time for guys."

"Right."

They dissected Sarah's year-end meeting for twenty minutes before Sarah switched gears. "So how badly do you want to meet your potential?"

Kiara rolled her eyes. "You're like a dog with a bone."

"Answer the question."

"Badly enough to learn defense."

"What if defense isn't enough?"

"Say *what?*" Kiara wrinkled her face.

"Don't get me wrong. Defense *will* make you all-ACC. But there's more you could be doing."

"Such as?"

"I don't know." Sarah exhaled deeply. "Hope I'm not hitchhiking."

"Out with it!"

"You could be a better leader."

"We covered this. I'll be leading by example, on both ends."

"That's great . . . as far as it goes." Sarah spoke softly. "You need to connect better with your teammates. You're—"

"How would you know? You're in friggin' Durham!"

"I've known you since you were nine. Face it, you're not approach-able. People are scared off by your intensity."

"You're saying I need a personality transplant?" Kiara huffed.

"No, you just need to push the connect button."

"Explain that."

"You can read people a mile away, but you choose not to relate. You freeze people out." Sarah lowered her feet from the dashboard. "We're not in grade school anymore. You're no longer the Black girl with the back brace who reads all the time and talks like a professor but can't remember what she's just heard. Your teammates are no longer competing with you for scholarships. You can let your guard down."

"*Now* who's the shrink?"

"I know you're self-sufficient," Sarah continued, "but you'd be happier with more close friends. I'm wonderful, of course"—she grinned—"but I'm not the only fish in the sea. Let people approach you. Besides, if you guys come together, you'll win it all."

Kiara tapped the steering wheel. "I wonder why Bob never brought it up."

"Improving your defense and conditioning is already a big ask."

"I guess."

"But you can do it all. Especially if you start practicing your social skills right now. Say, by driving an extra hour."

"Bitch."

"You see? You're a natural."

21

INFIDEL

Izmir, Turkey, 1979. Word of the commotion inside the nightclub spread rapidly, and as Leo was escorted to the police car, he ran a gauntlet of hateful stares, insults, and spit. Few things riled Turks as much as foreigners disrespecting their pious women. No one, apparently, had noticed Azra swilling whiskeys, one for one, with the infidel.

Passions cooled at the police station. The chief ordered that Leo's handcuffs be removed. When asked for his passport, Leo presented his military ID, explaining that his other documents were back on base. He made no effort to dissuade them from thinking he was American. Leo was released an hour later with a warning not to approach any more Muslim women while in Izmir.

Yeah, right. He knew what happened to refined gentlemen—they were mistaken for switch-hitters. Maracaibo had taught him that. There could be no hint of ambivalence. Players needed practice, and if he didn't swing the bat, he'd never hit the ball.

Besides, no harm had been done. His military status had worked like a charm, almost like diplomatic immunity.

Back at the barracks Leo tried to snooze but couldn't. Forty minutes until his shift.

"Hey, Latino!" Thompson said, returning from the bathroom. "You ready to get spanked . . . again?"

"In your dreams, my friend."

"Game on, you little shit." Thompson set up the chessboard and moved his pawn. "So how are you enjoying work?" Thompson always asked questions when it was his opponent's turn to move.

Leo moved his knight. "We have an expression in Spanish: Work is work."

"Same in English. What do you think of the dock system?"

Leo had never given it much thought. Eight docks handled two engines at a time. Each crew worked together on all aspects of repairing the jet engines. "It is okay."

Thompson moved his bishop into a forward position, asking, "You don't think it's inefficient?"

Leo blocked the impudent bishop's line of attack. "I guess. We spend too many time waiting for spare parts."

"Forget the parts, Latino. That's out of our control. I'm talking about the system. It makes no sense."

"I do not understand."

"It should be reorganized so everyone focuses on one phase: disassembly, repair, assembly, or testing. That way we get better, faster, and safer. Things would run better."

"But we would know less."

"Not necessarily." Thompson unleashed his queen. "After each mechanic learns one job, he would move to another phase and learn new skills. That way, we could work on six engines at a time, not two."

Leo thought about this while he moved his next two pieces. "Could be."

Thompson moved in for the kill. "We could push way more engines out the door, back into service."

"Maybe."

"Checkmate, sucker!"

"*Coño!*"

Losing to a redneck was as bad as being bored. The loss would eat at him his entire shift.

22

THE MATRIX

Chapel Hill, North Carolina, 1991. They were alone, Kiara sprawled on her beanbag, while her boyfriend sat on the edge of her bed. It was a rare moment of privacy, courtesy of her absent roommate. Craig fidgeted with his Miller Lite pop-top, eyeballing her. She cradled a carton of chocolate milk, her recovery beverage of choice.

"Seventy-four minutes, two goals, one assist, and ACC champion," Craig said. "Your days of griping are officially over, right?"

Kiara smiled. It was big of him to celebrate her triumph, especially when he was struggling. "Not sure. It's too soon to get complacent."

"Don't be modest. I can handle it."

Craig was right. He did understand and could handle it, unlike other guys she'd met. He accepted her demanding schedule, how little time she had to invest in a relationship. He relished her drive and commitment to excellence. Nonathletes didn't get her. Her mentality alienated all but the most self-assured, as some tried to prove they were even busier than she was. Craig wasn't a brainiac, but he was bighearted and secure. His dark brown eyes flashed with sincerity. They soothed her. White guys weren't normally her bag—dating them seemed like a betrayal—but he'd worn her down through lovable persistence.

"You're right—I *was* the shit!" she said, tapping her carton to his can.

"Damned right, you were! So, tell me, Miss MVP, how'd you turn it around? Gimme some pointers."

It was his turn to be uplifted. "I stopped fighting the system."

"System? What do you mean?"

She sighed. "Coach Jeffreys calls it the 'competitive cauldron.' We get scored on every drill and team activity. Rankings are posted weekly based on this elaborate matrix. It's Bob's way of teaching us to compete like men, without having to be on our case all the time. I finally bought into it, suppressing the more toxic parts of my personality."

"So toxic," he said, chuckling. "Did you hire a trainer?"

"Didn't need to. Sarah and my nutcase friend, Zeb, busted my butt."

"Cool. I still don't know how you guys deal with always having a target on your back—everyone gunning for you. We're top ranked, but we don't handle it like y'all."

"It's the cauldron. Every day in practice the competition is so intense we get used to it. Big games are fun, challenges, a piece of cake. The concept is 'sympathetic toughening'—if Bob's not making the shit up."

"Coach Scroggs should give it a try." Craig took a swig. "Still, do you ever wish you were a normal student? So you could go to Franklin Street anytime you wanted and not worry about it?"

"Sometimes but not now. We can win another national championship—if we stay on track."

He nodded. "But don't all the rules get to you?"

"What rules?"

Craig raised a quizzical eyebrow.

"Bob doesn't believe in rules. We have core values and principles we try to abide by. We self-regulate."

"Super cool. So deep down, why do you play? I mean, you're smart enough to have gotten an academic scholarship. And it's not like there's any money in women's soccer."

"Hey"—she tossed a pillow at him—"same with lacrosse."

"True, but I'm not brilliant. And I didn't want my parents taking on debt."

Kiara got up and kissed him on the cheek. "Nah, man, I'm an affirmative-action baby. People handed me everything. Soccer was my lifeline." She punched him playfully.

"Two dumb jocks. Seriously, why?"

"A lot of reasons. I play because nothing beats burying a shot in the upper ninety after beating my defender with a double scissors. I love competing. I love playing headphone karaoke with the girls. I love being a champion, part of the best women's program in the world."

"I get it."

"But nothing's perfect. It's hard to disconnect, find the 'off' switch in my brain. That gets old."

"I wonder . . . after you win national titles and make the national team, will you be satisfied then?"

"Duh! Why else would I train so hard?" Rubbing her neck, Kiara grimaced and then cast a suggestive glance at him. "All these pressures. Can you think of anything to get my mind off them?"

"I can"—he laughed—"but I'm worried about ranking low in that damned matrix of yours. It's enough to give a guy performance anxiety."

"Yeah, right. I guarantee you, a hot guy with a heart of gold and hands like yours will *always* rank at the top. Of course, you'll also rank at the bottom. My first matrix goes up tomorrow."

"First?" He kissed her neck tenderly. "I'm guaranteed to score?"

"Who knows? There's always a first time. But my money's on you."

23

DERAILED

C*hapel Hill, North Carolina, 1992.* Zeb taped the last box and surveyed the remnants of his dorm room. Talk about an unceremonious end, a senior year imploding. But, having made his bed, it was time to lie in it. *Off* campus.

January would be drearier than ever. No more cheering on Lynch and Montross at the Dean Smith Center or salivating over recruits like Stackhouse and Wallace. No more storming Franklin Street after big wins—at least not with friends, because he wouldn't have any. He could forget Spring Break. Just getting Mom to look him in the face, or Dad to converse without an undercurrent of disappointment, would take an act of God. Earning his degree, much less a doctorate in history, was now a pipe dream.

It was one thing to be expelled for absenteeism, bad grades, or smoking dope, quite another for having broken the honor code, to be branded a cheater. Living at home would be purgatory. Not that it was his parents' fault—they'd invested in him big-time, only to be humiliated. He had raised questions about his entire family. How excruciating it would be for them, as professors, to receive judgmental and pitying stares from colleagues. How painful, as education-obsessed Jews, not to have him earn even an undergraduate degree. *If I had just stayed on the meds*, he thought.

Zeb left Old East and headed downtown. He would miss this— strolling from the Old Well under the canopy of glorious oak trees, past ivy-covered colonial buildings and Silent Sam to Franklin Street. Sure, one could retrace these steps, but without living on campus, it would never be the same. Minutes later he walked into Chapel Hill Travel, whereupon Betty hugged him and escorted him to Mr. Cousins's office.

"So what brings you in?" the owner asked after they'd exchanged pleasantries.

"You said I could return anytime, sir. I was hoping to take you up on that."

Mr. Cousins raised his eyebrows. "It's been over a year. A lot has changed."

"Have the multisport tours stopped selling? I could come up with something new."

"Actually, they're doing great. They've been a gold mine."

"I was dumb to leave."

"Not at all. You liked creating more than you liked selling. I understood."

"Would you take me back, sir, if I committed to selling? I'd gladly do it all."

Mr. Cousins sighed.

"I've got more ideas," Zeb said. "History-based expeditions, gene-alogy tours."

"Look, I'm grateful for the job you did. You kept us in business, simple as that." The owner rubbed his forehead. "But everyone's heard about your predicament. It sounds serious. Will it be resolved soon?"

"Unlikely, sir."

"You know my business is based on trust and reputation."

"I do, sir. Sorry to have wasted your time."

A teary-eyed Betty squeezed him on the way out.

Zeb sat outside the rabbi's office, rubbing his clammy palms against his jeans. The truth wasn't pretty. He had never been much of a Jew, skipping services for years and praying to God sporadically, sometimes on a self-serving basis. Other than teaching his special-needs class—something that helped him as much as it did the kids—he'd been a no-show at temple since his bar mitzvah. *Now I turn up*, he thought, *when the shit hits the fan.*

His disappearing act hadn't made him happier, either. As a Jew in the Bible Belt, he was still a fish out of water. People were friendly, but the ubiquitous churches, endless references to Jesus and Bible study, everyone always dressed to the nines on Sundays—all of it made him feel lonely. But it had taken this crisis to drive him home. He needed the kids.

Would Rabbi have a choice? Mr. Cousins didn't, and he was only running a business. How could any rabbi entrust kids' education to a cheater?

"Come in, Zeb." After chatting briefly, Rabbi said, "I'm glad you're here—you saved me the call. But first things first, how can I help you?"

"That's okay, Rabbi. You go first."

The rabbi's face turned serious. "This has been a difficult period. I need to discuss something important. Last week, I was informed—"

"Rabbi, I'm so sorry for the trouble and embarrassment it's causing."

"Well, it's certainly not easy, that's for sure."

"I can resign immediately, if—"

"Resign? Heaven forbid!" Rabbi Norman shook his head vigorously. "I need you to teach more classes. Mrs. Miller is moving to Charlotte. We need someone to fill in, even for just one semester. You'd be perfect, if you could brush up on your Hebrew."

Zeb's eyes opened wide as saucers. "Are you serious? That would be awesome."

"I take it you accept?"

"Absolutely! Thank you!"

"Wonderful. There were three applicants, but I'll tell them no."

Tears pooled in Zeb's eyes.

Rabbi came around and patted his shoulder. "Not to push my luck, but how about joining Torah study? You would add so much."

"Thanks, Rabbi, but that's a bridge too far."

"You can't blame me for trying. Oh, and one last thing."

"Yes?"

"You *will* bounce back. I have complete faith in you."

"Excuse me?"

"The honor court," Rabbi said nonchalantly, dashing off to class.

Zeb returned home to find his dad drinking lemonade in the kitchen. He was back from teaching. Better him than Mom. Still, Dad would expect an update, so he poured himself a glass and took a seat.

Ever since the spat over ADHD meds, his father had steered clear of sensitive matters. Whenever they loomed, his dad gravitated toward conversational safe zones, usually scholarly topics. So he reported on his meetings with Mr. Cousins and Rabbi without broaching, or being pressed on, his expulsion from college.

"Teaching at temple will be good for you," Larry said pensively. "It'll give you a chance to take more pride in your Jewish heritage. Not just Southern."

"I *am* proud."

"They're not as incompatible as you might think."

"I didn't think they were."

Larry raised his eyebrows. "You know, historically, the South has treated us Jews pretty well. Even with some notable exceptions."

Zeb smiled. *Dad is off to the races again.* He eagerly took the bait, leaving his expulsion from UNC far behind. "Oh, yeah?"

Larry nodded. "America was the first country to offer us full citizenship. Believe it or not, Charleston was the most tolerant place of all. Jews could vote, worship freely, trade, own land, the works."

"Cool. And where were most of those early Jews coming from?" Zeb knew the drill by now.

"Mainly Spain and Portugal. They were fleeing the Inquisition. Some arrived in Charleston and Savannah in the 1690s. A number worked as translators for the British, dealing with the Spanish in Florida."

Zeb sipped lemonade and, as his father went off on this latest tangent, visualized a map of Europe. "What about the Russian and German Jews—the ones running from the pogroms? They went to New York, right?"

"You'd be surprised. Many settled in the South. By 1800 South Carolina had twice as many Jews as New York." His dad sounded like the professor he was. "Jews were a higher percentage of Whites in the South than in the North right up through the Civil War."

"That's interesting, Dad, but ancient history."

"Not really. Three times as many Jews live in the South now as in 1970." Larry rose to rinse his glass. "My point is, we're not alone, and we have it pretty darn good."

His dad was right. Anti-Semitism wasn't a major problem, not now. Yes, some still said "kike" and talked about "Jewing people down." Some frats and country clubs still banned Jews, but the harsher manifestations had disappeared. Pi Kappa Alpha—a Southern fraternity—had taken in his buddy Jonathan last year, and more Jews were rushing this semester. Society girls now dated Jewish men. Intermarriage rates had skyrocketed. In the countryside many fundamentalists had their "favorite Jew," someone with admirable qualities who represented an unbroken link to biblical times.

"Why do we have it so good?" Zeb asked.

Larry sighed. "Some of it, sad to say, is that the Black community is a lightning rod for prejudice. Probably because poor White people compete more with Black people than with Jews for jobs. Also Jewish immigrants to the South did their best to assimilate, to be 'more American.' Maybe White Christians treat Jews better because they feel guilty about how they treat Black people."

"Maybe so, but Blacks are being treated better, too."

Larry pressed his lips together, shook his head, and raised his hand. A stop sign. "Zeb, I veered way off course. Last night, your mom and I discussed how *you* need to be treated—after getting expelled."

Zeb felt his stomach twist. "What do you mean?"

His father puckered his lips. "I'm sorry, but we don't want you hanging around more than you need to. Make yourself scarce. Teach more, find a second job, whatever. Is that clear?"

Boom. "As crystal."

24

INVESTING

hapel Hill, North Carolina, 1981. Leo stared into the bathroom mirror. The Batman mask was still on properly, covering his eyes and nose. He wiped the lipstick off his cheek. After removing the bills from his Speedo, he slipped into his jeans, pocketing the tips. *One more gauntlet to run*, he thought. He burst out of the bathroom and dashed to the front door, where "Robin" was fending off an enthusiast attached to his thigh.

"Whoooeee, Boy Wonder!" the drunk woman shouted. "How about doing the horizontal mambo with me?"

It was the same lech who had slapped a twenty in his own Speedo during their last number, a superhero rendition of "Stayin' Alive." Unfortunately, her expectations had matched both her outsize tip and her buzz, so the bachelorette's sister had had to rescue him. As consolation, Robin had kissed the jilted woman on the mouth, eliciting cheers. Big mistake. Instead of being free and clear, Robin had a lovestruck fan to contend with.

When Robin disentangled himself, they sprinted to the car. "Sheesh," Marv said, shedding his mask and ducking into the passenger seat. "These women are getting clingier and clingier."

Leo turned on the lights and drove off. "What you expect when you make out with them?"

"Hey, I don't see you turning away your half of my tips. You ask me, you've got a sweet deal."

"I agree. It's not easy keeping up with Boy Wonder."

"And don't you forget it." Marv cackled. "You need to invest, dude—lay yourself out there. You have it in you, I know you do."

"I follow your advice, I'll get herpes before Spring Break."

"No risk, no reward. Let me guess, you're saving yourself for Becca?"

"Maybe."

"You guys done it yet?"

"Is none of your business, my friend."

Marv shook his head. "Try keeping your mask on. Chicks dig Batman. Or, better yet, dump her—Bible-thumpers are for the birds. I know a dozen babes who'd jump your bones, Latin lover and all. Why you date her is beyond me."

"Becca has a good heart and good brain."

"Right."

Leo concentrated on the median. Driving down unlit, winding country roads was difficult enough without fighting the urge to pull over and sleep. The fake persona, playing the extrovert, it all exhausted him—more so because he did it poorly and felt sleazy. There was also the risk of being recognized and transformed into a laughingstock. Audiences sensed his reticence; hence Batman was Robin's sidekick. "I'm not sure how much longer I'm up for this."

"Becca or the gigs?" Marv asked.

"The gigs."

"Don't tell me you're feeling cheap again? Dude, we're killing it! This is way more than you make at the Happy Store."

"I know, but it's not what I imagined when I left Venezuela. I keep thinking of grandparents."

Marv grinned. "What, giving lap dances doesn't live up to escaping fascism and chasing dreams in the New World?"

"Exactly."

"Dude, give yourself time. Four years in the service—you deserve a break. You could be a stud if you'd just lighten up. Remember, social skills will get you farther than all the intellectual crap."

Leo dropped Marv off. He waved goodbye and pulled away from the curb, knowing Marv was right. He'd have gone bonkers in Izmir had he not changed his attitude. As a wrench turner, he'd adapted to the physical discomforts—the summer heat, earsplitting noise, and long shifts. What he found unbearable, even as a loner, was the sense of isolation. In Maracaibo people who loved him had always been close at hand. Six thousand miles of separation was too far.

The best airmen, he had finally learned, were the ones who let loose, laughed, helped others. They played hard so they could work even harder. Relationships reenergized them, adding to, rather than depleting, their psychic reserves. He had passed on smoking weed and chasing prostitutes but learned to drink and deal poker with the best of them. Marv was right: Friendships were key.

When he arrived in Chapel Hill, he had felt as if he'd died and gone to heaven. He was thrilled to exchange F-16s for the less flighty Southern belles who graced his economics, political science, and business classes. Much to his relief, one had even become his first girlfriend.

He'd considered majoring in engineering—to build on his technical background—but Carolina didn't offer it, and the real money was in finance. Besides, decompressing and fun, not academics, would be his priority. There was no way the GI program would enforce their GPA standards. Carolina would round him out socially, and he could turn to weightier matters later, with his prospects much improved.

Tonight hadn't been a resume-building experience, but he'd earned enough to invite Becca to a fine dinner. *It's time to lighten up.*

Days later, at the Pi Kappa Alpha Fraternity house, Corbin, the pledge master, scowled at the eleven pledges facing him. Three fuckers hadn't even bothered to show up and had been spotted at Purdy's, chatting up women. Ladies' night had blown a hole in his lineup, and forty-eight brothers were watching this fiasco.

The pledges who did show hadn't prepared. Few had memorized the most basic information about their pledge brothers and big brothers. This from a class that, on paper, was exceptionally bright with a stellar GPA. How much time did it take to interview fourteen PBs and learn simple stuff? They just didn't give a shit. Only the overage Hispanic, Leo, had performed well. This class's failure reflected on him. Unacceptable.

The problem was arrogance. Word had it they had adopted the mantra, "We saved the house!"

Translation: The fraternity had been foundering, but the arrival of these studly dudes had turned things around. They lacked humility and a sense of brotherhood. Narcissism and pretentiousness might fly with the Dekes, Betas, or Phi Delts, but Pikas were supposed to be different: quality guys minus the self-importance and elitism. *Boy, do I have a job on my hands.*

Corbin slammed his fist on the table. "Coming into tonight, you sorry fucks each had two brothers in your corner, your big brother and me. You've lost us all now. Right, brothers?" A chorus of profanity erupted, the yells reverberating off the basement walls. "Now where the hell are those dumbfucks Kaufman and Hardy?"

No one was *that* dumb.

"I'll tell you where. They're at fuckin Purdy's!" Corbin paced the length of the line and stopped, like a drill sergeant. "Carmichael, who's fault is that?"

"Mine, Brother Corbin."

"Damn right it is." Finally, a correct response. "You're all to blame. Pledge brothers are supposed to communicate, keep each other in line."

Corbin moved on to Buchan. "What is that you're wearing?"

"A jean jacket," the pledge said, chomping on gum.

"Now why in hell would you be wearing that?"

"Cuz it's cool," Buchan said, pronouncing the last word "coo." His response elicited snickers and then the obligatory outrage. When his big brother approached, he handed over the jacket and spat the gum into a cup.

Corbin lectured on loyalty and trust before pausing in front of Leo, the one pledge who'd performed flawlessly.

"Bello, they teach you about unit cohesion in the army?"

"Air force."

"Smart-ass. You're *all* a bunch of jarheads!"

"They did teach us about it," Leo said, clearly suppressing a laugh.

Bello needed to be sweating bullets, not smiling. That was the downside of rushing a vet. He probably sensed that the brothers who had recruited him so assiduously didn't suddenly hate him. But he could not be allowed to treat this lineup as a farce. "What's so fuckin' funny!"

"Nothing, Brother Corbin," Leo said, addressing him properly for the first time.

"How do you get off making your fellow PBs look so bad?"

"It was selfish of me. I promise to suck next time." A torrent of *ooohs* and expletives followed.

"No one likes a wiseass, pledge! When we took you in, we thought you'd add maturity to the class—even if you do look like you're in high school. We never thought you'd have the social skills of a doorknob."

Hooting broke out, but Corbin signaled for silence. "Bello, you should've learned from Carmichael. The key is to uplift others, not emulate bad performance. *Comprende?* My God, we recruit a Hispanic and a Jew this semester, and this is how you repay us?"

Leo's head dropped.

"So this Saturday, at five a.m., it'll be Bello, Buchan, those bozos Kaufman and Hardy, and me picking up trash on Airport Road. We'll go until seven. Anyone's late, we'll do it again next Saturday."

Corbin dashed out, returning seconds later. "We'll have another lineup tomorrow night. Anyone who screws up will clean up after Gasoline Alley."

25

SPINELESS PENGUIN

ort Lauderdale, Florida, 1982. Leo weaved through traffic on Commercial Boulevard, hoping to make the contest in time. Otherwise they'd be heading back to Chapel Hill four days early. Driving in Myrtle Beach, their first stop, had been a comparative breeze—fewer spring breakers and no drawbridges. He cussed as another Sunshine State driver cut him off.

"Do me a favor," Gary called from the back seat. "You get stopped by a cop, *don't* tell him he's a spineless penguin trying to meet his quota."

"*Or* that he's making a mockery of the justice system," Marv added. "Where do you come up with this stuff, Bello?"

Leo smiled. But it hadn't been funny at the time—the cops behaving like Venezuelan policemen, him losing his shit, them getting arrested. Not an auspicious start to their Spring Break. Fortunately, such detentions were a revenue-generating ploy for the beach town and wouldn't go on anyone's record. "What happened in Myrtle Beach stays in Myrtle Beach."

"I hope so, because we're broke."

Soon Leo and Marv were in the restroom at Flanigan's Bar, donning the green Speedos they'd been given. The swimsuits had a yellow ruler imprinted on the front, so female patrons could take full measure of the men parading before them. Public humiliation was the price for their disorderly conduct back in Myrtle Beach. Leo dropped to the floor of the bathroom, cranking out as many push-ups as he could. When he jumped up, Marv followed suit, adding a hundred sit-ups to eradicate all traces of a gut. Neither of them concerned themselves with germs. "That's as pumped up as I can get on short notice," he said.

Leo smiled. "You got this, Robin."

"I don't know, man. This is embarrassing. I wish I had my mask."

"Me, too."

The music yielded to an announcement over the PA system. "Okay, ladies. In two minutes, Fort Lauderdale's finest studs will be strutting their stuff. So take advantage of our two-for-one special on well drinks."

Women squealed as Leo, Marv, and two other contestants marched onto the stage. Gary chatted up women, cultivating a fan base for Thing 1 and Thing 2. Promising free mixed drinks to whoever cheered for his buddies, he ordered a trayful of cocktails, emptying their coffers. Meanwhile, Macho Man, a hairless, arm-flexing bodybuilder, showcased his talent for swaying off rhythm. He seemed too muscle-bound to cross his thighs or throw a decent spiral. Latin Lover blew kisses to the audience, thrusting his pelvis forward but generating little enthusiasm. Thing 1 and Thing 2 came across as normal, handsome guys desperate for beer money. All four played to the crowd until the moment of truth.

"Ladies, we have your winners! In third place, winning twenty-five dollars: Latin Lover from FSU. Give him a hand!" There was moderate applause, mostly from a drunk girl who endlessly begged him to flex.

"In second place, winning seventy-five dollars, from the University of North Carolina: Thing 1!" Leo beamed as rowdy cheering broke out, interspersed with lewd invitations, and then tapped his heart twice and blew kisses. Gary flashed a thumbs-up.

"And now our grand winner of the 1982 Flanigan's Men's Hot Bod Contest, also hailing from the University of North Carolina: Thing 2! Give him a hand, ladies!" A roar erupted. Probing hands grabbed at Marv's calves.

"Have I got a thing for you!"

"I'll take care of your thing, all right!"

Gary raised his fists triumphantly. Free well drinks and the normalcy of his buddies had proved unbeatable. Gary high-fived them when they emerged from the restroom. "Dudes, we're *way* ahead— even after paying for drinks!"

"Enough for the rest of the week?" Leo asked.

"Yessir, thanks to Mr. Hot Bod here." Gary nudged Marv. "We can even treat our groupies."

Marv looked at Leo. "Might be time for Robin to switch roles with Batman."

"Not a chance, Boy Wonder."

Two weeks later, Leo strode into the Steele Building. The cubicles were manned by administrators who all had time to look up at him. Military bureaucracies were the same, overstaffed and designed to waste the time of enterprising individuals. Academic advising was more useful for younger students, but Dean Acosta was a nice person. Her affinity for veterans had shone through during orientation. They'd chew the fat, she'd give him a pep talk, and he'd be on his way.

"So how are things going?" she asked after inviting him into her office.

"Awesome, ma'am." He leaned forward in his seat. "We're in paradise. Everyone's super friendly; we won a national championship. No complaints whatsoever."

The dean raised her eyebrows. "And your classes?"

"They could be better."

"Your calculus professor tells me you got a D-minus on your last test."

His shoulders slumped. "It wasn't my best day, ma'am."

"And the *five* classes you skipped before the test? They weren't your best days either, I take it?"

Leo grimaced. *Why is she busting my chops? I'm hardly the only screwup out of four thousand freshmen.*

"How about Public Speaking?" she continued. "The average course grade is an A-minus. You got a D-plus on your speech. What happened there?"

"It was on Jimmy Buffett, ma'am. I overshot the time limit."

"By seven minutes on a five-minute speech?"

He looked down. "The musical clips took too long. I should've rehearsed more."

"More?"

"I should have rehearsed."

"Is that how you prepared in the military?"

"No, ma'am."

She frowned. "I'm looking at a police report from March 29. I doubt you remember much. With 25,000 fans celebrating on Franklin Street, it takes a lot to stand out, but you managed it. Listen, I was once a student, and I put on a few good drunks myself. Work hard, play hard—I get it. But, seriously, standing on top of a parked car, *peeing* on a girl's head? I wouldn't *believe* it if it wasn't documented."

"I didn't know I was doing it."

"Whew, that's a relief." She shook her head. "And not remembering your own name when the police picked you up? Having to check your license?"

"Not one of my finer moments, ma'am."

"Leo, we accepted you over more qualified applicants, people I now know would have taken better advantage of the opportunity. And unlike you, they were North Carolina residents—people UNC is supposed to prioritize. I serve on the diversity committee and, as a Hispanic myself, I went to bat for you, big-time. But with your 1.9 GPA, I have egg on my face."

"Sorry to have let you down."

"Not just me. And not just *you*. Your failure will hurt future Hispanic veterans, especially noncitizens. You understand I *can't* let that happen."

"I'll do better."

The dean shook her head. "You've ignored my warnings and treated yourself and this university with tremendous disrespect. I'm informing the VA that you'll be withdrawing from UNC. If it were up to me, you would leave at the end of this semester. But you'll be permitted to stay through the fall semester if you want, in deference to your military service. Your special parking permit for North Campus will be revoked immediately."

Dean Acosta twitched her head dismissively. The conversation was over.

26

"FAST FORWARD"

Chapel Hill, North Carolina, 1992. He's Not Here had a different vibe on weekday afternoons. There were no high-minded conversations with Professor Small and the gang. No live bands. None of the social electricity that prevailed late night. Instead, the beer garden attracted a handful of drifters who came to sprawl on the grass, drink cheap pints, and listen to tunes. As a student, Zeb stood out from the other patrons. Being the only tipper—albeit a small one—he was given free rein over the music.

These days Jackson Duvall escapism fit the bill. The singer-songwriter's music helped Zeb flee many things—parental glares, the whispers of former classmates, contemptuous glances from lifelong acquaintances. With no money to skip town, Zeb's mind did the wandering. His companion was the balladeer from Key West.

Duvall's music was therapy, pure and simple. It gave him hope. He would discover new passions and live them out, not vicariously but personally. Not being wealthy or a sailor-musician made things harder, but the details would be worked out. Besides, diving headfirst into life sure beat swallowing a bottle of pills or accepting a humdrum existence.

And Zeb was hardly alone. Legions of Duvall fans had adopted the same mindset, albeit to different degrees. Some never ventured beyond Duvall's hedonistic songs. Not him. How many times had Zeb grabbed an atlas to pinpoint the Caribbean and South Pacific islands Duvall had sung about? How often had he read the novels on which Duvall's tunes were based? The quintessential flip-flop-wearing, beach bum had introduced him to Faulkner, Twain, Pat Conroy, Flaubert, García Márquez, and Oscar Wilde. More than his college professors had done. Zeb had often scurried to a foreign-language dictionary to decipher lyrics written in Spanish, French, Creole, and Tahitian. Partying was the tip of the Duvall iceberg.

Kiara sauntered in and found Zeb on the grass. She waited for him to finish intently singing along with Duvall's anthem, "Fast Forward."

"Bravo. Jackson himself would be impressed," she said.

"Why, thank you." He grabbed an Evian from the ice bucket and handed it to her. His one true friend. Out of his league romantically, she'd become more important than a girlfriend. Not what he'd had in mind when he committed to training her a while ago, but things had worked out for the best. "A cold one for the Lady Tar Heel who'll bring glory to the USA," he said.

"Not as tasty as your Bud."

"Restraint goes with the territory." He smirked. "With greatness comes responsibility."

"Make sure to let the national team coach know I've made his roster."

"It's just a formality."

"Obviously. So, what's the plan?"

"I figured we'd drive to Key West."

"We? What's going on in that fertile mind of yours?"

"It's simple. I'm your Great White Hope. You're lost without me."

"Great White Hope!" Kiara spat out, guffawing. "I think fighter man here has suffered too many blows to the head."

"Hey, hey, hey!" He feigned hurt. "We're talking three College Cups, two national championships. That's not chopped liver."

"I see. Where, pray tell, do you keep your trophies?"

"Where, pray tell, was your fat butt planted before I trained you?"

Kiara giggled. "Where it is now . . . on a bench."

"You can drive down and fly back a week later." His eyes glowed. "Separate beds. I'll cover gas and your plane ticket. We split the motel."

"Got it all figured out."

"The man with a plan."

"You know, you really are a dumbfuck," Kiara said, her tone despondent.

"Ouch."

"I just don't get it. You were on such a roll. You'd brought your stats grade way up. You had a clear path to the doctorate program. How in God's name could you screw that up?"

"I thought you didn't believe in God."

"You really are infuriating," she said. "Answer the question."

"I don't know."

"So you're just gonna skip town?"

"What alternative is there?"

"Fixing things."

"They're unfixable." His eyes welled. "My name's mud. I can't get a job outside of Temple. Hanging around home is torture."

Kiara looked pained. "I can't go . . . for several reasons."

"Bummer."

"So you'll be headin' down to Captain Tony's?" Kiara said, referring to a Key West saloon.

"Yup." He jumped to his feet as "Mustachioed" began to play. "You'll love this one!" Zeb mangled the song as people gawked. "Not bad, eh?"

"The captain would be so proud."

Zeb sped southward on I-95, radar detector and cruise control working in tandem. His '77 Oldsmobile Cutlass, while no spring chicken, had proven more reliable than his friends. The rust bucket would make it.

Springsteen tunes carried him through to South Carolina, where South of the Border billboards beckoned him to stop at the attraction. The tackiness was unrelenting, interrupted only by a Hawaiian Tropic billboard featuring a bikini-clad beauty. He punched a button, and Carlos Santana displaced the Boss.

"*Oye, cómo va?*"

It was too soon to tell.

Bowie, Neil Young, and the Police powered him through to Daytona, where he slept at a rest stop. Traffic was heavier in South Florida, but the warm temperatures, palm trees, and U2 made the driving pleasurable. Visions of Sonny Crockett and Ricardo Tubbs, the *Miami Vice* duo, speeding past in a cigarette boat almost made him divert to Miami Beach, but he stayed the course. There would be enough vice in the Keys.

Driving past Pennekamp Coral Reef Park felt like a sin, scuba diving having topped his bucket list for a long time. He would return when he had money. Turquoise water now engulfed both sides of the Overseas Highway, and Zeb knew it was time. He had held off for eight hundred miles, saving the best for last. Inserting *A1A* into his cassette player, Zeb belted out "A Pirate Looks at Forty," "Migration," and "Trying to Reason with Hurricane Season," not missing a word.

It goes well, Carlos, he thought. *Very well.*

Islamorada was upon him, and he had no choice. Word had it that the Holiday Isle tiki bar had the world's best rum runners, and where cocktails flowed, other delights might follow. If there was one place to splurge before Key West, this was it.

The tiki bar oozed character, its low thatched roof extending to the water's edge. Hundreds of signed dollar bills and business cards—stuck to the underside of the roof and wooden support beams—lent intimacy, as if patrons intended to return. A mix of middle-aged and younger folk sat on barstools. Scantily clad cocktail waitresses pranced around, minimalist tattoos adding to their allure. A calypso band played melodies in the distance. A half-mile offshore, deep-sea fishing boats lined up, hauling in their catch. The vice president, he'd heard, vacationed here regularly, relishing the best sportfishing on the planet.

But sailfish held little interest for a land shark like Zeb. Two-legged, terrestrial creatures of the female kind appealed more. Predators needed fuel, so he ordered a rum runner, overtipping the waitress. Eight bucks poorer, he found a stool and took in the view. Boat captains docked at the pier, preparing to unload their catch. A white-faced angler leaned over the rail, sharing his lunch with the fish. Other land sharks got the jump on him, chatting up the ladies. *Sure could use a wingman*, he thought. Cruising solo smacked of desperation.

Too bad Kiara isn't here. She'll always see me as a friend, but no problem; I'll be the best damn friend I can be.

Downing his rum runner, Zeb headed for the Kokomo Bar. Rabbi Norman had been a mensch, not getting mad after he resigned and then telling him about this place. Who'd have figured, a reggae-loving rabbi? "Hey, *mon*, aren't a rabbi and his wife allowed to jam in the name of the Lord?" Rabbi had replied in a Jamaican lilt, laughing at his flabbergasted expression. If that wasn't a license to chill, what was? In his mind's eye, he saw the bearded scholar and his wife swaying to the rhythms of Bob Marley.

A three-piece reggae band held court over two dozen partiers, most with a rum runner in hand, swinging to the strains of "Stir It Up." The lead singer had Bob's intonations down pat.

Zeb ambled up to the only solo dancer, a striking Black woman with wavy, jet-black hair and toned arms. She swayed with her head back and eyes closed, twirling as if in a trance. Zeb rocked, sipping his margarita, beaming. When Miss Deadhead's eyes opened, she flashed a smile and then resumed her mesmerizing spins.

The band went on break, and Zeb stuck out his hand. "Thanks for letting me tag along. I'm Zeb."

"Abigay," she said, shaking his hand. "Anytime, sweetie."

Sweetie? Not good. He wasn't a teenager. "Can I buy you a drink?"

"Evian would be great, thanks."

Jeez. Was every hot Black chick addicted to bottled water? When he returned from the bar, Zeb said, "Is that an island accent I hear?"

She smiled. "Bahamas."

"Now that's cool."

"But I'm really from another world," she said airily.

"I hear ya. What world would that be?"

"The kingdom."

"Oh, I see. The kingdom!" What was this woman smoking?

"The kingdom of *God*."

Wonderful. I found the only Bible-thumping babe in all the Keys. "How do the beaches compare?"

"Compare?"

"The kingdom's versus Bahamas."

"Yes!" She giggled. "They're natural . . . supernatural!"

"Good answer. Where in the Bahamas are you from?"

"Congo Town. You've probably never heard of it."

"It's on Andros."

Abigay raised her eyebrows. "You've been?"

"Nope, but I love maps. A hobby of mine. One day I want to visit every country on earth."

"You're an ambitious young man."

"I'm not so young, Abigay," Zeb said, sounding every bit his age. "Do you live here?"

"Key West. But I'm heading to Miami to see a friend."

"A guy?"

"A girl—not that it's any of your business."

"I'm moving to Key West, seriously." His eyes sparkled.

"Look, you're an angel, but I've got to run." She pecked him on the cheek. "Here's my card in case you need help—realtors, plumbers, and the like. Thanks for the drink."

"Sure thing." He frowned.

Abigay left as the band launched into "I Don't Want to Wait in Vain."

Halfway across the Seven Mile Bridge, Zeb tossed Abigay's business card into the ocean blue, vowing never to litter again.

27

FLUORESCENT CLOCK

*C*hapel Hill, North Carolina, 1982. Two stunners stood at the cooler, debating whether to go for the Budweiser or Miller Lite. Neither of them had the freshman fifteen to worry about, Leo thought, so the discussion seemed academic. Fortunately, as the Happy Store's lone cashier, he was required to stare at them attentively. A dream job if ever there was one.

Meeting girls at the store boosted his reputation, and there was plenty of time to study between purchases. He also received an employee discount. If he didn't take full advantage of his platform—Leo didn't line up dates because he had a girlfriend—he certainly enjoyed the scenery. So long as the drinking age was eighteen, and the Tar Heels continued to kick butt, he'd be sitting pretty. After all, most of the party girls strolling around town were carrying his six-packs.

The downside of hawking goodies on Saturdays was not seeing William Fuller terrorize opposing quarterbacks in the tradition of Lawrence Taylor, or Kelvin Bryant rack up yards by the thousands. Peddling Famous Amos cookies didn't compare. He also missed seeing

Lump, the legendary Mic Man, keep students in stitches with his Robin Williams–like antics. Leo's stomach sank every time a roar emanated from Kenan Stadium. What great thing had just happened to the nation's third-ranked team? Thompson, his air force buddy, would be tickled by his frustration, having nurtured his interest through American Forces Network football broadcasts.

The girls approached the register with six-packs of Budweiser. Wearing sweaters and add-a-bead necklaces, they were clearly heading to a tailgate.

"Hey. You're in my econ class," the brunette said.

Leo pretended not to be surprised. "Yup, that's me. You enjoy the test?"

"Not at all. I need to drown my sorrows."

"I know the feeling." No need to mention he had aced it.

"Are you going to the court party?"

"I think so," he said. "Liquid Pleasure is playing."

"Awesome, see ya there."

"See ya." And people wondered if he missed his teller job.

After his shift, Leo returned to his dorm to find Becca waiting for him. His roommate was at the game, so he invited her up. He popped two beers, handed her one, and then switched on WCHL. Woody Durham's mellifluous voice detailed the Tar Heels' shuffled lineup and offensive formation. Becca turned down the volume and sat at his desk.

"Did you leave a copy of your test with Dean Acosta?" she asked.

"Yup, I left it in her mail slot."

"Another A?"

He nodded.

"Have you heard anything?" she asked.

"Nope."

"That's going on five weeks. She's stubborn."

He nodded. "So am I. I'm determined to stay."

Becca moved next to him on the bed. "You know, I love this new you. Intelligence is sexy."

"Touchdown!"

"Would you mind turning that off?" she said, frowning.

"It's the fourth quarter. We're only up by three."

Leo rose and approached the radio, as if closer proximity would transmit more support. The Tar Heels obliged, intercepting a pass. Unnoticed, Becca moved behind him. She grabbed his buttock with her hand. Leo froze and then shuddered, his panicked face unseen to her. He began sweating.

"Jeez, someone's tense." Becca removed her hand. "I can relax you, if you'll let me."

"Now's not the best time."

"It never seems to be the right time."

Leo thought of the broken hearts he'd left behind in Maracaibo, after the kidnapping. One weeping girl—no longer a virgin—had begged him to bring her to Angel Falls. He turned to face Becca. "I don't want to take advantage of you."

"You don't think I can fend for myself? It's been four months, and we still haven't made love."

"Niiice. I'm sure your minister would love to hear that." He turned up the volume.

Becca's jaw dropped. "I don't appreciate your throwing religion in my face. I may not be a saint, but I'm not a . . . Look, I love you, but I'm beginning to wonder if you have . . . issues."

Leo's gaze snapped away from the radio. "Issues? What issues?"

"Most men would be all over me—not that I know from experience. But I've got to ask, are you gay?"

"*Coño!*" He glared at her. Shaking his head, he pointed to the door. "Get the fuck outta my room!"

"I didn't—"

"Out!"

The nightmare had returned. Like an endless rerun, this time with audio. He lay down, shattered.

Slowly, Leo pulled himself from his stupor. He ambled to the mirror and took a long gaze. His torso was thin—more like a teen-ager's. Bernardo, the asshole rich kid from the country club, had once called him a Ken doll. He'd been right. He looked more like a delicate British aristocrat than a Latino. *I'm emitting the wrong signals, just like in Maracaibo. But are my signals, in fact, wrong?*

There could be no downward spiral. He needed to set things straight—now. But this had to be tackled in private. Fortunately, the postgame party was at Little Fraternity Court, away from the Pika house. And it was good that the Tar Heels had beaten Maryland. Bird-dogging conditions improved when moods were light.

The uplifting funk music pulled him up Cameron, his step peppier than expected. Liquid Pleasure always did the trick. A Miller Brewing truck was parked by the Phi Delt house, so he made a beeline for the free beer. Even with six taps, there was a line. Which was perfect, as he wanted to seem purposeful while assessing the talent. The onset of darkness made him feel less conspicuous. He would fill up and settle in a prime viewing spot. *Was I just being a nice guy with Becca?*

Wild Cherry's classic, "Play That Funky Music," had everyone around him crooning. Leo sang along, guzzling beer. Someone shoved him from behind. He spun around, clenching his free fist.

"Well, if it isn't my favorite econ guy!" the brunette from the Happy Store said, giggling. She had upgraded her sweater and lost her add-a-beads. She looked less preppy, even more attractive. Her blond friend yawned, looking away.

"Oh, yeah, then why'd you shove me so hard?"

"Mark it down to enthusiasm. You here alone?"

"Yup. The joys of working when everyone else is at the game."

She stuck out her hand as her friend took off. "I'm Kelly."

"Leo."

"You speak well for a foreigner."

He grinned. "So well you can tell I'm a foreigner."

"Are you Spanish?" she asked, chuckling.

"Venezuelan."

"Wow. Where'd you learn English?"

"Latin books are too flowery, so I read books in English as a teenager. In the air force, I read on my free time."

"Impressive. Not many people read for fun in a foreign language."

"When you live in a troubled country, you look for ways to escape. Step one is learning English."

She nodded. "Makes sense. It's sad you had to leave."

"I'll be an American soon."

"Now, that's way cool." Kelly raised her Carolina cup. "Here's to our brainy, handsome, soon-to-be American!"

He blushed. "Thank you."

"No, thank *you*. I knew there was something behind the Happy Store veneer. So where were you stationed?"

The conversation flowed too easily. She was beginning to like him—not part of the plan. Kelly was adorable, undeserving of being collateral damage. But Leo hadn't lied. No one was pointing a gun to her head. Hadn't Becca just scolded him for being too considerate? Who could say Kelly wasn't looking to get laid, like him?

Not finding her sidekick, they headed to Troll's. He sprang for a two-dollar pitcher of Old Mil Light, whereupon Miss Wholesome pounded him at the drinking game Quarters. When puking became a real possibility, he opted for plan B.

"Want to see my fluorescent clock?" he asked. Absurd pickup lines, if delivered sweetly, could be disarming. A gift from his interior designer aunt, the killer timepiece had varying geometric shapes for the second, minute, and hour hands.

Raising her eyebrows, Kelly said, "Whatever keeps you from blowing your cookies. We better stop at Hector's."

Soon, Stratos was serving them Greek grilled cheeses to go, the tinfoil warming their hands. They chowed down while strolling toward North Campus. They passed the infamous hedge where two buddies of his, Heeseman and Coop, had once awakened after a rollicking night.

"I'll bet you're glad I fell for your fluorescent clock line," Kelly teased. "You were looking pretty pale."

"Can't pull the wool over your eyes," he said, gently squeezing the back of her neck and kissing her.

They reached Carr dorm. "My roommate is at his girlfriend's," Leo said.

"What, she not like the clock?"

Moments later they were snuggling on the couch, listening to Steely Dan and telling kaleidoscopic time. The clock's incandescent colors faded in and out, and, in the dark, the effect was mesmerizing, almost hallucinogenic—minus the mushrooms. Leo kissed Kelly softly, and she responded encouragingly. Her scent was strangely familiar—alluring but wholesome. For the longest time neither strayed into risky territory, content to make out. She followed his lead with sweet passion. Loose girls, he knew, never showed this much self-control. Eventually, his own restraint ebbed, and, little by little, his hands rubbed her breasts. Startled, she tightened. Then she relaxed, trusting him. She slipped her hand under his shirttail, gently rubbing his back. Her tongue caressed his with just the right energy. No helicopter tongue.

Kelly pulled her head back and eyeballed him. "You won't believe me, but I've never done this. Swear to God. I'm not sure what's gotten into me."

"My Latin genes, alcohol—take your pick. But remember, Quarters was your idea."

He kissed his way down her body, lifting her sweater to reach her flat stomach. Leo paused. "Is it okay? We don't have to." Nodding, she helped him remove her jeans and panties. He stayed down, kissing, taking his time, generous. Kelly extended her arms, inviting him to come up, to enter her.

Then it hit him. The familiar, enticing aroma from earlier. The innocent scent—before the sex. He'd only encountered it in Maracaibo, with the girl whose virginity he had taken before fleeing to Angel Falls.

Enough collateral damage. I've proven myself.

"Kelly, you're amazing, but we gotta stop."

"Now? Are you serious?"

"I am. We'll talk later. You deserve better."

"Better? I know I'm a rookie and all, but I can't imagine there *is* better." Leo blushed. She hopped up, kissed him, and looked at him earnestly.

"What?" he said.

"I want to thank you, airman, for your service."

28

THREE!

Key West, Florida, 1992. Zeb strode along Whitehead Street, faster than he would have liked. The pastel-colored antebellum houses, draped in palm trees and tropical flowers, seemed like distant cousins to homes in Chapel Hill. Even the offices were eye candy. Some, like the Audubon House and Pan Am First Flight building, had rich histories, detailed in placards out front. He wondered if Hemingway had been on the inaugural flight to Havana in 1927. No matter. One day he'd buy a watercolor or two.

Minutes later, Zeb marched into Carousel for the second time. Again, he was struck by the cornucopia of visual delights. Sharks and a seaplane hung from the ceiling. Surfboards, palm trees, lizards, parrots, and nautical paraphernalia adorned the establishment. Taken together, the combination bar-restaurant-store-music venue resembled a quaint corner of a Caribbean village. So many patrons were wearing Jackson Duvall T-shirts that there seemed to be an unofficial dress code.

Hopefully, this visit would build on the last. The manager's assistant had suggested Zeb lose the khakis and collared shirt, and he'd obliged.

Moonshine preferred informality, much like her boss. Duvall's right-hand woman seldom listened to unsolicited pitches, but he'd been lucky.

"I hear you have a business proposal," Moonshine said, shaking his hand. "I have fifteen minutes, so let's jump right into it."

Zeb handed her a booklet. "Sure. My presentation is divided into four sections—"

"Sorry, give me a minute to read the summary. I'll absorb more."

"Take your time." He scanned his copy:

EXECUTIVE SUMMARY: FAST-FORWARD ADVENTURES

Proposed product: a Jackson Duvall–themed line of upscale "soft" adventure tours, branded as Fast-Forward Adventures.

Premise: a large and growing number of Jackson Duvall fans would jump at the chance to go on Duvall-themed tours with like-minded adventurers. Fans' demographics and psychographics favor this niche. They have the financial resources, vacation time, and passion to be loyal Fast-Forward clients.

Initial tours: Samba Queen (Brazil), Gringos and Yanquis (Mexico), Michener's Hideaway (Polynesia), Pura Vida (Costa Rica), Slow Boat (China).

Sample Brazil activities: painting a favela schoolhouse; samba lesson in Leblon; hoodlum drink (caipirinha) happy hour; Rio hang gliding (liability waiver); Portuguese lesson and feijoada in Salvador; Buzios surfing.

"Soft" adventures: snorkeling, surfing, hiking, whitewater rafting, kayaking, horseback riding, wildlife safaris, hot-air ballooning, glacier trekking, dune surfing.

Features: bilingual tour leader, four-star accommodations, four or five "elective" low-intensity adventure activities, JD-themed cultural activities, community-improvement activity, "must-see" sightseeing excursions, two-thirds of all meals, transfers.

Experience:

Travel coordinator, Chapel Hill Travel, part-time, 1990–1992

Developed and marketed multisport Spring Break Tours for college students (generated $700,000 in sales)

Studied history at UNC–Chapel Hill

Moonshine nodded slightly and set the booklet down. "So what gave you this idea?"

He sat straighter, held his chin high. "Jackson's music speaks to fans in different ways. Some obsess about his escapades in exotic settings. Some love his sense of humor and clever lyrics. Still others chill out or party to his music, escaping their humdrum life. Some weirdoes like me use his songs to learn about geography, literature, and languages, to get the most out of life."

So far, so good. She wasn't rolling her eyes. "All of us adore Jackson's adventurous spirit because it underlies his music. It gave him the imagination and courage to explore the world and live life to the fullest. He knew that people, places, and experiences would spur his creativity. So many of his colorful characters and wonderful predicaments come from his sailboat and seaplane adventures in far-flung lands. I've never met him, but, to me, Jackson's an adventurer at heart, like his grandfather."

Moonshine flipped through the pages. "You're an articulate young man, but the clock is ticking. Better get to the point."

He nodded. "Bottom line: Jackson Duvall and adventure travel are a natural fit. As for me, I'd be a good partner, because I have tons of experience crafting adventures to exotic countries. I've been obsessed with geography, foreign cultures, history, and adventure for a long time."

"And you're convinced there's enough demand?"

"Oh, yes," Zeb said, smiling. "Duvall fans are a far cry from the party animals portrayed in the media. Most are smart and successful—doctors, lawyers, businesspeople. They can afford international trips. Just as important, they *want* to take them—to have fun, explore, learn, make friends, do good, and recharge their batteries. Word of mouth will attract similar people who aren't already fans, so the target group will expand."

"Fair enough," she said. "Now this Gringos and Yanquis tour. Won't that offend the people whose business we need to succeed?"

Zeb flushed. "Good point. I can rework the title."

"You studied history at UNC. Great school. When did you graduate?"

"I didn't."

"Why not?"

"I had a problem with the honor court."

Moonshine raised her eyebrows. "Can you explain?"

He sighed. "I'd rather not, but I have references from my former boss and my rabbi."

She frowned. "Well, thanks for coming in, but I'm out of—" Moonshine's phone rang, and she grabbed it, waving goodbye. "Hey, Abigay. You have an update?" Zeb's ears perked up, and he looked at the manager hopefully, but it was clear his opportunity had passed.

Three days later Zeb stood on the deck of Turtle Kraals bar, nursing his Miller Lite and surveying the waterfront. A historic schooner was setting out on a sunset sail as diving, fishing, and reef expeditions returned. He wondered how this place had looked in the 1960s, when shrimping, turtling, and sponging thrived, or in 1513, when Ponce de Leon visited, finding so many green turtles he named an island chain the Dry Tortugas after them. The conservation movement had forced change, but the seaport still bustled.

Nearby a man in Civil War garb wiped sweat from his brow. It was pushing ninety degrees, but he was covered head to toe in a navy-blue uniform, complete with hat and boots.

"I take it you're Union?" Zeb asked.

"Yes, sir."

"Quite a ways from your supply lines."

"Actually, less than a mile, sir."

"Seriously? In Key West?"

"Fort Taylor remains in Union hands. It's our only port in the Deep South."

Zeb whistled. "Man, that's weird."

"How do you mean?"

"Union troops having to travel so far *north* to fight the Confederacy—to get to the center of the action."

"I see your point, sir, but our mission here is critical." The soldier pointed toward the gulf. "We're blockading Confederate shipping, to keep them from resupplying troops. Our ten-inch Rodman and Columbiad cannons do quite a job."

"When do you expect to engage?"

The soldier checked his watch. "In forty-seven minutes. We'll be going against blockade runners. They'll feel the full force of our artillery."

"Good luck. And thank you for your service."

"Sure thing, sir."

Zeb went inside, settling in next to the racetrack. He fiddled with his ticket. Now that Moonshine had nixed him, it was his best hope for extending his stay. Beer in hand, tummy nudging the speedway, he was ready. Other spectators gathered around.

Clark Whitt, the turtle master, laid his pen on one end of the track and slid open the door. The numbered box turtles seemed underwhelmed, none vying for pole position. To Zeb's dismay, Three appeared comatose, even by turtle standards. Hopefully, Three was in energy-saving mode. Or sandbagging.

Only when Whitt lined them up did the turtles move—two forward, two sideways, one backward. It figured. Backward. Like Zeb.

Whitt kept repositioning the reptiles to ensure a fair start. *Who feels more undignified*, Zeb wondered, *the turtles or Whitt?* Finally, the turtle master shot his cap gun, and they were off.

Or not. All five seemed intent on proving Newton's Law of Inertia. Spectators whooped and hollered. "Let's go, Three!" Zeb yelled.

Whitt artfully emceed the inactivity. Two suddenly took off with Three in hot pursuit. One, Four, and Five ignored the gun, perhaps tanking. The race was neck and neck, with Three nudging ahead at the last instant to snatch victory.

Jumping up and down, Zeb hollered. "Whoooeee! We won!" He dashed to the end of the track, picked up the champion, and planted a big, wet kiss on Three. "We did it! Whoooeee!" A Swedish tourist snapped a photo.

Whitt's voice boomed, "Okay, folks. I hope you enjoyed watching our little speedsters. All of you with Three tickets, meet me at the bar."

"All of you?" Zeb said.

Four candidates lined up, each hoping to select the key that would unlock the treasure box containing a cash prize. The pot increased fifty dollars each week, until there was a winner. Eight weeks had passed since the last payout.

Minutes later Zeb raised his arms in triumph. He treated the other finalists to a beer and then feasted on yellowtail snapper and a mojito, toasting Three. Four hundred dollars didn't erase the sting of Moonshine's rejection, but it was the best he could hope for. The world wasn't at the beck and call of college rejects.

A colorful sign across the marina advertised a scuba course. Bingo! If nothing else, he'd leave Key West with a certification and dive Pennekamp on the way home.

He scooped the garnish from his plate into a napkin and went out back. Whitt was loading the turtles onto his pickup. "Well, if it ain't the champ. What can I do you for?"

"Can I give this to Three?" Zeb said, holding up the parsley, cucumber, and lemon slices. "I figure he deserves something."

"No, you can't give it to Three," Whitt said, sounding more like a crotchety codger than cheery emcee. "But you *can* give it to all five of them." He guffawed, slapping Zeb on the back. "Now, that's a first, son."

Three hours later, after napping, showering, and stashing his winnings under the motel mattress, Zeb headed out again. Sunset having passed, he'd missed Mallory Square's performers. The unicyclists, sword swallowers, tarot-card readers, jugglers, fire-eaters, artists, contortionists, and acrobats had had to make do without him.

Just ahead on Simonton a guitarist played "Fire and Rain." Noticing the harmonica hanging inches from his mouth, Zeb requested Neil Young. Incredible renditions of "Old Man" and "After the Gold Rush" had Zeb clapping maniacally. He dropped two bucks into the empty jar, prompting the musician to throw in "From Hank to Hendrix." "You're awesome, man!" Zeb shouted, soaking it in before heading on.

He marched into the famed Pier House, carrying himself as if he'd booked the presidential suite rather than a single room at the Blue Marlin Motel. He made his way to the Chart Room. An exquisite model clipper ship perched atop a sill. Nautical charts and black-and-white historical photos adorned the walls. Pink and green florescent lights illuminated the well-stocked bar. A chessboard sat atop a wooden table. Scribbled on a blackboard were two notes: "Humpty Dumpty may well have been pushed!" and "Hemingway was never here, and Jackson Duvall just left."

Zeb snickered. He'd come for free hot dogs and popcorn, so humor and atmosphere were bonuses. After ordering a beer, he asked the bartender, "Did Duvall ever play here?"

"It was his first gig in Florida. He played for drinks. Bob Marley, too."

"No shit." Zeb grabbed his beer, hot dog, and popcorn, and moved to the table. Marley and Duvall—both of them, right here. Scarfing down his food, he imbibed and fiddled with the chessboard.

Zeb picked up a piece and twirled it around. A pawn. He smiled, a line from *Blazing Saddles* echoing in his mind: "Mongo only pawn in game of life." Like him. Actions had consequences, and, for the foreseeable future, he'd be a pawn, not a queen, bishop, or rook. The question remained: Could a pawn dig himself out of a hole—like, say, a newborn sea turtle?

He ordered a margarita.

"Three!" Zeb exclaimed. The little fella could be a mascot, not just a meal ticket. Though penned and powerless, Three had shown spirit, racing to win despite no obvious reward. He'd suffered, lugging his shell. Directionless at first—then moving backward—he'd recovered, finding his way. Obstacles blocked his path, yet he'd persevered, progressed by sticking his neck out. Once a pawn, always a pawn? Hell no.

"A journey of a thousand miles begins with a single step," Zeb said, drawing stares from other patrons. He visualized Gene Wilder and Lao Tzu hanging out.

Was Key West the first step? Was he headed in the right direction? Did speed matter? Should he only rely on himself or lean on others? As Rabbi always said, the questions were clearer than the answers.

One thing *was* clear. Unlike Three, he'd been blessed with free will. A powerful gift.

"Jeez, what's in this margarita?"

It was time to lighten up, so he took off. Minutes later he sat on a barstool in Captain Tony's, soaking up rhythm and blues.

"Excuse me, sir," Zeb said to the weathered man standing beside him. "Do you know the name of the band? They're amazing."

"Son, don't ever call me 'sir.' It's bad for my reputation."

Zeb nodded.

"They're called Mojo Hand."

Zeb drummed his hands to the beat. "Awesome song."

"'Boom Boom' by John Lee Hooker. He was a blues legend."

"Appreciate that. Can I buy you a beer?"

The old man chortled. "You buy *me* a beer? Good one!" He stuck out his hand. "Captain Tony. Your money's no good here."

Zeb grabbed his hand. "Oh my gosh! I'm Zeb. I'm honored."

"Don't be. I put my pants on one leg at a time." Captain Tony flagged down the bartender, directing her to serve him free Bud the rest of the night. He turned back to Zeb. "What are you doing in Key West? Chasing pussy?"

Zeb snickered. "Sort of. Won't be doing it long if I can't land a job."

"What are you looking for?"

"I applied at Carousel but didn't make it."

"Why not?"

Zeb's shoulders slumped. "I got expelled from college."

Captain Tony grinned. "Don't worry, son, I wasn't a choirboy either. Never made it past ninth grade. Hell, I quit school to bootleg whiskey during Prohibition. Also did some gunrunning."

"Holy shit! You ever get caught?"

"Once. Mobsters left me for dead in the Newark dump."

Zeb recoiled, shocked. "How come?"

"I cheated them. Used a phone to get early race results. I escaped here in '48."

"And the rest is history. Now you have your own charter business, your own bar, you ran for mayor—"

"Unsuccessfully. Lost three times so far, even with Duvall's backing. But I can't complain; I'm listening to 'Boom Boom' in my own damn saloon."

"So what's the secret?" Zeb asked admiringly.

The captain smirked and pointed to a patron. "Read his T-shirt."

A quote was imprinted under a likeness of Captain Tony: "All you need in this life is a tremendous sex drive and a great ego—brains don't mean shit."

Zeb howled. Maybe bouncing back wasn't a pipe dream. Here, it seemed, getting expelled could be worn as a badge of honor.

"So what's next?" the captain asked.

"Not sure. I'll run out of money in a couple weeks. Maybe I'll get certified in scuba and then return home."

Captain Tony studied him. "Nah, got a better idea. Wait here."

Ten minutes later, the captain returned with another man—slightly younger but with a similarly weather-beaten face. "This is a buddy of mine, Mel Fisher."

"Nice to meet you, Mr. Fisher."

"Mel. If you're gonna be a freshwater conch, drop the formalities."

Zeb nodded.

"Mel's a treasure hunter," Captain Tony continued. "He's been searching for sunken treasure for fourteen years. Mainly sixteenth-century Spanish galleons. He's got a team of divers. I was telling Mel about you. Says he'll hire you on a test basis, if you get your basic certification and pass the search-and-salvage course, which he'll pay for. It's hard work, but his crew lives rent-free aboard a houseboat. Crew are responsible for cleaning and maintenance."

Zeb beamed. "I don't know what to say."

"Better say something," Mel said, grinning.

"When can I move in?"

29

SHELL MONEY, PIGS, AND A CASSOWARY

*P*apua New Guinea, 1998. Kiara awoke shaking in the pitch-black darkness but couldn't remember having had a nightmare. She reached for the lamp, grabbing only air. Groggily Kiara got to her feet and bumped into a table before remembering where she was. She flipped the wall switch—nothing. A power outage. Welcome to PNG.

She stumbled back to bed, desperately wanting more sleep. But with no air-conditioning, she just lay there sweating like a pig. The shaking began again, only it wasn't her, she finally realized. *An earthquake!* Kiara scrambled for the doorframe, sheltering there, until the tremors abated.

Now completely awake, Kiara returned to bed, her mind racing. Why did catastrophes so often hit those countries least able to withstand them? Cyclones pounded Bangladesh; earthquakes battered Haiti. As if the rampant crime, poverty, and tribal conflicts hadn't already brought enough misery. Fundamentalist preachers would surely attribute Mother Nature's wrath to the locals' lack of faith—God's retribution. And they would be wrong, if for no other reason than Christians now outnumbered animists in PNG.

What's the cause-and-effect of all this misery? Kiara wondered. *Do recurring disasters cause poverty? Or do bad policy and poverty make tragedies worse than they need to be? It probably goes both ways.*

Apparently poorer Papuans had to cut down trees for fuel and to clear land for subsistence farming. Corporate logging, too, had led to widespread deforestation that, in turn, caused massive flooding and mudslides. *Port Moresby's building codes had probably made matters worse*, Kiara mused.

She stepped outside. Her neighbor's ramshackle house was intact, with minor debris scattered about the mostly flat roof. She wondered how the multitudes living in houses on stilts had fared. She would inquire later.

A letter had been left at her doorstep. Kiara shook her head. Neither snow nor rain nor, apparently, earthquakes . . . It was from Bob Jeffreys, her coach.

> Dear Kiara:
>
> I hope this letter finds you healthy and self-actualized. Suffice it to say, not too many of my girls have chosen to give back in the highlands of Papua New Guinea. We're all proud of you.
>
> I've often wondered if the *physical* courage I look for, and try to develop in my players, correlates with bravery in other facets of their lives—in relationships, career decisions, spiritual matters, or when it comes to taking intellectual and entrepreneurial risks for their personal growth. Finding a connection between physical and spiritual courage would obviously make me feel great, though I'm not sure there is one. But you, Kiara, *are* leading a tremendously consequential life, so hats off! If I were twenty years younger, I'd follow your example. (I still wish I'd gone into the Peace Corps.)

You may have heard about our new "Kiara tackling drill." It's mind-boggling how you transformed into a defensive stalwart! We'd never have made it to three College Cups, let alone won two of them, without your leadership. It's time to put that missed penalty behind you. All the greats miss big ones—Platini, van Basten, Rummenigge. Besides, winning three straight national championships would've been bad for our sport! Okay, not really.

Just to be clear, I'm *not* upset you turned down the women's national team; we have enough Tar Heels on it. You're representing your country in a different way—one that's more important. Give Marcus time. He'll come around.

You were smart to switch to psychology. And, no, I don't think your year at medical school was wasted. Hell, I left business school after a year, and I still benefit from the background I got there.

Meanwhile, Sarah's jokes are getting annoying. Damn girl is working at my summer camp. It gets old hearing her brag about scoring the winning goal against us, and how I blew it by not offering her a scholarship. The worst part is, she's right.

I'll end this letter with two points, one of them self-serving . . .

Glancing at her watch, Kiara set the letter aside. Whatever the requests, they could wait. She had a busy day ahead.

Ninety minutes later Kiara was sitting in the reception area of Ambua Lodge, waiting for her Papuan host, Alice, to finish setting breakfast tables. When she had finished, Alice scurried over and grabbed Kiara's hand, introducing herself. The two women took a seat, chatting about the tremors and Kiara's journey to the highlands.

Alice shook her head with obvious delight. "A Black female doctor from USA—I still can't believe it! Dr. Battle, you are a godsend."

"Please, call me Kiara. Besides, I'll be learning just as much from you."

And it was true. She wasn't used to admiring her peers, but Alice's humble letter had revealed an extraordinary woman. It took energy to manage her lodge duties—waitressing and leading tours—while moonlighting the way she did. It took courage and flexible thinking to question, and then reject, the foundations of her culture, risking ostracization or worse. It took self-control to present an amiable front, while waging a ferocious battle. Ambua's cultural and wildlife tourists had no clue. Ten weeks would hardly be enough to pick her brain.

Alice blushed. "Okay, Kiara it is. So, what are your first impressions of Tari, aside from the earthquake?"

"It's been fascinating, quite an eye-opener. People are so friendly."

"Really?"

"Absolutely. Whenever we drive by, villagers wave enthusiastically. They shout greetings and call out, 'Hello, White man!'—to the others, of course. It cracks me up. They keep waving until long after we've passed."

"You've been lucky," Alice said. "Most of the time, we fight."

"Over what?"

"*Everything*," she said wearily. "Land, women, pigs, fishing rights. Sometimes over freak accidents. If a clan thinks fair reparations haven't been made, they look for payback, which leads to war. Things got worse after last year's earthquake."

"How come?"

Alice sighed. "It destroyed entire villages. Tens of thousands were displaced. Many moved here, occupying land owned by the clans."

"I see," said Kiara thoughtfully. "Well, so far, my highlight has been the Huli wedding. It was incredible—the colorfully painted children, the elaborately dressed bride and groom, the pigs, and cassowaries. The best part was the bargaining over the bride-price."

"Intense, right?"

"And hysterical! I hope that's not rude. It's just, these tactical fits of outrage alternating with periods of calm, it made me bust out laughing—it's so *different* than anything I'm used to. And to me the most amazing thing was that after fighting so hard and for so long over the bride-price, the father then turned around and shared all the spoils! We're talking eight pigs, one cassowary, and a *bunch* of shell money. He didn't save any of it!"

Alice smiled. "He was sharing it with his *wantok*."

"*Wantok?*"

"That's how we live. Papuans believe that we're related to, and responsible for, many people. Not just family, relatives, and clan members but everyone who speaks our language, has the same ethnicity, and lives near us. Sick people, orphans, and the elderly are taken care of by members of their *wantok*. Men trying to raise a bride-price, or pay for a funeral, get help from their *wantok*. It's the glue that holds us together."

Kiara nodded. *In America, Alice could be a university professor.* "Fascinating. . . . So what's the plan today?"

"Someone will cover for me here. We'll be meeting a sick woman called Charlize."

"Alice, you realize I'm not a doctor, right? I'm barely qualified as a psychologist."

The Papuan chuckled. "I've only attended two NGO seminars. You will help so much. Shall I tell you her background?" Kiara nodded again.

Charlize had been feeling lethargic for months. Unable to sleep, work, or eat normally, she had frequent headaches and digestive problems. She was constantly catching colds but so far thankfully no infectious diseases. Hela Provincial Hospital had performed blood tests, but they revealed nothing.

Charlize had turned to a traditional medicine man who advised her that an evil spirit was living within her and causing the illness. The spirit was apparently a green dwarf with an affinity for women, but with the help of a shaman it could be hoodwinked into exiting her body. Charlize returned the next night, and several shamans performed a spirit dance. Donning grass skirts, long wigs, bird-of-paradise feathers, and elaborate makeup, they lured the evil spirit out of Charlize's body. Only she wasn't cured. Finally, two weeks ago, at the end of her rope, Charlize had pleaded for Alice's help.

Kiara tried to imagine Charlize's plight. Huli women lived and ate separately, because the men feared menstrual blood. Women cared for the pigs and worked the fields, growing sweet potatoes. They lugged cargo from the market, while their husbands strolled along beside them, unburdened. Girls received little education. Men made the important decisions, with the wealthiest taking two or three wives to enhance their status. Domestic abuse and rape were rampant. That was the reason Alice had established her one-person advocacy organization.

"I assume you explained to Charlize that she's suffering from depression and anxiety?" Kiara asked when Alice had finished.

"Not yet. We need to know for sure."

"What could be causing it?"

"Her husband will soon take a second wife."

Kiara flinched. *Work the woman like an ox and demote her when her tits sag.* "Makes complete sense. What's your plan?"

"You can examine and diagnose her. If we're right, we take her to a woman shaman."

"You just told me the shamans' magic didn't work. They couldn't exorcize the horny green dwarf!"

Alice's smile vanished.

There I go again, Kiara thought. *The same lack of respect. Here it'll get me into real trouble. Or, worse yet, get Alice in trouble.* "I'm sorry, Alice. You were saying . . ."

Alice waited as two guests walked out of earshot. "There's a woman shaman who casts spells to make husbands loyal, so they forget about taking a second or third wife. She makes a special compound, chants her incantation, and gives it to the wife, who hides it near the roof."

"And?"

"And then we hope it works."

"What's her track record?"

Alice cocked her head. "According to the shaman, it always works."

"You don't sound convinced."

"I have seen it *not* work."

Kiara suppressed a smile. "What happened?"

"The husband suspected what was going on and got his own shaman to counteract the spell."

"I see."

"Of course, it's possible that spells don't work at all," Alice said, no trace of emotion in her voice.

"Could be," Kiara agreed equally coolly.

Alice leaned forward in her seat. "But the woman shaman doesn't charge anything. If Charlize *thinks* the spell works, she will be more confident, and she might seem more attractive to her husband. He may not want to marry again. It cannot hurt."

Kiara grinned. *Now which of us is the trained psychologist?* "It certainly can't hurt. What's your plan B?"

"We advise Charlize to get a divorce, if you agree."

"I might be persuaded."

"Then comes the hard part."

"Huh?"

Alice wore a grave expression. "Charlize would need to repay the bride-price."

"Won't the *wantok* help?"

The Papuan shook her head. "Divorce isn't part of our tradition. Her parents might help, but she would need to depend on other women."

"Do they have any money?"

"Sure." Alice nodded. "A lot of women make ropes, bags, or skirts and sell them for money. They also own pigs. And remember, in some villages, women own the land, not men. It's dangerous for women to help Charlize, but they can."

"Interesting," Kiara said, considering the angles. "And what do the men think about this woman shaman?"

Alice recoiled and lowered her voice to a whisper. "Men *cannot* know about her. They would kill her for being a sorcerer."

The two women sat in silence for a moment, with the exception of Kiara's grumbling stomach. *Jesus, this kind of outreach has consequences,* Kiara thought solemnly. *Won't the men hurt Alice, too, if they find out what she's up to?*

"Sorry for asking, but aren't sorcerers *eaten* here?" Kiara said, wearing her most apologetic face.

Alice sighed, mentally queueing up her usual Westerner-reeducation talk. "It's very rare nowadays, but, yes, *some people* eat the flesh of sorcerers to protect against black magic. And, yes, *sometimes* warriors eat the flesh of their enemies to keep their spirits from taking revenge. That way the warrior lives longer."

Kiara swallowed a nervous giggle. "I have a friend whose favorite historian blames cannibalism on protein starvation," she blurted, grasping for any kind of reply.

Alice raised her eyebrow and pondered Kiara's odd statement. "That could be. There weren't any large animals here until colonists and missionaries brought their livestock. Ancient Papuans ate monkeys, spiders, insects, sometimes people. I guess pigs, cows, and Christianity changed those things."

"Well, let's pray the woman shaman succeeds without getting discovered," Kiara said, exhaling deeply.

The rest of that day Kiara and Alice spent visiting with Charlize and a few other Huli women in distress. When she returned home that evening, Kiara read the rest of her coach's letter:

I'll end this letter with two points, one of them self-serving:

First, when you return, I'd like to hire you for a sports psychology project. I know this isn't your specialty, but you'd be perfect. I need my ladies to find their voice during games—pack some bite while staying positive. By senior year you became a master at communicating bluntly without upsetting team chemistry. Also, I'm getting older and need better ways to handle players who are taking things too easy.

Second—and forgive me for dispensing pop psychology to a shrink—but time away from your PhD studies will be good for you. Your thesis supervisor will still be a jerk when you return, but you can use this period to improve.

During your last three years you did a remarkable job of connecting with teammates. Your awareness when it came to *them* was astonishing. But, despite our many long chats, I feel you only scratched the surface as far as self-examination. I suspect you're scared. You shouldn't be.

Sports are a laboratory of the human spirit. For four years I saw you in a high-pressure environment, and I, therefore, have special insight into your character. Know this: You have *nothing* to fear. All of us have flaws, but I assure you that yours are far outweighed by your inner beauty. For God's sake, you're helping kids in PNG! Look more deeply within yourself; you'll be pleasantly surprised. You just might find that you're a better shrink for it, and that your thesis supervisor isn't as evil as you thought.

See you in CH!

With affection,
Bob

Holy shit! First the earthquake and now Alice, Charlize, and Coach Jeffreys were shaking up her whole world. *I'm gonna need a double dose of melatonin tonight.*

Three weeks later they visited with Charlize's husband, who had indeed taken on a second wife. Charlize had already announced that she would repay the bride-price and pursue a divorce. In retaliation her husband was refusing to let her care for her children. Alice applied maximum pressure on the husband, using moral suasion, logic, and, finally, threats. In the end, he capitulated, allowing the children to be reunited with their mother. Alice promised to support the spurned Charlize at every turn.

For her part, before Kiara returned to America, she donated three quarters of the sum Charlize needed to raise for her bride-price. Kiara received word, once back in the States, that Charlize had recovered from her illness soon afterward.

30

SMOOTH SAILING?

Stuart, Florida, 2016. Leo tied the waterproof radio to the mast and tucked away the sail ties. Carlos, the CFO of REK Cruise Lines, stood on the dock, chatting with Leo's associate, Jake. Carlos didn't appear antsy, so Leo threw the covers below and resumed his preparations. The mental checklist he'd developed made the process feel routine.

As recently as a year ago Leo never mixed sailing with work. The water was his escape from the stresses of the concrete jungle. It also compensated for not having a girlfriend—ironic since he'd expected the sailboat to be a chick magnet. These days he mainly hosted corporate executives. Best-laid plans . . .

Leo dropped the centerboard and grabbed hold of the tiller. "Ready, guys." He had dropped the military sirs and ma'ams at the urging of his boss—respect without subservience.

"Carlos, why don't you come aboard first? Please watch your balance. You can join me on the windward side." When Carlos was seated, Leo said, "Go ahead and push off." Jake did so and climbed aboard quickly, pulling in the jib sheet without prompting.

Leo steered the Flying Scot toward Stuart's main channel, avoiding Sherwood Forest—a dangerous group of pilings. Jake turned the jib over to Carlos and raised the mainsail. Soon they were off, propelled by a balmy eight-knot breeze.

Jake shot him a nasty look.

Yes, I'm a Benedict Arnold, Leo thought, *but please don't sabotage everything. Not now. Not over a woman.*

Carlos beamed. "Now, this is really something. Turquoise water, wind, no high-rises—definitely worth the drive."

"Glad you approve," Leo said. "A different world from Miami, that's for sure. If we're lucky, we'll see dolphins."

"*Ojalá!*"

"Of course, if that happens, you have no choice but to appoint us agent!" *When did I become so nauseatingly smooth, such a glad-hander?*

Carlos grinned. "We'll see. With the fees you guys charge, it would be cheaper to steal your associate." He slapped Jake on the back. "A brainiac who can sail! Now that's a valuable commodity, especially for a cruise company."

"You got me there, my friend." *If only Carlos knew.*

"Just kidding. Man, the shrimp bisque and dolphin fish were awesome. The visit from the manatees, too."

"Glad you liked it."

The Dolphin Bar and Shrimp House never disappointed. Best to back off now, let the waves and breeze do their thing. He sat back and pondered the incredible turns his life had taken. Once a star-crossed Venezuelan, he was now an American—a senior relationship manager at Bank of America, no less—hosting the CFO of a public company on his own sailboat.

Thank God Mr. Walsh and Dean Acosta intervened all those years ago. Without their guidance he'd have gone nowhere. The onetime "axis of evil" had been anything but; their tag team had ultimately whipped him into shape. Even after Leo's GPA skyrocketed, Dean Acosta had insisted he transfer out of UNC, only relenting when Walsh threatened to torpedo his U.S. citizenship because he, too, "felt like a sucker" for having sponsored a deadbeat. The fact that she, Dr. Evil herself, had lined up his postgraduation interview with BOA blew Leo's mind. From that point on, his progress had been steady, if not rapid—credit training, retail lending, managing a branch, commercial lending, and foreign-exchange trading.

Leo had loved FX. Investing the bank's capital in promising currencies excited him. Helping corporations hedge risks associated with imports, exports, and capital projects was also stimulating. By recommending cost-effective forward and option contracts, he became a financial advisor, not just a salesman. Clients lauded his financial acumen, honesty, and, amusingly, his interpersonal skills. Still hungry for a bigger challenge, he'd enrolled in UF's executive MBA program at night.

Transferring to global finance five years ago had been another good move. After three years as an assistant relationship manager, he was now a senior relationship manager with a portfolio of ten corporations with annual sales of $400 million to $6 billion. How cool was that! Hell, REK Cruise Lines was the world's third-largest cruise company.

If only I could manage my personal life that well.

Carlos tapped Leo's knee. "Do me a favor. Recap the main points. I'll need to summarize your ideas to Julian. He's a busy man."

"Anyone too busy to come sailing must be," Leo said. The CEO was a notorious workaholic. "You asked us to participate in a two-hundred-and-fifty-million-dollar revolving line of credit, to be agented by JP Morgan Chase. You wanted us to commit twenty-five million dollars.

"If you decide on the revolver, we'd commit forty million dollars. REK can service the debt, and your relationship is important to us.

"But we also looked at larger questions. What are your *long-term* funding needs, and should they be met through short-term borrowing, as you're requesting, or through longer-term borrowing or a stock offering? What is your optimal capital structure? You with me?"

"Yup."

"We then analyzed three financial risks. First, foreign-exchange risk. Your strategic plan calls for three more five-thousand-passenger ships over the next ten years. Jake's model assumes five hundred and twenty million dollars per ship. If they're bought from the Italians and Finns, that exposes you to huge FX risk."

"Agreed."

"Next, interest-rate risk. The yield curve reflects expectations of higher interest rates. With the revolver you're requesting, your variable rate borrowings will soon become more expensive."

Carlos nodded. "That ties in with capital structure."

"Absolutely, I'll get to that in a second. Commodity-price risk was the last risk we assessed. Your ships consume an average of seventy-five thousand gallons of fuel per day. For the entire fleet, REK's exposure is huge.

"By not hedging your foreign-exchange, interest-rate, and commodity-price risks, your earnings become more volatile. Investors perceive higher risk. Riskier stocks have lower P-E ratios, hence lower valuations. But you know all that . . ."

"Never hurts to be reminded," the CFO said.

It was great Carlos didn't have a huge ego. Glancing at the angle of the waves, Leo turned upwind and scanned the water for dolphins. "By the way, we should reach Jupiter in twenty minutes."

"Sounds good."

He turned back. "Lastly, we identified two possible acquisition targets. They would be strategic and increase your cash flow per share. We did a discounted cash flow and comparable transaction-multiples analysis. Both point to the acquisitions increasing shareholder value."

"Acquisition targets are *definitely* Leo's thing," Jake said with a wry smile. Leo flinched.

"Maybe so, but he didn't tell us the names of the targets!" the CFO protested.

Leo patted Carlos on the back. "We're hoping you give us the mandate. We'll deal with M&A separately."

"Okay. How about financing structure?"

At Leo's prompting, Jake spoke. "We've assumed your ships operate for fifteen years before you sell them. Ideally, they should be matched with long-term debt or equity, not a five-year revolver. You generate tons of cash from operations, but your ten-year external funding need will be eight hundred million dollars.

"Because your business is unpredictable, you won't want to lever up much. Still, interest expense is tax deductible, so you can reduce your cost of capital by two-point-three percent if you increase your debt-to-enterprise value ratio to thirty-five percent. That would increase cash flow by two-point-four million dollars.

"You can handle the extra debt because your operating risk is lower than your competitors. I'm talking about luxury cruise operators, sellers of luxury land-based vacations, and smaller cruise operators. Your cruises are less vulnerable to swings in the economy, because they offer tremendous value, they're perfect for older Americans who are becoming an ever-larger percentage of the population, and because two-thirds of Americans have never been on a cruise—a sign of huge growth potential."

"So what specifically are you proposing?" Carlos asked.

Leo said, "On the funding side, two things. First, a five-hundred-million-dollar offering of ten-year bonds. You'd receive an investment grade rating of BBB– and a coupon rate of four-point-five percent. It makes sense to lock in when rates are at historical lows. Second, we advise a secondary equity offering of three hundred million dollars to preserve your borrowing flexibility. You'd remain solidly in the investment-grade range."

"You forgot one thing," Jake said, glaring at him. "With us, it's *always* about the relationship. Trust is paramount."

Leo bit his lip.

"Got it," Carlos said. "We have a lot to chew on."

"Everything's in the binder, but call us anytime," Leo said.

Carlos nodded. "One last thing. Why'd you guys go to all this trouble knowing that JP Morgan's been our agent forever?"

Leo grinned. *Because Bill Walsh told me to always shoot for the moon?*

"In reality, we want to be your primary advisor. JP Morgan is great, but they missed the boat on this one—no pun intended. The financing piece can boost your cash flow, smooth out earnings, and raise your trading multiple. Our acquisition targets can do the same. We hope that, by bringing you good ideas, you'll give us the chance."

"That's not all you're bringing me," Carlos said, pointing off starboard. A pod of dolphins approached. They marveled as the acrobatic mammals put on a show until finally swimming away.

Carlos and Jake went ashore in Jupiter so that Carlos could be chauffeured to Miami. So much could happen on that ride, Leo knew. Would Jake sabotage the deal? Jump ship to REK? Maybe both.

Actually, it made more sense for Jake to support the blockbuster deal, so that he could gain valuable experience, stay in the prestigious associate program, and get into a top MBA program. Why sink his chances for something that had already happened? Afterward, Jake could spill the beans about Leo's betrayal to their managing director. Such conduct would never be tolerated, not given the corporate culture. Justice would be served.

Leo reversed course, sailing solo like the old days, when he'd refused to invite work associates. Why had he broken his rule? Loneliness? Expediency? Whatever the reason, the slope had proven slippery. First, thanking a friend—a Merrill investment manager—for showing him some promising private-equity deals to invest in. He'd then hosted the friend and a potential investor from Venezuela on a private sail. His Merrill friend had won the business and invited more clients, until finally Leo had decided to do the same himself. He'd sold out, defiling a once-sacred activity.

And now debauchery had sullied the waters of his professional life. *Sleeping with my associate's girlfriend, a woman in her thirties? What in the world was I thinking?*

The pitch going off without a hitch was a testament to Jake's self-control. Under the circumstances, his barbs had been restrained. Beyond all that, Jake had shown self-assurance, gladly taking a back seat during the pitch, not requiring affirmation. If only he had had that same quality, Leo thought.

A sleek fifty-four-foot Beneteau came into view as Leo sailed past the final drawbridge. Next to his Flying Scot, the French sailboat seemed an altogether different mode of transport. Maybe one day but no time soon, thanks to his disgusting behavior.

Radioing the sailing center, Leo made his final tack and approached the U.S. Sailing Center dock. A volunteer helped him tie up. By the time Leo stowed everything, he'd mentally cued up Buffett tunes for the drive back to the office. He was in no rush. None whatsoever.

31

TAR HEEL BRED

hapel Hill, North Carolina, 2016. The UNC marching band launched into "I'm a Tar Heel Born," just as Zeb reached the midway point of Kenan Drive. "Damn," he muttered, picking up his stride. *Why can't I ever be on time—even when it matters?* The Chancellor's Club pregame party waited for no one.

He beamed as he entered Kenan-Flagler courtyard and sauntered past the makeshift bar and hors d'oeuvres stands. Baby-blue paraphernalia was ubiquitous. Philanthropic alums sang the fight song and clapped along, having set aside their cocktails.

Others, he knew, were opining on the basketball team's prospects and on the worthiness of multimillion-dollar academic projects. Waiters served delicacies and replenished drinks. Geniality prevailed.

Already, golf carts ferried the less mobile to the Dean Dome two hundred yards away. Tipoff wasn't for another hour, but warm-ups lured many, especially for the big game against Duke. All 21,750 seats would be filled, with most Chancellor's Club members—not him—courtside.

Some thought it strange he would take to these parties. After all, Zeb was relatively young, unsuccessful, and, conspicuously, not an alum. Nor did he aspire to live the high life. But these were his people, people who bled Carolina blue. Their allegiance to school often surpassed their devotion to God, a phenomenon that didn't sit well with local clergy. When pressed, alums would respond, "If God isn't a Tar Heel, why is the sky Carolina blue?" Zeb's grandparents had understood all this when gifting him the lifetime membership, and even as an expellee, there was nowhere Zeb would rather be. All the more after having missed the last three games.

Zeb moseyed to the bar and tapped Bob Jeffreys's shoulder. The coach seemed relieved. Chatting with Zeb was apparently less painful than the alternatives.

"I was beginning to think they booted you out," Bob said. "Where've you been—Mongolia, Madagascar?"

"Key West—for a wedding. I hung out with old friends for a while. Here, let me buy you a free beer."

"Too generous. Make it a Beck's, nonalcoholic."

"Nonalcoholic?"

"The price of being a spiritual titan."

"Gotcha." Zeb smiled, knowing the teetotaler could cuss with the best of them. He ordered their drinks.

"What's your history with Key West?"

"Funny you mention history. You ever hear of Mel Fisher?"

"The treasure hunter?"

"Bingo. I worked as one of his divers for two years. We found the *Nuestra Señora de Atocha*. A Spanish galleon that sunk in 1622. Mel had been searching for sixteen years."

Bob whistled. "Great timing on your part. It was worth a fortune, if I remember."

"Four hundred and fifty million. My share was minuscule, but it lasted a while."

"Must have. We didn't see you for, what, a decade?" The coach sipped his beer.

"Longer. After Mel, I traveled for two and a half years. Hit about thirty countries until my money ran out. Then I worked as a divemaster."

"Where?" Bob didn't normally pry into his personal life. Usually, they talked books, current events, and soccer.

"Lady Elliot Island, Sharm El Sheikh, Eilat, Maldives, Cozumel." He popped a deviled egg into his mouth.

"Fascinating. Why'd you return?"

"Three years in, I busted my eardrum. Money got tight, so I returned to Key West and worked for Hanns Ebensten. The guy was a pioneer in gay adventure travel. Taught me everything. But after eight years I decided to start a different type of travel business."

"You wanted to uncover the mysteries of history and nature."

Zeb nodded. "Wish I could uncover the mystery of making money. If things don't improve soon, we'll be evicted. . . . Anyway, enough about me. I saw your ladies spank the Seminoles. You guys dominated."

"It's about time. They've had our number lately."

Zeb raised his eyebrows. Who'd have guessed that Bob had won a World Cup title and twenty-two national championships? Or that, in his early days, critics had unfairly branded him as arrogant for a brash, take-no-prisoners approach that supposedly created Amazons? Never mind that most of the coach's critics had lost to him in lopsided fashion or that his male players never had to apologize for being domineering. By dismissing these criticisms as petty and sexist, Bob had reinforced his reputation.

If the coach had been maniacal early on, maybe it was insecurity. Would women's soccer and Carolina's fledgling program ever command respect? Had he been foolish to quit business school to coach a sport without a viable professional league? Was it smart to give up coaching the men? Would he ever boost his emotional intelligence enough to coach women effectively? Over time the insecurities—like the criticisms—died out, unsustainable in the face of Carolina's dynasty. Nowadays Bob dismissed unearned praise as much as he had unfounded criticism.

"I noticed you switched at halftime to a 4-4-2."

The coach chuckled. "Yes, protecting our big lead was pure genius. The box score should really credit me, not my automaton players, for the dazzling goals and stunningly creative assists."

"You realize sarcasm is the lowest form of humor?"

"I've always been a bottom-feeder."

"Seriously, I don't understand how your players go from kicking each other's butts in practice—from constantly being ranked against each other—to playing together like soulmates. How does that happen?"

Bob set down his Beck's. "People think our team is filled with alpha females. It isn't. But even so, building chemistry is a challenge. The main thing is to recruit character, but, even there, it's hit or miss. Accountability is a problem. Many players—especially the younger generation—are inoculated against criticism by their parents. They don't realize that overprotectiveness hampers kids. We need to make sure selfish players don't derail the team."

"Is that the hardest part of coaching for you?" Zeb grabbed some shrimp.

"No. It's finding the energy to confront players who are taking things easy. If I don't, our standards will erode. Can't let that happen."

"I hear ya. But I imagine you're smarter now as a coach?"

Bob chuckled. "When I first started coaching the women, my emotional IQ was about sixty. It's crept up over the years, and I think my teams have benefitted." His voice cracked. "I know my wife, marriage, and children have."

"Well, you're lucky that your passion helped your family life. Mine ruined it."

"I'm sorry," the coach said. Passing cheerleaders waved pompoms in their face. "What're you hearing from Kiara?"

"We had drinks last week. We were laughing about the old days." Zeb cocked his head. "Like when she ran away to Papua New Guinea to get away from her new thesis supervisor, and you wrote her a letter to keep her from quitting the program."

Bob smiled. "I remember. The guy had a problem with strong women. But she also needed to stop working on side projects without getting his approval. Anyway, she found the answer."

"Well, it looks like you've found your answers. Alessia Russo's been incredible. If Jessie Scarpa recovers her form, and if Emily Fox gets healthy, you guys will win it all."

"If, if, if." Bob pointed to the Dean Smith Center. "It's time to kick Duke's ass."

32

FLIPPING THE SWITCH

Western Rwanda, 2013. Knocking at the bungalow door woke Kiara from a dreamless sleep.

"Good morning," the cheery Rwandan woman said. "It's five thirty! This is your wake up!"

"Okay, thanks." Joviality at this hour was obnoxious.

After throwing on her hiking gear, Kiara strode to reception where the Jeep waited. She jumped in, sitting beside another comatose guest. Off they went in the dark, the guide handing them each a sandwich, fruit, hard-boiled egg, and juice.

Kiara tried to orient herself. Her lodge, perched on a ridge, faced the Virunga volcanoes in the heart of Rwanda's Parc Nacional des Volcans. PNV bordered Uganda and Congo, and they were two hours from Kigali, where she'd spent six weeks volunteering.

The sun rose, but a layer of mist still blanketed the five peaks. How might this place have looked when Dian Fossey arrived in 1966? Even now the "land of a thousand hills" was incredibly lush and undeveloped. Hopefully, they'd find some gorillas.

The guide spoke. "Today, there are around nine hundred mountain gorillas left on earth. Half reside in PNV. Only seven families have been habituated, and they often cross into Bwindi or Virunga. I must remind you that we could track eight or ten hours, over steep slopes with poor footing, and still not see them. There's no guarantee. You understand?"

They nodded.

"If we do find them, we'll spend no more than one hour. Are either of you feeling sick?"

They shook their heads vigorously. Human disease could kill the primates. If the ranger deemed them unhealthy, they'd forfeit the $650 permit fee.

Kiara felt a surge of adrenaline as they reached the park entrance. She hopped off the jeep and marched straight to the warden for her health inspection. Dropping her reserve, Kiara acted bright-eyed and bushy-tailed, the essence of health and congeniality. Declared healthy, Kiara joined the eight-person group, double-checking her camera and water supply. François Bigirimana, Fossey's porter from the 1980s, introduced himself as their guide, smiling broadly. Trackers, he explained, had been sent out hours earlier.

François led, and Kiara settled in behind him, the better to catch everything he did and said. The montane forest wasn't steep, but several hikers were already panting from the altitude. François stopped at clearings, giving them a chance to catch their breath and enjoy the panoramic views.

The terrain became steeper, the rainforest denser. As they climbed, mud and instability slowed their progress. One hiker, presumably too macho to wear long pants as instructed, griped about the stinging plants. François explained the stings were harmless, and that the pain would fade. Ahead a troop of golden monkeys with golden orange patches on their flanks and back were dazzling, as they jumped single file and seemingly nonstop from branch to branch.

"Nice bonus," Kiara said, and François smiled. She pointed to four volcanoes. "How high are they?"

"Between 11,500 and 14,400 feet. We're at 8,000 now."

"What was it like working for Dian Fossey?"

"Not easy. Dr. Fossey was a great scientist but a *very* tough boss. She liked gorillas more than people."

Fossey had famously captured, beaten, and humiliated suspected poachers. She'd held their cattle for ransom and burned their camps to the ground. "I hope she treated you better than she did the poachers!"

"For sure," François said, smiling. "But remember, there wouldn't be any gorillas left if she had only done research and taken census counts. Rangers were helping poachers capture baby gorillas for foreign zoos. She had to destroy traps and challenge the government."

A hiker pulled even with them. "Damn right, her tactics were needed! In *Gorillas in the Mist*, Dr. Fossey talked about a time when her four-man patrol managed to destroy 987 traps, while the park's twenty-four-man team didn't destroy a single one."

They entered a bamboo forest, François chopping a path with his machete. Periodically he mimicked the gorillas' vocalizations, imitating the way they ate plants, scraped bark from trees, and roughhoused. François munched on plants himself, and Kiara followed suit. When everyone had caught their breath, he resumed tracking. The microclimate was cold and misty, but Kiara found herself sweating.

François spun around, bringing a finger to his lips, and then pointed onward, through the leaves. Nine gorillas sat no more than forty feet away, feeding on bamboo leaves. "The Sabinyo family," François whispered. Guhonda, a huge silverback, crouched with his back to the hikers, unfazed. So this was what they meant by habituation, Kiara thought.

The group inched to within thirty feet, branching out, crouching. Most were too awed to snap photos.

"Guhonda eats seventy-five pounds of food daily. The females, forty pounds. Leaves, shoots, and stems from 150 species of plants. Sometimes bark, roots, and fruit."

Two infants took a breakfast break, wrestling and chasing each other. One did somersaults. An adult female, the mother or perhaps an aunt, barked, and they resumed eating.

"They're just like us," one hiker said.

François nodded. "Their DNA is ninety-eight percent the same."

A gorilla belched, apparently contented.

"Sounds like my husband," someone muttered.

François pointed to an adult female. "She's Guhonda's favorite. They do *jiggy-jiggy*."

In the blink of an eye the gorillas approached them, oblivious of the legally mandated twenty-two feet of separation. "Make yourselves small, look down submissively," François whispered. "Don't look Guhonda in the eye."

The silverback passed François, touching him affectionately on the shoulder. The hiker with plant stings rose to snap a photo. Guhonda roared, pounded his chest, and charged to within inches of the hiker. The man wet his pants and fell to the ground. Covering his head, he whimpered like a child. Guhonda moved on, having proved his point. Kiara snickered.

She was so entranced she didn't bother snapping photos. The hour passed in a flash.

On the return Kiara befriended a San Francisco businesswoman, Jill, who had also giggled at the pants-wetter. Jill promised to email photos of the troop from that day.

That evening Kiara joined Jill and others who had seen the gorillas. No one seemed exhausted. The exhilaration lingered, as each animatedly relived the highlights of the day. One spoke of spiritual rejuvenation, another of extending his stay to add another trek. Jill hoped to return and venture to Bwindi. Kiara listened rapturously, and, when they'd finished, she wasn't ready to retire. She and Jill moved to the lounge, ordered drinks, and settled onto the veranda overlooking the Virungas.

"So where else is your safari taking you?" Jill asked.

"Nowhere. Today was it."

"Your last day?"

Kiara smiled. "First and last."

"Ah, you're working. Well, if it's any consolation, today was the highlight of my entire safari. You chose wisely."

"Thanks." So many travelers played the one-upmanship game that it was refreshing to meet someone who didn't.

"So enough about gorillas. What've you been up to?" Jill asked.

"I spent six weeks volunteering with Psychologists Without Borders."

"Doing what exactly?"

Kiara sipped her wine. "I diagnose learning disabilities and teach strategies to compensate for them. So I did that, plus mental-health counseling—not my expertise, but they needed help."

"Wow, that's way cooler than what I do. How'd you get into it?"

She chuckled. "Sometimes I ask myself the same question."

"What do you mean?"

"I originally wanted to do medicine. I thought social sciences were beneath me—too soft."

"And?"

"I tutored this guy in college who told me later that I sucked at it—because I hadn't taught him according to his learning style. He was one hundred percent right, but I wasn't inclined to listen to lesser mortals." Kiara shook her head. "Eventually, I became fascinated by the diagnostic and learning aspects of psychology. Ironically, I found they were backed by hard science."

"And now you're a globe-trotting Mother Teresa." Jill's tone wasn't mocking.

"Yeah, right. I traveled because I wanted excitement in my life. I spoke at conferences where I could add on adventures. 'Mother Teresa' was rafting the class-five Zambezi and Bio Bio rivers, diving with sharks in Polynesia and Australia, hang gliding in Rio, paragliding in the Swiss Alps, trekking Patagonia." She sipped wine. "My assistant said I was trying to prove something."

"Were you?"

For some reason this woman was inducing diarrhea of the mouth. Kiara said, "I guess gallivanting made me feel I was grabbing life by the horns and facing my fears—heights, sharks. I felt powerful."

"You're using past tense. What changed?"

"I never guessed—even as a psychologist—that foreign *cultures* would affect me so deeply. The physical adventures were meaningless by comparison. When I travel—"

"You come alive!" Jill said.

"Exactly. The more alien the place, the better."

The reverse was also true. At home, Kiara was famously unobservant. Colleagues teased her about never remembering the names of roads, stores, or restaurants she saw daily. She felt no desire to explore or appreciate details. At work, too, she went about her responsibilities robotically—conducting interviews, administering tests, writing reports, and delivering lectures.

But escaping the familiar flipped the switch. Kiara became hyperaware, seeing and hearing everything. She picked up on nuances in behavior, lifestyles, fashion, cuisine, landscapes, and architecture. She peppered guides with questions on religion, history, art, music—everything.

"What else?" Jill said.

"I also like myself more. People don't annoy me as much. I show interest in others, even initiate conversations."

"That's admirable, considering how much you are forced to immerse yourself in others' lives."

"I'm kinder, more trusting when I travel—more patient and compassionate. Somehow, my brain chemistry changes." She blushed. "Tell me about you."

Jill rolled her eyes, as if suddenly afflicted with ennui. She described in rapid-fire fashion her job, travels, and hobbies. "Now," Jill asked, "how did you go from high adventure to treating Tutsi children?"

Kiara shook her head. "I wanted to help underserved women, so I hooked up with an outfit called Women Sports Corps. They had a camp in Kampala targeting at-risk girls, mostly refugees. I worked there as a soccer coach and trainer. The people were amazing. This Rwandan mother I met had two soccer-crazy daughters, and she filled me in on the hardships in her country. I decided sports wasn't the best use of my time. My best friend, Zeb, learned about Psychologists Without Borders and made Rwanda happen."

"That's fascinating. What did you focus on, the learning disabilities part? I imagine there's less need for counseling since the genocide was so long ago."

"You'd be surprised. The mental-health crisis is still huge. Survivors and prisoners still need counseling—badly. And the trauma people feel affects learning. Debilitating flashbacks and memory problems can make students appear cognitively disabled."

Jill nodded sadly. "It must've been weird dealing with Hutu prisoners."

"It was."

"I can't imagine they're suffering half as much as the survivors."

"They aren't. Most survivors, many of them children, saw family and friends brutally killed, often with a machete. Everyone saw dead and mutilated bodies. PTSD is rampant."

"That's hard to fathom."

"That's just the beginning. Eighty percent of the survivors are women and children. Most don't have enough food, housing, or money for schooling. They're anxious and depressed. Some are suicidal."

"And the perpetrators"—Jill frowned—"how are they suffering? From a belated sense of guilt? Why should anyone care?"

Kiara smiled, learning she didn't have a monopoly on insensitivity. Jill didn't sound like your stereotypical San Franciscan. "Most served eight or more years in prison and never expected to leave. Cells were overcrowded; prisoners were malnourished, had poor health care, and were attacked. When released, most were terrified about how they'd be received."

"Poor babies," Jill said derisively. "Again, who gives a shit?"

"I feel your disdain, but if Rwandan society is to recover, they need to overcome mistrust and fear. That'll only happen if they address the needs of the entire population." Kiara cringed. She sounded like a bureaucrat toeing the official line.

They sipped wine, gazing at the silhouettes of the Virungas. *Can it get any better than this?* Kiara wondered. *Too bad I can't hit the pause button.*

"Your work must've given you tremendous satisfaction," Jill said.

"It didn't change much, not in the big scheme of things. But it did make me happier. Like talking to you."

"Thank you," Jill said, seemingly touched. "But don't forget the gorillas. They made you happy, too."

"Absolutely. I just feel bad they spent so much on my junket."

"Girl, you earned every last penny. Don't you *dare* feel guilty—leave that for the prisoners!"

The Virungas disappeared into the clouds, prompting the others to leave. Insect, bird, and monkey calls took the place of the views. Jill leaned over and removed lint from Kiara's hair, gently pushing the strands back in place.

Kiara felt drawn to Jill in a way that felt strong, despite their short time together. "Thank you." Was it butterflies? Personal electricity? Neither made sense. Jill was certainly gorgeous, but she had been around striking women before and never felt this way. Once upon a time, an old teammate had even teased Kiara for not opening herself up to women romantically—something many female athletes were inclined toward. But as much as Kiara might have wished she were gay after some of her more unsuccessful relationships with men, she had never felt that desire. Somehow, Jill aroused different feelings. She was highly intelligent and inquisitive but not pretentious. She had no filter, which made her hilarious and believable. That she openly professed her admiration meant a lot. Somehow Jill made her feel emotionally safe, like she wanted to spill her guts.

When they'd reached Jill's bungalow, Jill took Kiara's hand in both of hers. "Listen, I'm happily married to a wonderful man, and I don't want anything about that to change," she said slowly, studying Kiara's face, which was a mask of surprise. "So if you come inside with me, this will be the only time we'll ever be together. I might be making some assumptions here, but I'm going to take my chances anyway, because I think you have an extraordinary soul, and I don't want to let you go just yet. I have slept with one other woman, back in college, so I might even have some idea what I'm doing." They both cracked a smile at that. "But all of this is totally your call, no pressure from me whatsoever. You'll get the Sabinyo photos regardless."

The next morning Kiara didn't feel weird about what had happened at all. Unlike Jill, she hadn't ever slept with a woman before, but it felt clear to her that something special—affection, tenderness, mutual respect, and appreciation—had passed between them. They were two kindred souls brought together for a short time in a unique setting—a successful short-term relationship.

The two women rose before their wake-up call. Although Jill's transfer wasn't until the afternoon, she joined Kiara for breakfast. When it came time for Kiara to leave, Jill whispered, "And don't you dare feel guilty!"

"I know," Kiara laughed. "Leave that to the prisoners."

Afterward Kiara's driver stopped at the Kigali market, where she bought a painting celebrating the rebirth of Rwandan culture. They passed the Genocide Museum, which weeks earlier had implanted altogether different images. They would remain with her as long as her memories of Guhonda.

But how long would the rest stick—the faces of her Rwandan counselors, teachers, and students? Her happiness from a meaningful job well done? Her newfound sociability? Her gratitude for being born in the land of opportunity? Only time would tell.

33

BOBBY HURLEY

hapel Hill, North Carolina, 2017. Chewing on her pen, Teresa glanced at her watch for the third time in fourteen minutes. She ambled to the conference room and checked emails for another five minutes.

"It's three," she called. "You ready?"

Zeb joined her. He seemed relaxed, almost cheerful. That wouldn't last.

"What's up?"

Small talk had never been their thing, and it would make her lose her nerve, so she dived in. "A lot, actually. I've held off saying this, but you need to know. Moving to this office—and paying less rent—won't solve our problems. Not even close. We need to make major changes—now—or we'll be out of business. Fire me if you want, but I can't keep quiet anymore."

Zeb's jaw dropped. "What kind of changes?"

"I've got an audio montage I'd like you to listen to. It's not meant to be disrespectful."

He sat back, crossing his arms.

"You don't realize how blunt you are. You usually make valid points, but you're alienating people left and right."

Zeb raised his eyebrows.

"Your interview with NBC is a good place to start, since it was picked up nationally. Judge for yourself whether you need to be more diplomatic."

She played an audio clip of him responding to a reporter:

> Why *shouldn't* I speak out about the things they lie about? All their hidden charges, for example—porterage, drinks, tipping, excursions that aren't included, currency-fluctuation surcharges. All their false claims about departure guarantees, room categories, guide qualifications, group sizes, the duration of excursions, downtime, meal choices, philanthropic support. Shall I go on? How on earth can travelers assess value when companies misrepresent what they're offering? No wonder none of these guys have an A-plus rating with the Better Business Bureau like we do.

When the clip ended, Teresa said, "The last time you spoke out like this—during the National Tour Association conference—we lost our ARC license. How are we supposed to improve the industry, or help travelers, if we go out of business?"

Teresa played the second clip:

> Seriously, Sally, how can you possibly go to Indonesia, a top-five country in terms of culture and natural history, and spend all your time on the beach or in spas? Did you even *read* my proposal? We're talking Borobudur, Prambanan, orangutans, Komodo dragons, Balinese dancing, a gamelan orchestra, biking along rice terraces, cooking and batik lessons, whitewater rafting. If all you

want is sun and fun, fly to Fort Lauderdale and save yourself eight thousand dollars. You're *killing* me!

Teresa paused the recording. "Sally took her business to A&K, and we lost three thousand dollars in profits. *She's* killing you? *You're* killing you, Zeb. Every itinerary doesn't need to be a masterpiece. Sometimes we should listen to our clients. They pay our bills. Here's another beauty."

George, our terms and conditions give us the right to terminate our relationship with clients who demonstrate "unreasonable behavior or attitudes," as defined by us. We sent you three proposals, all of which took countless hours to develop and which you accepted and asked us to book. In each case, after we'd made *all* the hotel and service arrangements, you changed your mind, asking us to start again with completely different parameters. Maybe you should consult a shrink.

Teresa paused the recording. "You'll remember we discussed charging a two-hundred-fifty-dollar nonrefundable trip-development fee up front, allowing one free change in bookings and collecting a change fee of one hundred fifty dollars for each subsequent change. You felt it was wrong to charge people before they were completely satisfied, although these fees are standard in the industry. Everyone respects your idealism, but we need to be reasonable."

He nodded. "Next?"

Peter, do you really think it's ethical to have us craft a complex itinerary—one that took thirty-six hours to develop—and then shop it around to our competitors so they can copy it and undercut us by fifty dollars per person? Do you have any sense of decency?

Teresa sighed. "This could have been prevented with a trip development fee. I know Peter's a jerk, but why didn't you just match the competitor's price, given all the time you'd invested?"

"Who needs assholes like him?"

"Who needed to pay rent before being evicted? Let's turn to our suppliers."

Alonso, I love the lectures on Jorge Luis Borges and subaquatic archaeology of Patagonia. We'll be including them in our Argentina tour.

"The problems here, Zeb, are content and cost. First, people who didn't major in comparative literature won't know who Borges was. And most travelers aren't interested in Patagonian subaquatic archaeology. Tango, polo, wine tasting, and cooking would lure more clients. Second, the two private lectures will add four hundred dollars to the price. That's too much."

Zeb shook his head. "We have a responsibility to teach our clients the distinguishing aspects of these countries. Most don't have the background to judge this for themselves. Our ideal clients want to be told what spinach to eat. They've entrusted us to do that."

"I think you've romanticized the situation," she said gently. "We can count on one hand the number of clients who are Renaissance-man wannabes. Most want to do what they want to do. They won't pay up for bad-tasting spinach."

"Our clients aren't most people." Zeb leaned forward in his chair. "You're underestimating them. They're dying for new experiences, to learn, to challenge themselves intellectually, spiritually, and physically. Just because no one else is offering these things doesn't mean there isn't a latent demand for them. We need to lead the market, not be slaves to it. Otherwise, what's the point? Does America need more commodity tours? I'd rather quit. There's got to be some purpose to all this—something beyond lining our pockets."

She felt a lump in her throat. "I agree. But can we at least give clients a choice of lectures and cultural-immersion experiences, instead of deciding for them? It would lower our risk."

"I guess."

"Also, when choosing suppliers"—she twirled her pen in her fingers—"can we look at pricing and execution, not just their creativity and educational content?"

"Yes, but I'll never compromise on the quality of our guides." Zeb seemed both shell-shocked and bemused. "You're pulling a Bobby Hurley on me."

Teresa chortled. The Duke point guard's whining and gesticulations had been so over-the-top that his coaches produced a highlight video of his antics and forced him to sit through it. His behavior had improved. "Here's the last clip."

> To be honest, Mrs. Ostrander, if you dislike ground travel, you should probably go on the Tauck tour. Our India tour has sixteen hours of driving; theirs has eight. Yes, our tour visits two tiger sanctuaries, theirs none, but if you have to travel in November, you probably won't see any tigers anyway. They're hard to see until April.

Teresa frowned. "Who were you working for, us or Tauck? We needed that business. Honesty's one thing. Being sacrificial is another."

"Teresa, complete honesty is the only way to run a business. Not only is it the right thing to do, but in the long run, the market rewards honesty. We earn loyalty and referrals by building trust. And if I'm wrong, so what? What's the point of winning if you're misleading people? That's cheating."

A knot of emotion lodged in her throat. How could she not love him? What faith the man had. After a decade of doing things his way, they were still struggling. But if they were to fail, they'd do so together. If she still had a job.

Zeb came around the table and hugged her. "Cheer up. If we go under, you can always work for the NSA—your surveillance skills are top-notch."

"We can't go under, Zeb," she said, sniffling. "Being a spook isn't on my bucket list, and, besides, you'd be lost without me."

"Is that so?"

"Seriously, let me be your buffer. When you feel yourself getting pissed off, stay in the background, let me speak with the client. You be the brains, and *I'll* be the personality."

"The beauty and the beast."

She smiled through her tears. "If the shoe fits . . ."

They would never overtake Tauck or Nature Expeditions International. But maybe they'd become solvent. Maybe she'd earn her third bonus. And Zeb? His condo, wife, and golden retriever were long gone. But maybe he could still find happiness.

34

SNIFFING MESSES

eston, Florida, 2016. Leo released the girls for their water break and ambled to his SUV to retrieve more soccer cones. Their ball movement needed to be faster—two touches maximum—and without turnovers. That meant improving their positioning, moving together. Every player needed an outlet option when possessing the ball. They needed to get their act together.

He returned to the field and placed the cones. The next drill would address their mistakes. *But what about mine?* Sometimes Leo felt like a puppy being trained, his nose constantly being rubbed in his own messes. *Have I learned?* Hopefully. Why else would he drive to Weston to coach these girls instead of training a team back in Fort Lauderdale?

For years Leo had disassociated himself from Venezuela and its people. Now he craved their company. Coaching in "Westonzuela"— which teemed with Venezuelans—allowed him to stay connected. Mothers brought tasty *tequeños* to team meetings and parties. Fathers cussed in familiar terms—roaring *coño* or *verga*—whenever their daughters didn't live up to expectations. Hispanics filled half his roster, instilling enough comfort to warrant the one-hour round trip three times a week after work.

Not that Leo's pedigree impressed the families. When the club had announced him as the replacement coach, parents had asked, "You're from Venezuela? Shouldn't you be coaching baseball?" Many of the girls dreamed of earning a scholarship and their success depended on development, attendance at prestigious tournaments, and exposure to the right recruiters. Some parents had paid for club dues and private training since their daughters turned nine. Sometimes subtly, usually not, they conveyed their hope the investment would pay off, which meant landing a scholarship. Many thought him not up to the task—a Venezuelan with a meager USSF F license.

It didn't help when he kicked off the inaugural meeting by pooh-poohing the notion that scholarships were the yardstick for the girls' success. Irate parents had protested until Wendy, the technical director, quieted them down. Two players from last year's team, he explained, had received numerous scholarship offers from schools that were third-rate academically—far below the caliber of his student-athletes. Neither set of immigrant parents had understood that although tuition would be free, their diplomas would be worthless. Each family needed to be fully informed.

One mother had questioned his college-advisory credentials, observing that he'd "barely got off the boat himself." Conceding he had no formal qualifications in that area, he pointed out that he'd attended UNC, a public Ivy, thanks to help from a mentor. Scholarships to selective schools required strong transcripts. He would take care of the soccer piece; they needed to emphasize academics. Instead of hemorrhaging, his roster had increased.

Wendy and another woman approached. The visitor looked familiar, a cross between Diana Ross and a Jamaican sprinter. Striking.

"How's it going?" Wendy asked.

"Frustrating," Leo replied.

"Be patient. There's only one Barcelona."

"I guess."

"This is Dr. Battle, a Weston FC alum. She played for your alma mater."

Leo shook her hand. "I read about you in the alumni magazine. You were a shoo-in for the national team before quitting to save the world."

She blushed. "Thank you. It's Kiara."

"Forget the world," he said. "How about saving my team?"

"Looks like you're on the right track."

"I'm not so sure. Have you been back to Chapel Hill recently?"

"I live there," Kiara said.

"Lucky dog. What're you doing here, visiting old haunts?"

"Pretty much." Kiara pointed to a player juggling a soccer ball. "Your number fifteen's got potential."

"She does." Leo smirked. "But you know what your former coach says about players with potential."

"It means they ain't done shit yet!" Kiara said on cue.

"Jess is talented, but she's a turnover machine. She wants every pass to be worthy of Messi."

Kiara nodded. "I had that problem myself."

"Well, then," Wendy said, patting Kiara on the back, "maybe you could speak to her?"

"I'd be glad to."

Leo pumped his fist. "Awesome! Oh, and it couldn't hurt to mention Bob Jeffreys and the Tar Heels."

"My, you're a shy one," Kiara said.

"In reality, I am. But whatever works. By the way, a Dukie visited last week. She also played here."

Kiara sighed. "That would be Sarah. She's got horrible taste in colleges but is otherwise tolerable. Claims to be my best friend."

"Small world. I've got to get back to my girls."

When practice ended, Leo gathered his players. "Not bad, ladies. You cleaned things up. Much better moving after you pass, creating space, hitting your targets."

"*Coño!*" one player said. "Was that a compliment we just heard? From *Coach?*"

"Must have a hearing problem," said another.

"Better get it checked out."

"Sign the whole team up. Might be contagious."

"We'll get a group discount," Jess said.

"Very funny, ladies. Let's calm down." Once they got on a conversational roll, it was hopeless. On the pitch, they listened; off it, it was like herding cats. Not that he wanted to muffle them. His girls were awesome. They didn't spend their lives at a shopping mall or depend on boyfriends for self-esteem. They were self-assured with a strong sense of identity. They avoided drugs and excelled in the classroom, despite having little free time.

"Today is Carmen's birthday," Leo said. Cheers broke out. "Señora Maria Eugenia has baked one of her famous chocolate cakes." Whooping and hollering. "You're each allowed *one* piece—you hear that, Jess?" Boos. "Other moms brought *hallacas* and arepas." Boisterous cheering. "Ladies, indulge responsibly. We have a tournament next weekend."

After chatting with Jess, Kiara joined Leo and Wendy for a late dinner at Lucille's. Leo noticed how Kiara hung on his every word, smiling at even his bad jokes.

On the drive back, Leo pondered the ironies. Having betrayed Jake, he surrounded himself with wholesome people. Having disdained sports, he coached soccer. Having dumped his homeland, he desperately missed it.

As a cocksure teenager, he'd seen his countrymen as shallow and materialistic. Frivolous pursuits sapped Venezuelans' ambition for important things. Few discussed literature, how to live a good life, or how to make a unique contribution to the world. Men obsessed over sports and politics. Women fixated on fashion, recipes, and travel. The ambitious sought riches so they could spend even more time on trivialities. If the system sucked, people were to blame.

Or so he had thought. At some point, he'd lost the ability to divine the innermost thoughts of every Venezuelan. That made it harder to conclude they were all idiots. Moreover, having fun no longer seemed shallow. Singing, dancing, sports, and drinking weren't ends in themselves, but pastimes that brought people together, serving as social lubricants and mood enhancers. Fun helped people recharge their batteries, to feel loved, so they could experience joy and chase goals with greater vigor. Pursuing happiness didn't stifle ambitions; it made them more attainable. His Abuelita Merche, a rabid Barca fan, had understood this.

Leo pulled into his garage and sat, thinking. *How long will I be sniffing my own messes? It's time to clean and disinfect. Will Jake let me? Will the bank?*

35

SNAFU

Chapel Hill, North Carolina, January 2017. Zeb was lathering his hair when the phone rang. He rinsed, toweled off, and scampered for his smartphone. After redialing the office, he learned that he needed to speed things up. "Be there in a few." During high season there was no such thing as personal time.

"It's the Peru group," Teresa said the second Zeb entered the office. "We lost the space at Machu Picchu Sanctuary Lodge and seven cabins on the *Amazon Clipper*."

"That can't be. We sent deposits and have written confirmations. Final payment isn't due until next week."

"Apparently, there was an administrative snafu. Double booking."

Zeb's eyebrows pulled toward the bridge of his nose. "In both places? Tell them we'll wire the balance today and to hold the space."

"I already tried—no dice. They're sorry."

"Sorry! We're talking twenty-six people leaving in thirty-four days. Let me handle it."

Two days later the Beijing operator informed Teresa that the Tibet visas for their museum group had been denied. Moreover, Hao Li, the world-renowned lecturer they had booked, could not lead the group because of illness. Five cabins aboard the *Yangtze Explorer* were no longer available, even though they'd been fully paid for up front, and the group was due to arrive in seventeen days.

Zeb slammed his fist on the desk. "We've never had our Tibet visas rejected, except for journalists. And Hao Li? The guy's a health nut. I don't buy his sickness for a second."

The following day their Namibia operator informed them that the intercamp flights were sold out, as was the all-important Wilderness Lodge at Sossusvlei. Ground travel not being feasible, two of five camps could not be visited.

Teresa sighed. "Talk about snakebitten."

He shook his head. "It's my chickens coming home to roost. This is about the public comments I made about reform. Mongo strikes again."

"Zeb, you're *not* a pawn in the game of life. So stop that. But, if I understand you right, we're being blackballed?"

"Damn right. All three of these operators have worked with us for over a decade. Unfortunately, they also work for our eight-hundred-pound-gorilla competitors. They must've threatened to cut off all business with them, if they operated our groups."

"What now?"

"We've got to quickly find new operators and make alternate bookings. I'll call the consul general for the visas. See if you can find another air-charter company in Windhoek—with a good safety record."

Over the next few days irate clients bombarded International Expeditions with calls. Most had received their final travel documents but were now being asked to accept inferior itineraries and accommodations. Huge discounts did little to mollify them. Most clients canceled and demanded full refunds. Zeb offered them customized private tours for the same price as the group tour, but few accepted.

Complaints against International Expeditions mounted at the Better Business Bureau. Travel magazines publicized the three group-tour cancelations. The financial hit was threefold—lost profits from the canceled tours, wasted advertising expenditures, and losses on the subsidized replacement tours. The company's Better Business Bureau rating dropped from A-plus to C-minus, damaging their reputation and causing sales to implode.

36

RAPPROCHEMENT?

Fort Lauderdale, Florida, January 2017. Kiara sat on the water, gripping her paddle, waiting. Marcus tugged at his life jacket and cursed a noncompliant buckle. Finally, he slid his kayak into the shallow water. She nudged it back toward him so he could settle in.

Years had passed since they had spent meaningful time together without other family members present. For Kiara it felt bizarre, though something of a relief, to be among the mangroves and not on the soccer fields at Regional Park. Her dad, though, seemed completely in his element, as if kayaking—and not soccer—had been his early life's obsession. "Which way you want to go?" she asked.

"I'm thinking the red route. It's three miles. Heads north, then loops back through an area with sea turtles."

"Sounds good."

They babbled about crocodiles, the Heat game, the humidity—about anything but soccer. Or maybe that was how it seemed to her. After all, men were experts at talking endlessly about irrelevancies. Maybe her dad had moved on unscathed from the profound disappointment of her career choice. If so, more power to him, but he still deserved far more than the perfunctory apology she had offered years ago.

How long could she sustain this nonconversation? Such a relief, being a crack psychologist.

They paddled across West Lake, entering a narrow channel. As they became enveloped by vegetation, silence seemed more appropriate. Nature commanded reverence, as if they were in church. They glided along the meandering channel, taking care not to collide with elevated roots, a foot away on either side. Occasionally, a resting night heron or wood warbler lifted off, frightened by the sound of paddles brushing against branches. Neither sun nor mosquitos were a problem, the rays blocked by the canopy, bloodsuckers evaded through movement. Though Ann Kolb Nature Center spanned only 1,500 acres, Kiara felt thousands of miles away from Fort Lauderdale.

Her dad looked serene. She wondered if he was recalling his youth in Trinidad. He had often reminisced about expeditions taken with his father and brother—hiking the Northern Range, snorkeling the Buccoo Reef, birding in Arima Valley. After his career-ending injury, he had returned to these places, relying on wilderness therapy to recover emotionally. He should have gone back a third time—after she walked away from soccer.

The channel opened into a small lake, and Kiara pulled even. "Pops, I've been meaning to tell you this, and I'm embarrassed it's taken so long"—she breathed deeply—"but I'm really sorry for the way I quit soccer. I let you down. You deserved a whole lot better."

Marcus stopped paddling and sat in his kayak, seemingly befuddled. He appeared to be clearing the cobwebs from his brain. "It's okay," he finally said. "I understand."

"It isn't okay. All those years of training, the money spent on tournaments and travel—all down the drain. The showcases on Thanksgiving and Mother's Day"—her voice cracked—"spent away from home."

"It balanced out. We didn't pay for college."

"You know what I mean. I'm so sorry."

"Stop apologizing," Marcus said. "Let me give you an analogy."

He was big on analogies. Everything related to soccer or business.

"In accounting we can handle business costs two ways. One option is to expense them, because they're cash out the door, totally consumed, and don't provide long-lasting value. The second option is to capitalize them, treat costs like an asset because they're an investment with enduring value."

"Not if the assets are immediately mothballed."

"I couldn't disagree more. You didn't spend your youth hanging out at the mall or fixated on boyfriends. You hung out with *me*. We drilled, studied, and dreamed together. Those memories will last a lifetime."

"But I dashed those dreams just as we reached them." She stroked against the current to keep her kayak level with his.

"When *you* reached them. I was along for the ride. It was you, not me, who did the suicide drills, the Cooper tests. You who got up at four thirty a.m. for three summers to train before work."

"Okay, but who in their right mind invests all that and then denies herself the benefits, while shattering her dad's dreams? I must be nuts."

He shook his head vigorously. "Your highest calling isn't being a member of the national team and entertaining soccer fans—or me. Sometimes I forget that—because of my own issues."

"What do you mean?"

He sighed. "Look, I'm grateful I could support my family, especially as an immigrant. But being a CPA isn't the most exciting thing in the world."

"And soccer filled the void."

"*Economist* articles only go so far. Pathetic, I know."

"Not at all." She swatted at a cluster of gnats. "Most of my friends' dads spent most of their time hanging out with buddies or golfing. I'm grateful you didn't. So is Mom."

"I guess I was also worried we wouldn't bond as much."

Kiara snickered. "One reason I quit was my identity got too tied up in soccer. Everyone looked at me through the prism of the game."

"Like those poor Hollywood stars who aren't taken seriously when spouting off about current events."

Kiara smacked her paddle into the lake, drenching him.

"No, you do have a point," he said. "It was silly of me. With your work, trips, and volunteering, there's tons to discuss. And FIFA isn't going away."

She nodded. "You know, Pops, I have issues, too."

"Isn't that a job requirement for shrinks?"

She doused him a second time. "I'm serious."

"I was pumped to talk about the weather, but go ahead, fill me in."

Kiara sighed. "To begin with, there are two things I'm supposed to be in my profession: compassionate and nonjudgmental. I'm neither."

"Wrong," he said emphatically. "You're both."

"For God's sake, I don't even *like* most people!"

"Hey, your compassion is helping people learn better and regain their mental health. You don't need to be their best friend. Look at surgeons. Mostly their bedside manner sucks, but they fix the problem. Other people can offer sweetness therapy."

"I'd be sweeter if I was less judgmental. I'm sweet when I'm around LD or disadvantaged kids. But around others, especially the kids' parents, I can be nasty."

"Then you better get yourself some help."

"One thing I don't get are the differences I see within the Black community."

"Differences?"

She exhaled deeply. "When I see fellow islanders or other Black immigrants, they're really on top of things. Their kids get evaluated, and they get the help they need. But way too many Black kids born here are neglected. Pops, if I didn't volunteer in the schools, I'd never see most of them. It's heartbreaking."

Marcus nodded. "It's tragic, but it doesn't surprise me. We immigrants are in much better shape. More of us went to college, and more of us are married, so we earn more. We can afford to get the help we need."

"Why the difference?"

"Black people born in America had a radically different experience."

"Islanders were slaves, too," Kiara said. "Our forefathers moved on."

"Apples and oranges," Marcus replied, shaking his head. "In the islands, slavery was abolished sixty years sooner. That's *three generations* more time for people to recover. Plus, the islanders' masters were far away in Europe. When they rebelled, they faced less resistance."

"Did they win?"

Marcus whistled. "All over. Jamaica, Barbados, Grenada. In Haiti, they fought and won their independence—against Napoleon no less! The point is, all that history affects the way islander descendants feel today. It boosts their spirit. That's much different than it was for Black people born in America. They won their independence much later and had to endure continued racism living among their former masters for generations. Keep that in mind, and you'll be more understanding."

"I never thought of that."

"It also didn't help"—Marcus hesitated and bit his lip—"that the Great Society programs almost destroyed the Black family."

Kiara recoiled in shock. "Whoa, now, Pops! Let's not get crazy. I'm no history major, but even I know those programs helped Blacks tremendously."

"In many ways, they *did*," Marcus said, laying his paddle atop his legs. "They reduced poverty and saved many lives. But they also created perverse incentives with the way they were designed."

"I doubt that. I think you've been reading too many *Economist* articles."

He grimaced. "You're a student. Study two things. First, look at Booker T. Washington's research on Black marriage rates, homeowner-ship rates, and the percentage of two-parent Black families in the early 1900s. You'll be dumbfounded—Black people outperformed Whites in many key areas. And remember, this was *after* slavery but *before* the Great Society. Then look at Harvard professor Paul Peterson's analysis of the Great Society's impact on Blacks. I'll leave it at that."

"My next pleasure reading," Kiara quipped. But the frontal assault on her long-held beliefs made her stomach turn.

They paddled side by side toward the observation tower that jutted out from the sprawling vegetation.

Marcus pointed at an ibis in flight.

She smiled. Obviously, he'd moved on. She would, too.

Kiara stared at her father with melancholic admiration. He could easily have been an economist or political scientist. Instead, he worked on tax returns. Important work, certainly, but not where his heart was.

Marcus paddled toward the narrow channel marking the final stretch.

"You've given me a lot to think about," she said.

"No Messi moves."

"No, but I can now work my compassion muscle harder."

"Just make sure it doesn't atrophy," Marcus said, grinning.

"God help me. I wouldn't want to turn into a Republican."

Marcus shot her a coy look. "Hey, hey, hey—some Republicans are okay, right?"

"Oh my God, you're kidding me." She shook her head. "Does Mom know?"

"No, and please don't tell her—she'd have a fit."

"Forget her, I'll have a fit. Talk about betraying your own. Seriously, Pops, how can you vote Republican?"

He cringed. "Didn't you hear a word I said—about incentives, the Black family? Did your auditory thing kick in again?"

Squeezing the paddle tightly, Kiara hissed, "No, it did *not* kick in. At least LBJ's heart was in the right place. The rest is detail."

"Kiara, getting the details right is everything. You should have learned that from soccer."

"Maybe that's why I quit." It wasn't, but she couldn't help saying it.

Marcus flinched, as Kiara started paddling furiously away from him. *Back to square one*, she thought.

37

CHICKEN SOUP

*C*hapel Hill, North Carolina, January 2017. Zeb walked out of Ye Olde Waffle Shoppe, patting his tummy. The trifecta of blueberry pancakes, Belgian waffles, and fresh orange juice had more than hit the spot. His buddies, too, had been in fine form, coming through with ample basketball scoop and knee-slapping jokes. Fun of a different sort awaited him now.

Rabbi Norman was a hoot—a brilliant one at that. Nobody could teach Torah the way he did. Equal parts elucidating and entertaining, he made the scriptures accessible. Rabbi quoted Mel Brooks, Monty Python, and Captain James T. Kirk in the same breath as Abraham, Maimonides, and Rashi. Only last week he'd cited Reba McEntire's "Fancy" when discussing a Leviticus statute protecting daughters. When it came to knowing human psychology, biblical history, geography, and Hebrew—and throwing American and Jewish culture into the mix—Rabbi was untouchable. His free-flowing, enlightening associations might have impressed LSD trippers. But Rabbi's commentaries weren't whimsical; they were grounded in his encyclopedic knowledge of the Bible, Talmud, and the commentaries known as midrash. His love of Americana merely amplified his scholarship.

Rabbi gushed whenever students offered perspectives he'd never considered. "Wow, that is *really* good! Thank you, Rabbi Alice," he'd say, elevating the student to clergy status. He would then pepper the student with questions so they might elaborate on the new interpretation. Sometimes, inspired by the new line of thinking, he'd launch into a spontaneous commentary, improvising like a jazz musician. Unanswerable questions posed no threat; in fact, Rabbi relished them as much as any answers he could deliver. In his mind they reflected deep thinking and led to further study.

Rabbi could be frustratingly democratic, exclaiming, "Yes, yes, and yes!" when students offered contradictory, logical interpretations. "There's no right answer," he'd say with a grin, "unless I say so!" Half-baked comments, though, met with friendly barbs that invited more precise thinking next time around. Rabbi saw all biblical figures, even the patriarchs, as deeply human, with strengths and flaws everyone could learn from. His doctorate in family counseling helped him extract such lessons.

Rabbi teased students to show he liked them. He also poked fun at himself. Relaxed students, he must have figured, learned more.

But Rabbi wasn't a saint. He had no patience for clergy with absolutist tendencies. A common refrain: "Whenever you hear a rabbi or priest say, 'The Bible says,' run!" Neither did he have any use for ivory-tower intellectuals who had no clue about the real world or for hermit scholars who didn't share their knowledge.

He also had no tolerance for rudeness. Low-level transgressions—especially speaking on smartphones during religious services—earned offenders an icy stare. More grievous offenses—failing to treat strangers with sufficient warmth or treating some Jews as second class because they had married into the faith, were insufficiently observant, or were born in Latin America—really ticked him off. No one could be made to feel unwelcome at Temple. He scolded impolite people right then and there.

"All right, *kinderlach*, enough kibitzing. Let's get started," Rabbi said, as Zeb took a seat.

Together they recited the prayer for the study of Torah. "We ended at Exodus, chapter seventeen. The Israelites are kvetching to Moses—this time because they're stuck in the desert without enough water. Anna, will you please read verse four?"

"Moses cried out to the Lord, saying, 'What shall I do with these people? Before long they will be stoning me!'"

Rabbi said, "Now, the second clause says לעם מה אעשה. Does anyone know what the *lamed* in front of לעם signifies?"

All eyes turned to Daniel, the only student who knew Hebrew.

"It means 'with.'"

"Correct. Does it have other meanings?"

"Sometimes it means 'for.'"

"Right again. A third meaning is 'to.' So going back to the verse, Zeb, what are the three possible translations based on the original Hebrew?"

Zeb found the verse. "The first is: 'What can I do *with* these people?' Moses is exasperated—at the end of his rope. He doesn't know what else to do with them. The second translation is: 'What can I do *for* these people?' Here Moses is compassionate. How can I help them? The third is: 'What can I do *to* these people?' He's angry. How can I punish them?"

"Well done."

"So who knows what was intended?" a Lutheran student asked.

"The Shadow knows," Rabbi quipped, recalling the pulp hero from the 1930s.

"Seriously, the Bible says—"

"Jim, never go with 'the Bible says.' It'll say whatever you *want* it to say. Whoever translated this text from the original Hebrew into English had to make a big decision: whether *lamed* meant 'with,' 'for,' or 'to.' That decision made all the difference. When we extrapolate, we're taken in different directions. That's why we look at the Hebrew and various possible English translations."

"Which is the right translation?" Jim pressed.

"We can look at the context and make assumptions, but there's no definitive answer. Even in the Talmud, eighty percent of the questions go unanswered. Debated yes, definitively answered, no. Daniel, please update us through the appearance of Amalek?"

Daniel straightened in his seat. "The Israelites are losing their faith because there's not enough water. God instructs Moses to strike the rock with his rod. Water runs from it, and the Israelites' thirst is satiated. Next Amalek appears and decides to attack them."

Rabbi chuckled. "Oscar Wilde said, when God wants to punish us, he answers our prayers. Be careful what you wish for! You got your water; here's Amalek. Why might that be?"

"God provided a common enemy so that the Israelites would stop fighting among themselves?" Daniel asked.

"Maybe, but as we'll see throughout the Bible and modern history, it's usually when we fight among ourselves that anti-Semites attack. Other possibilities?"

Zeb spoke. "The Israelites weren't behaving faithfully, so Amalek was their reward. Karma and a teachable moment."

"That would be my guess," Rabbi said. "Who is Amalek? What does he represent?"

"Wasn't he the grandson of Esau?" the Lutheran student asked.

"Correct! What else?"

Blank stares led Rabbi to elucidate. "Amalek is the anti-Semite par excellence. You remember Haman, the villain from Purim, the high-ranking minister who tried to kill all the Jews in Persia? Well, Haman descended from Amalek. Amalek becomes an archetype of evil."

"There was more than one Amalek?" a student asked.

Rabbi nodded. "You've heard the saying 'So many Hamans and only one Purim . . .' Okay, we have a bunch of Israelites—former slaves who weren't soldiers—wandering around the desert with little to eat or drink. How's the fight against Amalek likely to go? What's the point spread?"

"Not good."

"Who does Moses look to for leadership?" Rabbi asked.

"Joshua."

"Yes, John Derek from *Ten Commandments*! So what happens?"

Daniel summarized. "Moses climbs a hill with the rod of God in his hand, and Joshua heads to battle against Amalek. Whenever Moses's hand is held high, the Israelites prevail; whenever his arm tires and drops, Amalek takes the upper hand. Aaron and Hur support Moses's arms for good and the Israelites triumph."

Zeb raised his hand. "The arms were a symbol—a visual aid—for the Israelites. They could see they won with God's help and lost without it. If the Israelites had defeated Amalek easily, they'd have thought the victory was their own doing. They needed to be taught to have faith in God."

Rabbi nodded. "Well done, Rabbi Zeb." He rose to wipe the whiteboard and write several words in Hebrew. "And now for something completely different!" he said, mimicking John Cleese. In Rabbi's Flying Circus, anything went. They were discussing blood avengers and sanctuary cities when the alarm rang.

"All right, *kinderlach*, that's it for today."

Zeb thanked Rabbi, stuffed a fiver in the charity box, and headed out. It was a lot to part with, given his current circumstances, but Torah study made him kinder and humbler. Chapel Hill would benefit, as he and others fanned out in a better frame of heart.

Until his divorce, he'd avoided Torah study like the plague. Torah-thumpers were no better than Bible-thumpers. Real history mattered, not ancient hearsay. Eventually he learned otherwise. Wise people took Torah seriously, even if they didn't take it literally. Just because Sarah didn't conceive at age ninety didn't mean students couldn't learn from biblical events—how to live a good life. Study was therapeutic, chicken soup for the soul.

He needed crates of the stuff, having failed with his wife, Hannah. She had paid a huge price for his expulsion from UNC. If he had only graduated, he'd have been less obsessed with proving himself in business and would have invested more in their marriage. Insecurity from one failure had led to the second.

Hannah had tolerated his unwillingness to plan, save money, or discuss anything other than his passions. She had stomached his refusal to go back on ADHD meds. She'd supported his dedication to a struggling business. The breaking point had been living with a husband who shared little beyond the mortgage obligation.

Or maybe it was hubris. After all, why had he been expelled? Why had he underperformed in business? At UNC he'd held himself above the members of the honor court, refusing to answer their legitimate questions. In business, he'd assumed that low sales only meant buyers were uninformed, undervaluing his tours and that they would come around eventually. If the direct cause of their divorce was his insecurity over being expelled and underperforming in business, then the ultimate cause was hubris.

With all that baggage, five bucks was a pittance.

Zeb walked into the office, prepared to extend the morning's equanimity as far into the day as possible. Teresa deserved some workplace serenity, relief from his intensity.

No sooner had he sat at his desk than she accosted him. Her face was red, her forehead sweaty. "The National Tour Association just decertified our deposit insurance. Apparently, we no longer meet their financial-strength standards. Read their letter."

He scrutinized the document and set it down. "They really had no choice under the circumstances." He rubbed his eyes and exhaled deeply. "There's worse—no sense keeping it from you. Our buddies in

L.A. and Boulder just learned about my honor-court issue, the expulsion, everything. They'll be broadcasting it to the world any day now."

"No, you can't be serious!" Teresa said, her eyes bulging. She plopped into a chair. "What do we do?"

His shoulders drooped. She deserved so much more. Her loyalty, faith in him, and hard work—all wasted. He looked down, shook his head, and fought the tears. "I'm so, so sorry, Teresa. I failed you, big-time." His voice thickened. "You better update your resume." And then he lost it, covering his face and turning away.

She approached him, hugged him hard, and didn't let go until the phone rang.

38

GROUNDING

Miami, *Florida, January 2017.* Transit passengers passed by Leo's table in the airport lounge, some scurrying, others sauntering. *Thompson will be one of the relaxed ones,* Leo thought, as he repeatedly folded and unfolded his cocktail napkin. *And why not?* American Airlines' new director of aircraft maintenance loved airports. Even back in Izmir, it was clear that he'd attend the College of Aeronautics and work for a major airline. Still Thompson had to be comatose after the overnight flight from Saõ Paolo. He'd be eager to get back to his wife and kids but, hopefully, they could catch up before he connected to Fort Worth.

Thompson approached the table. Surprisingly chipper, the Texan bear-hugged him, lifting him into the air.

"*Bienvenido a Miami,* redneck!" Leo said upon hitting the ground.

"All that reading, and you still ain't mastered English!" No corporation stood a chance of rectifying Thompson's discourse.

"But I did learn to kick your butt in chess, my friend."

"Yeah, yeah." Thompson gave him the once-over. "You look good."

"Thanks, but looks are deceiving. So what'll you have?"

"Water. I'm dehydrated."

After ordering, Leo asked, "How are Joy and the kids?"

"Fine, we still love Dallas. Joy's running an online clothing business—keeps her busy while I'm on the road and the kids are in school. Now what's this about looks being deceiving?"

Leo shook his head. "I slept with my colleague's girlfriend."

"What the fuck?"

"I know."

"I thought you learned your lesson in Izmir," Thompson said and chugged Evian.

"Guess not. I can't explain it. I'm a fuckup, except when I'm not."

"I assume you're screwed at work? No pun intended."

"Not really, but I feel terrible."

"You should."

Leo nodded.

"Dude, you should be way past sewing your wild oats. At least stay in bounds. I don't get why a stud like you has to do that shit."

"I don't have an answer."

"Maybe a shrink would. You need to see one."

"Maybe so."

Thompson glared at him. "Not maybe, definitely."

"Okay."

"Now that I've crushed your spirit, it's time to pulverize you on the battlefield. I can't let your shit-talking go unpunished."

Beaming, Leo motioned inward with cupped hands. "Bring it on, my friend!"

Thompson snorted while retrieving a travel chess set from his luggage. "Game on." He glanced at his watch. "There's time for me to spank you twice before my flight leaves."

"I didn't realize you had a three-week layover."

Fort Lauderdale, Florida. The janitor knocked on the open door to Leo's office at the Bank of America.

"Wow, six forty already? Sorry, Frank, give me a few minutes."

Leo powered down his computer and changed clothes. Within five minutes he was merging onto I-595 West. He'd be late to practice, but the girls knew what to do. Tuning into NPR, he settled in for the ride. Hopefully, the bias would be less unsettling than the traffic. Tomorrow, he'd be back to Glenn Beck. Alternating viewpoints wasn't easy, but it was necessary, no matter what his colleagues thought. Maybe he was nuts.

Kai Ryssdal spoke over *Marketplace*'s fading theme when Leo remembered it was Thursday. Damn! Switching off the radio, he punched the speed dial.

Bill Walsh's voice came through strong. "About damn time! Sheesh, young people these days. Give them an inch, they'll take a mile."

"Sorry, Bill. The week's passed by so quickly."

"As did last week."

His mentor had a point. Staying in touch was the least he could do. "What can I say? I'll do better."

"What's new?"

"Well, I screwed up royally."

"What, the cruise line not like your pitch?"

"No, that went fine. But I hooked up with my analyst's girlfriend."

"You slept with her?"

"I feel terrible."

"Hey, it happens. Too bad for the guy, but if he can't hold on to his pussy, that's his problem, not yours. If there aren't any wedding rings, it's not a huge deal. Apologize and move on."

"In reality, it's not that easy." *Sorry, Jake, I was just proving my manhood—to myself. No blood, no flagrant foul.*

"I wouldn't worry unless it messes with your work."

"It does, but whatever. How're you doing?"

"Awesome! Being single again suits me. I'm delegating more, traveling, chasing the ladies myself. Know any?"

Leo laughed uneasily. "I'm glad you're having fun."

"Oh, I meant to ask, when do you present your acquisition targets to REK Cruise Lines?"

"Next week. If Jake doesn't quit on me."

"He won't if he knows what's good for him. Do me a favor, let me know what REK decides—before it reaches the papers. Know what I'm saying?"

He shook his head. "It's not that easy, Bill."

"I know, but we're practically family, right?"

"Right."

"Family help each other. Gotta run."

Leo pulled into Vista Park and, as he grabbed his bag and ran onto the soccer field, the girls greeted him warmly. *They* were family.

Later that night Leo felt weird as he lugged two unwrapped fifths of liquor up the staircase and past residents of the apartment complex. He'd never been a boozehound. He made his way to the unit number his secretary had provided him and rang the bell. His heart pounded. It was time to face the music. Footsteps approached and the door opened.

Jake scowled. "What the—Get the hell out of here!"

"Look, I'm really sorry to bother—"

"Bother me? You've got to be friggin' kidding." Jake's nostrils flared. "It's not enough you screwed my girlfriend. Or that I still slave for you twelve hours a day? Now you intrude on my free time? Get the hell out!" He slammed the door shut.

"Jake," Leo shouted. "You're one hundred percent right. There's no excuse for what I did. There's no reason you should hear me out. But *can* you please? For two minutes? I beg you."

Slowly the door opened.

"You seriously think Grey Goose and Jack Daniels are going to calm me down?"

"If it's any consolation, I hate myself, even more than you hate me."

"Oh, that's rich."

"Not just for what I did to you. Two minutes . . . please?"

Jake shook his head as if he were crazy to invite him in. Leo entered meekly, setting the liquor on a side table. They proceeded to the tiny living room and took a seat. This had to be excruciating for him, Leo thought. The enemy had invaded his sanctuary.

"So I'm not the only one you screwed over?" Jake said. "That supposed to make me feel better?"

"I want to share things I've never told anyone."

"Oh, goody. Two minutes."

It was best to keep it clinical. "When I was seventeen, I was kidnapped and held for ransom. I was locked in a storage room. My parents had no money, so the kidnappers sold me to a thug. He handcuffed me at gunpoint to the legs of a table. I was forced to bend over. He raped me three times. Once was with a plunger. When they found me, I was still handcuffed, sitting in a pool of blood . . . and semen. My anal cavity had been perforated. There were bruises on my thighs, scratches on my back. The police never told my family, thank God.

"I didn't leave my room for a week. I had no pain meds, so I couldn't sleep. It wasn't hard to fake being sick. I quit my job. My parents forced me to return to school, but my grades plummeted. I began questioning the signals I was sending out. Why didn't I like what other red-blooded males liked—drinking, sports, chasing women? Why was I bookish? Why would kidnappers hand me over to a homosexual?"

Two minutes had passed, but Jake wasn't holding him to it.

"This wasn't a sin I could share with anyone, least of all our priest. I tried to off myself with pills but failed. My parents grounded me, thinking I'd turned to drugs for recreation.

"When I came out of hiding, I went crazy. I chased women. They liked me because of my blond hair. I slept with many ladies, maintaining relationships with none. Proving my manliness was all that mattered. Then, as if being an asshole wasn't enough, I beat up a gay man. He was hospitalized."

"What the fuck!" Jake said.

"What the fuck is right. My best friend, Federico, finally put an end to it. He talked sense to me and orchestrated a way out of the morass. A member of the club where I worked lined up a job for me at a wilderness lodge. It was in the middle of nowhere, where I could do no damage. A guest at the lodge became my mentor and brought me to the States."

Jake was wide-eyed, so Leo continued. "Listen, I'm hardly the only rape victim in the world and—"

"Yeah, but being a male victim takes it to another level."

"I'm not sure women would agree."

"And a *plunger* . . ." There was empathy in Jake's voice.

"It doesn't give me a license to hurt people." He sighed. "Life's full of setbacks. Most people bounce back better than I have."

"That wasn't just any setback. You're seeing a psychologist, I assume."

"No, but I'm improving—"

"Jesus, you've got to be kidding me!" Jake slammed his fist down on the cushion beside him. "How can you look at me with a straight face and say that?"

Leo's head slumped.

Jake was breathing noisily. "You may not be beating up gay men anymore, but you're still doing damage. Why do you think you're here right now?"

"You're right."

"What are you going to do about it?"

Leo sighed. "First, I want to apologize again. I'm deeply ashamed of what I did to you, truly. Second, I'll let top management know. It's time to take responsibility. Third, if they don't fire me, I'll arrange for you to have another boss. Working in a new area might benefit you, round out your training before business school."

"You're forgetting the most important thing: counseling."

Leo nodded.

"If you get counseling—serious counseling—we'll keep this private. I'll stick by you. I have no interest in ruining your career or switching divisions. Linda wasn't right for me—not that that in any way excuses what you did." Jake pointed to the counter. "But I'll be needing a *case* of Grey Goose and another of Jack."

39

GODSEND

Chapel Hill, North Carolina, February 2017. Everything took enormous effort. Every task—getting out of bed, shaving, showering, dressing, and driving to work where he'd be presented with unpayable bills and bad news—tapped Zeb's limited reservoir of strength. The International Expeditions sign outside the office depressed him further.

Zeb walked through the front door to see Teresa, her eyes twinkling, doing a jig. Something was up because irrepressible joy had been nonexistent, and she was hardly the manic type. He forced a smile, tried to soak in the gaiety.

"How much do you love and respect me, boss man?" Teresa asked after coming to rest. "Anything less than total admiration and sucking up, and I'll quit!"

That she hadn't already quit had been a minor miracle, stupid really. Something in his spirit craved a break from the stress and sadness. What else was there to do? He dropped to one knee, brought hand to chest, and conjured his inner Debby Boone. He crooned the opening to "You Light Up My Life."

"Please, please stop!" Teresa said, cackling. She seemed torn, as if the amusement might be worth the pain.

Zeb blushed, his ears beet red. "Whatever you got better be good, because that was humiliating."

"Trust me. It's good enough for me to demand an encore and video-tape it." After a second fit of giggling, Teresa quieted. "Here's the deal. You remember the itinerary you did for Mrs. Nazarian?"

"Sure. The aborted Trans-Caucasus trip—Armenia, Georgia, and Azerbaijan."

"I figured it shouldn't sit on the shelf, so I sent it to National Geographic Expeditions. They loved it and, with minor changes, want us to operate it for them. They asked for more itineraries, so I sent Indonesia, Guatemala, and Himalayan kingdoms. They'll be offering those as well."

Zeb's jaw dropped.

"They admire our business ethics and the reforms you're pushing for. They don't buy the accusations our competitors are leveling at us," she added. "They're ready to sign a multiyear mandate if you agree. Ta-da!"

His eyes bulged. "National Geographic? Incredible. You're a god-send, Teresa."

"Aw, shucks, you really know how to flatter a girl."

"This makes us a serious player."

"Yup."

"Are there any contingencies that would kill us—minimum ad spend?"

"Nope. We just need to cost in a special lecturer and a four-hundred-dollar-per-person contribution to Geographic. We keep one hundred and fifty dollars if the tours are canceled."

"Unbelievable."

"I am." Again, she broke into a jig.

He clapped. "We should celebrate. Call Jim—we'll go out."

"Tonight?"

"Whenever. My calendar's wide open."

That evening Zeb stood on the front lawn of the Carolina Inn, nursing his Blue Moon and admiring the venerable establishment. It was a dead ringer for George Washington's home at Mount Vernon, the perfect venue for Fridays on the Front Porch. Who wouldn't want to rock out under the stars and willow oak trees, partake from the cash bar, and feast on ethnic delicacies?

Sometimes Zeb favored folk or bluegrass, but rock fit the bill tonight.

He sang along to Steely Dan's "Haitian Divorce."

Someone tapped him on the shoulder. He turned and beamed. "Well, if it isn't my new partner-slash-marketing director." He raised his bottle to Teresa. They clinked beers.

"Partner? Wow, I must be good! I take it you got approval from the board?"

"It was unanimous. Where's Jim?"

Teresa rolled her eyes. "Couldn't come. His regular poker game with the guys. He sends his regards."

"You all right? This was supposed to be a celebration."

"I'm just frustrated." She tossed her bottle in the recycling bin. "We're drifting apart."

Zeb nodded sympathetically. "I'll be back." He went to the bar and returned with two margaritas.

"An umbrella drink to solve my problems."

"Look, I'm no authority on marriage, but giving Jim time with his buddies seems like a good thing."

"I agree." She sipped her cocktail. "We just don't have much in common anymore—besides Wylie, that is."

"I hear ya."

"The thing is, he's still a great guy. He's loyal, devoted, supports us well."

Zeb shifted his feet uncomfortably. "You sure you want to get into all this with your boss?"

"Partner." She smirked.

"Ya got me. Spill your guts then."

"Bottom line: Jim's boring as shit. All he cares about is making money, playing golf, tailgating, and the beach."

"Doesn't sound too bad to me," Zeb said, chuckling. "Don't knock making money."

"Sorry"—she squeezed his arm gently—"I know you're struggling. It's selfish, but I want more."

"What do you mean?"

"It's his mentality. I can't remember the last time he said anything evenly remotely interesting. Intellectually, spiritually, he hasn't grown much since we were eighteen. What's worse is that he doesn't seem to care. I'm dying of boredom."

"Don't kill me"—Zeb whispered—"but didn't Jim skip college for a good reason?"

"Damn right. He knocked me up and did the honorable thing. I shouldn't be complaining, but that's how I feel."

"What do you expect him to do?"

"He's boring because of how he chooses to spend his time and money."

"What's wrong with football games? I go all the time."

"There's nothing wrong with sports. I'm a fan. But there's more to life. He could audit courses. Do volunteer work. Mentor entrepreneurs. Learn a language. Get involved at church. Go to classical concerts. God forbid he should ever read a classic."

"Don't forget poker."

"Seriously, he's letting life pass him by."

"He's a good dad."

"True, but I want *more*." She downed her margarita. "I wish he was more like you."

He blushed. "Now I know you're drunk. Let's not go there."

Teresa took his hand. "I'm serious, Zeb. Lord knows you're a pain in the ass. But I never get bored around you. You're always learning. You're on a mission—not to pad your pockets but to build a new type of company, to introduce products that enlighten. You're pushing the market in the right direction. You're passionate about interesting things."

Zeb gently freed his hand. "Don't romanticize what I've done. I lost my wife, my condo, my dog. And for what? I'm in my forties and can barely pay my bills. If I was such a genius, everyone would be buying. And it was you, not me, who reeled in Geographic. Without them, we'd be pushing up daisies."

"Thank you for that." She kissed him on the cheek. "But don't you see? The market is responding to your ideas. It just took time. Other big fish are waiting to be caught."

Zeb felt a tingling. She was cute, brainy, and spunky. But it wasn't right, even if her marriage was on the rocks. "Well, now that my money problems will soon be over, how about I treat my talented partner to dinner at the Lantern?"

"Talented? Not *gorgeous*?"

He cocked his head. She never missed a thing.

40

ASIA SUCKS

hapel Hill, North Carolina, February 2017. Kiara pulled into the empty parking lot at Southern Community Park. The Murphys hadn't arrived, so she sat back and shut her eyes. She needed to get her mind right. Owen was a great kid, but training any kid on a Saturday morning sucked, especially with his Dragon Lady mother in tow. But it was her own damn fault.

Next time she'd know better than to fire off a scathing email response, no matter how idiotic the provocation. Luckily, Vicki had interceded on her behalf. Otherwise Kiara would have been reported, censured, or worse. Somehow, Vicki sensed that another apology wouldn't defuse Mrs. Murphy's anger. Free training for Mrs. Murphy's soccer-obsessed son was the only way out, and, not wanting to work for a disbarred psychologist, Vicki had proposed it.

Kiara lugged the equipment bag to the field. Dragon Lady had evidently been substituted by her equally charming husband. He and Owen were passing the ball back and forth.

After exchanging pleasantries, Kiara said, "Your mom said you're studying Asian capitals."

"Yup, a real blast."

"Did you write out the note cards—country on one side, capital on the other?"

"He did," Mr. Murphy said. "But he still can't remember them."

"Not to worry. Owen, why don't you run a warm-up lap and meet me by the far goal? Bring your cards." He took off. "It's good you're spending time with him. He needs that."

"So do I." The lawyer gave her a sheepish look.

"Good to hear."

"My wife's leaving me."

"I see." She stopped fiddling with the equipment bag. "I'm sorry."

"I'll wait in the car and get out of your way."

Now there's a good boy, she thought. Chastened sure beat arrogant.

Kiara laid two cones on either side of the penalty marker. Beside each she placed a stack with half the note cards—twenty-four countries—and six soccer balls.

"Okay, Owen, listen up. You're what's called a kinesthetic learner. That's a fancy way of saying you learn best when you're physically active. Understand?"

"Yup."

"Your mom says you love soccer and want to get better at it. I figured we'd combine the two, training and studying."

He nodded.

"You know how to shoot with both feet?"

"Sort of."

Kiara showed him the proper shooting technique and then explained the drill. "Start behind the right cone. Drop to the ground, do two push-ups, and pick up the stack of note cards. Say the country twice, spell it once. Flip it over. Say the capital twice, spell it once. Lay the stack down and shoot on goal. Read the country and capital one last time. Got it?"

He looked uncertain, so she demonstrated the drill. "Aim two feet inside the side post to give yourself a margin for error. You'll be retrieving every ball that goes wide or over the crossbar."

"What'll you be doing?"

"Don't you worry about me. I'll be in goal."

"Asia sure has a crap load of countries," he said, shaking his head. "That's one hundred and ninety-two push-ups."

"Soccer takes strength. Plus, the exercise will help you learn." She walked toward the goal and signaled for him to begin.

Owen dropped to the ground, did two push-ups, and jumped to his feet, forgetting the note cards. "Shit." He grabbed the stack. "Never heard of this country. Bhutan. Bhutan. B-H-U-T-A-N." He flipped the card. "Thimphu. Thimphu. T-H-I-M-P-H-U." He set the stack down and booted the ball right of the post.

"No worries. Keep going."

Afterward, Kiara gave him a water break before explaining a drill that combined dribbling and sit-ups.

Owen looked at the parallel lines of cones, each separated by fifteen inches. "Twenty-four times with each foot? You've got to be kidding."

"Yeah, it'll really suck getting an A, leading your team in scoring, and having girls notice how buff you are."

He grinned. "Asia still sucks."

Two days later Kiara walked into International Expeditions and, for the first time ever, wasn't attended to immediately. Teresa, Zeb's freshly minted business partner, was on the phone ordering Post-it notes and staples.

"You look swamped," Kiara said, when Teresa hung up.

Teresa sighed. "It's not easy wearing the pants—I mean, skirt— around here."

Kiara chuckled.

"So you here for your next adventure?"

"Yup. Is Mr. Jolly in?" Kiara said.

"He's headed to the Loop with Bob Jeffreys and assistant coach Theo. You can probably still catch them."

"Nah, let the boys have their meal." Kiara took a seat. "I hear you landed National Geographic Expeditions. Impressive."

"Thanks."

"How'd you guys turn things around?"

"You mean, aside from Zeb unleashing me?" Teresa grinned.

"Exactly."

"Well, Mr. Jolly has become more self-aware."

"Yeah, right." Kiara snorted. "And how, pray tell, did he achieve this enlightenment? By sitting under the Bodhi Tree? Listening to a sensible female?"

"Let's just say, the Bobby Hurley behavioral-modification technique came in handy." Teresa winked.

Kiara looked befuddled, so Teresa elaborated. Kiara listened with mounting astonishment.

"Holy shit," Kiara said, "that's great stuff. You just solved my problem."

Standing in McCaskill Soccer Center, Kiara stared at her old mentor. Was he still helping her grow? Bob Jeffreys had always advocated getting out of one's comfort zone, and what could be more unnatural than telling the winningest coach in history how to improve—even if he'd requested it? Unnatural or not, with the entire team assembled, it was time to put aside any misgivings. Hopefully, her sweat wasn't too noticeable.

"I'm truly honored to be here, although it feels surreal. Bob asked me of all people to talk about on-field communication, the goal being, of course, to improve team chemistry. I really hope this session is useful because I'll never be able to repay Bob and Theo for everything that they did for me. Now, because I wasn't able to attend as many games as I would have liked, I used A/V footage to study the team's psychological dynamics. Some of you may think the clips I'm about to show are embarrassing. They're meant to be *instructive*."

Fortunately, there were no rolling eyes or yawns. "There's something else you should know," Kiara continued. "Bob invited me to speak not only because I'm a psychologist who used to play soccer here but also because I once epitomized the worst in on-field communication. Your issues pale in comparison to the piss-poor attitude I showed my freshman year. I was so individualistic, and communicated so poorly, that, although I was the number-three player in the nation coming in, I sat on the bench most of my freshman season. I wouldn't play defense, I was aloof, and, when I did communicate, I was rude and cutting." She sipped water. "You can imagine what that did for team chemistry. I was a cancer, so the coach did what he had to do. But . . . the story ends well. We went on to three straight national championship games and won two."

The players applauded.

"Okay, here's a lowlight video of the Virginia, Wake, and State games. Let's jump right in."

They watched as the referee blew his whistle and raised an arm to signal offsides on the Carolina left-winger, Jill, who walked toward the Carolina half, eyes downcast. The Heels' midfielder, Cindy, barked, "C'mon, Jill. What's that, four offsides in one half? You're killing us! Get your fucking act together!"

Kiara paused the video. "In the two previous games Jill had three goals and one assist, averaging sixty-five minutes a game as a starter. Since that encounter, Jill hasn't contributed a point, and her minutes dropped to fifteen. She hasn't started a game since. Theo tells me Jill's confidence has evaporated. Regaining it is one of the team's priorities."

Cindy, seated near the front, bowed her head.

"Cindy, you had every reason to be frustrated. That was, in fact, her third offsides, and one of them was critical, preventing a win. But when you see that clip, what goes through your mind?"

The midfielder rubbed the nape of her neck. "Honestly, it hurts. I didn't realize how mean I was. I got caught up in the heat of the game, but that's no excuse." Cindy glanced over at Jill. "I'm really sorry."

"How did your words affect the team?" Kiara asked.

"Jill's our second-leading scorer, and I crushed her confidence."

"Did you cause her struggles?"

"No, but I could have helped—not made them worse."

"How?"

"By choosing better words."

"Such as?"

Cindy shrugged. A senior piped up instead: "Be more positive, offer a suggestion."

"Give me an example?"

"Something like, 'Their back line is tricky; try a curling run.'"

Kiara clapped her hands. "Perfect!" She played the next clip.

A Virginia striker manhandled Carolina's center back, firing a rocket that almost scored. Carolina's goalkeeper marched up to the defender, screaming, "Stop playing like a damn wimp!"

Kiara coaxed a more constructive response: "Remember the game with Clemson, when you dominated. We need that toughness now."

The players responded effectively to two more situations, so she felt comfortable closing. "Look, this isn't like basketball. There are no time-outs; you largely need to coach yourselves. You need to communicate effectively, providing positive and negative feedback. How you communicate affects chemistry, and chemistry is way more important for us than it is for Neanderthal men. It's okay to be blunt, but stay positive. This handout provides examples of good communication. Study it, and, please, kick Duke's butt on Sunday."

"That was quite a tour de force you put on," Bob said after the meeting ended.

Kiara smiled.

"The Bobby Hurley treatment was effective," Theo said.

"I got the idea from International Expeditions."

"From Zeb?" Theo was clearly confused. "He seems more like the dreamy intellectual."

"It was Teresa. She's sharp as a tack. You guys should really let her handle your travel arrangements."

Bob nodded. "We'll check them out."

"Good," Kiara said. "Now, switching gears, you were concerned that performance standards would erode, because you don't have the same energy to confront players who're taking it easy in practice."

"Exactly."

"Any chance you'll retire in the next five years?"

Bob shook his head. "Not a chance. Dean Smith regretted retiring too early. He's still teaching me from his grave."

"I'm hitting the final stretch," Theo said.

"I recommend you hire a brilliant young assistant coach," Kiara said. "Someone to run the practice drills and hold the ladies accountable. Someone to groom as your successor—way before he or she is needed. That would extend your longevity."

"You found someone," Bob said knowingly.

Kiara grinned. "There's a world-class youth coach in Raleigh."

"I agree. Reggie would be ideal."

She smiled. Coach was usually a step ahead.

When Theo left, Bob asked, "How are your parents?"

"Mom's great. She's now a charge nurse at Cleveland Clinic. Dad's fine, but he's pissing me off."

"How?"

"Can you believe he's a Republican?" She scrunched up her face.

The coach smirked. "Capitalist pig! Sound the alarm!"

"Seriously, a Black immigrant?"

"I thought shrinks were supposed to be tolerant and non-judgmental."

"Bob, tolerating heartlessness isn't a virtue."

"America is full of heartless Republicans, Kiara. Some of them even coach soccer."

41

SUCH FINE CAUSES

*L*ighthouse Point, Florida, February 2017. Leo held the tiller, check-ing the telltales and boat traffic. Saturdays were busy, giving him a pretext for staying on the periphery of the conversation. Listening to his friend, Enrique, give estate-planning advice to Marco, a Merrill Lynch client and Hugo Chavez–supporting *enchufado*, was more than Leo could stomach. Talk about a good sail ruined. A trio of dolphins appeared, but Leo kept the sighting to himself.

"It's not like Maracaibo," Marco said. "There we could afford three servants, a membership at Club de Las Americas, the works."

Chavez-Maduro largesse went to such fine causes, Leo thought.

"You're in good shape," Enrique said. "The penthouse condo is mortgage-free, and the structure I'm recommending would secure the future for your middle-aged son and grandchildren."

Marco grimaced. "Not if I die and my son spends it all on alimony, cocaine, sports cars, and supermodels."

"If you want, we can set it up so he can't invade the principal. Income distributions can be controlled by a trustee."

"You realize Bernardo overstayed his visa?" Marco asked.

At the mention of Bernardo, Leo squeezed the tiller so tightly his arm trembled. The vessel deviated from his intended point of sail, causing the jib to luff. Leo corrected it.

Enrique's eyes widened. "Really?"

"Is he legally able to sign the papers?"

"Bernardo doesn't need to sign anything, but getting arrested would derail everything. He needs to keep his nose clean, no pun intended."

Marco sighed. "We did our best, but he's always been trouble. Maybe it's the dyslexia."

"I'm sorry."

"Can he get asylum?"

"It's doubtful," Enrique said.

"We're not Chavistas, you know."

Leo gasped. *Not anymore. Not after looting your country.*

The dolphins swam off.

42

BIG BROTHER

C*hapel Hill, North Carolina, February 2017.* The Federal Trade Commission examiner was frowning when Zeb arrived on the doorstep of International Expeditions at 8:08 a.m. Once inside, Zeb offered her a cup of coffee, but she declined. He handed over the requested files. The audit would last a day or two—enough time for her to wade through traffic reports, bank statements, client records, invoices, and supplier emails. The FTC, she reiterated, had concerns about the manner in which International Expeditions conducted its business.

At 4:00 p.m., the examiner approached Zeb.

"Thanks for your cooperation. I have all I need. You'll need to come to D.C. to answer further questions."

43

THE DIPLOMAT

hapel Hill, North Carolina, February 2017. Zeb was mouthing an apology to his old mentor: He had to take this telephone call. Professor Small smiled amiably and rose to examine the travel photos on the walls.

When Zeb hung up, he said, "I'm sorry, that was the chairman of the FTC."

"Whoa, hobnobbing with the heavy hitters."

"Not by choice, but, thank God, things worked out. I was expecting to be fined after the mass cancellations. Turns out, we got a clean bill of health—ethically at least. They'll be fining three of our competitors."

The professor returned to his seat. "For anticompetitive business practices?"

"Yup. Blackballing our suppliers. The examiner saw that we'd never been canceled on before by our operators—not after sending deposits—then, all of a sudden, we had three. They got suspicious."

"Especially after your NBC interview."

"*And* my comments at the trade conference," Zeb added. "Anyhow, they want me to come to D.C. to discuss reforms. The FTC will be working with Congress and the Justice Department to revamp regulations and enforcement—across many sectors, not just travel. They'll force industries to adopt strict rules on disclosure, along the lines of what I was pushing."

"Bravo. That's a huge step forward." Professor Small clapped. "Will the NTA reinstate your deposit insurance?"

"I doubt it. We're honest, but we no longer meet their financial-strength thresholds."

"And your ARC license?"

Zeb cocked his head. "I'm hoping they reduce their bond requirement. I'd say it's fifty-fifty."

"Why did they audit you in the first place?"

"Several competitors reported us after the mass cancellations."

"Which they caused." The professor shook his head.

"How about we discuss an expedition that went swimmingly?"

"You received feedback?"

"No, but when things go wrong, we get bombarded by emails and calls before the evaluations roll in. So tell me about it."

Retracing David Livingstone's 1841–1851 exploration of southern Africa hadn't been without its issues. Professor Small suggested modifications to the itinerary and lodging and handed Zeb expense reports and sealed trip evaluations.

The professor continued, "They were a great group—adventurous, inquisitive, not a bad egg among them. You had the right mix of history, adventure, wildlife, and Livingstone's life. The lectures on the Scramble for Africa, Boer Wars, Bushmen, Zulus, and Cecil Rhodes all went well. Your notes made my job easy."

"How about the adventures?"

Professor Small whistled. "Ms. Levine's raft flipped on the Zambezi, but she had insisted on going and raved about it afterward. The elephant trek, lion walk, and great-white-shark encounter were outstanding. Stellenbosch wine tasting was okay."

Zeb opened the envelopes and quickly scanned the overall trip and lecturer ratings. "All 'excellent' except for one 'very good.' That was from Dr. Engle, who'll croak before he utters the word 'excellent.'"

"Engle was my favorite—cantankerous old goat." Small chuckled.

"It seems your research on sub-Saharan wild grains, domesticable mammals, and tribal political structures came in handy."

"Handy as my jump hook. If only Livingstone had stopped at the Sahel, I'd have won Engle over. My expertise ran out in the north."

"Bummer."

"Seriously, your expedition was better than every other trip I've led for schools and museums. If you'd like, I can talk to UNC and recommend you."

"Thanks, Professor, but I don't stand a chance."

"The honor-court deal?"

"Yeah."

"Travel is run separately from academics. Have you tried?"

"No. Locally, my reputation is shot all across the board."

Small leaned forward in his chair. "Maybe it's time to restore it."

"How do you know I wasn't guilty?"

"You think I'd have led your tour if there were *any* chance you were dishonest? I know. You were my best student."

"I appreciate that."

"What actually happened?"

Zeb sighed. "I got charged for helping a student cheat on the final exam."

"The operative word being 'charged,' of course. Which must mean you didn't do it?"

"I did it."

Small raised his eyebrows. "There must've been a reason . . ."

"He had a learning disability."

"That doesn't justify cheating."

"No, it doesn't."

"Did you show contrition?"

"There was nothing to apologize for."

"Help me out here," Small said. "Cheating is *wrong*, but you had nothing to apologize for?"

Zeb rubbed his eyes. "My statistics professor wasn't like other UNC professors. Other teachers totally understood that students have different learning styles; they were prepared to make accommodations. This guy was an outlier, old school. Students were either dedicated or lazy. 'Dedicated' meant they learned well under a lecture format."

"That shocks me." Small massaged his chin. "Carolina is usually way ahead of the curve on this stuff. It's drilled into us. I assume he allowed extra testing time?"

"He offered up a single day and time for students who, as he put it, 'needed extra time for some unfathomable reason.' The other LD student couldn't make the time slot. Take it or leave it, our Good Samaritan said."

"So you went to the extra-time session and gave the other guy the exam questions in advance?"

"No, we both went to the regular session. I was damned if I was gonna be the only learning-disabled loser needing extra time."

"And?"

"Keep in mind, this other student was brilliant. His shows play on Broadway. But he was a visual-kinesthetic learner."

Small nodded. "A different kettle of fish."

"Entirely. So the guy gets fidgety. He gets up and walks around. He's told he can't. To compensate, he starts bouncing his legs, probably unconsciously—and again he's scolded by the proctor. He stretches his arms and legs—stopped again. He sits there. I can tell he's panicking. He's about to walk out and flunk, this brilliant guy. He knows his stuff but can't prove it under this testing format. He's sinking fast."

"And?"

"I slipped him my answer sheet. He told me no thanks."

"But the proctor saw you."

"Yup. And reported me to the honor court."

"What did you say?"

"I told them the professor had screwed the guy over, not just on the final exam but all semester. I was compensating for it. There was no way the guy should have failed. The professor had failed *him*, I said, and should be apologizing to both of us."

"You told them that?"

"Verbatim."

"Ever the diplomat. I wish you'd come to me. I could have testified on your behalf."

"I should've."

"How were things left?"

"I was booted one semester before graduation. It's on my permanent record. No good university will accept me. But at this point I don't give a crap."

"You sure about that?" Small looked at him earnestly. "Listen, I've got a class, but I'd love to discuss this further. I'll send you the trip report, and thanks again."

"Sure thing."

Small got up to leave. "Oh, do me a favor: Let Teresa be a buffer between you and anyone who pisses you off."

"She already is."

"Well done, Mr. Ambassador."

44

SETTLING UP

Machiques, Venezuela, February 2017. Leo's back still ached from falling off the horse. He could have used several days to recover but, with the arrival of the FedEx package, one would have to suffice. His last day in Venezuela had to be productive—and matters had to be handled with discretion—so he rose from his parents' living-room couch and took off alone in the family clunker. *Hope I have more luck than on the horse trek.*

Ten minutes later Leo ambled into Bocados restaurant. An assortment of regulars, all men, were eating breakfast and chattering loudly. Leo made his way to a booth where the private detective sat alone. They shook hands, exchanged pleasantries, and drank a *cafecito*. The detective slid two manila envelopes toward him. Leo opened the first and scrutinized the photographs and documents within. The headshot of the hairdresser revealed he had aged well in spite of the assault. Absent was his expression of terror, a look that would remain etched in Leo's memory forever. The envelope also contained a mortgage statement confirming that, like many Venezuelans, the hairdresser's family had stayed put for decades.

The contents of the second envelope brought hope, not consternation: evidence of Bernardo's longtime involvement in drug dealing. Unfortunately, the detective couldn't prove that Leo's former classmate had orchestrated the kidnapping outside the Club de las Americas. Had he not been abducted and sodomized, he'd never have assaulted the hairdresser or required the first envelope.

"*Gracias, amigo.*" Leo paid the man and left.

Minutes later the Banco Mercantil branch manager was staring at him, mouth agape. Clearly, he had never fielded such a request. Nor did the manager seem inclined to comply. Leo applied pressure and, in the end, accomplished his mission.

Leo drove to the outskirts of town, pausing in front of a dilapidated house. The street numbers being nonexistent or faded, he removed a photo from the envelope and compared the houses. Seconds later he was ringing the doorbell. He shuddered as he remembered the pain he'd inflicted, unprovoked. How dirty he had felt—*still* felt.

A dog barked, and the door opened. A smiling lady spoke, "*Buenos dias.* How can I help you, young man?"

"Good morning, señora. I'm Leo. Does Juanjo Dias live here?"

"*Claro*, he's my son. Come in, I'll fix you a *cafecito*."

"Thank you, but I've just had one. I'm fine waiting here."

"Suit yourself."

A sleepy-eyed Juanjo came to the door. Upon seeing Leo, he jumped back, his eyes bulging. He froze, trembling.

Leo looked down. *Is it any wonder he remembers my face?* "I promise, there's nothing to be scared of."

Juanjo stammered, falling silent.

"There's no need to say anything. My name is Leo. I just paid off your parents' mortgage. Here's the receipt for $26,490, dated today, from Banco Mercantil." Leo leaned inside and left it on a table by the door. "The canceled note is attached to the receipt."

Juanjo no longer looked as if he might wet his pants.

"I know this won't make up for what I did," Leo continued.

"Nothing will. I'm deeply ashamed. I hope you were able to reconstitute your life and that God blesses your family. He certainly won't bless me."

Juanjo stepped forward. "You hurt us tremendously," he said, timid at first. "For years, we lived in abject fear, wondering when you or someone like you would return to finish the job. Me, I could bear that, but not my mother. We'll accept the payment, but I won't thank you. We both know this gesture, so late in coming, will comfort *you* as much as us. Now, please go."

Leo bowed his head and backed away, tears streaming down his cheeks.

Back in his parents' living room, Leo thought everything seemed to have shrunk—the coffee table, picture books, television, phonograph, and sofa. His parents, too. Only his sister, Carina, seemed larger, having grown into her outsized responsibilities. How many hours had he spent in this cocoon, reading, listening to classical music, or conversing as they were now? Was it delusional to think he'd mostly been contented?

"Are you in the moon again?" Leo's mother, Leonor, squeezed his leg. "I said, how are things in Charlotte?"

"Sorry, Mamá. Everything's good, but I miss you guys."

"We miss you, too. But we're proud of everything you're achieving."

"*Gracias.*"

Leonor chuckled. "Of course, we showed you exactly what not to do."

"That's not true." Leo blushed.

"It is, and that's okay. We're thrilled you escaped."

"Please, Mamá."

"No, the smart ones played the game, or they left, like you. Your father and I were *bobos.*"

Leo shook his head emphatically and looked squarely at his father,

Chuchu. "In reality, you were patriots, fighting the good fight. It took guts to take on the Chavistas—to not play their corrupt game."

"For what?" Chuchu said, rubbing his neck. "So we could sink our business, lay off employees, and let them go hungry? So we could join protests that were immediately crushed by Cuban-trained soldiers? So you could send us money and medicine every single month? No, Leo, an unwinnable fight is a stupid fight."

Leo winced. "Let's talk about the future. I have some joyful news to share."

"I just knew it!" Leonor said, jumping to her feet as she hadn't done in years. "You're engaged, *hijo*—finally, thank God! Come give me a hug."

"It's not that, Mamá," he said, feeling his ears turning red. "All in good time. This is more important."

Immediately, Leonor's face grew puffy, and, although not given to melodramatic outbursts, she broke down, blubbering. Carina brought her tissues.

"I'm sorry, son," Chuchu said. "She'll get over it."

Leo embraced his mother, but she was inconsolable. "What is it, Mamá?"

Sniffling, she said, "We've suffered a lot, your father and I. But we've always been happy. You know why?"

"Tell me."

"Because we have each other. Yes, we've been fools, but love helps you endure almost anything." She wiped away the tears and exhaled deeply. "We want the same for you and Carina. More than anything, I want you to find someone."

A lump lodged in Leo's throat. He fought the urge to weep.

"Enough with all the drama," Carina said. "If you're not engaged, what is it?"

Leo snickered, grateful for her intervention. "Here's the deal. I spoke with George Akst, a top immigration lawyer in New York. He runs Akst and Akst. They're smart, compassionate, and they speak Spanish."

"Nice buildup, bro. What's the bottom line?"

"He can get all three of you into the U.S. You'd qualify under political asylum. How's that for a surprise?"

"Oh, that is a surprise," Leo's papá said. "That gives us lots to think about. Please thank Mr. Akst."

His mother hugged Leo perfunctorily.

"I appreciate it, bro," Carina said, as if he'd bought her a Mars bar.

Apparently, some people took longer to process big moments. Still, it was irritating. "I've got to take care of something. I'll be back in an hour."

There's no point giving Mamá false hope, Leo thought. *A decades-old crush isn't enough, even if Clara* did *overlook my mortifying tumble yesterday.*

Soon he and Clara were seated at the Café Pink, one of the few hygienic restaurants that hadn't been looted during the economic depression. Leo smiled as he eyeballed the *pabellón criollo* in front of him. He waited for Clara to dig into her *hallaca* before attacking his shredded beef, black beans, rice, and plantains. Charlotte had nothing to compare on either the culinary or female front. But he needed to pace himself. "You threw me for a loop yesterday," he said.

"Forty years and a change in hair color will do that." She smiled warmly. "It was fun messing with you."

"Any more Lenin quotes and I would've vomited."

Clara chuckled. "When I mentioned *tequeños*, you looked as if you'd seen a ghost."

He nodded. Memories of that fateful afternoon at the Club de las Americas had indeed flooded his mind. Working as a janitor-handyman, preparing for the New Year's Eve festivities. Awkwardly refusing Federico's offer of the tasty snack. The confrontation with Bernardo and its catastrophic aftermath. He forced the abduction from his mind. "I can't imagine Bernardo approved of losing his blond bombshell."

"He had no say. I dumped him the next day."

"Smart girl. I never liked him."

"Smart man. . . . You never showed up that night."

Leo pushed a plantain around his plate. "What, so I could watch you make out with a jerk at the stroke of midnight? No thanks."

"Let me guess. You spent New Year's Eve reading Dostoyevsky."

"Probably."

"You know"—she looked at him earnestly—"you made literature class fun with all your questions."

"*Now* you tell me."

"What can I say? I was an idiot, hanging out with other idiots."

"You're certainly no longer that," he said. "Are you a professor?"

"A professor in search of students. With all the strikes and power outages, I haven't taught in a while. I do business consulting, but, with foreign investors spooked, there's precious little of that." She smirked. "It's outrageous how they insist on private-property rights and free-market policies."

"Funny, you don't fit my idea of a Soviet factory worker."

"Not grim enough?"

"Oh, plenty grim. Too feminine."

She beamed. "What, I overdid my transformation from Farrah Fawcett to Cindy Crawford?"

"Not in the least." He held up his *tequeño*. "You know, the club's tasted better."

"True, but the company was abysmal."

He wondered if assholes still ruled that place. "So, no Bernardo to worry about?"

"Or hair-color changes."

"Smart girl."

45

DECENT STUDENT, LOUSY JEW

hapel Hill, North Carolina, February 2017. Zeb popped his head into Rabbi Norman's office, looking for his assistant. No luck. Faye was being indispensable elsewhere.

Rabbi looked up before Zeb could escape. "Come in! I'm so glad to see you."

"Thanks, Rabbi."

"I wish more people would drop in."

Zeb smiled, wondering how a man who was so charismatic on the *bima* could be so self-effacing off it. Hopefully, Rabbi wouldn't mention his prolonged absence from services. Apart from Torah study, he'd long felt out of place here, and it wasn't something he wanted to discuss. "The truth is, I just needed to drop off some forms."

Rabbi cocked his head. "You don't think the truth is overrated?"

The clergyman was smiling, but it was clear that he wished to engage. He'd never been a ritual-first rabbi or hermit scholar. Counseling and teaching were in his blood, and that was where he shined. A little conversation couldn't hurt.

"I do have a holdover question from Torah study," Zeb said.

"Wonderful! Have a seat. Ask away."

"How much of Exodus is real history?"

"Does it matter?"

Rabbi loved to answer questions with questions, but two could play at that game. "Wouldn't Torah lose its authority if it wasn't accurate?" Zeb asked.

"Can't we take Torah seriously without taking it literally?"

"Yes, Rabbi."

"Can't Torah help even people who don't believe in God?"

How did one cry uncle? "Yes, Rabbi, nonbelievers can learn as well. Torah is filled with people facing life challenges and moral choices. We can learn to be better people." The reply was a good one, Zeb knew, but the real question remained: After years of Torah study, was he anywhere near the person he *should* be?

Rabbi was already running with Zeb's response. "Exactly! But, to your question: There's lots of evidence that the Exodus from Egypt is true. Richard Elliott Friedman summarizes it better than anyone. He studied at Harvard, Cambridge, and Oxford."

"Not too shabby. But I believe doubters say there's no archaeological evidence. That two million people spending forty years in Sinai would've left some trace."

Rabbi smiled. "Remember, Sinai hasn't been combed. There have only been a few major excavations, and it's incredibly difficult to find objects buried more than three thousand years ago. To give you an idea, an army vehicle was lost in the Yom Kippur War and found forty years later, in 2013, under fifty-two feet of sand! Can you imagine three thousand years?"

"Nope. Still, with so many people, you'd think they'd have found some remnants."

"There's every reason to believe that a *smaller* group left in the

Exodus—and that they were Levites, the tribe of priests. The textual evidence is overwhelming."

"But doesn't the Torah mention a huge number?" Zeb asked.

"The earliest mention of the Exodus—and one of the two oldest texts in the Bible—was the Song of the Sea. The Israelites, led by the prophetess Miriam, were singing to God after Pharaoh's army was destroyed at the Sea of Reeds. The song said that 'a people' left Egypt, but it never mentioned how many took part in the Exodus. It was *four hundred years later* when a priestly source added a number to the story: 603,550 Israelite males, plus their families."

"How do we know it was the Levites who left?"

"Many reasons. First, Moses is identified as a Levite in the Torah. Second, the Song of the Sea describes God as leading these people to the sacred mountain site of his throne's temple. Among the Israelites, only the Levites became temple priests."

Zeb shifted in his seat. "Okay, but just because the Levites were the only priests, doesn't mean they had any connection with Egypt or an exodus."

Rabbi chuckled. "Among the Israelites, only the Levites had Egyptian names."

"Any other evidence?"

"A ton, Zeb. The second passage in the Torah that is older than all others is the Song of Deborah, another prophetess. She sings a hymn after the Israelites defeat the Canaanites. Like Miriam's Song of the Sea, the Song of Deborah is written in an archaic style of Hebrew much older than the rest of Exodus." Rabbi sipped water. "Which means it's closer in time to the events being described—more accurate. Here's the key: The Song of Deborah, which is set in Israel, lists all ten tribes—Judah and Simeon were still separate—but it *doesn't* mention the Levites. The only outliers."

Zeb's eyebrows raised. "They hadn't arrived yet?"

"That's what Friedman concludes." Rabbi let it sink in. "There's tons more—but I need to give you some background."

"Okay."

"Remember, the Five Books of Moses weren't transcribed by a single person. Scholars have concluded the Torah was written by four different sources over the period 1,200 to 400 BCE."

"Why four?"

"They studied the text in great detail. There are factual inconsistencies, contradictory regulations, and major differences in style, vocabulary, and theology."

"Any examples?"

"Sure. Take the name of God. God is known by several names. El Shaddai emphasizes His power; that was how He was known to the patriarchs. Elohim is the supreme deity. Adonai is His most sacred, intimate name, how He became known to Moses. That was when the Israelites become a special people with a unique faith."

"Okay, so how does this relate to an exodus consisting only of Levites, not *all* Israelites?"

"The four sources are J—Yahwistic, E—Elohistic, P—Priestly, and D—Deuteronomic. Three of these writers, E, P, and D, are traceable to Levite priestly authors."

"And?"

"*Only* the Levite versions of Torah tell the *entire* story of the plagues and exodus from Egypt. The non-Levite source (J) skips from Moses saying, 'Let my people go,' to the people's already having departed Egypt. No details."

"Suggesting the Levites alone were in Egypt," Zeb said, eyes widening.

Rabbi nodded and then offered more evidence to his eager student.

Zeb sat back, nodding in amazement. "Wow, that's a powerful argument. What a shame it's wasted on me."

"It's never wasted, Zeb. You're a wonderful student."

He snorted. "Decent student, lousy Jew."

"Why would you say that?" Rabbi looked concerned.

Zeb chuckled. "I don't go to services. I don't own a tallith or yarmulke. I don't know the *v'ahavta* prayer. I can't give a lot of charity. I've missed the last two chances to go on mitzvah days. The one thing I do is Torah study, and that's because it makes me feel better. Need I say more?"

"No, you're unquestionably doomed. But it's funny. You bear a remarkable resemblance to this teacher who for years inspired our learning-disabled kids—those who would have otherwise fallen through the cracks."

Zeb felt a lump in his throat.

Rabbi had a gleam in his eye. "Ritual isn't the highest form of spirituality. Some people, like you, grow more in other ways; that doesn't make them less Jewish. We're a people for whom deeds are as important as beliefs. Look how many people benefit from your insights during Torah study, how many kids you helped as a teacher, how, honestly, I'm sure you treat your clients." He sipped water. "That's not to say you wouldn't feel happier if you got more involved. Maybe there is room to raise your game. That's not for me to judge. But, as your rabbi, I'm asking you to lighten up on yourself. You've gone through a lot over the years with your learning disability, the divorce, your business, your aging parents."

"Thank you." His voice cracked. "The thing is, I feel different, like a fish out of water."

"How so?"

"Well, for one thing, my political views make me a black sheep. I'm sick of people assuming I'm immoral or ignorant."

"You'd rather be around people you always agree with?" Rabbi asked.

"No, that would be boring. I wish people would be less judgmental."

"What do you mean?"

"They assume conservatives don't care about the poor."

"Do they?" Rabbi grinned. "You realize Conservative congregations have far more Republicans than Reform?"

"Yeah, but they're heavy on Hebrew—and you're not their rabbi."

"Too kind."

Zeb glanced at his watch. "Sorry, Rabbi, I need to make my own exodus. Thanks a ton."

"My pleasure. Remember, there's no Torah study this week." He whispered conspiratorially, "I'll be meeting again with Senator Lindsey Graham. He likes to keep his pulse on Jewish communities in the South."

Zeb's jaw dropped.

"Keep that under your hat. I'd like to keep my job."

46

ZINGERS

Chapel Hill, North Carolina, March 2017. Ruth sent a topspin backhand whizzing by Zeb at the net. He floundered, stumbling momentarily, but righted himself and beamed. She had controlled most of the points with spin and placement, but he had retrieved and counterpunched effectively. Not this time.

"Jeez, Mom, that was child abuse."

"Thanks, sweetie. I know you laid it up there, but on my birthday, I'll take it."

"I didn't—not on purpose anyway." He handed her a ball. "You're getting your form back."

For years mother and son had cleared their calendars on her birthday. Chapel Hill Tennis Club was Ruth's destination of choice because she wanted help with her game. Her strokes had lost their pop, and her footwork had become erratic. She'd always been an A player, but her form had dropped, resulting in demotion to the B team. Ruth bristled at being "relegated to irrelevancy," as she put it. She was not a happy camper.

Off the court it was a different story. Family relations were as close as Zeb ever remembered them. His mom had mellowed, dispensing sweetness, as if making up for lost time. Maybe it was no longer raising a problem child. Maybe the stings of his expulsion and divorce had worn off. Possibly she felt guilty for forcing meds on him or less pressure after achieving her goals. The reason didn't matter.

Ruth was less enthralled when Zeb aced her to cap off a tight set. Of course, she would have been offended had he let up on her.

"Nasty son," she said, motioning toward the clubhouse. "Lunch is on you, and I'm ordering a Bloody Mary."

"Actually, I planned lunch for us at Wendy's. There's a Baconator special."

Ruth slapped him on the shoulder. Soon they were seated at a reserved table overlooking the pine forest. After they had ordered, Ruth asked, "So what's new?"

Business was still their comfort zone—like father and son discussing football—so that was how he led off. "A lot. You remember how the Florida Museum of Natural History chose six of our wildlife safaris?" She nodded. "Well, this week UNC Alumni Travel picked eight of our European and Asian tours. We're hiring two employees to handle the volume."

"Bravo." She raised her glass. "I'm so proud of you."

"Thanks."

"I guess it helped being a Carolina grad and all."

Zeb dropped his mozzarella stick. "What are you talking about, Mom? You know I never graduated."

"Oh, yes. . . . Sorry, dear."

"No worries. There's more good news."

"Let me guess. You and Hannah are reconciling. You'll be giving me grandkids?"

After the divorce Ruth had transformed from Hannah's disapproving mother-in-law to her biggest advocate. It had taken Hannah's being shunned by her own family for Ruth's goodwill to sprout. Zeb's ex-wife was now flawless.

"No, not that," he said.

"A shame. So, what is it?"

"You remember Professor Small?"

"The name rings a bell."

"You remember . . . my mentor. He came to dinner several times years ago and recommended I get my doctorate in history."

She nodded. "And so?"

"Professor Small led our David Livingstone expedition. Without my knowing it, he approached UNC to discuss my honor-code violation. He vouched for my character and explained details they hadn't known before. They reviewed my case and—"

"Honey, it's been decades since you cheated. How long do you have to keep paying for one mistake? Look at everything you've achieved since. It's just not right."

Zeb paled. "Mom, I didn't *cheat*. I tried to help someone who was getting *screwed*. Anyhow, Carolina expunged the incident from their records. I now have a clean slate, and I'll be returning part-time to earn my degree. I'll no longer be an embarrassment."

"That's wrong, Zeb. You've never been an embarrassment—not to me, not to your dad. I remember now, you got expelled because you're special. There was a lapse in judgment, but you were heroic." She caressed his cheek. "I always knew you'd succeed. You were too good to give up on. And look at what you overcame, accomplishing so much more than people without your challenges."

Heroic? Too good to give up on? Haven't I always come up short? There was a frog in his throat. "Thanks, Mom." *Did I ditch my meds to sabotage myself and spite her?*

"I'm ready for another Bloody Mary," she said.

"I've got a better idea. Let's talk about your real birthday present. It's a genealogy tour of Morocco and Israel. Anytime you want to go."

"Oh, dear." Tears welled in Ruth's eyes. "I don't know what to say."

"Simple. Say that you'll go."

She sighed. "My dean has been pushing me to take a semester off to recharge my batteries."

"We could dig into family history," Zeb mused. "There are things I've wondered about a long time."

"Really? Like what?"

He whistled. "Where do I begin? For one thing, how on earth did Nonna, a female Jew, become a physician in a Muslim country like Morocco back in the 1940s?"

Ruth smiled. "Your grandmother was extraordinary and was blessed with progressive parents. Also, Morocco was very tolerant."

"It's cool they weren't meshuge."

"Not crazy at all. During World War II, when King Mohammed was asked by the Nazi Vichy government how many Jews lived in Morocco, he replied, 'I have no Jews, only Moroccans.' And he invited Morocco's rabbis to attend the throne celebrations."

"Impressive."

"And Essaouira, where my family was from, was Morocco's most progressive city." Ruth sipped her drink. "Port cities are usually that way. It was a trading post for a thousand years, offering goods from the Trans-Saharan caravan trade to the world. What's with the funny look?"

"Nothing," he said, chuckling. "I've just never heard you talk about this stuff before."

"You'd rather I talk shareholder value?"

"Absolutely not."

"An earlier king," she continued, "encouraged Jews to settle in Essaouira to manage trade with Europe. They once represented forty percent of the city's population. When the French took over, many learned French so they could work in government and French-owned businesses. Nonna was a standout student, one of only two women accepted into the local medical school."

"Fascinating," Zeb said. "I'll have my ground operator check if we can visit her home and school. And Nonno's, too."

"That would be special."

"So things went downhill in 1948?"

Ruth's expression saddened. "Rioters killed forty-four Jews after

Israel was formed. Your grandparents stuck it out until 1954, but Moroccan independence was inevitable, and they feared what would happen without French protections. So they immigrated to Israel."

"Wow, that's tragic. What was Nonno's profession?"

Ruth pushed away her empty plate. "Your grandfather dreamed of being a concert pianist, but the arts weren't a priority in a fledgling country with hostile neighbors and such a harsh environment. He was a tailor by trade, but he farmed the land. I do remember him playing piano during the 1956 Suez Crisis. The radio broadcasts were terrifying, and his music calmed everyone down."

The waiter served them bowls of lime and peach sherbet.

"So why did you choose business?"

Ruth sighed. "In Israel I was exposed to varying influences. We lived on a kibbutz. The communal farm had a utopian mix of Socialists and Zionists. Some of them pioneered drip irrigation and transformed desert into farmland. But we often came across capitalists who set up businesses, developed the cities, and would later make Israel the start-up capital of the world. Zionists came in all stripes. I guess the entrepreneurial side won out."

Zeb dipped into his sherbet. "How did that sit with Nonna? I can't imagine she appreciated your training the next generation of labor-exploiting capitalists."

"There were tensions. She had devoted her life to healing the sick."

"The acorn had fallen miles from the tree. Why'd you leave Israel?"

Ruth tapped his arm. "My, you're full of questions. At the time, Moroccan Jews were second-class citizens in Israel. European immigrants had all the power. They discriminated against Moroccans, supposedly for shunning agricultural work and being hot tempered. So after farming Israeli land for nine years, your levelheaded grandparents decided to emigrate. Charlotte was paradise."

Zeb grinned. "And you became a capitalist."

She nodded. "Nonna came to understand that I did worthwhile things as a business consultant. Meanwhile, Israel was transforming itself into a dynamic country because of free-market reforms. Business was no longer an embarrassment."

"You were no longer a bad Jew." Zeb smiled.

"Or a good one. I didn't go to temple as much as Nonna would've liked. But I founded the Jewish-Muslim Friendship Council in honor of our Moroccan roots, which did earn me brownie points."

Zeb smiled. He wasn't the only mediocre Jew in the family. Nor was he the first to disappoint with his career path. "It couldn't have hurt that you entered academia."

"No, it didn't," Ruth said, seemingly surprised by the insight. "I'm sure my career choices were influenced, on some level, by our family's precarious situation in Morocco and Israel."

"Interesting. Did the anxiety you all felt go away after you made it to America? After all, you saved money and lived without hard-core discrimination here."

"Much of it, but not all." She waved a spoonful of sherbet in the air. "As Jews, we've never had it as good as we do in America. We're blessed. But history tells us we're always one severe economic recession away from being scapegoated. One reason why we're so liberal politically."

"How do you mean?" he asked.

"Our deep commitment to social justice and repairing the world— *tikkun olam*—is unquestionable. But there's more to it."

"I'm all ears."

"We also support lavish government spending on the poor—even during good times—because it reduces their suffering when things get bad. They're less likely to blame the Jews."

Zeb signaled for the check. "Basically, more government spending insulates us from anti-Semitism."

"Lessens it. That's partly why we vote to pay higher taxes."

"But don't tax-and-spend policies cause the bad times?"

Ruth frowned. "Let's not lose our moral compass, okay? Not on my birthday."

"Now you sound like Nonna." He smirked. "Guess I'll have to become a history professor before I get any respect."

"Not to worry, sweetie, you'll surely graduate by fifty."

Zeb beamed. Zingers were just what he needed from her. A sign she wasn't slipping. "Mom, your A game may be back, but your personality is firmly stuck on C."

47

THE MOST
BEAUTIFUL ROSES

Maracaibo, Venezuela, February 2017. Leonor left her apartment before sunrise, with Chuchu tagging along. Nothing—not the rampant crime, oppressive heat, or their decrepit bodies—would dissuade her from the trek. Driving wasn't an option given the scarcity and price of gas. Leonor's only concession had been to move up the departure time.

They stuck to the lit avenues, praying the power outage would hit later. Passing Central Hospital, they headed up Milagro and turned west at Óptica Joel. On they walked, Chuchu toting water and Leonor the roses. They spoke only when necessary. The sun rose as they reached Urdaneta Park. Leonor ignored her parched throat, marveling that her husband's sciatica hadn't acted up. Maybe it had. A man outside McDonald's munched on an Egg McMuffin. They pressed on, passing the mall and reaching the unguarded entrance to El Cuadrado Cemetery at 6:25. Early enough to talk to her brother in peace.

They followed the perimeter path. Out-of-control shrubbery blocked most views, but Leonor had no trouble finding Oswaldo's grave—not after resorting to bribery to secure an idyllic spot. Blotting her record had been worth it. He deserved the shade of an araguaney tree. He also deserved more than two visits a year.

Leonor's breathing quickened, as they approached the familiar grove of trees. She rubbed the bouquet, beautifying the arrangement.

"Oh, shit!" a man shouted.

"Be careful, dumbass!" a second man barked.

Leonor stiffened. Profanity here was inappropriate at any hour, but so early in the morning it was frightening. The place should have been deserted.

Chuchu grabbed her arm. His index finger was drawn to his lips. "Come this way." He led Leonor away from the commotion, stroking her back.

They climbed to a vantage point shielded by vegetation. Three plots over from Oswaldo's grave, two men were desecrating a tomb. One sat in obvious pain, nursing his foot. Next to him lay a rectangular slab of concrete, presumably removed from the grave and dropped by accident. The second robber scavenged like a jackal.

"What in Lord's name is he doing?" Leonor asked.

"They're looking for jewelry, gold teeth, bones. To sell."

"That can't be. It's unconscionable."

"It's not just the graves of commoners," he said. "Last year it was Rómulo Gallegos, the former president!"

"Why bones?" She was almost in tears.

"They sell them to *paleros*."

"The black-magic priests?"

Chuchu nodded. "The skulls and bones are used in initiation ceremonies."

"*Qué horror!* I know Santeria priests sacrifice chickens and other animals. But human bones?"

"*Paleros* are different. They're also from Cuba, but it's a different thing."

"My God, what have we come to—stealing teeth, jewelry, human bones. There's no respect anymore."

"That's what happens when an entire generation suffers economically, thanks to generations of corrupt rule by the elite." Chuchu sighed. "People lose faith in government, science, and traditional values. They turn to black magic to solve problems. I'm not making excuses, just explaining."

"Hogwash." She glowered at the grave robbers. "Chavez practiced Santeria—he dressed in white for months. These idiots are copying him."

"It's not that simple, sweetheart. Hey . . . wait!"

Leonor bolted down the hill. She headed toward the intruders. "Leave him alone, you shameless sons of bitches!"

Chuchu lumbered after her. "Wait!"

The kneeling scavenger looked at Leonor as if he she were a gnat. He cradled a human skull in both hands. She screamed, "*Hijo de puta!*" He cussed back at her. Leonor smacked him on the head with the bouquet. He pushed her away with one arm. She came back at him, kicking him in the thigh. The robber shielded the valuable skull from her blows, his handgun hanging uselessly from his belt. The other thief, still holding on to his injured foot, cackled, unable to contain himself. Leonor pummeled the scavenger, shouting, "Have you no respect? No sense of decency? Get the hell out of here!"

"Look, I'm sorry, lady. If this is your family, I'll return the skull."

"It isn't, you *pendejo*! But you'll replace it immediately, or I'll give you a *coñazo* you'll never forget."

Chuchu arrived to find one robber being browbeaten, the other in hysterics. He waited, ready to intervene. There was no need. Cowed, the scavengers returned the skull, replaced the gravestone, and left.

Tearfully, Leonor walked over to her brother's grave. She laid the mutilated roses on the headstone and sat beside it. Chuchu caressed her head. "*Mi amor*, these roses are truly the most beautiful ever." He left to give the siblings their space.

48

HIGH-FLIER

Miami, *Florida, February 2017.* Leo gazed out onto Biscayne Bay, its turquoise channels spreading like tentacles to Brickell Key and downtown Miami. Somehow the city's skyline enhanced nature's splendor. He followed Virginia Key's coastline to the golf course where he had once, as a junior banker, sliced balls into the deep. A rare break from the grueling routine of climbing the corporate ranks. But he had made it. The once-penniless immigrant was pitching acquisitions to the CEO and CFO of the world's third-largest cruise line—from the comfort of their penthouse conference room.

He giggled inside. *Who would have guessed? Batman-stripper turned investment banker.* Julian, Carlos, and two aides were still studying the financials projected onto the whiteboard. Jake sat opposite them, thumbing his smartphone.

When enough time had lapsed, Leo spoke. "Today, as you can see, we're bringing you two possible acquisition targets, A and B. The projections assume that you implement our financial recommendations in conjunction with each acquisition. Make sense?"

"It does," Julian said.

"Great. So let's dig into option A. Strategically, it offers several benefits. You would expand into the potentially huge Chinese market. And you would diversify your customer base, no longer relying overly on any single market."

"But the risks are significant."

"Absolutely. You would have to fine-tune your product to meet local preferences in a way that doesn't dilute your brand."

"Much easier said than done," Carlos said.

"For sure," Leo said. "You'll need to go beyond modifying language and cuisine—and those, in themselves, are challenging. Jake's research shows the Chinese take shorter vacations, so you may have to shorten your cruises to four nights. They have different shopping preferences. They buy Cartier and IWC watches and other big-name brand items. That'll affect inventory management and cost. And, unlike the Brazilian and Italians, the Chinese don't want nonstop entertainment."

"All true," Carlos noted, "but it extends further. The Chinese look at cruising differently. They see it as a means to gamble and shop. If cruising is to grow, we'll have to convince more of them to see it as a way to relax and explore new places. So at the same time we're catering to their tastes, we're trying to change them. That's not easy. It'll be expensive."

"Great point." Leo flipped to a new slide. "But, in reality, you can mitigate the risks. Take a look. We assumed, first, that you would retain the leading marketing consulting firm in China to help modify the product, increase brand awareness, and change consumer perceptions. Second, you would work through travel agents, not sell directly. Your gross margin would drop, but building a strong distribution network is key, and your SG&A expenses would drop. Less need for advertising."

Julian shook his head. "Leo, we'd have to make the right call on a range of key issues, each one more complex than the last. We're talking product, sales, marketing, operations. Carnival took a bath after entering China; it took them a long time to turn the corner. And we haven't even discussed the political risks of operating in a Communist country or the opportunity cost of investing in China and not in other viable markets."

"I'm sorry, Julian. I somehow forgot to mention that we're recommending a fifty-fifty joint venture, not an outright purchase."

The CEO nodded. "That makes more sense. That's what Royal Caribbean did. Who's the partner?"

"*Partners*, plural. China State Shipbuilding Corp. and China Investment Corp. They're strategic and local. They can help you make the right calls."

"Our in-country eyes and ears," Carlos noted. "It cuts down on our political and regulatory risk."

Leo leaned forward in his seat. "In reality, we feel there's a risk in not acting soon enough, of falling too far behind Carnival and Royal in the world's next growth market. China is now Royal's second-largest market, up from forty-fifth place only ten years ago. A joint venture limits your risk and investment, while gaining you a foothold." Leo turned to Jake. "Can you walk them through the valuation numbers?"

Jake nodded. "Sure. First, a technical point. We assumed capital expenditures will increase by one hundred and ten million dollars because two ships need to be retrofitted. You would expand shopping areas and add bumper cars, disco roller-skating, and basketball courts."

"Fair enough," Julian said.

"We analyzed the impact of the acquisition on REK's enterprise value using both the discounted cash-flow method and multiples of cash flow." Jake flipped the slide. "Both methods yield valuations far above your current level. You'll notice our base-case assumptions are conservative. Exhibit C is a sensitivity analysis showing the acquisition would increase shareholder value under all but the most pessimistic scenario." Yet another slide. "We also looked at the impact on REK's credit-risk profile. Look at your key leverage and cash-flow ratios. We anticipate a debt-rating upgrade from Standard & Poor's and Moody's. So not only would you narrow the strategic and valuation gap with Carnival and Royal, but you'd become more creditworthy."

Julian rose. "Thank you. This is excellent, but let's take a break before looking at the second acquisition."

"Sounds great," Leo said.

Carlos smiled. "I peeked. Looks like an entirely different animal."

"That it is. The ultraluxury niche and outside Asia."

Leo pressed the hands-free button. His mentor only seemed to call when he was speeding on I-595. "Good morning, Bill."

"Well, it's done. The evidence you sent me is with my buddy at ICE. Bernardo's days in the U.S. are numbered."

"You sure?" It was hard not to cheer.

"Absolutely. This country isn't high on illegals or dealers. Deportation is the best he can hope for."

Leo smiled. "Fantastic. I owe you."

"What else is new?" Bill guffawed. "So how was your trip to Venezuela—aside from playing private eye?"

"Eventful. Part amazing, part bad."

"Start with the bad."

Leo swerved to avoid a slowpoke. "I fell off a horse. I was probably the only sober man in Venezuela to manage that."

"No shit. You need to visit my ranch."

"I do."

"So what was the amazing part?"

Leo flipped the sun visor down. "I've been wanting to get my family out of Venezuela. So I spoke to this immigration lawyer in New York. On my trip we learned they'll qualify for asylum. Awesome, right?"

The telephone line fell silent. "You there, Bill?"

"Sure am." His tone was peculiar. "You do remember it was me who got you out of Venezuela?"

"Of course, I remember. . . . Oh, shit!"

"Some nerve," Bill said. "I'm good enough to get you out but not your family? You hand the business to a stranger when I offer the same services?"

"I'm really sorry! You're one hundred percent right. It slipped my mind."

"Yeah, right."

"I can't explain it. I feel terrible."

Bill huffed. "A lot of good that does me."

"I'll make it up to you."

A pregnant pause. "Well, maybe you can. How did your meeting with the cruise line go?"

"Fine."

"Did you pitch your acquisition targets?"

Leo's hand tightened on the wheel. "We did."

"Will they be acquiring them?"

"Not sure yet."

"Well, let me know—*soon*. Gotta run."

49

CORINDA TWOFER

reensboro, North Carolina, February 2017. Kiara forced herself
to smile politely at the triumvirate of inquisitors facing her.
Sitting there, they seemed as nondescript as the municipal
building they worked in. If only her case were so bland. But the North
Carolina Board of Psychology didn't convene for routine matters.

The head of the Probable Cause Committee whispered to the psychologist who had researched the case. The investigator excused herself,
as the third committee member pulled out his agenda and flipped
through it. More wasted time.

She had never liked Greensboro—too much concrete, too commercial, and devoid of character. Yes, it had stunning neighborhoods
and hosted the PGA and ACC basketball tournaments, but "Greensboring's" best attribute was being close to Chapel Hill. Maybe she'd
been soured by the city's civil rights history—the 1960 Woolworth
lunch counter sit-ins and the 1979 Greensboro massacre. Race relations had certainly improved since Klansmen killed five Communist
Party members who were rallying in favor of Black textile workers
but not nearly as much as in, say, Charlotte, where savvy leaders had

expanded opportunities for minorities. Bottom line, aside from giving guest lectures at UNC-G and attending Springsteen and Police concerts as an undergrad, she'd had little to do with the city. Today's proceedings weren't likely to change her opinion.

Once the investigator returned, the director led off, "Dr. Battle, I think it's fair to say we're perplexed by your request for a meeting, under the circumstances."

"How so, Doctor?" She probably should have memorized their surnames.

"As I understand it, when Dr. Neal detailed the allegations in her letter dated March 24, you responded saying the charges were accurate. Do you still believe that?"

"Yes."

"And you admitted to behaving unprofessionally during two counseling sessions with Mrs. Murphy?"

"Correct."

The director perused the report. "And without recounting the specifics of your demeaning comments, you understand they were in clear violation of Section 3.03, Harassment, of the Ethics Code?"

"I do."

He frowned. "And you admit to going out on a date with Mrs. Murphy's husband, the father of your patient?"

"Yes."

"And you understand that dating Mr. Murphy violated Section 3.05, Multiple Relationships, of the same code?"

"Yes, Doctor."

"Then what else would you like to add?"

"Some details that will provide context." She sighed. "First, Mr. Murphy told me that his wife had asked for a divorce; there was no chance they'd reconcile. I know I still shouldn't have gone. Second, our date lasted one drink, one hour, *tops*. There was no physical or emotional intimacy and never will be. Any implications to the contrary are one hundred percent false. I'm sure Dr. Neal verified that."

Dr. Neal nodded.

"It was a huge mistake, and it's not one I'm ever going to repeat."

"Is there anything *else* you'd like to say?" the elderly board member asked. He seemed to sense there was more.

Kiara exhaled deeply. "I've thought about my strengths and weaknesses. I've concluded I should limit my dealings to two patient groups—kids with learning disabilities and disadvantaged kids. I'm uniquely positioned to help them. I'm less suited to dealing with other patients, who deserve more empathy and respect than I've shown. If I'm allowed to resume practicing, I'll target these underserved groups."

Ninety minutes later Kiara pulled into her driveway and heard the ping of an incoming text.

Sarah: How'd it go?

Kiara: Okay. I'll find out next week. I'm guessing one-year suspension.

Sarah: That sucks! Next time try a robot ☺

Kiara: Pervert! That's NOT what it was about.

Sarah: Okay, lonely heart. Gotta go.

Kiara went inside, grabbed an Ultra, and plopped on the couch. She turned on the Classical Masterpieces channel. The soothing strains of "Capricho Árabe" took some of the edge off. But not all. *Where does a nonbeliever shrink go for solace when her best friend and Segovia aren't delivering?*

To the Jesus freak, of course. Would her mom respond reflexively—invoking the Lord and reciting scripture—or would she offer pragmatic recommendations with a spiritual twist, as she sometimes did? Kiara muted the television and pressed speed dial. When Corinda answered, Kiara brought her up to date.

"What *always* helps you when you're depressed?" her mother asked.

"If I knew that, I wouldn't be calling."

"Come on—you need to think. When are you happiest? It's not a trick question."

It wasn't. Helping others helps yourself, her mom had taught her. Sarah had called it the Corinda twofer.

"Love you, Mom. You're the best. Say hi to Pops."

Three days later Kiara was sitting opposite Ruth, her longtime mentor and friend. Ruth leaned forward and patted Kiara on the knee. "Enough about me. You look sad today, and it's not because of my problems."

Kiara looked about Ruth's living room and grinned.

"What's going on? I might be able to help," Ruth said. "In fact, I'll bet you came here to let me help you—and thereby help myself."

Kiara chuckled. "Can't pull one over on you."

"Not even with my rotting brain. So out with it!"

Outwardly, Ruth seemed little changed apart from her graying hair. She still flashed that winning smile. She peered with searing intelligence. She looked fit. Her posture was ramrod straight.

But everything had changed. Ruth no longer taught or consulted, and she'd relinquished the chairmanship of Ellevate under duress. Quite a downshift. Years ago, Bob Jeffreys had invited Ruth to speak to his team as one of the rare figures who'd conquered the worlds of business and academia. The whole team had attended Ellevate's enlightening panel discussion, and they'd been offered membership in its network of 135,000 professional women. Kiara had never followed through—too busy. She and Ruth had only reconnected when Kiara took her business course as an elective. Much later, after becoming friends, Kiara had learned Zeb was her son.

Kiara sat back on the sofa. "I got suspended for a year. I insulted the mother of a patient and then dated her estranged husband. There was no romance or sex, but it was colossally bad judgment. I let loneliness get the better of me."

"Ooh, that is bad. But you're human. Early on I had some rough years with Larry, and, under the wrong circumstances, I might easily have gone astray myself. . . . So aside from not dating patients' fathers, what else did you learn?"

"That I hate counseling adults," Kiara said, exhaling deeply. "I need to focus on LD and disadvantaged youth."

"Is that the best you can do?" Ruth looked disappointed. "You're rearranging chairs on the *Titanic*. Sorry to be so blunt, but what do you expect from a half-demented woman like me?"

"Not sure I follow." Kiara ignored the d-word.

"It's not complicated, Kiara. You pinpointed the problem yourself: loneliness. You need to focus on your personal life. Find a soul mate."

"Oh, that."

"Yeah, that."

"Just snap my fingers, and Prince Charming will appear."

Ruth's eyes twinkled. "Let me tell you, he'd come running—from the five hundred block of Rosemary Street, to be precise."

Kiara winced. "I can't risk it. Zeb's my closest friend on the planet."

"There are worse things."

"Look, I've really got to run." Kiara squeezed Ruth's hand. Two interrogations in one day were more than she could handle. "Let's do this again—soon."

"Better be. I'll be drooling in my soup before long." Her words were grim, but Ruth was grinning, clearly invigorated.

Kiara left with a bounce in her step.

50

YARDSTICK

Chapel Hill, North Carolina, March 2017. Zeb hadn't a clue as to why he was attending graduation. He hadn't taught the special-needs class in eight years, Wednesday afternoons were inconvenient, and he had declined Rabbi's invitation. Yet here he sat among excited families chitchatting in hushed tones. He had to admit: The temple sanctuary had a good vibe.

Rabbi spotted him from the *bima* and scurried over. Placing his hand on Zeb's shoulder, he said, "It's wonderful to see you."

Zeb rose to shake his hand. "You too, Rabbi."

"I saved you the chair next to me. You'll be handing me the diplomas."

Zeb grinned. *Who is he, Yoda?* "It would be my honor."

Rabbi began the ceremony by congratulating the students in a heartfelt manner. He honored their achievements, thanking the parents for their support. The religious school director followed with administrative announcements. "Pomp and Circumstance" played, as Rabbi Norman took center stage, beaming and rocking his head.

He called the name of the first graduate. Rachel and her parents approached the *bima* to receive hugs, kisses, and a handshake. Rabbi spoke of how deeply moved he was by Rachel's resilience and generosity of spirit. She had undertaken her project to clothe the poor with great energy, continuing long after the prescribed time period. Rabbi wrapped his arms around the huddled family, blessing them. He urged Rachel to continue along her Jewish path, reminding her that Temple would always be home. When he handed her the diploma, Rachel squeezed him as if she would never let go. When they returned to their seats, the music resumed until the next family reached the *bima*.

Standing by Rabbi's side, Zeb could feel the affection and devotion. A man who loved so genuinely received tons of love in return. *He is one lucky man.*

But it wasn't luck, was it? Rabbi had earned his reward. He gave so much to Chapel Hill—not just to Jews—and did so quietly, never calling attention to himself. Making others happy made him happy. No matter that he drove a Corolla and lived in an ordinary house. He was a winner if ever there was one.

"Jeez, what the hell is going on out there?" It sounded like five lacrosse players were jumping up and down on the metal staircase.

"Not sure," Teresa said. "I'll take a look."

A burly man was lugging a dolly with three large boxes.

"It looks like a delivery," she said. "Are you expecting something? I didn't order any supplies."

Zeb approached the foyer. "Nope."

Teresa opened the door for the perspiring deliveryman.

"Thank you, ma'am," he said breathlessly. "I sure hope this is International Expeditions. These cases weigh a ton!"

"Cases of what?" Zeb asked.

"I have no idea, sir."

Teresa checked the return address. "What the . . . it's from Jabulani."

"South Africa Inbound?"

She shot him a look. "How many Jabulanis do you know?"

"Looks like wine," Zeb said. "I wonder why?"

"Beats me."

Teresa tackled the boxes. Ten minutes later she popped into Zeb's office. "You got a second?"

"For booze, always."

"Not just any booze. Jabulani sent the best of the best. I checked it out online. One case is Leeuwenkuil Heritage Syrah 2015. It won the International Judge's Prize for the best overall red wine at South Africa's premier wine competition."

He whistled. "Awesome."

"The second is Spier 21 Gables, a Chenin Blanc 2016 that won the best overall white wine."

"Cool. The third?"

"Rustenberg Peter Barlow 2015. The Best Cabernet Sauvignon."

"Any note?"

Teresa handed him a sealed envelope. Zeb opened it and read aloud:

My Dear Friend Zeb,

I hope this letter finds you healthy and in good "spirits!"

Please accept this wine as a gesture of appreciation for everything you have done.

When you brought us on as your South Africa operator, you had no need to promote Natal. You had enough business in Cape Town and Kruger that you didn't have to take on new risks. There was no existing demand for Zulu culture among American travelers. And when you did commit to Natal, you could have chosen any number of larger, White-owned operators instead of my unproven services. But you trusted me. That in itself was a blessing that validated my services and boosted my confidence.

For you then to invest so much money promoting my home province, and to send so many travelers to us over the last seven years, was something I could never have dreamed of. Thanks to you, I can now afford to send Nandi, my eldest, to university in London. She will study medicine and return to help our community. And if things continue, Lwazi will be following in his sister's footsteps. Never in my wildest dreams could I have imagined this good fortune!

Your support has given my family a bright future. And I can now offer higher wages and better benefits to my employees. Please toast yourself and Teresa with some South African wine!

Forever grateful,
Jabulani

Zeb wiped away a tear.

Teresa smiled. "You feeling less unworthy about peddling tours for a living? It's about time. You're quite the savior."

"Yeah, yeah. Academia's loss was the Third World's gain."

"The only thing I want to gain is a buzz! Which of these suckers do we uncork first?"

Most eighty-one-year-olds would have taken it easy, especially if they were already set financially. Pearl Burnett was having none of that. She'd worked hard all her life and wasn't ready to spend the rest of it watching *Dr. Phil* or playing canasta. But her priorities had shifted. With her children and grandkids taken care of, she could turn to making Chapel Hill work for all its people. She cherished her hometown, but, even now, some folks were still being left behind. The Rainbow Dinner, which brought together people of all races and religions, was her contribution. The year's event needed to be perfect, like the twelve that had preceded it. She had forty minutes to tie up loose ends. No sweat—not for her.

Pearl had been pulling things together since she was a little girl on a sharecropper's farm. She was so good at cooking that, when her mother died, her dad gave her free rein over the kitchen. She used ingredients that grew out back or nearby. Her talent led to a succession of jobs. She worked for two White families and a restaurant before landing a job as chef at a UNC fraternity. Working long hours, Pearl became a surrogate mother and big sister to several of the brothers, keeping them in line whenever they tried to sleep through classes or hang around the wrong people. Several times Pearl intervened to help "her boys" escape trouble from the police or their own parents. She saw no irony in bailing out pampered White boys. She helped whoever needed it.

After ten years, Pearl moved on, opening her first diner, Pearl's on Rosemary. On her first day, she had $45 to buy ingredients for breakfast and $28 to make change. She earned enough money at breakfast to buy ingredients for lunch, using lunch profits to buy ingredients for dinner. At closing time, she had $145. Many students, including Michael Jordan, James Worthy, and many of "her" fraternity boys, devoured her country biscuits, fried chicken, and pies regularly enough to boost their cholesterol count.

Over time her business sense, culinary talent, and work ethic propelled her to the front line of Triangle-area restaurant owners. Within fourteen years, she owned restaurants in Raleigh, Durham, and Chapel Hill. Along the way, she married and divorced an abusive leech. Pearl hired children, grandchildren, and people down on their luck, including former prison inmates and substance abusers. One of the fraternity brothers did a story on Pearl for his hit network series, *NC Revealed*. Prominent food critics dined at her restaurants, invariably leaving impressed. *Good Morning America* and television food shows booked her. President George W. Bush invited Pearl to the White House. UNC Press published her recipe book. Sociology professors interviewed her for the Southern Historical Collection. The sharecropper's daughter was a quasi-celebrity.

Pearl wondered how the event would go. With Zeb's contribution, it could be a big deal. She suddenly felt an adrenaline rush. It would easily carry her through the next four hours.

Guests of all conceivable stripes arrived at McDougle School. They milled about, sipping on cocktails and listening to the jazz quartet. When it was time to eat, guests were encouraged to "sit down with a stranger and leave with a friend!" They feasted on a smorgasbord of Southern, Latin American, Chinese, Thai, and Italian dishes, donated by numerous restaurants and organizations. They were regaled by the Spirit of Praise Choir, an Afro-Peruvian dance troop, Paperhand Puppet Intervention, Diversity Strings, Hong Yan Choir, and the Seventh-Day Adventist Church Choir.

Pearl took the microphone and thanked everyone. "In all these years, we've never pushed an agenda," she began. "The only thing we've wanted was for people to know, understand, and love each other more. This year I'm breaking my rule. I hope you'll agree it's for a good reason." A few encouraging murmurs.

"Last year a dear friend of mine, Zeb, came to me with this ridiculous idea. I needed to get my DNA tested, he said, to find out where in Africa my family came from and then go visit. Now don't get me wrong—I love Zeb—but I thought to myself, 'This is one crazy White boy!'" The guests hooted. "I wondered if he'd been smoking weed or needed more travel business. Just kidding—he's doing great."

She scanned the audience. They seemed engaged. "Anyhow, Zeb told me about how his temple had done a DNA study of its members. Many ended up traveling to Eastern Europe to see the towns, synagogues, and graves of their ancestors. They also visited concentration camps. They came back deeply affected. They learned what their ancestors had gone through and how strong they were. They felt pride, more tied to their people."

Pearl wiped perspiration from her brow. "I decided that's what I wanted for my family. I was always proud of my African heritage, but other than going to church and celebrating Kwanzaa, I never thought about it much. I was too busy putting food on the table and raising my kids. Anyway, I took the DNA test and learned my ancestors were from the Akan tribe. They're from Ghana and the Ivory Coast. So that's where we went. And I'm telling you"—she nodded slowly—"it changed our lives." Cheers broke out, and she felt chills.

"My grandkids, especially, felt a pride they never had before. That will carry them a long way. Tonight I'm going to show slides from my trip. Why? Because I'm hoping everyone digs into their own backgrounds, whatever they are. But first, Zeb, I want to thank you from the bottom of my heart." Tears filled her eyes.

Zeb tapped his heart and blew Pearl a kiss. Kiara leaned over and kissed him on the cheek.

After the slide show the attendees peppered Pearl with questions. She concluded by announcing that Zeb would gladly arrange genealogy tours "at cost" for anyone who was interested. Pearl was still embracing Zeb long after the standing ovation ended.

51

JELLYBEANS

*F*ort Lauderdale, Florida, March 2017. Leo sat opposite Dr. Rubin, admiring the magic-marker children's drawings that adorned the office walls. In front of him, on the table that separated them, lay a humongous jar of jellybeans. Framed diplomas from UVA and Harvard hung in the corner, providing reasonable assurance that the psychologist could minister to the needs of adults, as well as children. He had not chosen unwisely.

Still, after two sessions—120 minutes in all—it was time to get a move on. Dr. Rubin's open-ended questions had elicited rambling responses, and the exercise seemed directionless. Why couldn't he be more targeted, especially after receiving two pages of self-assessment notes? These consultations weren't cheap. Time for doc to prove his shrinking chops.

"Do you mind if I offer some impressions?" Dr. Rubin said.

"Please."

"I'll start by addressing the questions you posed. Do I think, as a clinician, that you might have some kind of social anxiety disorder?

No, not from what you've told me here. From what I can see, you seem to be experiencing some of the physical and emotional symptoms of trauma, which can look a lot like social anxiety. You may avoid some common social situations because of this. But no, I don't think you have social anxiety."

"I see."

"Second, you're wondering if you are a 'closet homosexual,' as you put it."

"In reality, I've got nothing against gays."

"That's not really the point, though, Leo. You clearly have something against *yourself*. You are fixated on whether your demeanor is too refined, if your physique is too trim—you worry a lot about your dislike of 'manly' things like getting drunk, chasing women, and most sports." Here, the doctor paused. "You wonder if you might somehow have unintentionally invited those men to assault you."

"And?"

"I think these worries you have about your masculinity are all deeply rooted in inaccurate stereotypes about what it means to be a gay man." Dr. Rubin paused again, gauging Leo's response. "And I always want to leave the door open for you to tell me who you are and to define your sexuality on your own terms. But, for better or worse, no, Leo, I don't think you're gay." Leo shifted in his seat, uncomfortable. Dr. Rubin let the moment pass without pressing on just yet. When the therapist judged the moment was right, he offered his final insight: "But regardless, no sexual orientation is an invitation to or justification for rape."

Leo's face was anguished. "Then what's the matter with me?"

"Not a lot, honestly. You're just extra shy," the doctor said simply. "It may occasionally pose problems for you, sure, but there's nothing *wrong* with you. My colleague, Dr. Murray Stein, says the world needs more people who are quiet, thoughtful, and introspective. People who don't shoot off their mouths first and ask questions later. I think he's right."

"If I'm so shy, why did everyone think I was arrogant?"

"Those traits aren't mutually exclusive. Most likely, you were shy as a child because your tastes, interests, and manner weren't popular in the culture in which you lived. There were few social rewards for someone with your mentality. You didn't have many friends, which exacerbated your shyness. The important thing to know is that the assault you suffered wasn't something you invited or deserved in any way. It was the violent act of someone with very serious problems, and the fact that you were put through this experience is a matter of extreme bad luck and nothing else. And you prevailed. You are now free to thrive and be happy."

"But I'm arrogant."

"Maybe a touch. Early on, it might have been a useful defense mechanism. If you fostered a superiority complex, it protected you from the teasing you were experiencing all the time."

"And later?"

"Later your surplus of confidence, shall we say, was earned. You accomplished a hell of a lot, professionally and even socially—and as an immigrant, no less. Hats off to you."

"I have UNC to thank."

"And your parents. But remember, you're still a bit shy. If you're happy in your cocoon, then great. It's only a problem if you aren't enjoying life. In that case, we can work on it. Otherwise, I wouldn't worry."

"What about my relationships with women? Can I change those?"

"That will take time and more work, but, yes," Dr. Rubin said. "It's possible now because you've learned that there's nothing wrong with you. The assault was random, unrelated to who you are as a person. You've got nothing to prove to yourself or anyone else. That should help shift how you approach your interactions with women and what you're actually hoping to get out of them."

"That's great, doc, but I still want to work on my shyness."

"Fair enough. For now, have a jellybean."

52

PERSPECTIVE

hapel Hill, North Carolina, March 2017. The receptionist at the UNC Rehabilitation Clinic smiled and waved Zeb through while speaking into her headset. He strolled to the physical therapy wing, where Hannah was busy with a patient. He waited outside, looking in.

He had never tired of watching her ply her trade—not as a patient, spouse, or ex. She shined, her self-assured manner making her even cuter. People bloomed with praise, shrunk with criticism. He had once acted on that knowledge, penning an effusive letter to the clinic director upon his own discharge. One thing led to another and—

Why had he stopped praising her? Somehow, he'd lost respect for her. As he obsessed over International Expeditions, Hannah's life and career goals had been subsumed by his. She refused to complain as he mismanaged his business and neglected their marriage. She accepted his foibles. How he had wished she would have just blown her top. Anything to prove she wasn't a doormat.

Hannah's patient was atop the treatment table on all fours. She placed a broomstick-handle across his lower back. When he extended his left arm and right leg in tandem, the pole fell to the floor. She showed him how to stabilize his hips. Next time, the patient completed six reps before dislodging the pole. She replaced it and had him start anew.

Hannah had paid a huge price for his disrespect. Marrying outside her religion had earned her the scorn of her family. She had sacrificed having children because they'd been unable to feed more than two mouths. After the divorce her family had shunned her for failing to hold the marriage together and—he suspected—for the embarrassment that failure had caused them. Hannah's position at the clinic was lower than it would have been, and Zeb knew it.

It had taken strength, not weakness, for Hannah to stand by him. How hard it must have been to keep her mouth shut, even when she knew he was wrong. His chest ached.

Hannah ripped off the disposable table paper and replaced it with a new sheet. Spotting him, she left the treatment room.

"You got a minute?" Zeb said.

"Barely." She led him to a vacant room. "What's up?"

Zeb handed her an envelope. "It's the fifteenth. Thought you might need this."

"Oh, thanks." Hannah's face flushed. "If you're in a bind, I can—"

He usually transferred the funds. "Not at all—things are great. Is the clinic ever going to bring you on full-time?"

"I doubt it." She sat, inviting him to do the same. "There are PT grads every year, so the clinic holds all the cards. No need to pay up for an old fogie."

"Old at forty-one? You can run circles around newbies."

She smiled. "I'm guessing you didn't come here to give me a pep talk."

"I'm not sure how to say this." He rubbed his neck. "I know I'm years late, but I just want to apologize. For everything."

"That's long gone, Zeb. I've moved on. Anyway, you already apologized."

"Not the right way. I need to do it right—if not for your sake, then mine."

Hannah rolled her eyes. "What is it, Yom Kippur? All right, start groveling."

Zeb recited the litany of wrongs he had committed, sparing nothing. They stemmed, he said, from his arrogance and insecurity. He should have let her help with the business as she had begged to do. When Zeb finished, he waited expectantly.

"Look, I'm not sure what you want from me." She sighed. "Yes, I'll accept your apology. And I'm glad you figured everything out."

"I appreciate that, more than you know."

"We just need to fix our lives," Hannah said tenderly. "Make something good out of them."

"Here's the thing. I think yesterday set me on my way. It was like God was hitting me over the head with life lessons."

"What do you mean?"

Zeb described the graduation ceremony. "I've never seen anything like it. Everyone was in tears. And it wasn't just a passing moment. There was deep gratitude on both sides. You could tell Rabbi felt as blessed as the families. I've had the wrong yardstick all along."

"I wish I'd been there." She checked her watch. "Anything else?"

"I learned yesterday—twice in fact—that there's more to what we do than peddling tours."

"No joke—I could've told you that. You've never been a Mongo."

Zeb winced, remembering the *Blazing Saddles* character who was buffeted throughout life. "Our Zulu operator was able to send his kids to university in London."

"That's awesome. I'm proud of you."

"Then there's Pearl Burnett."

"Pearl?" Hannah perked up. "How's she doing? I love that lady."

"You love everyone. She's doing great. We sent her family on a genealogy tour of West Africa, and it really helped them. She did a slide show at the Rainbow Dinner. Now she's telling everyone to explore their past."

"Too bad you aren't following her advice."

He gave her a quizzical look.

"Blowing off your parents' tour of Israel and Morocco." She shook her head. "Look, if you've had this epiphany, great. But make sure it's not just words. No one likes a hypocrite."

"Ouch! You're way more outspoken than you used to be."

"That works better for me now. Besides, you didn't used to take it gracefully." She winked and rose to her feet. "Gotta go. Thanks for the moola."

53

TIKKUN OLAM

*C*hapel Hill, North Carolina, March 2017. The mellifluous strains of Bach's "English Suite No. 6" filled Memorial Hall. Kiara snuck another peek to her side. Amazingly Zeb was still transfixed, his unwavering smile suggesting serenity. Sir András Schiff had tamed the hyperactive beast. For Zeb to have lasted past intermission was a miracle. With a smile of her own, she returned to soaking in the virtuosity of the Hungarian pianist, one of the all-time greats.

Kiara nudged Zeb, as they exited the historic theater. He twitched. "What? Did I screw up, clap at the wrong time?"

"No, I wanted to commend you."

"For what?"

"Not snoring."

He huffed, feigning hurt, while she giggled. The night air was pleasant, as they headed to 411 West Italian Cafe. She ordered the bruschetta and seafood linguine, Zeb the gnocchi and wood-grilled salmon. Both sipped pinot grigio.

"Look, I appreciate all this, but there really was no need," Kiara said.

"It's the least I can do. Hell, five teams followed Bob Jeffreys's lead. We're handling the travel arrangements for all of them, thanks to you."

"That's what friends do."

Zeb winced, and she felt as if she'd slapped a Labrador. Apparently, crushes didn't die easily. Or maybe it was something else. "You sure there's nothing else to all this?" she asked suspiciously.

"Jeez, can't hide anything from you shrinks."

"Technically, I'm not practicing anymore. . . . Oh, is *that* why we're here? You're checking up on me."

"I was worried."

Kiara relaxed. "Look, I'm fine. Next topic."

He nodded as they served themselves bruschetta. "Can I at least ask you about your profession? There are things I've always wondered about."

"Shoot."

"Cool. Do shrinks always analyze everyone around them—like family, friends?"

Kiara grinned. "We do tend to notice things and infer. Even as a girl, I watched people constantly—how they dressed, walked, spoke, behaved. I looked for patterns: this person is a policeman; that one's a doctor. It's more of a natural ability than a learned skill. But I try to bite my tongue when I'm not working."

"Whew! Are you as good at analyzing yourself as other people?"

"Not according to Bob Jeffreys. Many psychologists understand themselves quite well, but I'm still working on it. My peers and supervisors helped me with their feedback during training. We were held accountable, which forced me to be more introspective."

Zeb nodded. "How hard is it to disconnect from your cases after hours?"

"Not hard. I don't work in hematology or oncology, so I don't see life-and-death situations. I deal with kids. There's always something else to try if a particular approach isn't working."

"Sounds like a good gig."

"I can't complain. And my colleagues are more down-to-earth than physicians."

The waiter served the entrées.

"So how are you handling all your free time?" Zeb asked.

He was impossible. "You're counting on seafood linguine to keep me from walking out."

Zeb snickered.

"I'm fine, seriously," she said. "In fact, it's liberating. I work out more, hang out with your mom, and I'm auditing Mandarin and Comparative Literature."

"The world is your oyster." He raised his wineglass to hers. "You're handling expulsion way better than I did."

"I'm way older than you were. So how'd you come up with András Schiff?"

"I didn't. It came from Teresa; she thinks of most of my good ideas. She and her mom saw him years ago."

"If she was a shrink, I'd steal her from you."

"If she was a shrink, she wouldn't have so many good ideas."

Zeb seemed different these days—more confident, less cocky. Women would like that. He deserved the best.

"How are things going with Marcus?" he asked.

"So-so. He says he's finally okay with me quitting soccer, but we're still working through our issues. His listening to Rush Limbaugh doesn't help. What else? I did a consulting project for Bob. It went well, but I'll be ready to move on once my suspension is over."

Zeb raised his eyebrows. "What's wrong with what you're doing?"

"Nothing, but it's too ad hoc. Plus, it's a drop in the bucket compared to what's needed."

"What, one mind at a time isn't enough?"

Kiara gasped. "You realize *A Mind at a Time* was my bible! It's why I gave up medicine."

"Great minds," he said, beaming. "You were saying?"

"So here's the deal." She set down her wine. "I love working with special-needs kids. But I keep thinking back to Rwanda. I counseled traumatized patients and worked directly with LD students, but my biggest contribution, I'm sure, was training psychologists to diagnose and treat better. Helping them become self-sufficient."

He frowned. "You want to train psychologists?"

"No. Very few students have their learning style assessed by a psychologist. I want to train *teachers* to do a better job of assessing and teaching to individual learning styles. That way we can keep kids from falling through the cracks."

Zeb whistled. "Jeez, that's a tall order, expecting teachers to do all that."

"You're right. Differentiated teaching takes a while to master, and lesson planning takes longer. But most teachers can handle it if they're trained well and mentored."

"I guess you'd be helping way more kids by training them instead of individual students."

"Exactly."

Zeb twirled the pasta around his fork. "Wouldn't you miss dealing with the kids one-on-one? They're basically the only people who don't annoy you."

She slapped his shoulder playfully. "It would be worth it."

"But, seriously, can you avoid getting pissed off at teachers? Parents weren't your strong point."

"Which is the reason we're sitting here," she said. "I'd have to control myself. The board will kick me out for good next time."

"How will you even train these armies of teachers?"

She leaned forward. "Dr. Mel Levine, the guy who wrote *A Mind at a Time*, founded this institute called All Kinds of Minds. It analyzes learning differences and provides counseling. They're great at helping kids with severe learning problems. They used to train teachers, but that effort fell off. I'd like to reinvigorate it."

"Wait a minute! Wasn't Levine the guy who molested kids and committed suicide?"

"That's right." She sighed deeply. "On the one hand, he was a genius who helped countless kids with his revolutionary diagnostic methodology that was incredibly humane compared to the standards of the time. His research showed that kids who were deemed lazy by society weren't in fact lazy at all and that many kids who couldn't read didn't have a low IQ. But it's also true that he was a sick predator who deserved worse than to die by his own hand."

Zeb grimaced. "You wouldn't mind being associated with that evil?"

"The institute disassociated themselves from Levine back in 2008. They continue to do important work, so why throw the baby out with the bathwater? His victims paid a humongous price. Why not ensure that their suffering helps others?"

"Fixing the world, huh?"

"*Tikkun olam*," she said.

"Preparing to become my bride, I see." He grinned. "That's music to my ears."

"Bach's 'English Suite No. 6,' to be precise."

"In D minor, to be *more* precise."

54

FRUITION

Chapel Hill, North Carolina, March 2017. Zeb grabbed two Yuenglings from the fridge and returned to his sparsely furnished living room. Abigay was focused on the framed photograph in her hands. Twenty years had passed since he had tried to chat her up in Islamorada, but the Bahamian woman still captivated him. She was whip smart, with a track athlete's body and wavy black hair.

Abigay set down the picture. "You have a thing for Black women?"

"She's my best friend. That was taken after a training session. A few weeks before I met you in Islamorada. You and Kiara, the lucky two."

"Absolutely."

Zeb remembered tossing Abigay's business card into the Gulf of Mexico all those years ago. This encounter promised a better outcome, regardless of whether she stayed over or not. He turned on Netflix and navigated to *Luther*. "Too bad I'm up against Idris Elba. I'm not sure I like my odds."

"Oh, you mustn't give up," she said, sounding so Commonwealth. "If there's no fifth season, I'll have no choice but to fall in your arms!"

He beamed. "From your lips to God's ears."

"Honestly, I'm impressed you watch this stuff."

He brought a plate of cheese and pâté from the kitchen. "Hey, Bahamians aren't the only former colonials."

"True, but you take Anglophile to a whole new level," Abigay said. They had compared notes on *Foyle's War*, *Endeavour*, *Inspector Morse*, and *Shetland*.

"Which should lead you to one inescapable conclusion: I'm the refined hunk of a man you've been searching for all your adult life."

Abigay laughed. "Actually, you're not far off. But let's not risk messing up what we've accomplished." She rose. "Call of nature."

Abigay's take on the last two decades had been enlightening. Moonshine, who still ran Carousel, had instructed her to monitor his progress. They would revisit his Fast-Forward Adventures proposal if he proved himself. Abigay had stayed abreast of developments through Google Alerts and internet research. More recently, they'd seen his press releases on National Geographic Expeditions, UNC Alumni Travel, and the Florida Museum of Natural History. Moonshine had finally agreed it was time.

Not that they didn't still have concerns. How would a company specializing in historical and genealogy tours promote Jackson Duvall–themed tours? Would the differences in content and mentality make focus and execution difficult? Did he have enough staff? The right type of staff? A botched foray into travel could damage Duvall's brand.

Thankfully, his idea of dividing the business into two divisions, International Expeditions and Fast-Forward Adventures, had eased their concerns. Zeb had thought through enough details, and proposed enough solutions, to inspire confidence. The licensing agreement they'd signed was huge. The "Samba Queen" and a newly developed "Crossed Spears" tour would be up and running in Brazil and East Africa. Carousel's formidable marketing arm would lend its support.

"You're right," Zeb said, when Abigay returned. "Friends *is* better. That way I can crash at your pad on my next trip to Key West."

"Always playing the angles."

They listened to the *Luther* theme song, "Paradise Circus," sitting transfixed until their hero bagged the villain. Then they headed to the Dead Mule Club, where bartender Sam mixed tasty margaritas and explained that the litmus test for Southern literature was the inclusion of a dead mule. They toasted the late Jerry Mills, UNC English professor and founder of the club. Zeb dropped Abigay off at the Carolina Inn, promising to visit her in Key West by year's end—to treat her to a grouper sandwich and the winning box turtle at Turtle Kraals.

55

TEAM PLAYER

harlotte, North Carolina, March 2017. Sitting outside Mr. Renfro's office at the Bank of America headquarters, tapping his shoes, Leo felt like a schoolboy waiting to be handed back an exam he knew he'd aced. Last year had been a crazy one—the home-run REK deal had been followed by a string of doubles and triples. No wonder the performance reviews had been delayed. *Will my portfolio grow? How big will the bonus be?*

The managing director invited him in and got right to business. "First things first: REK was a blockbuster deal, obviously. Being lead underwriter on their bond and equity offerings, and advising on their acquisition, catapulted us up the league tables. Your team generated huge fees and established us as their key financial advisor. It couldn't have gone better."

"Thank you, sir."

"We normally hold bonus checks until next month."

"I understand." Leo's excitement mounted.

"However, circumstances warrant breaking that tradition."

"Yes, sir."

Renfro handed him an envelope. "Inside there's a bonus check for $240,000."

Leo's jaw dropped. "My gosh, sir. Thank you so much!"

"Don't thank me. And I mean that." His boss's expression was grave.

"Of course, sir. I've already thanked Jake and the others, but I'll thank them again. It was truly a team effort."

Mr. Renfro looked like he'd been served a plate of broccoli. "Leo, I received some repugnant news. It came to me through a couple of credible channels, including HR. They're saying you had intimate relations with your analyst's girlfriend. Is that true?"

Leo gasped. He felt like Mike Tyson had slugged him in the gut. Blood rushed to his head. "Um . . . I . . . yes, sir, it's true. I'm deeply ashamed."

"You should be. If I had my way, your bonus would be zero, *nada*. There's no room for sleazy behavior here, no matter how talented you are, no matter the fees you generate." Renfro was breathing audibly. "You spoke of the team, but you've made a mockery of the very idea."

"I'm not sure what to say. I'm—"

"Now I was overruled on your bonus. The attorneys figured it was better to pay you. But there's one area where I couldn't be overruled. You'll find a pink slip along with your bonus check. Today's your last day, Leo. You can no longer access the bank's computer files."

Leo turned ashen.

"It was your own doing, son."

"I know, sir."

"Anything else?"

Leo exhaled deeply. "Just that I understand. I deserve it, and I'm truly sorry. I hope Jake's work will be recognized. He played a huge role in our wins." Leo's voice thickened. "I promise you I'll learn from this. I *will* be a better person."

"Don't promise me, Leo. Promise *yourself*. Now, if you don't mind, I have more appetizing matters to deal with."

56

SCHOOL CHOICE

hapel Hill, North Carolina, April 2017. Kiara sauntered into Four Corners and immediately had flashbacks. She'd relished so many roundball victories from these barstools. The tavern's name derived from the stall offense that Coach Dean Smith had used to close out games. Its walls were adorned with photographs of iconic moments. The largest image, taken on March 29, 1982, showed the basketball being released from Michael Jordan's fingertips with seventeen seconds left in the national championship game. The freshman's shot ended twenty-five years of frustration. Thus began a golden era when "storming Franklin Street" became a regular occurrence.

That night was epic for off-court escapades as well. Kiara still cracked up thinking about Leo's misdeeds. Living large was what *she* needed to do—without attracting the men in blue, of course. Kiara made her way to a booth where Zeb sat with a pitcher and two mugs. He hugged her and poured the beer.

"So, what's new?" Kiara asked.

"Lemme see," he said, scratching his chin teasingly. "Well, I inked a joint-venture agreement with Jackson Duvall's management company."

"Yeah, right."

Zeb nodded, his dreamy expression leaving no doubt. "For a full line of Duvall adventure tours."

Her jaw dropped. "My God, that's been your dream forever. That blows my mind." Kiara leaned across the table and squeezed his hands.

"Mine, too."

"And a *joint* venture! Hilarious."

"What do you mean?" he asked.

She winked. "The Jolly *Reefer* Band."

"Jeez." Zeb cringed. "How about you?"

"I've been busy, but nothing that glamorous. The main news is, I don't suck as bad as the bureaucrats thought."

"Really?" He feigned astonishment. "Why not?"

She slapped his arm. "Some patients from the free clinic filed a protest with the Board of Psychology. They weren't happy with my one-year suspension."

"Awesome. What did they say?"

Kiara smiled ironically. "That my services are—get this—uniquely valuable and that withholding them would compromise their children's mental health. They're insisting I be reinstated quickly or else they'll take legal action."

"Is this serious?"

"Bob Jeffreys seems to think so."

"What's he got to do with it?"

"Nothing and everything." She sipped her beer. "Without me knowing, Bob met with the board and submitted a statement attesting to my character and my record as a student-athlete and alum. Apparently, I'm stubborn as a mule and outwardly rude, but deep down—don't puke now—I have a heart of gold, and my highest aim is to help the needy. I made a colossal mistake but have learned from it. Given the sum total of my record and the needs of my patients, Bob said I deserve leniency."

"Bingo."

"Word has it the suspension will be reduced to six months." She pumped her fist.

"Fantastic! That must make you feel good."

"Even shrinks need validation."

"I hear ya." Zeb refilled their glasses with beer. "So . . . have you finally narrowed down what you're going to work on?"

She grinned. "I may have expanded it."

"How come?"

"Pops told me about Polly Williams."

"Who's she?"

"That's what I said," Kiara said, chuckling. "Polly was an important state legislator from Milwaukee. She served for thirty years, and, back in 1989, she authored America's first-ever school-choice legislation."

"Got it. Remind me about school choice."

She sighed. "As you know, public school students generally have to go to their neighborhood school. These schools mainly get funded through property taxes. This means there's a correlation between home values and the quality of the public school."

"Meaning poor folks get stuck with lousy schools."

"And it's hard to escape poverty if your school sucks, no matter how smart or hardworking you are."

"No shit." Zeb fiddled with the coaster.

"Meanwhile, families with more money can choose where to live based on the quality of the public school. Or they can send their kids to a private school."

"And Polly Williams?"

"She was African American and got tired of seeing poor Black kids get the shaft. So she worked across the aisle with the Republican governor, Tommy Thompson, and they crafted a school-choice program."

The waiter brought menus.

"And why are you so obsessed about all this?" Zeb asked. "You come from Weston, Florida. You don't exactly match the profile, even if you are Black."

Kiara frowned. "We weren't always from Weston. When my parents came to America, they lived in a poor neighborhood. Also, I had a learning disability, an auditory-processing disorder. But I was lucky. My teacher, Mrs. Foster, championed my needs early on, and, later, soccer got me into a school that could really help." She swallowed to get rid of the lump in her throat. "Most kids aren't so lucky. Poor people, recent immigrants, and special-needs kids often get shafted. That's just wrong."

"No argument there," Zeb said. "My grandparents were poor immigrants, and I have ADHD."

"Yeah, but Chapel Hill has some of the best public schools in the country."

"Doesn't mean I can't empathize. . . . You still haven't defined school choice."

"Patience, grasshopper. The basic idea is that public education money follows individual students to the schools that best fit their needs. That can mean public, private, charter, or magnet schools, home-schooling, online education, and—get this—special-needs tutoring."

Zeb gulped down his Yuengling. "Are all these options available?"

"Depends entirely on the program. Some allow parents to choose any traditional public school within their district. Other programs allow kids to go to any public school, charter school, or magnet school within their entire region. Some programs are even broader."

"What about vouchers?"

She sipped beer. "Vouchers cover private schools. Some or all of the public money set aside for the child's education goes to the parents in the form of a voucher. They can use the voucher to pay some or all of the tuition at a private school."

Zeb raised his eyebrows. "Seems to me that draining money from public schools would make them worse."

"That's a popular misconception. The voucher dollar amounts are carefully capped so that public funding per student doesn't decline. In fact, if anything, the per-student funding at the public school usually *increases* after the voucher student transfers to the private school."

He smirked. "Now that makes no sense at all."

"How about I give you an example?" she asked, leaning forward. "Say a public-school student in Durham uses a voucher to transfer to a private school. Say that Durham budgets $11,500 per public-school student. Of the $11,500, say $6,400 is the instructional cost, and $5,100 is the cost of support services—building maintenance, administration, transportation, food services, and capital expenditures. Now, if the public-school student transfers, the public school's out-of-pocket cost decreases more than $6,400—closer to $11,500. Why? Because the student consumes food services and transportation. So—"

"Jeez, that's convoluted. What you're really saying is that the voucher amount for the private school is always set lower than the public-school budget per student."

"Correct."

"Okay, so choice has been around since 1989," Zeb said. "Does it work?"

"Generally, when given enough time."

"How do you know?"

"Test scores and graduation rates have gone up; so has college enrollment. The evidence is overwhelming."

"Where hasn't it worked?"

"Louisiana." Kiara quaffed beer. "Their voucher program worked terribly because they got the regulations all wrong. They meant well but screwed them up. They made sure that only the worst private schools—the ones that were losing students and desperate for money—participated."

"How were the regulations screwed up?"

"Schools weren't allowed to charge any tuition beyond the voucher amount. They were forced to administer the Louisiana state test to students. They couldn't choose from any of the other national tests. They couldn't set admissions criteria. Voucher programs in other states also target poor students, but they have more flexibility, so good private schools participate. Not in Louisiana."

"Bummer," Zeb said. "How does school choice affect teacher pay?"

"Overall, it helps. Some teachers—the unmotivated ones, those with few skills—lose out, but salaries mostly go up."

"How come?"

Kiara smiled. "Choice brings competition. Schools have to compete for students. Schools with good teachers attract more students and generate more revenue, so they can afford to train and pay teachers more. Bad schools are incentivized to improve. Competition improves quality."

"Not, I'll bet, at the schools that lose kids to private schools."

"You'd lose that bet. Test scores actually improve at public schools that lose students."

"That blows my mind," Zeb said, whistling. "So how does all this affect your plans?"

"I'll focus on helping the disadvantaged and learning disabled."

"That's focusing?"

Kiara grinned. "I'll train teachers to assess learning disabilities and teach to individual learning styles. For the disadvantaged, I'll push school choice."

"Is there enough overlap?"

"Tons. School choice helps both groups. Special-needs kids are helped because education savings accounts are often part of school-choice programs. Parents can withdraw their special-needs kid from the public school and have public money deposited into a savings account. That money can be spent on customized learning services."

"Like what?"

"Specialized therapies, specialized private tutoring, online learning programs, community college."

"Cool. Sounds like the next wave of school choice."

"Absolutely," Kiara said.

"And how, Mother Kiara, will your work help minorities?"

Kiara snatched the coaster from Zeb's fidgeting hands. "Black and Brown kids have learning disabilities at the same rate as White kids, but they're diagnosed much less frequently. They need to be screened as early and expertly as White kids, so they don't fall through the cracks."

"Amen. You'll be working with All Kinds of Minds?"

"Yup, we worked out a deal."

"Stupendous, but with all this talk of choice, I need to look at the menu."

"Me, too."

"I'm thinking ribs and beer"—Zeb glanced at the widescreen TV—"with a Wake romp over Duke thrown in."

"The Julius Peppers are looking good to me."

"You athletes—always sticking together."

"Just like your baby backs."

57

PIÑA COLADAS

hapel Hill, North Carolina, April 2017. Zeb scurried past Teresa, but there was no chance of escaping unscathed. Not at the stroke of five, not decked out as he was. She looked as if she'd just seen a streaker and began grinning like a Cheshire cat. He felt himself flushing.

"My, my! The slacker is looking so dapper."

"I figured . . . um, uh," he stammered.

"I'm kidding, Zeb. It's not a sin to leave on time and have fun."

Zeb headed west on I-40. With any luck, he'd arrive in Charlotte in two hours—just enough time to scarf down food and make it to tango class. He set his playlist and sat back, happy to let Spotify take charge.

Things started off with Carlos Gardel and "Por Una Cabeza," the richness of his voice transcending the recording technology of the 1930s. Zeb belted out the lyrics, unconcerned with his mangling of the language. Goose bumps ran up and down his arms. He thought of his long-ago trip to Buenos Aires, when Milena Braun, the lead dancer for Rojo Tango, had given him his first tango lesson. She had lit the fire in him, so much so that he'd practiced his dance steps in the Ezeiza Airport bathroom before his flight home. Somehow he'd allowed the fervor to dissipate. It was time to recapture it.

Zeb walked into the ballroom as the class was starting. From the number of students, it was evident tango fever had spread throughout the Carolinas. So many takers for the one-hour class and three-hour *milonga*. Students paired up as the two teachers, a husband and wife named Carly and Alex, commenced stretching exercises.

"Do you have a partner?" a thirtyish woman asked.

"Nope." He offered his hand. "I'm Zeb."

"Mary."

"Your first class?"

"Actually, it's my fourth, but I dance like it's my first. Lucky for you, we change partners every few minutes."

"How come?" he asked.

"They say we learn more that way."

He grinned. "Got it."

Carly and Alex demonstrated the *double ocho* with such elegance and attitude that Zeb knew the class was in good hands. Zeb and Mary struggled but giggled. Zeb's next partner, a genial lady in her fifties, guided him while seeming not to. Carly approached, showing him the correct posture, arm position, and walking technique. Three partners later, Zeb was feeling like less of a hippopotamus.

"Switch!" Carly announced.

Zeb stopped in his tracks, wide-eyed. His ex-wife smiled at him.

"Lordy, *someone* learned how to scrub up."

"Hannah!" He hugged her. "*You* dance tango?"

"As of three weeks ago. It was my friend Fred's idea, and I remembered how you raved about tango. We're now hooked."

"Well, I'll be damned," Zeb said.

"Mom seems to think so."

"Listen up, folks," Alex called out. "The next step is a bit sensual, but don't worry. You can hold your partner by the arms if you prefer."

Zeb stepped back. "Don't let me keep you from . . . er, Fred. Hope he's treating you well."

"My gay friends always treat me the best. I think he'll forgive us." Hannah caught Fred's eye; he flashed a thumbs-up.

"My lucky day."

In his mind's eye, they were back at Cat's Cradle the day he first met her—long before he became her physical therapy patient. A reggae band jammed, and Hannah was swaying with two girlfriends. The two friends danced showily, checking for admirers, as much into themselves as the music. Hannah looked like an angel, immersed in the music, her smile and free-flowing hair emanating joy. She had allowed him to join her, to partake in the moment.

Now, as they clasped hands and he braced Hannah's back, while Carly talked them through the *sandwich-to-gancho* steps, there was a powerful sense of fitting. And with the inevitable missteps came chuckles, not annoyance or embarrassment. Before he knew it, it was time to switch partners. During the *milonga* session, single men vied for the attention of the shapely Chapel Hill woman with twinkling green eyes. Zeb took off early but not before introducing himself to Fred and satisfying himself that Hannah was in good hands.

Teresa stood at Zeb's desk, her lips pinched together.

"*Please* listen to me," she said. "Making clients sign this character clause is playing with fire. It'll alienate them."

"Not if they have good intentions."

She clenched her fists. "Let me get this straight. We tell them that International Expeditions will only do business with people who behave politely and ethically, that offending clients will have their tour canceled and deposits returned, and that *we* will determine what constitutes rude or unethical behavior. You don't think that'll piss them off?"

"You don't think many consumers behave badly?" Zeb asked, too calmly. "That we're not better off without them as clients?"

"I didn't say that."

"So, what's the problem?"

"The problem is"—Teresa sighed—"the minute we're off the hook with regulators, you pick a fight with our clients. We *finally* get a level playing field with our competitors, and you want to drive clients into their hands. Hell, *I* wouldn't sign this contract. It's offensive." She turned away. "I'm going for a walk."

Teresa headed to Cameron, her mind spinning. So much had gone right. With National Geographic, UNC Alumni Travel, and the Florida Museum of Natural History coming on board, they were on a roll. Students couldn't sign up fast enough for Professor Small's summer expeditions; the trips earned them credits.

Why is he so reckless? Maybe too much had gone right. The reversal of the honor court's decision, UNC's apology, and the invitation to finish his studies free of charge. Maybe Zeb was feeling indestructible.

And he was neglecting important matters again. Hadn't he learned his lesson with ARC? There was no way now—not with her added responsibilities—to keep him on track. And the new hires didn't have the experience to fill that role.

She gazed at the Old Well, modeled after the Temple of Love at Versailles. As a kid, she had posed for photos in front of the neoclassical rotunda. She'd drink from the marble fountain, emulating the good luck tradition of UNC students on their first day. Teresa walked over now and sipped the water.

It was time to get back to the office. She skirted Coker Arboretum. In high school she and Jim would stroll, arm in arm, along the trellis covered with purple wisteria and yellow jessamine and admire some of the four hundred species of ornamental flowers, trees, and shrubs. They'd canoodle and share dreams. *Can we ever get that back?* Something to reflect on—when she didn't have to prevent an unforced error. She walked quicker.

58

LIFENET4FAMILIES

ort Lauderdale, Florida, April 2017. "I'm opening the doors!" boomed Big T. "The line's over a block long."

Leo prepared for the human deluge. He had wrapped three hundred sets of plastic cutlery in napkins, filled the water and coffee dispensers, and donned a blue hairnet. Two volunteers stood with him behind the food counter.

This felt nothing like his first day. Then he'd stressed about what he would see, how he'd respond, and how the homeless would react to him. All that fear had vanished. The only awkwardness now was parking his newish car next to the throng waiting to eat.

"We're ready!" responded the manager, and in they came.

The customers proceeded smoothly along the food line. Mostly that was because of Big T's eagle eye and bloodhound sense of smell. A former drug addict, he could spot junkies a mile away and kept most of them out of the soup kitchen. Leo served chicken or meat loaf, and a coworker ladled out soup, veggies, and mashed potatoes. Most customers said, "God bless you," before moving on to the desserts. Like Leo, they were unemployed. Unlike them, Leo had never uttered the words "God bless you" to anyone who hadn't sneezed. That would change, he vowed.

After ninety minutes, Leo switched roles, handing out yogurt, filling water pitchers, and wiping off tables. Washrags needed to be dipped into buckets of soapy water. Leo went about his duties maniacally. He sweated profusely, smiling throughout. It was soothing to perform humble tasks, to serve the homeless.

These people neither hoarded nor wasted anything. They shared leftover food. Aside from the few druggies who slipped through Big T's net, none acted entitled. No one tried to sneak food out. Would he behave so ethically? Where were the glaring character flaws that explained their predicament? Most were good people buffeted by adverse circumstances.

Big T slapped Leo on the back. "You're getting the hang of it."

"Thanks, my friend."

"Keep it up, you'll be stealing my job," the giant said, smiling.

"How'd you get started here?"

"After I got out the army, I worked construction. Fell off a thirty-foot ladder, broke my back. VA health care screwed me over. Then I screwed myself, getting hooked on painkillers and racking up bills. I was on the street, eating here until Mrs. Ostrander offered me a job. I kicked drugs, been holding down this job going on two years now. Ain't never letting it go. God gave me a miracle: Lifenet. Now I'm paying it forward."

"That's awesome. Does your back still hurt?"

Big T chuckled. "Hell yeah, always will. But I'm good enough to work."

Leo walked to the bathroom, slipped off the hairnet. He looked in the mirror. The monstrous lump in this throat wasn't visible. *I will never pity myself again.*

He had the punishment and humiliation coming all along. Sure, it was ironic he got fired just as he was understanding himself and treating people better. But the sooner he settled his karma bill, the sooner he could move forward. He needed this time-out. Counseling, church, and volunteering were all that mattered now.

His Pika fraternity brother, Corbin, told him he was "eating his spiritual spinach" and would "come out stronger in the end." His air force buddy, Thompson, agreed, "You're fixing what needs fixing." He hadn't given his mentor, Bill Walsh, a chance to weigh in.

When Leo's shift ended, he headed to Walmart. He bought two carts of nonperishables and supplies and shipped them to Venezuela. The toilet paper alone would cheer up his family and Federico. Perspective—the day's lesson to him.

Charlotte, May 2017. Pollo Tropical was nowhere to be found, so Leo pulled into a Wendy's. Instead of using the drive-through, he went inside, figuring he'd get a Diet Coke refill and mingle with his fellow Charlotteans, but women in pants suits and men in blazers made him feel as underdressed as the homeless people he had served. Gym shorts were apparently meant only for the gym.

Two hours later, after showering and changing into a new suit, he drove downtown. The Queen City's oak trees, antebellum houses, and well-tended gardens brought a smile to his face. Still, it felt weird being so far inland. There would be no open-water sailing, hanging out at the beach, or walking about town in flip-flops. He missed his U-17 soccer girls.

Leo parked under the Bank of America tower and ascended to the eighteenth floor. The receptionist escorted him to the corner office where a silver-haired gentleman, Mr. Swofford, greeted him with a genuine smile, rare among investment bankers. After they'd exchanged niceties, the managing director said, "I know Rosemary gave you the grand tour when you interviewed. But since I was out, I wanted to meet you before you started."

"I appreciate that, sir."

"Call me Tom." Swofford leaned back and eyeballed him from behind his desk. "So what questions can I answer for you?"

"The main one is why you hired me sight unseen."

The director smiled. "Heidi's been my deputy forever. I trust her judgment. Besides, the others agreed with her."

"I see."

"Plus, we know what you accomplished in Florida."

"Do you know about my screwup?"

"I do," Swofford said, eyebrows raised.

"Pardon me for asking, but you strike me as old school."

"I am."

"What made you overlook my blunder?" Leo asked. "It was bad."

"It was horrendous. But I'm looking at the full picture."

"You mean the fees I can generate?"

Swofford shook his head. "That's a bonus, but, no, I judge mainly on character."

Leo snorted. "Forgive me, Tom, but that makes no sense. Most folks in Florida would rate my character in the negatives."

"Not the person who knows you best. Jake called me from Palo Alto."

Leo recoiled in surprise. "Jake? He's the guy I screwed over."

"Jake practically begged me to hire you." Swofford was grinning. "He went over the deals you guys worked on and told me how you topped off his bonus—to the tune of seventy thousand dollars. He said it came out of your own pocket—*after* you'd been fired."

"It was the least I could do." Leo's eyes glistened. "It made me feel better."

"Jake said he refused the money, but you wouldn't take no for an answer. Apparently it was the only way you could forgive yourself."

Leo shifted in his seat. "As I said, it was self-serving."

Swofford walked over to a framed *Sports Illustrated* cover hanging on his wall. The cover commemorated the UNC Tar Heels, 2017's newly minted basketball champions, and featured Joel Berry, the Tar Heels' point guard, celebrating after overcoming untold adversity. "The best ones bounce back." The director returned to his seat. "You also wrote a stellar recommendation letter that got Jake into Stanford's MBA program."

"I didn't write anything that wasn't true."

"He assured me there were extreme extenuating circumstances behind what you did. He wouldn't elaborate but insisted they wouldn't be a problem in the future. I believe him."

"Why, sir?"

"Because Jake called back twice more to press your case."

Leo's eyes widened. "So that's why Heidi recruited me out of the blue."

"Yes, sir."

"*Please*, call me Leo."

Tom chortled. "We're gonna get along fine. Listen, this is off topic and none of my business, but how's your family doing? I know Venezuela's going to pot."

"They're surviving, that's about it."

"Are you going to sponsor them?"

"They won't leave," Leo said glumly.

Tom's jaw dropped. "Why in heavens not? Are they too attached to home?"

"It's a combination of things. Starting over is tough. Plus they want to fight for change."

Tom nodded admiringly. "Patriots."

"They also want to protect my relatives' graves. Robbers steal all kinds of things."

"I get it."

Tom summarized his expectations. As SVP of corporate finance, Leo would oversee six relationship managers who handled the bank's largest accounts. A military veteran himself, Tom wanted his best fighter pilots out front, pitching for bond and equity deals. He wanted the A team leading when it mattered most. Leo *was* the A team. He needed to step in to close deals, even at the risk of ruffling subordinates' feathers. Clearly, Tom didn't like to lose. He was a polite Southerner, but there was fire in his belly.

Lifenet had given Big T a second chance. Tom was now doing the same for him. *I'll never let him down,* Leo thought.

59

YOU SOUND LIKE GRANNY

Moorea, Polynesia, April 2017. The smiling resort attendant handed Sarah and Kiara ice-cold washcloths and fruit juice. "*Merci beaucoup,*" Sarah said, wiping her sweaty forehead, face, and neck. "It looks like guava."

"*Oui, c'est guava,*" the Polynesian confirmed.

Kiara emptied her glass in a flash. "Yummy!" Not a word she had ever said before.

It was clear that two-star hospitality didn't include porterage, so they thanked the receptionist, grabbed the key, and rolled their bags toward the beachside bungalow. The palm trees—tall, bending, and randomly distributed—seemed like distant cousins to the stubbier ones planted throughout Florida in a more manicured fashion.

"Watch for falling coconuts," Sarah said.

"Killer fruits!" Kiara grinned.

"You'd be surprised. There've been nineteen documented, coconut-related deaths."

"How on God's green earth would you know that?"

"Try reading your own *Lonely Planet*. Here's another factoid: During World War II, in the Philippines, the Japanese threw coconut bombs at American troops. They were filled with acid and hand grenades."

"Lovely but, if it's okay with you, I'll ignore the coconut hazard."

They approached the lapping waters and veered toward a thatched-roof bungalow. Once inside, Sarah made a beeline for the window and gazed at the crystalline waters. "Incredible. The South Pacific makes Myrtle Beach look like sewage."

"You should take up poetry."

"It's like no place I've ever been. Or ever will visit. Just look at all the colors!"

Sarah was right to be awestruck. A dozen hues, ranging from emerald green to turquoise to sapphire blue, graced their waterside canvas. No matter what James Michener said, there was no way Bora Bora could be more beautiful than this. Not with Moorea's waters, lush mountains, and white powder beaches. "It's a dead ringer for Jordan Lake."

"Exactly."

"I'll take this one," Kiara said, pointing to the bed under the ceiling fan. "I flew three more hours than you, and I put up with your snoring."

"Witch."

Kiara collapsed on the bed and gawked at the rotating blades. Twenty-one hours to Papeete, a two-hour layover, one-hour ferry to Moorea, and a taxi ride. She needed the rest.

Ten minutes later Sarah blurted out, "I'm sweating like a damn pig. It sucks we couldn't get into the Med."

"No shit." Club Med had air-conditioning. It was also sporty, singles oriented, and reasonably priced. They had passed on the luxury resort with over-the-water bungalows because it attracted a mix of honeymooners and elderly travelers. No sense paying a fortune to watch newlyweds canoodle and listen to seniors whine about malfunctioning hearing aids.

Clearly, they had erred. "Wanna take a dip?"

"You sound like Granny."

"Wanna look for lemon sharks and moray eels?"

"Hell yeah! The surf can't be hotter than the air."

They slipped into their swimsuits. "Did you find a safety deposit box?" Kiara asked.

"Nope."

Kiara slid some bills into a Ziploc and stuffed it into her bikini top. Sarah gave her a funny look.

"What? You never know."

Sarah locked the valuables inside a suitcase. Grabbing their snorkels and fins, they made their way to the beach.

"How about asking that guy where the reef starts?" Kiara said, gesturing to a Polynesian wiping down an outrigger.

"*Pas de problème.*"

Soon they were swimming toward a spot two hundred yards offshore. Kiara cradled her arms underneath and kicked smoothly, as silver needlefish darted away. She smiled through her snorkel. Winning race medals was nothing compared to taking in marine life and enjoying endless underwater visibility. A parrot fish crossed her path and seemed to be swimming intentionally in one direction. Coral alert. She adjusted course, following the mosaic of colors. A sea cucumber lay on the seafloor, and Kiara broke into a spasm of giggling that briefly dislodged her mask, releasing bubbles to the surface. As teenagers, they had lifted these creatures from the Florida surf to watch them "pee."

The reef came into view. Lifting her head from the water, Kiara spat out her snorkel and, sounding more like an eighth grader than a doctor, shouted, "It's here!" Sarah gave a thumbs-up and caught up. Side by side, kicking against the current, they hovered above the reef, scrutinizing everything while ensuring their fins didn't destroy corals thousands of years in the making. A school of butterfly fish passed, their vibrant black, white, and yellow stripes forming an abstract backsplash. A sea urchin clung to a rock, its spiky needles less than a foot from Kiara's exposed skin. Countless species eyeballed them over the next forty-five minutes—damselfish, angelfish, snapper, puffer fish, a moray eel, and, best of all, clown fish.

Fatigue set in, so they treaded water. "It looks like we drifted quite a ways," Sarah said.

Their resort lay a quarter mile to the right. "We sure did. What's that place?" Kiara asked, pointing to the left. "It can't be Club Med?"

"That's exactly what it is. Outrigger man told me to avoid it. Overzealous security."

"Do you see what I see—or rather, don't see?"

Sarah winked through her mask. "No guards."

"Gotta love their zeal."

They kicked continuously until they came to within twenty feet of the beach. They could now stand.

"Damn! The sons of bitches returned," Kiara said.

"Now what?"

Kiara's attention turned from the security guards to the guests. Most looked fit, in their mid-twenties to forties. Some played volley-ball on the beach, while others lounged by the pool. A number of them sipped cocktails at the tiki bar, flirting visibly. Several snorkeled nearby. All wore necklaces of orange and white beads. "I've got it!"

"I'm listening."

Kiara turned her back to shore and removed the Ziploc. She handed a twenty-dollar bill to Sarah, keeping the second for herself.

Sarah stuffed the bill into her top. "We're gonna bribe the guards?"

"No, that would be unethical," Kiara said. "We're going to pass our-selves off as guests. Here's the deal. One of my colleagues who's been to five Club Meds explained how it works. You see the plastic beads around their necks and wrists?"

"Yes."

"Everything in the resort—drinks, store items—are paid for with them. Beads are used instead of cash. They're waterproof, detachable, and easy to hold on to."

Sarah splashed away seaweed. "That's fine, but if you hadn't noticed, we don't have any beads."

"It can't be tough to get them. Apparently, folks spend half the day quaffing drinks; there's no way reception is resupplying beads for four hundred guests." Kiara removed her fins. "There's got to be bead stations sprinkled about the resort. Probably near the beach bar and pool."

"Makes sense. So we split up, find the stations, and use cash to buy beads. Then we dangle them around our necks like everyone else."

Kiara nodded. "They'll be our passport. Tomorrow we'll be walking through the front gate instead of swimming in."

Twenty minutes later they were necklaced and playing a spirited game of beach volleyball. Adrenaline carried them through three games, but then exhaustion took hold. Grabbing beach towels from an attendant, they crashed under a *palapa* for a couple of hours.

Upon waking, they ambled to the beach bar for fruit juices. They collected their beverages and planted themselves in chairs facing the crystalline waters. "The wind sure picked up," Kiara said as a catamaran whizzed by. "Glad we don't have to swim back."

"You got that right."

"So tell me . . . I know you're a White House economist and do quantitative analysis on important stuff. But give me an example of what exactly you work on?"

Sarah looked at Kiara as if she were a Martian. "Seriously, with this setting, these views, you're interested in my work?"

"We can walk and chew gum. Let me guess. You project a rosy economy, cook the budget numbers, and take two-hour lunches?"

Sarah laughed. "Boy, are you clueless."

"Well?"

"I've done all kinds of stuff. I developed subsidy models to calculate taxpayer costs of federal credit programs. I created early warning systems so credit agencies can adjust underwriting guidelines based on policy, the budget, the economy, and projected portfolio performance. I've modified credit-scoring models so agencies can better identify their target beneficiaries." Sarah sipped mango juice as a catamaran passed. "Right now, I'm prioritizing high-risk areas at the Department of Veterans Affairs and developing corrective action plans. With 370,000 employees and a budget of two hundred billion dollars . . . Your eyes are glazing over."

"Not at all. That's impressive, seriously. How about for fun?"

Sarah sighed. "The White House Christmas Party is cool. But overall, my social life sucks. D.C. has the worst ratio of single men in the country."

"Damn. And I thought I was hard up."

"It's so bad I'm thinking of buying a sex robot."

Kiara spat out her mango nectar and howled. "Can you get one with a good personality?"

"Absolutely. They customize them." Sarah looked at her with feigned seriousness. "Here are my criteria so far: Has a Latin-lover accent. Doesn't snore sixty seconds after sex. Gives awesome foot massages. Takes out the trash without being asked. And turns into a pizza at the stroke of midnight. Whaddya think?"

"That should cover it," Kiara said, snickering. "If you can get one without an ego and who doesn't get jealous, it might be better than the real thing!"

Two musclebound vacationers hovered, but Kiara's glance made it clear she preferred androids. Having finished their juices, they moved to the water and stood waist-deep. Tiny fish swam by, occasionally nibbling at their legs.

"How about you?" Sarah asked. "It's great they shortened your suspension. Any men on the horizon?"

She chuckled. "Pops always says, 'Every bread has a cheese.' Somehow, I haven't found mine."

"Not even with Zeb?"

"There, it's the opposite problem."

"What do you mean?"

"I told Coach Jeffreys he should let Teresa handle his team's travel arrangements. He did, and a bunch of other UNC teams followed his lead. Meanwhile, I've spent lots of time with Zeb's mom because she's in decline—we've been friends for years." Kiara exhaled deeply. "Anyhow, Zeb now thinks I'm Mother Teresa. He has the hots for me."

Sarah snorted. "He's loved you for years."

"Whatever. It's not happening."

They giggled at the fish still nibbling at their legs. A boat with scuba divers took off for a nearby reef.

"You know he's a gem," Sarah pressed.

"I know, but I'd die if I were to hurt him or drive him away." Despite the warmth of the ocean breeze, a shiver ran down her spine.

"Zeb's not like most men," Sarah said. "He loves your strength. You guys are soul mates."

"Forget it. He's like a brother. Besides, I've got my sights on someone else."

"Damn! Now that sounds interesting. What've you been keeping from me?" Sarah splashed water in her direction. Kiara ducked, laughing, and splashed back.

"Last time I visited my parents, I stopped by Weston FC. I met this Latin guy, Leo, who coaches there part-time. We grabbed dinner, kept in touch, and—"

"Now, he's moving to Charlotte," Sarah interrupted, her smile fading. "You forget, I went back to Weston, too. A week before you."

"Oh, that's right." Kiara licked her lips, tasting salt. They headed back to their lounge chairs.

"You don't think he's too old? He's fifty-six."

To Kiara, Sarah's tone was odd—casual but forced. She probably hadn't met somebody who mattered in a while. But how did she know Leo's age?

"Not at all," Kiara said, hiding her annoyance. "He could be *sixty*-six for all I care. We might have something."

"Might?"

"Apparently, he has a checkered past with women." Past Sarah's shoulder, two women were throwing a brightly colored beach ball back and forth.

"How so?"

"I'm not sure. But he vowed to do better. I was impressed by his openness."

"Right—his looks had nothing to do with it," Sarah said with a smirk.

A familiar voice shouted out, "Oi! Missy and I are heading to dinner. Would you care to join us?"

Kiara spun around. It was the spunky British woman whose face she had walloped with one of her volleyball spikes. The woman had laughed it off and jumped right up.

"We'd love to, but I'm not sure if we're allowed," Sarah said.

"Why wouldn't you be?" the British woman said. "Let me guess: You flew in this morning and don't know how everything works."

Kiara exchanged glances with Sarah. "We didn't exactly arrive the traditional way."

"Whatever do you mean? Why so cryptic?"

Missy stepped forward and whispered conspiratorially, "Did you guys sneak in?"

"You could say that," Kiara said, embarrassed. "We tried to book a room, but none were available. So we made what you might call a wet landing."

"Brilliant!" the other Brit said. "I'm Pam, and, no, my swollen face won't hold a grudge. Your secret is safe."

"So is that a 'yes'?" Missy pressed. "They don't check ID for meals."

Sarah rubbed her chin. "Hmm, we could cancel our other reservation. What do you think, Kiara?"

"That's a tough one, but I say we grace the Brits with our presence."

"It's settled then!" Pam said. Kiara and Sarah borrowed sarongs and flip-flops and followed their hosts.

Kiara beamed when she saw the buffet tables. Feasting on

Polynesian and European dishes at sea level would be a blessing after four consecutive airline meals. And as befitted a French resort, the quality of the cuisine was excellent. They were joined by Pam and Missy's two girlfriends who had spent the day snuggling indoors with two handsome Italians.

During dessert they were approached by a *gentil organisateur*, the activity leader responsible for making everyone feel welcome. The French GO explained that tonight's cabaret show—to be performed by *gentils membres*, or guests—needed volunteers. Four female roles remained uncast for a comedic rendition of *Swan Lake*. Male guests outfitted in tutus, wigs, fins, and balloon boobs would join them. Would they please help him out? Pam, openly lusting over the Frenchman, immediately accepted on behalf of all four.

The minute Frenchy left, Sarah said, "You realize you signed up two illegals to dance in the limelight in front of hundreds?"

"No better way to flaunt your goods and find men," Pam said. "But stay away from Frenchy, he's mine."

"I hope we don't wind up in a Polynesian jail," Sarah mumbled. Kiara cracked up.

The show got off to a rollicking start. The cross-dressing swans, all wearing fins, performed a series of ballet jumps. Most tumbled, causing their boobs to explode. The British-American foursome, wearing tutus and inner tubes, entered stage left and, prompted by Missy's uncere-monious shove of Sarah, launched into an unchoreographed session of bumper-car dancing. Uproarious laughter broke out as grim-faced Pam repeatedly bounced off the more powerful Kiara, like a pinball. The Club Med photographer later told them he took more shots of this show than any all season. "Don't worry," Missy assured them, "we'll order extras for you."

Afterward at the bar, Kiara mused, "I've never had this much fun in my life."

"It doesn't have to end," Missy said.

Sarah chuckled. "I'm not sure we should press our luck."

"Poppycock!" Pam said. "Jill and Kim haven't used their beds the last three nights—lucky cows. You might as well sleep in our suite—unless you'd rather stay at your place."

"I gotta admit, it's wonderful having AC."

"And *us!*" Missy insisted.

"And you. It's just, we're used to paying our way. It doesn't feel right."

"The beds will only go to waste," Missy said. "Besides, you tried to pay."

Kiara set her margarita down and slapped Sarah's leg. "I don't know about you, but I really don't want to sweat all night. We haven't slept in days."

"Then it's settled!" Pam said.

"How do we repay you?"

Missy's eyes twinkled. "One day you'll write a book, *Club Med on Six Dollars a Day*, and dedicate it to Pam and me. In the meantime, we'll organize a girl's trip to Washington."

"Deal, but only if you let Sarah and me leave a massive tip for the staff—enough to cover all four of us."

"It's always about money with you Yanks!" Pam said, shaking her head. "Now, where did Frenchy get off to?"

60

CHALLAH

Chapel Hill, North Carolina, April 2017. Zeb sat on the edge of his parents' sofa, tapping his feet and glancing at the antique clock. He had bolted work early only to twiddle his thumbs in solitude. But he knew better than to rush his mom. Grabbing a *National Geographic* from the coffee table, he flipped through it. Jane Goodall's exploits soon made him forget the hour.

"I'll be there in a minute," his mom announced.

These days that meant ten. "No worries."

"Turn on CNBC if you like. The market's up two percent; they're expecting a Fed rate cut."

"I'm busy with chimps."

Finishing the article on Gombe, Zeb laid the magazine aside. So much had changed for his mother. Pillboxes, blood-pressure readings, and Post-it notes had replaced teaching, board of director's meetings, and tennis tournaments. She had drawn the line at using a walker but was only a fall or two away from having no choice. A live-in was on the horizon—either that or moving to an independent-living community. His dad gave her space because hovering offended her. Some days—like maybe today—it could be hard to notice any cognitive decline. But he'd learned not to get pumped by the upticks.

Few knew of her dementia. Her decline—inexorable—would be long and cruel. But there were positives, and he preferred to focus on those. Growing up, he had only been kissed by her several times, invariably after an award or achievement. Love seemed conditional. Nowadays his mom was an affection machine, caressing and squeezing him at every turn. The physical connection—holding her arm as he escorted her around, helping her get in and out of vehicles—warmed his heart. He relished the opportunity to show his gratitude. She had attacked his attention and organizational deficits vigorously, preparing him to succeed. Both of them ached to express their pent-up love. Now her condition allowed it to flow.

Conversationally, too, things had changed. It was no longer always about how his studies or business were progressing. She still cared—it was she who advised him to target older clients with Fast-Forward Adventures, and to pay more attention to overhead—but she no longer used his updates as a measuring stick. Maybe his mom no longer blamed him for getting expelled. Maybe she now understood the social cost he'd paid for taking meds. Or maybe he'd accepted that, without her intervention, he'd have languished. Whatever the reason, things were good.

Ruth emerged sooner than expected, hugging him tightly and kissing him on the cheek.

"You look beautiful, Mom."

"Purple does wonders for the mature lady." She posed.

"You look awesome in any color."

"Michael Kitchen and Martin Shaw will be knocking at my door, right? Your father better watch out." She was *on* today.

Zeb grinned. "He'll blame me, I'm sure." His dad pretended to be jealous of the stars of *Foyle's War* and *Inspector George Gently*, two British crime dramas he'd recommended.

They drove to Temple, and, walking inside, Ruth whispered, "Afternoon is a strange time for Torah study."

"Rabbi had a schedule conflict."

Students were chatting and fiddling with smartphones as Zeb escorted his mother into class. "*Shalom*, y'all," he said, and they were greeted in return. Rabbi was discussing something with his administrative assistant, so Zeb grabbed a rugelach from the table, handed the cookie to his mother, and settled her into a seat. He returned for a cup of coffee, preparing it to his mother's taste.

Rabbi took inventory of the attendees, chatting as he scanned. Apart from a core group of regulars, it was never clear who would show up. Some students were professionals with busy schedules. Others were older and susceptible to illnesses. Still others were frequent travelers or part-time residents. Rabbi's face lit up when he saw Ruth.

"Ruth Ackerman! It is so good to see you. You look great."

Ruth blushed but was clearly tickled. "Thank you, Rabbi. It's wonderful to see you."

"How's Larry?"

"Busy, which is good. Keeps him out of my hair."

"Tell him I said hi. He's welcome to join us if he leaves his puns at home. . . . Class, Miriam brought challah."

There were cheers, and Zeb's mouth watered. The loaf of braided bread—set next to the coffee—had looked warm, spongy, and crusty. Whether it was sesame or poppy seed Zeb wasn't sure, but it was certainly infused with honey.

"Will you be reading it?" one woman asked. Kids weren't the only ones who reveled in his playful interpretations. Some read palms or tea leaves; Rabbi used challah to impart wisdom.

Rabbi's eyes twinkled. "I might be convinced—if my scholars promise me brilliant commentaries. Man does not live on bread alone." A chorus of groans. "Of course, a super-size slice would seal the deal."

He lifted the platter and inspected the challah from all angles. Zeb knew that Rabbi's brain was in overdrive because he'd never heard the same homily twice.

Rabbi set it down. "Challah consists of flour, water, yeast, and salt. These are the most basic of ingredients. But only combined do they make a miracle: bread. So it is with life. For the miracle of life to be fully lived, we also need a combination of the most basic ingredients: family, friends, goals, and dreams."

"Thank you, Rabbi."

"You're welcome. Anyone want to comment before we turn to Torah?" Rabbi looked around. "Ruth, have at it."

"Well, your reading evokes many feelings and raises many questions."

"Good!" Rabbi said. "Questions are usually better than the answers."

Ruth sighed. "Rabbi, for most of my life, getting the right proportion of those ingredients—family, friends, goals, and dreams—has been difficult. Figuring out how much time and energy to devote to each is key. Misjudge, I've come to learn, and the result is bad, whether it's challah or your life."

"It's challenging to get these things right," Rabbi said. "You're far from alone."

"Another question is timing," Ruth said. "Whether the four ingredients must be handled together, or whether they can be dealt with sequentially, with some ignored in the short run."

"Interesting. Please elaborate."

Ruth hesitated before proceeding. "I'm ashamed to say, I damaged my challah. I neglected certain ingredients too long. I gave short shrift to my family while pursuing professional goals and dreams. My family should've been a bigger piece of my goals and dreams—not just tossed overboard." She seemed on the verge of tears.

Several students exchanged looks. Zeb wiped his brow. This was new ground.

Rabbi didn't flinch. "Ruth, women have it much harder when it comes to juggling priorities. It's a tough balance to strike, especially for someone of your abilities. But, in any case, you're dead wrong."

Ruth recoiled, speechless.

"The evidence is clear." Rabbi pointed to Zeb. "Your challah came out stellar. Zeb enriches this community—just ask dozens of our special-needs graduates—and, professionally, he's been a visionary, the hottest name in travel. Your challah, Ruth, is made of the right stuff. If you tossed some ingredients overboard, well, you must have thrown some flotation devices overboard, too, because everything is here now, and it's all in just the right proportion. Ya done good!"

"It was Larry who salvaged our challah from the depths," Ruth said sadly.

Zeb squirmed. Classmates fidgeted with their pens and cell phones.

Rabbi shook his head. "Look who Zeb brought to class. Give yourself some credit. But let's talk about this privately."

When his mother had her mind set, nothing could stop her. "I changed, but only after I started losing my mind. I have early-stage dementia. There's nothing like looking down the barrel of a rifle to make you less selfish."

One student gasped, covering her mouth.

Zeb embraced his mother. "Mom, you've never been selfish—not now, not ever."

Ruth looked around. "Sorry to get so personal, everyone. I'm hoping y'all can learn from my mistakes."

Rabbi walked over and hugged her. "Thank you for your courage and generosity."

The rest of the class proceeded normally, biblical drama superseding the Ackerman family saga. On their drive home, Ruth said, "I'm sorry for that embarrassing spectacle."

He felt a pang of shame. "I wasn't embarrassed, Mom. Your heart was in the right place, and that's what matters."

"Not much I can do about it now. But I was sharp today, right?"

"As a tack."

Ruth beamed. "It won't last but I said my piece." She looked at him. "I really am sorry, you know. About everything."

Zeb felt a frog in his throat. All he could do was nod.

When they reached the front porch of his parents' house, the door opened, and Zeb's father and Hannah walked out. Both were dressed elegantly. Zeb smiled, anticipating his mother's shock.

"What the devil!" Ruth said.

Larry smirked, noting to Hannah, "She means me. You can do no wrong."

"Tell that to my boss," Hannah joked, as Larry led them all inside.

Zeb escorted Ruth to the living-room sofa. A wide area had been cleared of furniture and the carpet. "Have a seat, Mom." Ruth's eyes widened in excitement.

Larry clasped his hands. "Honey, we have a surprise for you."

Hannah jabbed at her smartphone, and within seconds, the tango beat of "La Cumparsita" played from the Bluetooth speaker. "Ruth, we're taking you to Buenos Aires."

Zeb took Hannah's hand and led her to the center of the living room. They began with the *basico* and progressed to more intricate steps. Ruth smiled, tapping her feet in rhythm. The exhibition was unrehearsed, but they pulled it off. The *sandwich-to-gancho* elicited a "Mercy me!" while the *sacada* and *parade-to-forward rock* drew cheers. Together, Zeb and Hannah seemed as comfortable as a well-worn glove. When the song ended, Ruth stood and clapped energetically.

"Honey, we're just getting started," Larry said. "Hannah's a great teacher. Here, put your dancing shoes on." Zeb stood, mouth agape, as his parents danced the eight-step and *ocho*, two steps Ruth could handle despite her flagging coordination. When Ruth became fatigued, they feasted on Rasa Malaysia delicacies that had been delivered to their home.

Afterward Hannah whispered to Zeb, "Remember, I only did it for *her*." She nodded at his mother.

"I know."

Zeb arrived back at his apartment to see a melancholy Teresa sitting on his front step. His heart sank. This was obviously bad. The joy of Buenos Aires vanished instantaneously.

"Uh-oh. Trouble?"

"Of a sort," she said.

61

AMBUSHED

Raleigh, North Carolina, May 2017. Kiara bounced her foot repeatedly as the moderator and other panelists at the table chatted and giggled. Their levity made sense. Each had decades of professional experience in education; she had months. They were joined at the hip ideologically; she was the outlier, a sacrificial lamb. The televised Education Summit was a big deal. There was the opportunity to advance good policy and receive accolades. There was also the risk of dealing reform a setback, of being personally humiliated.

"Ninety seconds!" the producer announced.

Memories of her eighth-grade debate with Sarah brought a smile to Kiara's face. Back then she'd been an overconfident snot, relying on improvisational thinking rather than preparation. That wasn't an option here—not with so many kids depending on her. Somehow, only nine months after having her license suspended, and three months after being reinstated, Kiara was the designated advocate for school choice, her name put forth by the governor. Three weeks of cramming wasn't nearly enough, but it would have to do. Sarah's instructions? Kick ass. If only it were that simple.

Jim Wiles, the *Charlotte Observer*'s education correspondent and debate moderator, swiveled toward the camera. He welcomed the audience, framed the school-choice issue, and offered brief bios on the panelists. Nigel Tolliver was a veteran history teacher and union leader; Judy Pinkleberry, a senior analyst at the Network for Public Education. The moderator immediately established these two as heavyweights relative to Kiara Battle, who received the paltry description of "conservative" school-choice advocate and psychologist. Kiara almost interrupted him but took a deep breath instead.

Wiles launched the first salvo: "Critics say that by subsidizing private schools, school choice will destroy American public schools and undermine America. Nigel, do you agree and, if so, why does it matter?"

"I do agree, Jim. There's a long tradition of common schools in America. These schools embody our classless, democratic principles. We are—always have been—a country of immigrants. Public schools have always been the most effective way of educating our citizenry, of knitting together millions of immigrants from different lands. I shudder to think what this country would be without this unifying force."

"Judy?"

"Nigel is right. Public schools allow children of all classes to be educated together. This engenders mutual respect. That is essential to the functioning of our democracy. Anything that threatens our public schools threatens our democracy."

"Some high stakes," Wiles noted. "Do you agree, Dr. Battle?"

"Absolutely. But I have a different take."

"As might be suspected," Wiles said with a cheeky grin.

"You're one hundred percent right," Kiara said. "My parents were Black Trinidadians who immigrated to America. They lived in a poor neighborhood for years."

"Interesting," Wiles said. "And your take?"

"What Nigel and Judy are saying sounds great, but in practice few public schools conform to the common-school ideal. You've all heard of James Coleman, the University of Chicago sociologist. His research shows that public schools tend to be the most exclusive, segregated schools. Ironically, he found that religious schools are more integrated." Kiara ignored Nigel's smirk. "Catholic schools in Chicago and New York City bring together kids of widely differing circumstances—far more than most public schools. And—"

"Wait a minute—" the union leader tried to interject.

"Please, Nigel, let me finish. There's tons of research on how school choice affects integration, and it's overwhelmingly positive." Kiara cleared her throat. "My view, as someone who attended an all-minority elementary school for three years, is this: Disadvantaged students should be free to go to the widest possible range of schools, and not kept out of a particular school because of its cost or location. School choice offers the best chance of creating the common-school ideal you talked about."

"No doubt Nigel was going to raise the issue of creaming," Wiles said, "before he was interrupted by Dr. Battle. Creaming in this context, of course, meaning that with school choice, the disadvantaged and weaker students will be left behind in bad schools, while good students will be taken into the best schools. Judy?"

Judy nodded. "That's definitely a concern, because private schools are selective in who they accept. With school choice, we'll be creating elite academies for the few, and second-rate schools for the masses."

Kiara repressed a smile. She'd seen double-teams on the soccer pitch. Triple-teams? Not so much. "I disagree for two reasons. First, although some private schools are selective, many good school-choice options aren't selective. Parents can choose from among all the traditional public schools within their district, region, or state. They can choose charter schools, magnet schools, and most parochial schools. The Catholic schools I mentioned earlier are no more selective than public schools, and they graduate tons of well-prepared, low-income kids. Lastly, some private schools—like the one I went to—aren't academically selective."

"Your second point?" Wiles said.

Kiara smiled. *My cramming wasn't in vain!* "Twenty-five studies have looked at test scores in public schools after they lost voucher students to private schools. Twenty-three found scores improved, one showed no effect, and one found they declined. So the idea that bad students are being left behind in bad schools is wrong. School choice introduces competition, incentivizing all schools to improve."

She quickly sipped water. "I'll add a third point. People who worry that school choice will lead to educational inequality forget our system is already unequal. Rich people already benefit from school choice. They can move to a neighborhood with great public schools or send their kids to private school. Poor kids are trapped in terrible schools. School choice gives them opportunity."

"Not if their parents don't know the difference between good and bad schools," Nigel said.

"Whoa!" Kiara exclaimed, recoiling in her seat. "Are you saying poor kids will wind up in bad schools regardless because their parents are incompetent?" *Is this guy really that clueless?*

"I wouldn't put it like that," Nigel said hesitantly. "I'm saying poor parents have a ton of problems to deal with, including drug issues in some cases. That makes it harder for them to evaluate schools."

Kiara decided not to go for the jugular. Nigel could be classist and wrong without being racist. *Maybe.* "Look, some poor families do have trouble evaluating schools—but most don't. Evidence shows that being able to make a consequential decision for their child's future shakes many parents out of their despair. They feel empowered and rise to the challenge. We see the same thing with tenant management of public housing."

"I heard you say, 'many parents,' but not 'most parents.' What about those who *don't* react this way?" Nigel persisted.

"*Most* school-choice systems have outreach programs—parent liaisons and information centers," Kiara replied coolly. "They help families learn their options and choose appropriately."

"And when parents fail to take advantage of these resources?"

"It happens, just like it does with wealthy parents," she said. "The point is, even when children have negligent parents, they're better off with school choice."

"Hold on, you'll have to explain that one," Wiles said.

Kiara smiled. "The fact that other parents are choosing between schools forces *all* schools to compete if they want to attract and retain students. Like I said before, test scores increase even for students left behind."

Judy shook her head. "Many private schools won't want to take on special-needs students because they're more expensive to teach and accommodate."

"I disagree," Kiara said. "School-choice programs offer richer scholarships for special-needs kids. I experienced this firsthand. I have a learning disability, and my private high school recruited me, not just because I played soccer, but because my voucher amount was large."

Wiles raised the issue of vouchers siphoning money from traditional public schools, leaving them underfunded. Kiara explained in detail—the same way she'd done for Zeb in Four Corners—how voucher amounts were set below the budgeted cost for each public-school student, meaning that transfers increased per-student resources for the traditional public school.

Wiles rummaged through his notes, seemingly desperate. Then he grinned. "Dr. Battle, if school choice is such a panacea, how do you explain the abysmal results in Louisiana?" Wiles was now addressing most questions to her.

"I can't," Kiara said, shaking her head. "Jefferson Parish did horribly. They got an F in Brookings' Education Choice and Competition Index. Meanwhile, go figure, Orleans Parish got an A, second best in the country. Obviously, setting up a choice program isn't a guarantee of success. They need to get the details right."

"Please elaborate."

Kiara took a deep breath. She explained how, ideally, school-choice programs offered a mix of traditional public schools, magnet schools, charter schools, affordable private schools, and online education. Parents should receive clear information on school performance. Less-educated parents should receive support in choosing schools. Teachers should be trained in differentiated instruction. Schools should reevaluate teacher credentialing requirements, the curriculum, and the length of the school day. School safety should be assured. Entrepreneurial school leaders should be attracted and rewarded. Bad schools should be closed if they didn't improve. Kiara posited that Jefferson Parish got many things wrong, while Orleans got them right.

Nigel grinned. "Your Republican buddies blame Jefferson on too much regulation." It was clear he considered the notion ridiculous.

"Buddies?" Kiara snorted. "I've never voted Republican in my life, but I'll support whatever gets poor kids educated. I *was* one of them, so it doesn't matter to me who proposes the solution. In Louisiana, regulations probably were to blame—"

"Let's move on," Wiles said. "Kiara, do you support any of the teachers' union demands?"

"I do. Teachers should have more say in the design of school-choice programs. They've been given little input but will be scapegoated for any failures. They should also have more say in their development training. Teachers spend nineteen days a year in training at a cost of eighteen thousand dollars per teacher, but it does little to improve their teaching or student performance. That's because bosses choose the training."

"Well said," Nigel said.

"Where do you think the unions are wrong?" Wiles asked.

"When they say school choice doesn't work and isn't needed," Kiara said. "They should explain why a *third* of California teachers send their own kids to private school. Also, unions shouldn't focus only on salaries and benefits; they should emphasize professional development. Higher-skilled teachers will command higher pay."

Judy scowled. "Let me get this straight: You expect unions to invest in advanced training so their teachers can jump over to nonunionized charter and private schools?"

Kiara's stomach tightened. Three weeks of cramming hadn't forestalled every pitfall. "Good point. I may need to think that one through."

"I think so. Another thing: How are poor kids supposed to get to these other schools? If they don't have transportation, isn't it a false choice?" Judy grinned and shared knowing glances with her allies.

"Most educational savings accounts allow some money to be used for transportation. But, yes, that is an issue. I don't have all the answers."

"You don't say! No worries, Kiara, we won't tell you how to reorganize the psychology profession."

The moderator chuckled.

Kiara bit her tongue. Restraint would win more converts than anger. "I do know many states are working on transportation fixes. Technological solutions are hopefully on the horizon. We'll see how it plays out."

In Washington, D.C., Secretary of Education Mercedes Miller's eyes sparkled. Neither she nor her aides had expected much—not after Wiles had rejected their preferred school-choice advocate. They had tuned in with a sense of foreboding, thinking it might be a disaster. But Dr. Battle had stolen the show, promoting reform in a refreshing way. Secretary Miller smiled. Her gorilla-tracking friend, Jill, had been so insistent about this woman. *She was right. Kiara Battle is the real deal.*

Just as the president had been right to pick her as secretary. Many had thought her stupid for accepting the position. After all, compared with her peers in the cabinet, her role was symbolic. How much could she accomplish when federal dollars accounted for only 8 percent of primary- and secondary-school funding? States, communities, and private organizations—not the federal government—established schools and colleges, developed curriculums, and determined requirements for enrollment and graduation. No wonder the Department of Education had by far the smallest staff of any cabinet-level agency.

But Miller had no intention of doing what was expected, which was almost nothing. In a strange way, her position was liberating. Free of the scrutiny and outsize expectations that accompanied more powerful posts, she was in a better position to set her own agenda. It was also auspicious that the president—rare among Republicans—didn't favor abolishing her agency.

Her mandate—collecting information on what worked in education and disseminating it to teachers and policymakers—would be pursued vigorously. She would not be a figurehead. The D.C. social circuit held no interest. She knew what worked: school choice. It had worked wonders back in Florida and elsewhere. They needed to spread the word and mollify the unions, which was why Jill had insisted she watch Dr. Battle. If things progressed as she hoped, American students would owe a debt to the mountain gorillas of Rwanda.

"What'd you guys think?" Secretary Miller asked.

"It went better than expected," the chastened senior aide said. He had favored skipping the debate.

"I'll say. Can one of you guys get the numbers—the size of the viewing audience, polling data?"

"Yes, Madam Secretary," the junior aide said. "I'll also gather stories and op-eds from the Charlotte, Raleigh, and Greensboro newspapers."

"Perfect. What else?"

"Well," the senior aide began, "if you're thinking of approaching Dr. Battle—"

The secretary smiled. "That's exactly what I'm thinking."

"You know she's not one of ours."

"I gathered that."

"Of course, neither was Polly Williams," the aide said, "and that turned out to be a positive."

The secretary smiled again. She loved other opinions, especially when they matched hers. "Exactly!" she said, remembering the late 1980s. "Ms. Williams was a huge benefit—to students and to us."

"Dr. Battle compares favorably," the junior aide said. "She's supersmart, telegenic, and African American. It's hard to think of a better messenger."

"No question," the senior aide said.

"She's also savvy," the secretary said. "Notice how she didn't snap when the think-tank bitch made her snarky remarks? And how she admitted she didn't have all the answers? We need that woman on our team."

"I'll contact her," the senior aide said.

"Let Jerry handle it," the secretary replied. "He's earned it."

"No problem."

"Okay then. Onward, happy warriors!" Miller exclaimed, unconcerned that one aide was crestfallen. No doubt he would raise his game and bounce back. Competition had that effect—on people and institutions. All her life, she'd succeeded by outcompeting people who had attended more prestigious colleges or received higher degrees. It was time to make schools compete to earn the business of the kids they served. And so, as her aides left, she returned to honing her speech for the National PTA Convention.

62

NO MATTER
WHAT HAPPENS

hapel Hill, North Carolina, May 2017. Tears streamed down Teresa's face, and she wiped them with the back of her hand. All those years in the trenches together. All the obstacles surmounted, the disasters averted. Everything she had learned from him. All the confidences he had placed in her. *And this is how I'm repaying him?*

Zeb gave her a hug. "Hey, don't feel sad and don't feel guilty. When I really needed you, when no one would touch me a with a ten-foot pole, you stuck by me. You should have bailed years ago. Instead, you kept us afloat and sacrificed your family life.

"I don't blame Jim for threatening to leave, and can you imagine what that would do to Wylie?" He collected himself. "They need you even more than I do. And you need them. And remember, no matter what happens, I'll owe you forever."

Two Saturdays later Zeb answered the front door still in his bathrobe.

A man held a crate and envelope. "Good morning. Are you Mr. Ackerman?"

"Sure am."

"I have a delivery for you. He's in good shape."

"He?" Zeb asked with raised eyebrows. He took the envelope and opened it. "Thank you."

> Zeb,
>
> I heard about Teresa and figured you could use the company. Clark Whitt is retired now but still remembers the "nutcase" who tried to reward the winning turtle. He agreed you would take great care of Three in his golden years. (I explained how different your life path would've been without him.) Hell, this fella covered more ground on Delta than he ever did at Turtle Kraals! Enjoy.
>
> Hannah

63

THE PRETENDER

Chapel Hill, North Carolina, May 2017. Zeb felt his stomach twisting inside as he waited to be introduced as an expert panelist on the Keys to Business Success forum. In the last couple of weeks, he'd discovered that he was a pretender, not a real entrepreneur. The event sponsor, Launch Chapel Hill, would be sorely disappointed.

It seemed like a sick joke. The first rule in business was to hire the best people, the second to *retain* them. With Teresa's departure, International Expeditions would founder. She'd been the glue that held everything together. *How can I tell attendees to do something I haven't done?*

Teresa's departure to focus on family had made complete sense. But he'd made her decision so much easier—by neglecting so many important tasks and by setting ill-conceived priorities, he'd left her in perpetual scramble mode. Part of being a good entrepreneur was being a good manager. *I'm not.*

It figured the auditorium would be two-thirds full and that Kiara would be sitting up front.

He went onstage, shook hands with the moderator and Leo, and took his seat. At least the atmosphere would be relaxed, since he and Leo had mutual friends. Leo's investment-banking background would provide a useful counterpoint to his small-business experience. They chitchatted until the moderator introduced them to polite applause.

"Zeb, maybe you can lead off by telling us what you think the keys to entrepreneurial success are."

"Sure, be glad to. I'd highlight a few things. First, vision. Make sure your product or service solves an important problem or makes life better for people. Second, differentiate your offering from those of your competitors—define your target market, both demographically and psychographically. Third, be ethical. In the long term it's your only option."

"Leo?"

"Peter, in my experience, the single most important factor, by far, is hiring the best employees and keeping them. Vision and differentiation are important, but without capable, motivated, and loyal employees, business will suffer."

The knot in Zeb's stomach grew tighter.

"You see things differently then?" Peter asked.

"I agree on ethics," Leo said. "And vision is useful, but few businesses offer a revolutionary product or service."

"My company's tours are, in fact, unique," Zeb said.

"Maybe so, but, with all due respect, how many blockbuster years have you had? Innovation on its own doesn't lead to success."

Zeb felt his ears redden. Perspiration made his forehead itch. *I should have been more discreet about my struggles.*

"Here's what I've discovered," Leo continued. "First, successful companies have a well-designed system to ensure standardization and consistently high quality and to ensure that institutional knowledge is retained. Otherwise, businesses are vulnerable to employees performing inconsistently and to top-notch employees leaving."

"Anything else?" Peter said.

"Second, even if you have a revolutionary product, you're nowhere unless you master distribution. Otherwise, cash flow will suffer. The key is: How do you reach your target clients frequently enough in a cost-effective way? What good is a better mousetrap if you have negative cash flow and are destroying value?"

"Zeb?"

Kiara was watching him, pity etched into the furrows of her forehead.

"Some innovative companies suffer early on but succeed in the long run."

Peter nodded—too sympathetically, it seemed. "What are the most important traits for an entrepreneur?"

"Oh, there are a number," Zeb said. "Tenacity, passion, managing fear, flexibility, and self-confidence. Being willing to go against conventional wisdom."

"I'd add managerial awareness to that list," Leo said.

"Expand on that—if you would," Peter said.

The investment banker leaned forward in his seat. "The successful entrepreneur makes sure that managerial and technical aspects of the business aren't neglected, while he or she focuses on product development and big-picture goals. Many passionate visionaries go out of business because they don't take care of the knitting."

Zeb rubbed his neck. Where was this coming from? Teresa hadn't even announced her resignation yet. "Look, if every entrepreneur got bogged down with minutia, there'd never be any innovation. Yes, enterprises must be managed, but management doesn't replace vision. My advice is don't shy away from pursuing yours."

Scattered cheers. Zeb exhaled deeply.

"What do we need to do to prepare the entrepreneurs of tomorrow?" Peter said.

Leo nodded. "As an immigrant, I know America's university system is unequaled. But we need to do a better job educating our younger students. We also have a technical-skills and business-knowledge gap. Our businesses should offer more internships and apprenticeships to give young people training and exposure. Technical schools should be expanded. I know this from my own mechanics training in the air force, which set me on the right path."

Who's writing Leo's talking points? Zeb wondered. The guy was ridiculously smooth.

"Okay, we have our first question from the audience," Peter said. "Please introduce yourself, and then ask your question."

"My name is Kiara Battle—"

"*Doctor* Kiara Battle," Leo corrected.

Kiara smiled. *Too warmly*, Zeb thought.

"Is there room for special-needs students to work in businesses, maybe even your own, as apprentices or interns?"

"Zeb?" Peter said.

"I spend lots of time with LD kids, and I know they can achieve a lot. But I think each business should decide for itself what works best for them—whether an intern will add value or not. Details matter."

"I see," Kiara said. "And you, Mr. Bello?"

"There's always room for these young people, and businesses benefit in the process. Many special-needs students—those with ADHD, for example—are more creative than non-LD kids. There's always a suitable role. And laying the groundwork for more entrepreneurs is beneficial to our country."

Thunderous applause broke out, led by Kiara.

The questioning resumed once calm was restored.

64

UNRAVELING

hapel Hill, North Carolina, June 2017. What his father, a political science professor, was doing in the basement of Phillips Hall, the math building, was a mystery, but under the circumstances, Zeb didn't care where they met. He entered the lab, hugged his dad, and shook hands with the chairwoman of the mathematics department. Evidently, his father had arranged for a tour of the facility and hadn't wanted to cancel on her at the last minute. Which was fine. He'd join his dad on the tour, and they could deal with his tribulations later.

It soon became clear how this visit would be of interest to a modern historian. Phillips Hall, the chairwoman explained, had played a vital role during the Cold War. With the threat of nuclear war looming, the superpowers had developed fallout shelters to escape total annihilation. This shelter had been built in 1959 to protect the UNIVAC 1105 supercomputer and its staff of thirty. One of only three ever manufactured, UNIVAC was a crowning achievement in technology and a key part of the U.S. Office of Civil and Defense Mobilization's plan for saving American civilization in the event of a devastating atomic attack. The chairwoman showed them the supercomputer and detailed its capabilities.

Afterward, they walked to the Carolina Coffee Shop and chose a booth where they could talk freely. Larry ordered French dip, Zeb the pulled pork with pimento cheese.

"That tour was awesome," Zeb said, sipping his iced tea. "You sure know how to pick them."

"I missed my calling."

"So did I, apparently."

Larry's eyebrows drew together. "So, what happened exactly? Something about a lawsuit?"

Zeb exhaled deeply. "One of our clients got hurt zip-lining in Costa Rica. The brake system failed, and she suffered a horrifying injury. She's fine now, thank God."

"Thank God is right. . . . I guess you'll be relying on liability insurance?"

Zeb's ears got warm. "The problem is, things were sucking, and premiums were skyrocketing, so I let our coverage lapse. I never got around to reinstating the policy when things picked up. Teresa was on me about it before she left."

"Jesus, Zeb. I'm not sure what to say. . . . At least the corporate shell will protect your personal assets."

"I wish." Zeb rubbed his eyes. "We still have a partnership. We were working on forming a corporation, but I got swamped and—"

"What the hell." Larry shook his head. "That's irresponsible. What about liability waivers?"

"They won't hold up in court. It turns out the zip-line operator had prior mishaps. We'll be deemed grossly negligent for not knowing."

"How on earth were you supposed to know?"

"I'm not sure." Zeb chugged more tea.

The waiter served the food and refilled their glasses.

"What in God's name was Teresa doing? All this admin stuff—due diligence, insurance—wasn't that her responsibility?"

"She was a godsend. I screwed up. I had no system; I let things get away from me. I ignored things I found boring. Now eight people are losing their jobs."

"Please, not a word of this to your mom—until we figure out how to break it to her."

Break it to her was right, Zeb knew. He was the first in the family to go backward. His grandparents—peddlers and seamstresses—had saved their pennies so that his parents could go to college and become professionals. Now, instead of continuing the progression—becoming a doctor or lawyer—he had regressed by becoming a businessman and then failing at it. "I understand. It would crush her. I can barely look at myself in the mirror."

Larry held Zeb's forearm and stared into his eyes. "There's no need to be ashamed. I mean that. People go out of business all the time. We're proud of you."

"Yeah, right. Nonno and Nonna must be rolling over in their graves."

"You're wrong, Zeb. You've always run your business ethically, demanding the same of your clients and suppliers. You practically offered a public service, promoting genealogy and history before there was money in it. Then the market moved your way, proving you were right. Look at the jobs you've created, both in your business and in those who copied you. Be proud of yourself. Your grandparents would be."

Zeb wiped a tear from his cheek. Then he grinned. "So Alex Keaton can hold his head high?"

What a roller coaster their relationship had been. Early on, his dad had been a reliable ally. Things had changed when his mom prevailed with Zeb taking meds. Maybe his dad felt betrayed. Or maybe he'd resented his dad for not battling harder. Relations deteriorated further when Zeb became, as his dad put it, "an Alex Keaton double." The precocious capitalist from *Family Ties* hadn't been an ideal role model, given the family's heritage.

For a decade, not a fortnight passed when his dad didn't email him a *New York Times* opinion piece on the Republicans' misguided policies. Invariably, he responded with right-wing op-ed assaults on liberalism. Eventually they realized they had the same core values. They were like two baseball umpires who had the same moral strike zone but who called balls and strikes differently because one or both had deficient eyesight or an obstructed view.

"Hold it very high," Larry said. "You forget. I married a business professor. Seriously, you can go in any number of directions—finish your degree, take it further. You still have options."

After lunch Zeb headed to Fetzer Field to watch the latest crop of footballers. *Any number of directions*, he mused. He thought of Three's racing days at Turtle Kraals. Had the little guy always hurtled toward the finish line—lifting others—or had he sometimes searched for a new target? Had he been able to reroute and improvise?

A soccer ball landed a few feet ahead.

"Sir, you mind getting that?"

"No problem," Zeb said, leaning into a kick. "Just hope it ends up where it needs to."

65

GONE

Maracaibo, Venezuela, July 2017. Leonor broke into sobs the moment she hit her living-room sofa. That she had managed to maintain her composure so long astonished Leo. He slipped in beside her and took her hand. He kissed it, calming her. "Nocturne in C," his father's favorite piece, began playing from the speakers, and Leonor blubbered anew. Leo angrily signaled for Chopin to be silenced.

Never seeing his father again wasn't something Leo had contemplated. Only five months ago, in this very room, Papá had been the picture of vigor, physically if not emotionally. He should have pushed them harder to emigrate, not taken no for an answer. *This would never have happened in Charlotte.*

"Where's Carina?" Leonor asked about her daughter.

"She's settling things with the priest. Federico is driving her."

Clara walked in from the kitchen. "Señora Bello, try some chamomile." She served a cup, caressing the widow's shoulder.

"*Gracias*, sweetie."

As if life wasn't a whirlwind before this, Leo thought. Now it all seemed so trivial—the months of counseling with Dr. Rubin, making amends to those he'd hurt, returning to work after Jake's intervention, hitting pay dirt on his VC investments, joining a biotech's board of directors. The minute he fixed his priorities, this happened. Maybe it was karma. Too little, too late.

The lone witness to Papá's death had described him as heroic, fighting off grave robbers half his age. To have ever doubted Papá's bravery was laughable. If only he could have been there to stop them from knocking down Mamá and stabbing his father. And why had Papá died? So the bastards could peddle Aunt Victoria's skull and gold teeth to a black-magic charlatan.

The cup of tea and change in music took effect, and Leonor began reminiscing. She was single-minded—as if on a mission to imprint the family legacy into his mind. Not yet ready to talk of Chuchu, she spoke of his parents, recounting details Leo had always meant to ask about.

Leo's grandfather, Eduardo, the civil engineer turned Basque Nationalist revolutionary, grew up in Pamplona, the son of a military captain. A virile teenager, Eduardo ran with the bulls during San Fermín, surfed monster waves at Mundaka, and rode horses with abandon. He studied at the University of Navarra, moonlighting as a midfielder on Lagun Artea's fútbol team.

"What turned Abuelo into a revolutionary?" Leo asked.

Leonor shook her head sadly. "The Spanish Civil War. Or rather General Franco, Spain's fascist leader. He asked the Nazis to carpet-bomb the Basque town of Guernica and to send in their tanks. They did, targeting civilians and refugees and killing seventeen hundred people. Eduardo quit university and joined the Republicans—the Reds."

"And how did a builder wind up on death row?" Leo asked.

"Well, Eduardo masterminded two devastating attacks on Franco's barracks in Madrid. They captured him and sent him to El Dueso. Eduardo's father was well connected, but he was a *Franquista* and refused to intervene. Only a last-minute intercession by a businessman secured his release. Eduardo fled to Venezuela by ship."

"What about Abuelita Merche?"

"She was the best—like a second mother to me," Leonor said, misty-eyed, as she recounted Merche's story.

A Catalan aristocrat by birth, Merche had grown up in a mansion along Barcelona's Gran Via. Servants combed her hair and dressed her in lavish gowns, yet she had none of the haughtiness common to her class. What she did have was artistic talent. Periodically she traveled to Mallorca to study painting under her uncle, Hermenegildo Anglada Camarasa, whose works hung at the Musée d'Orsay and the Reina Sofía museum. Merche's family spent summers in San Sebastian and weekends in Calella de Palafrugell, an idyllic fishing village on the Costa Brava.

Merche's family was in San Sebastian when the Civil War broke out in 1936, as were Eduardo and a surfing buddy. They warned Merche that Franquista forces were closing in and that, as Catalan Republicans, her family should flee. Merche's father demurred, but Eduardo insisted. Franco was aiming not only to tap Basque raw materials to control Spain's industrial production but also to cut off Republican-controlled areas from France. Eduardo knew the escape routes to Barcelona through France's Basque country and promised to organize everything free of charge. Winning the favor of the elegant Catalana—seeing her mischievous twinkle—was reward enough. Eduardo's warnings proved prescient, when General Mola's forces rolled into San Sebastian one week later.

"How did Grandma Merche's life in Barcelona change?" Leo asked.

"Merche stopped everything she considered frivolous. No painting, socializing, or traveling. After all, Franco had Catalonia in his sights."

"If Grandma's family was well-off and supported the church and free enterprise, why were they Republican?"

"Same as with the Basques. The Reds offered the Catalans autonomy; Franco didn't. Also, Merche's family supported greater social and political justice. They had voted to abolish the monarchy in favor of a liberal republic. But things got terribly out of hand."

Leo leaned forward. "What do you mean?"

"The radicals and Communists were burning churches. They'd have executed Merche's father at the drop of a hat."

"So if Grandma couldn't put in with the Reds, what did she do?"

"She volunteered as a nurse's aide at a hospital. It was a nonpolitical way to do good. But that was the tip of the iceberg."

"How so?"

"Merche risked her life by helping nuns elude danger. Remember, nuns had taught her at Colegio Jesús María. Now they were being accused of poisoning children with sweets. One was shot for refusing to marry a militiaman who had stormed the convent. Another was thrown down a mine shaft after being forced to swallow her rosary beads."

Leo shook his head in wonder. "My God, super high stakes for a teenager."

"For anyone. But Merche did allow herself one indulgence: She kept in touch with Eduardo, in secret. Her parents would never have approved, since he was a Basque revolutionary."

Merche was relieved to discover that, despite being a Red, Eduardo was a devout Catholic and opposed to the harassment of clergy. He supported her scheme to help nuns escape rape and murder. Each week a different nun would arrive at Merche's house while her parents were out. She outfitted each nun in a stylish dress and hat, applied rouge, and made sure her hair was perfectly coiffed. Transformation complete, the nun would be whisked away under cover of darkness and transported to a convent in the Nationalist zone.

And so it was that Merche, a Republican, spent her Civil War years moonlighting for the Nationalist underground, Leonor told them with pride.

When Merche married Eduardo, she was disowned. Never mind that Eduardo's well-to-do relatives had pioneered steel fabrication in Navarra. The Huelins had arrived in Spain from Southampton,

England, in 1777 and shined ever since. In Malaga they had built a leading wine, dried-fruit, and sugarcane-exporting business, and 250 years later the workers' neighborhood was still called Huelin, in honor of Edward Huelin, the humanitarian visionary.

In Barcelona—where market conditions forced the closure of the Málaga factory—they became successful financiers and philanthropists. Merche had done the unthinkable, marrying below her station.

Undaunted, Merche followed Eduardo, eventually boarding a Caracas-bound ship with three children in tow, including Leo's father. Her devotion wouldn't be reciprocated. When Eduardo's construction business in Venezuela foundered, his insecurities led to dalliances. The couple separated, and the onetime aristocrat ended up working as a flight attendant, cheerfully serving meals to passengers on Avensa Airlines. Later Merche managed a boarding house for Maracaibo-based pilots and flight attendants. She sent her kids to school in Barbados and Jamaica so they could learn English and live in a more wholesome environment. Her positivity inspired everyone. Never a hint of bitterness over her riches-to-rags story.

As Leo listened to his mamá, he felt special to be part of Merche's bloodline. Even Eduardo had seemed heroic until he ran into bad luck. Insecurities could plague anyone. It would take time to absorb the import of everything he'd heard.

What mattered now was getting mamá to listen to reason. Life in Charlotte would be good for her and Carina. His sister was already on board—enthusiastically.

Three days later Leo was awakened by the sound of the flight attendant's voice over the public address system. "We'll be landing in Charlotte in twenty minutes. Please return your trays . . ." Beside him sat strangers, not mamá or Carina. He felt a knot in his stomach. It made no sense, his mother's refusing to abandon a deceased husband, still loving the country that had killed him, where positive change felt like a pipe dream. And poor Carina. What a bleak future . . .

Leo felt lonelier than ever. Untethered, too. And it could get worse: He needed to tell his dear friend, Kiara, about Clara, his new significant other.

He also needed to apologize to Zeb, whose help he needed. The apology was long past due.

66

GIMGHOUL

hapel Hill, North Carolina, July 2017. Kiara struggled to match Teresa's stride as they speed-walked toward Gimghoul. Somehow, being able to run a five-and-a-half-minute mile was of no help: She, the athlete, was sucking wind, while the office worker chattered nonstop. It was embarrassing but, now that she'd actually had her license revoked—not just suspended—humiliation was in order. Neither the Board of Psychology's warnings nor her suspension had put a dent in her overconfidence, so now all that remained was for her to pick Teresa's brain as part of her own postmortem.

"You heard about the legend of Gimghoul?" Teresa said.

"Nope."

"The castle is coming up soon. It's one of eight in North Carolina. There's lots of intrigue around it."

"Give me a taste." She kept her comments short, the better to keep pace.

"It's home to a secret society that college students founded back in 1889. They had some noble Arthurian mission, a code of chivalry. They called themselves the Order of the Dromgoole. Later, the name was changed to Gimghoul."

"Sounds medieval," Kiara said.

"Legend has it that, in 1833, a young man named Dromgoole was madly in love with a girl who had another suitor. They fought a duel, and Dromgoole was killed. He's buried under a bloodstained rock behind the castle."

Kiara chuckled. "Dead and buried—like my career."

"I don't believe that, not for a moment."

"Oh, yeah? Tell that to the All Kinds of Minds Institute. They dropped me like a hot potato when I lost my license. What's more, I deserved it."

"Hogwash."

Kiara wiped sweat from her forehead. "I was the one who recommended the poor girl transfer to Estes school. Two weeks later she tried to off herself and almost succeeded."

"If she was being bullied, it was the bully's fault, not yours."

A dense tree line came into view. "Confidentially, the girl had been struggling with a learning disability. I thought she'd get more personalized attention and learn better."

"Of course," Teresa said. "Parents send their kids to private school for that very reason."

"But I should've followed up after the transfer, to see how things were going. Let me ask you: What's Wylie's experience been like at Estes?"

Teresa slowed. "Educationally, it's been excellent."

"How about with bullying?"

"Truthfully?"

"No, I would prefer you lie," Kiara said, instantly regretting her response.

"Wylie was bullied until we intervened. Look, you can't be expected to know every school."

"I should've known *that* school. Her parents trusted me."

They entered the forest, with the contours of Gimghoul now visible above the trees.

"How's Zeb doing?" Teresa asked. "I've been scared to call him since he shuttered the business."

"You shouldn't be scared."

"I left him high and dry."

"Yeah, right," Kiara said. "After how many years? You had good reasons; Zeb knows that."

They reached the castle. "It's beautiful."

"I think so," Teresa said. "The artisans were French. It took thirteen hundred tons of stone to build and cost fifty thousand dollars. A lot of dough in 1924."

"All for a secret meeting place."

"Crazy, right?"

"Normally, I'd agree," Kiara said. "But I better stop making snap judgments. People get hurt."

"Not as bad as Dromgoole."

67

BASQUE IN GLORY

Saint-Jean-de-Luz, France, August 2017. Along the Saint-Jean-de-Luz waterfront, fishing boats returned to port, tourists snapped photos of macaroon bakeries and historic houses, and beer-swilling locals debated politics at the café where Leo sat engrossed in his book, *The Basque History of the World*. Finishing a passage, Leo looked quickly to the southwest, only to smile self-consciously and sip his txakoli. Hendaye train station, where General Franco had met Adolf Hitler on October 23, 1940, was thirteen kilometers away—not visible. Though embarrassed, he was in brighter spirits than either fascist had been on that day. He could immerse himself in the war without having to outfox or browbeat a potential ally.

The Basque wine got Leo's mind going the way caffeine did for many. It tasted okay—not great—but drinking it, as Zeb had advised him to do, connected him with the people whose blood he shared and whose history he'd grown to admire. It had taken his father's death to inspire this adventure. Well, that and consulting with the psychologist, Dr. Rubin. No longer did he have to radiate success or manliness while on vacation. He was free to explore his roots and to pay homage to the memory of Eduardo, his late grandfather. The revolutionary's exploits and death-row experience had given him courage during the assault long ago in Venezuela. Kiara, too, had urged him on, herself having taken a heritage tour to Africa.

Zeb had overlooked nothing. Had he still been in business, the itinerary could easily have been a prototype for a World War II Resistance tour. Sure, it was pricey, but Leo would have willingly paid double given the quality. Besides, he'd unwittingly humiliated Zeb during the entrepreneurship panel, and he knew by now that an apology wasn't enough, no matter how sincere.

Ever the oddball, Zeb had agreed to arrange the tour only after Leo promised to read Mark Kurlansky's masterpiece cover to cover. Having to read such a book was like having to accept a free snorkeling trip to Bora Bora. Already, he'd purchased ten copies to hand out as Christmas gifts. No people had a more fascinating history. And he'd now get to relive some of it himself.

"Lieutenant Bello?"

Leo glanced up at a brawny dark man in his twenties. "Oh . . . yes."

"I'm your guide, Fermin Goikoetxea."

He was Spanish, not French. They shook hands. "*Mucho gusto.* Leo."

Fermin frowned. Obviously, the man considered himself Basque, not Spanish. "Nice to meet you," Leo quickly said in English.

Fermin nodded. "Have you had anything to eat?"

"No, but I've had lots of txacoli."

"How was your adventure up north?"

"Adventurous. Zeb warned me that I wouldn't be visiting the Louvre. But I had no idea I'd be changing into fighter-pilot gear and jumping out of a plane."

"In tandem with an instructor," Fermin pointed out, taking a seat.

"True, but, last time I checked, Basques didn't fly missions for the Allies."

Another frown. "No, but they saved hundreds who did. Would you have rather blown up barracks?"

"I guess not."

Nonetheless, Operation Comet had gotten off to an intense start. Parachuting over northwest France had made his heart pound faster than it ever had. After landing in a wheat field—no incoming fire, thankfully—the instructor had handed him a map and compass and bid him adieu. Leo had navigated six kilometers to a safe house, a farm, where he overnighted. Over food and wine, the wartime farmer's grandson regaled him with stories about pilots. They poured over evocative photographs and newspaper clippings from the era. The next morning, he had taken the train to Paris. There, a "female agent" met him and accompanied him, inconspicuously, on the train to Saint-Jean-de-Luz. Upon arrival, he had made his way, as instructed, to the men's room, exiting to Avenue de Verdun via a hidden service door. Thus, he had slipped past any lurking German inspectors and headed to the Ocean Hotel Café to rendezvous with Fermin, the smart aleck.

"During the war," Fermin began, "Basque guides rescued over seven hundred downed pilots, taking them from Occupied France to Spain. Many of the fliers returned to England so they could resume the fight."

"That's incredible. I read they also helped political refugees and Jews to escape, and that some were former smugglers who knew the footpaths across the Pyrenees, how to descend mountain passes without being detected by French, German, and Spanish sentries. What I don't understand is why were they so helpful?"

Fermin sighed. "It was emotional. Many had relatives and friends who had been deported to Nazi concentration camps, especially Mauthausen. Thousands were executed. Basque guides saw the fight against Hitler and Mussolini as an extension of their fight against Franco."

Leo whistled. "Wow, respect."

"Sir, I recommend you stop drinking txacoli. Please hydrate, eat, and rest. Room 104 is yours." Fermin handed him the key. "I'll pick you up at eleven thirty p.m."

"You mean *a.m.*"

"No, *p.m.* We have a long night ahead, Lieutenant. Please recharge your batteries."

Fermin took off, as Leo pondered the hardships of being a downed fighter pilot and insensitive business panelist.

After dark they set off southward, following a stream they could hear but barely see. They climbed 1,600 feet, traversing Mt. Xoldocagcagna and descending to the Nivelle Valley. In Saint-Pée, Fermin pointed out the old Gestapo headquarters. During the war, he explained, it wouldn't have been visible at night because of the blackout enforced by the Germans. They scurried past it and headed toward the mountain village of Sare. Navigating another mountain pass, they trekked along a creek, tripping over branches and into ruts. Suddenly it dawned on Leo that this route matched one described in Kurlansky's book.

"Fermin, are you, by any chance, related to *Florentino* Goikoetxea?"

The guide stopped and faced Leo. "He was my grandfather."

"My gosh, that's unbelievable! What an honor."

"Thank you."

"Two-hundred and twenty-seven rescued pilots, if I'm not mistaken," Leo said. "Mr. Florentino was a hero."

"He helped pilots, refugees, Jews, even German deserters. Thanks to God, he wasn't arrested by the Gestapo like most guides."

"Thank God is right. How many people worked for *la ligne*?"

Fermin resumed trekking. "Around one thousand and seven hundred. They had agents throughout France and Belgium."

The exertion wore down Leo's exhilaration. They approached the Spanish side of the border where, during the war, the blackout gave way to the lights of Irún and Hondarribia. Here the risks for escapees mounted: Although Spain was technically neutral, the Guardia Civil would hand them over summarily to the Germans. That was why Fermin and Leo crossed the border at 4:00 a.m., when sentries would be less alert. Zeb was a simulation monster.

"I hope that was the hardest stretch."

"Possibly."

Ahead, the Bidasoa's rushing waters could be heard. With visibility so limited, Leo felt a pang of nervousness. Fermin unpacked some wet-weather gear. "Be careful with the current."

Once waterproofed, Leo stepped into the river on Fermin's downstream side. "Is it always this strong?"

"Sometimes."

Leo slipped, but Fermin grabbed him before he could be swept downriver. They made it across, overcoming slippery rocks and underwater branches. After repacking their gear, they hiked three kilometers to Sarobe Farm, where they feasted on omelets, cheese, and red wine, topped off with hair-raising war stories. Before allowing Leo to slumber, the farmer insisted he wash up and change into local clothes, lest the Guardia Civil raid them. After three hours of shut-eye, they were off again, hiking along secondary roads to the town of Rentería.

At the train station, Fermin said, "Lieutenant, when you arrive in Bilbao, go to the British consulate. They'll smuggle you to Lisbon or Gibraltar and then to London. God willing, you'll not be shot down again." He smiled and, role-playing over, added, "Sir, please forgive me. I misjudged you badly. You will make a wonderful ambassador. Please tell America about my people—*your* people."

"You can count on it, my friend. We'll keep in touch."

They hugged, and Leo jumped aboard. The journey from Saint-Jean-de-Luz to San Sebastian, twenty minutes by car, had taken them nine hours. Had the Bidasoa been raging, it might have taken sixteen hours. Thankfully, Zeb had arranged for him to dally in San Sebastian before proceeding to Bilbao. Apology finally accepted.

Even downed pilots needed their rest and relaxation, so Leo took his on La Concha beach, watching the waves—some ridden by surfers—roll in. It was hard to believe Copacabana or Ipanema could top this. He took a dip—too cold for a long swim—then plopped back onto his towel. He averted his gaze from two topless Scandinavian women to avoid appearing like another gawking American. Elderly men played *petanque*, punctuating their good and bad tosses with passionate outbursts. A man in North African garb built a magnificent sandcastle, inscribing *Eskerrik Asko*—thank you—alongside it. Onlookers from the promenade above marveled, dropping coins to acknowledge their gratitude.

Hunger was setting in, so Leo ambled to nearby Old Town. A basilica carved into the side of a mountain almost lured him in, but he sought nourishment of a different kind. Basque chefs, now considered some of the best in the world, made *pintxos*, snacks atop small pieces of bread that, according to Zeb, were not to be missed. And so he window-shopped along Calle 31 de Agosto, peering into a succession of *pintxo* bars, salivating like a Pavlovian dog.

Finally, he stepped into one. The question then became which delicacy to choose—the competition was brutal. Would it be mango, pâté, and Iberico ham; spinach, mushroom, and shrimp; *bacalao* cod, Iberico ham, and onions; or crab and salmon? He felt paralyzed until he realized it was a false choice. He ordered one of each, along with a carafe of txakoli. Fifty minutes later, passed out on La Concha, he felt like the happiest beached whale in the world.

That afternoon Leo met with Father Jose Javier Monte, a Basque studies professor at Deusto University. The Jesuit had spent thirty-five years as a missionary in Latin America before returning to Spain. In Argentina he had crossed paths with fellow Jesuit Cardinal Bergoglio, the current Pope Francis. Father Monte now doubled as a priest and educator, dedicating more time to research and writing, less to teaching and ministering. Working at the San Sebastian campus suited him because it was closer to Hondarribia, where he lived and loved to fish. *How does Zeb find these guys?* Leo wondered.

"Do you mind if we speak in English?" Father Monte asked.

Leo recalled Fermin. "That's fine with me."

"Zeb sent me the names of your ancestors in Basque country. I researched them, but, sadly, my findings were limited."

"I understand. What did you learn?"

"Two things. First, I traced one branch of your family to late-eighteenth-century France."

"France?"

"Not surprising, really. Basques inhabit both countries. The earliest ancestor I could find was Nicolas Apat. He was a colonel in Napoleon's Grenadiers regiment, cavalry. No details beyond that."

"Napoleon! That's some detail." Leo felt as if he'd been injected with adrenaline.

"When the emperor was defeated, Nicolas fled to Spain. He stayed within Basque country, settling in a village called Arizkun. He married a local girl and worked as a carpenter."

"Where is Arizkun?"

"In the Baztan Valley, in Navarra," Father Monte said. "It's isolated and was even more so back then. The people still observe traditions going back to pre-Roman, pagan times."

"They aren't Christians?"

"They are. Basques are among the most devout Catholics in Europe. But in this remote valley, Catholicism is mixed with supernatural beliefs."

"What happened then?"

"The family lived in Arizkun, until your great-grandfather moved to Pamplona. He loved horseback riding and, back then, serious riders entered the military. Living in Pamplona allowed him to move up the ranks."

Leo nodded. "And what about Eduardo, my grandfather?"

"That was the second thing. I assume you know he and Merche separated after she arrived in Venezuela?"

"Yes."

"Well, Eduardo then returned to France to join the Guernica battalion."

"Guernica? I thought that was 1937, during the Spanish Civil War?"

"The bombing, yes," Father Monte said. "The *battalion* was named in honor of the victims. The battalion played a crucial role at the end of World War II. In 1944, as the Allies fought their way east toward Germany, the Nazis left twenty-five thousand troops in southwestern France. They were dug in along the Atlantic coast in concrete bunkers. The Guernica battalion, mainly Basque veterans of the Spanish Civil War, heroically drove the Nazis from their bunkers despite being outnumbered. They deserve some of the credit for liberating France."

"Fascinating. What then?"

"Eduardo returned to Venezuela but died soon afterward. He never got to see what the country turned into."

Leo raised his eyebrows and started to speak but hesitated. Having gone to Catholic schools and overheard comments over the years, he knew Jesuits were all over the board ideologically. They were the church's leading intellectuals and, as such, remained unpredictable. In Latin America they leaned left, promoting a collectivist philosophy that appealed to Indigenous peoples and Castro admirers. In Europe Jesuits leaned conservative, supporting monarchs and the military. But not uniformly so. Allegiances varied widely, especially in Basque country, where support for self-determination often outweighed ideology. Where was Father Monte on the map?

"I gather you spent many years in Latin America," Leo said.

"I did."

"Including Venezuela?"

The Jesuit nodded. "Before returning to Spain, I oversaw Caritas."

"One of the few agencies allowed to run soup kitchens and first aid."

"Correct."

"How do you feel about the Venezuelan bishops?" Leo asked.

Father Monte smiled. "You really mean, do I support their opposition to the Maduro regime? Or perhaps, how can the Pope—whom I'm blessed to know—remain quiet in the face of Maduro's anti-Democratic measures and human-rights violations? How can he not support the National Assembly as the only legitimate organ of sovereignty, with Juan Guaidó as its leader? Or maybe even, how could the Vatican send an ambassador to Maduro's inauguration when the election was illegitimate?"

"You frame the questions better than I ever could. Forgive me—I know they're not what you agreed to discuss."

"Not at all. I'm glad you care about more than your family history."

"I take it you sympathize with the opposition?"

The Jesuit sighed. "I care about alleviating suffering, as does the pope. What do you suppose would happen to Caritas's clinics and soup kitchens if the Vatican were to end relations with Maduro?"

"I agree things aren't so simple. But, with all due respect, why does the pope fiercely denounce capitalists, while giving leftist autocrats a free pass? That's hard to stomach when so many Venezuelans, including my family, are suffering."

"What do you suggest?"

Leo sighed. "I suggest that the Holy Father follow John Paul II's example. Can you ever imagine John Paul sending diplomats to legitimize Jaruzelski's dictatorship while it was squashing Solidarity? John Paul was with the democrats all along and played a pivotal role in Poland's winning freedom."

"His Holiness was a unique individual and was Polish himself. And remember, the Russians' one-hundred-forty-year occupation of Poland, followed by the Communists' long domination of it, boosted the church's influence in a unique way. Catholicism became a point of identification for Poles." Father Monte was sounding more professor than priest.

"Granted, but is there any question that John Paul's courage and leadership boosted the church's popularity in a huge way?"

The priest grinned. "None whatsoever. But Pope Francis isn't Venezuelan, and he has a different disposition."

And ideology, Leo thought. Having lived under Argentina's right-wing dictatorship, Pope Francis had become a die-hard leftist. "So nothing serious can be done?"

"As you Americans say, there's more than one way to skin a cat." Father Monte eyeballed Leo. "What institution in Venezuela, do you think, enjoys the highest approval rating among the public?"

"The National Assembly they just elected."

"It's the Catholic church with fifty-seven percent approval. That's twenty points higher than the National Assembly. Moreover—and this is important—the fifty-seven percent includes half of those identifying with *Chavismo*." The Jesuit sounded like a political consultant.

"Fine, but what good is popularity if the church won't use its influence to change things?" Leo said.

"Not everything is visible. We have a vast network of priests throughout the country who can win over the hearts and minds of people on the fence."

"Hearts and minds won't win against machine guns, tanks, and torture," Leo said.

"Remember, most generals and colonels still attend mass, thank God. And the message they hear will soon be changing. Sermons will be standardized, like the talking points you hear in America. Have faith. The church will help transition Venezuela back to democracy."

"From your lips to God's ears—or at least the pope's."

Father Monte chuckled. "I assure you my words aren't that weighty."

They must have been, Leo thought.

The priest retrieved a flash drive from his drawer and handed it over. "Here's a copy of the research I did. Email me if you have any questions."

"You're leaving?"

"I need to catch me a *merluza* or *lubino*," the Jesuit said, already jettisoning his grammar. "Man doesn't live on bread alone."

Back in Charlotte, Leo reached for his cell with the lethargy of a jet-lagged traveler who had traversed too many Pyrenees. Checking the caller ID, he scrambled to a sitting position. It was Clara.

"Capitalist pig speaking, can I help you?" he said, teasing her for the conversation they'd had during his horseback jaunt.

"At this point, *any* meat would be welcome," Clara said.

"That bad?"

"Let's just say, there's nothing here to match the *pintxos* you sank your teeth into."

"You've been talking to Mamá."

"Twice a week. So tell me about your trip. I want to hear everything."

Leo covered the high points—the Resistance reenactment, his face-to-face with Father Monte, meetings with his second cousins.

"How are you processing it all?" Clara asked.

"Too early to tell."

"Any initial impressions?"

Leo sighed. "Just that I'm a know-it-all who doesn't."

"My gosh, a modern-day Socrates. Stop fishing for compliments. You know you're brilliant."

"I know I'm sharp in some ways," he said. "But when it comes to understanding the people who matter the most, I've been an idiot. I've been judgmental and wrong."

"Look, we don't need to dig into this, if it's too personal."

He reclined on the sofa again. "I think we're past that, don't you? Unless it's making you uncomfortable."

"Not at all, and I'm sure my rates are cheaper than Dr. Rubin's." Clara giggled. "You were saying?"

"Well, on the one hand, I idealized—romanticized—the distant and unfamiliar. My grandparents, particularly Eduardo. I was like a crow drawn to shiny objects. At the same time, I undervalued my own parents. And with Papá, it's too late. I'm ashamed."

Clara whistled. "That's a load. Don't you think your parents would want you to idealize your grandparents? And you're hardly the first to not fully appreciate your parents early on. Better late than never."

"It's more complicated than that."

"Why?"

"I allowed my admiration for my grandparents"—Leo's voice cracked—"to detract from, almost deplete, my regard for my parents.

Here's what kills me: My success is due to the love and support I received from my parents—their single-minded devotion to my education and to family over business success. It was precisely those qualities I disdained in my parents that catapulted me to where I am. My parents gave me the self-confidence to achieve so much I felt I could then look down on them. Take it a step further—if my parents had been ultra-ambitious and self-absorbed—more like Eduardo—I'd have been less successful."

"Ironic, I'll agree."

"I wish I could've told Papá how much I admire his courage." Leo fought the lump in his throat. "Not just for fighting off the robber. For bucking the *Chavistas* all those years. For not working side deals, while everyone else was earning kickbacks, living like kings."

"Look, I get it. But I had lunch with your parents every week, and one thing was clear: Your father understood and loved you deeply."

His eyes pooled with tears. "Maybe so, but I need to change my life. Do something worthier, something to honor my parents and grandparents."

"You'll find a way." Clara sounded confident.

"Easier said than done."

"True. You'll probably need help from a spiritual guru—someone to guide you along the way."

He smiled at the mischief in her voice. "Like who?"

"I know someone who moonlights as an economics professor and business consultant."

"Would this guru happen to have big brown eyes and sexy legs?"

"Do those things matter?" she asked.

"Absolutely. Would such enlightenment be administered by phone or in person?"

"Oh, that depends entirely on how many rabbits George Akst can pull out of his immigration hat."

68

GUIDE STARS

Chapel Hill, North Carolina, August 2017. Zeb couldn't help smiling as the seventh-grade girl delivered her presentation. It was so obvious now. He should never have quit teaching altogether. The joy and perspective these kids gave him would have benefited his business immensely. They were special—less for their "needs" than for their souls and creativity. Thank God, Rabbi had invited him back to teach this class. *Without these kids, I'd be lost.*

When Rachel had finished, Zeb jumped to his feet, clapping. "Great job! Sometimes I think I learn more from you guys than the other way around."

Rachel returned to her seat, blushing. Her classmates waved their arms eagerly.

"Okay, we have time for one more. Matthew, you're next."

"Spaceman!" a classmate bellowed.

Matthew dashed to the podium. "Why is God special to me?" he asked, restating the prompt. "That's easy! Because he created the stars. And I know Gordon Cooper agrees."

Zeb laughed. "Good start, now bring it home."

Matthew shot him an I-got-this wink. "We all know the Mercury astronauts studied celestial navigation here, at Morehead Planetarium. Well, on Gordon Cooper's solo mission around the earth, the navigation system broke down. Imagine that! He had to use the constellations and guide stars to make his reentry window. It turned out that Gordon's landing was the most accurate of all the Mercury missions. All thanks to God's stars!" Matthew tapped his heart twice and then pointed to the heavens. "That's all, folks!"

"Awesome, Matthew! Love the creativity," Zeb said.

Matthew bowed and returned to his seat.

"Okay, guys, that's it for today. Don't forget to practice your bar and bat mitzvah portions, and to use Khan Academy for your schoolwork. Shalom, y'all!"

That afternoon, Zeb escorted his mother into Triangle Care. They signed in and, as Zeb scanned the waiting room, he recoiled sharply, nearly upsetting Ruth's balance. After steadying her, Zeb led her to the far side of the room, away from the gentleman he'd spotted.

"Why do we have to sit here?"

"Walking is good for you, Mom."

No sooner had they taken a seat than Ruth's name was called. Zeb accompanied her to the nurse, grabbed a *Men's Health* magazine, and returned to his chair.

"Good luck finding anything interesting," the gentleman called out. "'Eating According to Your Blood Type' was almost readable."

Zeb grunted.

"It's been a while," the man said.

"Yup," he mumbled, staring at the table of contents.

"Was that your mother?"

"Yup." Zeb pretended to focus on an article.

"My wife was diagnosed with early-onset Alzheimer's. We've been coming here seven years."

He looked up. "Are you saying this stuff actually works, Professor?"

The gentleman chuckled. "Professor? I haven't been one for quite a while. But, yes, cognitive training works if you do the home exercises. I wish we'd known earlier."

Zeb nodded. That corresponded with what he'd read. The ACTIVE program supposedly boosted memory by 60 percent, with the gains holding for six months or more. "Makes sense." Hopefully, the guy would now shut up.

The professor cleared his throat. "Zeb, I never got a chance to apologize."

Zeb shot him a sardonic smile. "For what, ruining my life? You couldn't have tried that hard: I've been in Chapel Hill ever since."

The man's shoulders slumped. "I resigned my professorship the year after you were expelled. Two years later than I should have." He sighed. "I let my personal problems affect my teaching. At home, I was an inattentive father, and as a result my son turned to drugs—heavily. I was incredibly angry and shortchanged anyone else who needed special attention. I neglected my learning-disabled students. I'll carry that to my grave."

Zeb's nostrils flared. "You realize I would've had my doctorate in history by now, lived a completely different life?"

"I can't say how sorry I am—truly. I let down so many people— you most of all. That was *not* how the university trained me to behave. Still, you managed to bounce back incredibly. You're a household name in travel."

"Professor, we filed for bankruptcy two months ago."

"My God!"

At last, the man shut up. Zeb turned to the article on blood type, but soon discarded the magazine. He texted Kiara, asking her to thank Corinda for having recommended ACTIVE. And then he waited.

69

HAPPY CAMPERS

C*hapel Hill, North Carolina, August 2017.* Fetzer Field was almost empty now that all the day campers had left. Kiara's brother, Brian, was picking up cones, her dad gathering jerseys. It seemed like old times, cleaning up after their training sessions. Except, now, she hadn't needed to whine to be included. Far from it. She had been the head honcho of Kiara Battle Soccer Camp, directing the drills while the youngsters executed. Things had gone like clockwork for two whole weeks. Quality work, lots of laughs, no egos. A wave of satisfaction welled up inside her.

Could this mark an upswing in fortunes? It sure beat lying in bed for days after having her license permanently revoked. How pathetic she, the psychologist, had been. Thankfully, her family had come through, as they always did, when it mattered most. Her dad had been incredible—conceiving of the camp, pushing until she relented, and then convincing Bob Jeffreys to assign his camp's marketing person to promote hers. Because the Triangle was a hotbed of girls' soccer, enrollment had maxed out in nine days. Brian had taken time off work to help out. Her mom had come along for moral support. All hands had rushed on deck enthusiastically.

And, boy, had she needed the support, after a patient almost died. Her arrogance had led to multiple failures—making snap judgments, not researching the new school, not contacting the parents after the girl's transfer. And she'd acted this way *after* the Murphy fiasco, *after* getting suspended. Nothing had put a dent in her arrogance.

Had the camp finally managed to do what the Board of Psychology warnings and suspension couldn't? For Leo, LifeNet4Families had done the job, infusing him with humility and gratitude. Of course, training eighth graders in soccer—retrieving errant shots, tending to injuries, treating them like VIPs—didn't compare to waiting on the homeless, but maybe serving others would help her. Something was percolating inside. Could it be the start of what she needed?

She felt a tinge of sadness. The two weeks had gone by so fast. Brian approached with an equipment bag. "All right, boss woman, where does this go?"

"The trunk would be great. I've gotta wash everything before returning it to Bob. Come back for a hug."

Marcus strode toward them, beaming. "I don't know about you guys, but I had so much fun. A lot of work, but, my Lord, it was worth it."

Two hours later the family sat at Stoney River waiting to feast on succulent steaks. Brian beat Marcus to the whiskey shrimp, earning a glare once reserved for Sarah. Kiara grabbed parmesan fries while Corinda savored the lobster soup.

"Mom, how did your afternoon go?" Kiara asked.

"Great, actually. I didn't know what to expect, but Ruth's doing well. The cognitive therapy seems to be helping."

"Awesome. And Zeb?"

"He was there, typing whatever Ruth dictated. She's documenting her dementia experience in a book."

"Wow, that's courageous," Marcus said. "Is Zeb bouncing back?"

"It's hard to tell," Corinda said. "I avoided the topic of business like the plague. But he had a gleam in his eye. Maybe it's because he's getting a master's in education."

"Zeb's resilient," Brian said. "Like you, sis. You two need to date."

"Please. He's like a brother."

Brian's eyes squinted with feigned anger. "Hey, I didn't see *his* ass sweating at camp for two weeks!"

"This has all been so great," Kiara gushed. "I'll be sad to see you go."

"Good, then it's settled," Corinda said with a mischievous grin. "Brian has three vacation days left. You both should come for the Caribbean Carnival in Florida. You can bond, enjoy Trini culture, and eat home-cooked meals. Your dad will cover the flights, right, Marcus?"

"I know my role in life."

"The truth is, I had been hoping to hang out with Leo," Kiara said sheepishly. "But it looks like we're gonna stay friends."

Brian nodded empathetically and then blurted out, "Then it's you and me in Miami!"

Kiara grinned. "Start fitting your costume."

70

HUMILITY

Research Triangle, North Carolina, September 2017. Three hours after leaving Charlotte, Leo dashed into the UNC Center for Public Television. The drive had taken longer than anticipated. Meredith Summers, the program host, met him and escorted him to the studio. After freshening up, he took his appointed seat. They chatted until the recording session was due to begin.

"You ready?" Meredith asked.

"I better be," he said, wiping his sweaty palms on his trousers. He'd delivered many high-stakes interviews over the years, but this one meant more. Done right, this could propel him to doing even more with his life and making his family proud.

When the producer signaled, Meredith smiled and peered into the camera. "Thank you for tuning into *Our North Carolina*. Today we're pleased to host Mr. Leo Bello, founder of the nonprofit organization American Bridge, which conducts research and promotes bipartisan initiatives in key policy areas. Mr. Bello, welcome."

"I'm thrilled to be here. Please, call me Leo."

"You have quite a story, Leo—growing up in Venezuela, immigrating to the U.S., and becoming one of America's top investment bankers. You obviously lead a busy life. What made you decide to found American Bridge?"

"I've been blessed. After serving four years in the U.S. Air Force, I was allowed to become an American citizen. This country gave me opportunities I would never have had elsewhere. In reality, I owe it everything. I want to show my gratitude by helping make things even better."

"What needs to change?"

Leo sighed. "There's way too much polarization. In a democracy, you expect—need—diversity of views. Coming from Venezuela, I know this more than most. But things have gotten out of control, on both sides."

"How so?"

"The narratives are warped. One side looks at America and sees the glass as eighty percent empty. America is unjust, materialistic, a bully, it abuses its power, and is systemically racist. America isn't exceptional in any positive sense."

"The other side?"

"The glass is ninety percent full. America is a tremendous force for good, having liberated more people, and lifted more people out of poverty, than any country in history. Racism hardly exists. The police rarely mistreat minorities. Wealth inequality isn't a problem."

"So who or what causes this polarization?"

"I think it goes beyond ideological differences or President Trump's feisty personality. Ultimately, I think it's about humility. Too few of us are humble enough, and that leads to polarization."

"So talk to me about humility."

"Well, I'm as humble as they come," Leo said, grinning. "Seriously, humility is important because it helps bridge differences. There's a professor at Pepperdine, Brian Newman, who's researched this extensively, and he's discovered that people become less defensive and more willing to take in information that challenges their views when they're humble. Humility allows people to think others could know something they don't know or have experienced something they haven't. Humility allows us to see the humanity in people with different political beliefs. Prideful people often assume that people who disagree with them are stupid or immoral."

"So more humility would reduce polarization."

"Meredith, it would do way more than that. Humility helps peoples' physical health, mental health, and relationships. It fosters spirituality."

"Fine, but that's much easier said than done."

Leo nodded. "Too many people equate humility with weakness or low self-esteem. That's wrong. It takes strength and self-respect to admit mistakes and make amends."

"Okay, so how do we get people to be more humble?"

"So glad you asked." He smiled. "There's an amazing, research-based workbook on how to have more humility. It was developed by folks at VCU and Georgia State. I believe it should be taught at every university, completed by every adult, and discussed at churches and temples."

"What does this magical workbook do—in a nutshell?"

"People do practical exercises to learn humility—not just in their decisions but emotionally as well. They learn humility toward others and then toward themselves, which is the hardest part." Leo wiped perspiration from his brow. "People learn how to think of their achievements and abilities in the big picture, how not to exaggerate the difference between their abilities and those of others. The exercises open people to experiences that value the other person. They cultivate gratitude. People learn how not to pass judgment, because there is more going on than we can possibly know. People examine their limitations and much more."

Meredith rubbed her chin. "I imagine humble people are more intellectually honest and fair."

"You're spot on. And, as you're suggesting, honesty and fairness reduce divisiveness."

"So how will American Bridge reduce polarization?"

"We'll push for progress in promising areas," he said. "Education will be first up."

"Education? There's a battle royal going on."

"There is, but there's also common ground. No one wants human potential to be squandered, with all the suffering and lost productivity. Both sides want every poor child to get a good education."

"Is that even doable?"

"Difficult but doable. We know what works. School choice works. Dr. Kiara Battle—from the Education Summit—is my advisor on this."

"How about the politics?" she asked.

"Attitudes are changing. On this issue voters are becoming less entrenched. In the Florida governor's race, DeSantis beat a charismatic Black candidate, Gillum, because one hundred and fifty thousand African American mothers voted for the school-choice champion." Leo sipped water. "Another positive: School choice doesn't require higher spending, taxes, or cross-subsidization. There's no robbing Peter to pay Paul."

"The teachers' unions oppose choice," Meredith said.

"We feel the obstacles can be overcome, if union concerns about training and other issues are addressed, and if credit is shared. We just need Republicans and Democrats to listen to one another, to stop assuming opponents are stupid or immoral."

"More humility."

"Absolutely."

"Will you run for political office?"

Leo chortled. "Not a chance, Meredith. I know better!"

Afterward, Leo drove to Bar Taco to meet Kiara. Surprisingly, Zeb was there, too. He thanked Zeb again—personally and in front of Kiara—for his life-changing Basque adventure. They feasted on gourmet mini-tacos, Kiara and Zeb imbibing margaritas, while he had a Diet Coke. When it came time for him to leave, Zeb hugged him, and Kiara kissed him on the cheek.

Leo sang most of the way back to Charlotte.

71

LARGER IMPACT

hapel Hill, North Carolina, September 2017. Zeb and Kiara
lingered at Bar Taco, each finally taking an Uber home. Too
pumped to crash, Zeb watched two episodes of *Grantchester*,
wishing his own love life were as animated as that of the British vicar.
He checked his emails one last time. Leo had made good time back to
Charlotte:

> Hey Zeb,
>
> I had a blast with you and Kiara.
>
> One thing I didn't get to say. My previous apology
> for being such a jerk during the entrepreneurship panel
> didn't go far enough. Founding American Bridge has
> given me time to research issues and ponder them. I now
> realize how right you were when you championed ethics
> as the key to business success. I was an ass when I dis-
> missed your point. I was also wrong:

Dishonest selling, as you tried to explain, hurts referrals, repeat business, reviews, public image, and employee morale—all of which reduce profits. They call into question the trustworthiness of financial statements. All these increase the risk to investors, raising the cost of capital and further eroding profits.

Given all this, we might expect operators to deal honestly, if merely out of self-interest. Too often this isn't the case, as you pointed out.

I know you went out of business. But I'm convinced your obsession for improving business ethics had an impact far beyond Chapel Hill. Your crusade invited scrutiny from regulators, across many industries. American business practices will improve, revitalizing our economy and restoring trust in the free market. This will brighten job prospects for millennials and the poor. You may well have prevented a political lurch to the left, staving off draconian reforms that would make our system unrecognizable. Countless Americans will benefit. So hold your head high, my friend!

Honored to know you,

Leo

72

GINI OUT OF THE BOTTLE

harlotte, North Carolina, March 2018. Last week's campaign launch had been a blast, but now, sitting here at NBC studios with Audrey Pinkerton seated across from him, Leo knew things were getting serious and the stakes higher. The butterflies didn't concern him—he'd prepared thoroughly, and this wasn't his first TV rodeo. Audrey couldn't be any tougher than Meredith had been months ago. And if she was, so what? Sarah, his newly appointed policy director, had briefed him on economic and budgetary matters, while Kiara had tutored him on education, his signature issue. Nothing more to do.

Audrey scanned her notes, and, when the producer announced forty-five seconds, Sarah jumped in to adjust his tie and massage his shoulders.

"Good afternoon, thank you for tuning into *Politics Today*. This is Audrey Pinkerton. My guest today is North Carolina gubernatorial candidate Leo Bello. Mr. Bello, welcome." She flashed what looked to be a fake smile.

"Good to be here."

"Six months ago, you spoke with UNC-TV. They interviewed you about American Bridge, the nonprofit you had recently created. It was to be your commitment for years to come. Here's a clip from that conversation."

> Meredith: My last question. Will you run for political office one day?
>
> Leo: Not a chance, Meredith. I know better.

"So I ask you," Audrey said, "was American Bridge just a platform to gain name recognition? How can voters trust what you say?"

"Whoa, I see we're off to the races," Leo said, his eyes widening. "In reality, I never intended to run. I founded American Bridge to find common ground between the two political parties. I wanted to change the tenor of our rhetoric, reduce the spite. AB's work will continue, but the truth is, I'm impatient. I decided to lead by example."

Audrey shook her head. "Then how would you explain your record of abusing women—and men, for that matter?"

Leo recoiled in shock. "What the hell?"

"My sentiments exactly." She checked her notes. "Our investigation revealed that you beat up a gay man in Venezuela, sending him to the hospital. While stationed in Turkey, you harassed a married Muslim woman. And in Florida you were fired for sleeping with the girlfriend of a subordinate."

Leo's breathing quickened. He scanned the set. Several mouths were covered. Sarah was staring at him, blinking rapidly. How in the world had these incidents come to light? Two were overseas; none were on his public record. His stomach tightened—it was Bill Walsh, his confidant.

"Look, Audrey," Leo said, "I'm no saint, but you've cherry-picked the facts. You have ten percent of the story. When I was seventeen, I did beat up a gay man. I later begged his forgiveness and paid off his parents' mortgage, but that stain will stay with me even after I die. And, yes, I did betray a colleague, something I'm deeply ashamed of. But I got counseling and made amends—to the point where my victim intervened to get me rehired by the bank."

"It sounds like you were sanitizing your record so you could run for office."

"Absolutely not."

"That sounds awfully similar to 'not a chance I'll run.'"

Leo sighed. "Audrey, I'm running for a couple reasons. Partly, I want to repay America for giving me a better life. But I also want to atone for my mistakes. Tomorrow I'll release a detailed statement responding to your allegations, and voters can decide." He forced himself to smile. "Will you be asking me any policy questions?"

Audrey grunted. "You portray yourself as a bleeding-heart conservative who cares about social justice. How does this square with your support for free-market capitalism?"

"Now that's a fair question," he said, nodding. "It goes back to my experience in Venezuela. Venezuela once had a large middle class along with, of course, some rich and poor folks. Chavez came along, vowing to equalize things. His intentions may or may not have been noble—who knows—but the middle class shrunk, while the number of poor skyrocketed. And in Venezuela the poor truly suffer." Leo sipped water. "To me, a compassionate system regularly takes care of the bottom twenty percent, raising their standard of living. To others, though, it means reducing the income gap between rich and poor. That's a huge distinction."

"Why?" Audrey asked.

He tried not to sound professorial, but it was hard. "Evidence shows that these objectives are mutually exclusive. Policies that consistently raise the income of the poorest also tend to increase the income gap between rich and poor. And policies that consistently reduce the income gap tend to lower the standard of living of the poor."

"That makes no sense," she huffed.

Leo chuckled. "Everything I say is backed by OECD data—hardly a conservative bastion."

"You're referring to the Organisation for Economic Co-operation and Development?"

"Yes. I'll get to the data but let me explain first. A worker's income is tied to his productivity. Productivity, in turn, depends on investment. For example, a worker using a new plant, equipment, or computer is more productive than one saddled with old tools. Meanwhile business owners and financial investors invest more when their rate of return goes up, which happens when capital-gains taxes and corporate income tax rates drop. Workers do better when investors do."

"Ah, the old trickle-down economics."

"Don't laugh," Leo said. "I saw it firsthand in Venezuela. As you know, the oil industry dominates there and is capital intensive. When Chavez expropriated Exxon's and Conoco's assets in 2007 and failed to reinvest enough, oil production plummeted fifty percent. Some of it was the loss of technical expertise, but inadequate investment was key. Workers got laid off, and wages went down."

"Okay, so assuming enough investment, workers will earn more, but business owners will make even more. Why is that?"

"One reason is that owners risk more. If they profit, they pay a big chunk to Uncle Sam; when they lose, they bear the losses alone. But I'll give you a better answer."

"I'd appreciate that."

Leo explained how, compared with other models, America's free-market system delivered both higher inequality *and* higher living standards for the poor. American investors and business owners earned high risk-adjusted returns for a number of reasons. The U.S. domestic market was the largest in the world. American businesses could hire and fire with ease—not the case in other countries. American entrepreneurs could form new ventures quickly with few bureaucratic hurdles. Capital gains and corporate income tax rates were lower, although that was changing. The Federal Reserve's massive quantitative easing boosted returns to investors.

"Fine, so the fat cats are doing well," Audrey said. "How about American workers?"

"Great question. Let's look at OECD numbers—their 2020 Better Life Index." He glanced at his note card. "Sweden is seen as a worker's paradise, but their household disposable income per capita is $31,000. In America, it's $45,000—forty-five percent higher. Sweden's household net wealth is $300,000, less than half of America's $632,000."

"What about Germany and Japan?"

Leo smiled. "German income is $34,000, thirty-two percent lower than America's. Their net wealth is $260,000, only forty-one percent of America's. As for Japan, the numbers are $30,000 and $306,000—not even close."

"Averages hide a lot," she said.

"Not that much. I assume you mean inequality. Let's look at Gini coefficients."

"Gini?"

"Sorry," Leo said. "This does get a bit technical, but you and your audience will easily grasp it. A Gini of 1.0 represents maximum inequality—that is, one person owns all the income. A Gini of zero means everyone earns the same income. But, of course, everything depends on the integrity of the data that is used to calculate the Gini."

"And?"

"Well, most calculations of America's Gini don't factor in $1.9 *trillion* in annual redistributions to poorer Americans. Why not? Because the Census Bureau doesn't count them as income. That's *two-thirds* of all transfer payments, including Medicare, Medicaid, food stamps, earned-income tax credits, and over ninety other government payments." Leo shook his head, the truth still hard to believe. "Keep in mind, the poorest twenty percent of Americans get eighty-four percent of their disposable income from government transfers; the next poorest fifth receive fifty-eight percent."

"*If* that's true, it's significant," she said.

"It is true. And what's more, the Census Bureau doesn't even report household income *after* the amounts paid in taxes. An accurate Gini would look at income after all transfer payments *and* tax payments. Makes a difference, because the top forty percent of American earners pay eighty-two percent of all taxes."

Audrey frowned. "I'm not sure I buy your numbers."

"They're not mine. One of the authors of the analysis served as assistant commissioner at the Bureau of Labor Statistics—twice."

"So bottom line?"

"If you factor in all the transfer payments to the poor and all of the taxes paid, inequality in America has grown by two percent, not twenty-one percent, over the past fifty years."

"What about the Gini?"

Leo nodded. "The U.S. Gini would be 0.336—not 0.48—if it was calculated with all the transfer payments and taxes paid. France's Gini is 0.30, Germany's 0.29. If you ask me, slightly more inequality in return for thirty-two percent higher per capita income and two hundred and fifty percent the net wealth per capita is a good trade-off."

Audrey turned to education, questioning Leo's priorities. She noted that only a minority of North Carolinians supported vouchers and educational savings accounts, whereas a majority felt school funding was too low. Leo pointed out that the approval and disapproval percentages reversed themselves when respondents were given the details of the programs and funding levels. Moreover, five of six studies found that teacher salaries increased at public schools under school choice; the sixth showed no effect.

Audrey moved on to other issues, portraying Leo as a doctrinaire conservative. He pushed back with some success on immigration, but, walking off the set, Leo knew he'd been hammered. Sarah's long embrace said it all. Carolinians wouldn't take kindly to stories of philandering. His policy messages had been drowned out, and they'd have to go into damage-control mode.

And on top of that, he'd lost a mentor. Bill Walsh could go to hell.

The coming weeks brought cheer, as the press release squelched the allegations and ABC reported that Leo had volunteered at LifeNet4Families, donating heaps of groceries and tutoring homeless men.

A dozen Pikas hosted "Meet Leo" events in their hometowns and urged him to "trust in the brothers!" At the reception they touted his military service, smarts, and character. Leo was warmly received. It touched him to see so many taking time off work to chip in.

But, in the end, Leo lost in the primary, his free-market beliefs dooming him with liberals, his womanizing and pro-immigration stance alienating conservatives. A disgruntled Texan—his onetime benefactor—had played kingmaker in North Carolina. The only positive: Exit polls showed bipartisan support for choice. They'd all been schooled.

73

BRIGHT STARS

hapel Hill, North Carolina, August 2018. Zeb opened the front door and almost spit out his bagel. The sonofabitch stood there, rubbing the back of his neck. *What is this guy thinking?*

"I'm sorry to drop in," Zeb's former statistics professor said, "but I didn't think you'd agree to see me."

"The odds would have been long, that's for sure."

The professor puckered his lips. "It looks like you're heading out, so I'll be brief."

"I'll give you two minutes."

The professor nodded. "I run a biostatistics firm in the Triangle. I founded it after I stopped teaching, and, fortunately, we're doing well. We've got this managerial track position available on the development side. I'd like to offer you—"

Zeb blinked. "What?"

"We're looking for a smart, hardworking person who—"

"No, thanks." Zeb pushed past the man.

"I just thought—"

"Nope, I'm all set."

"I see," the professor said, looking crestfallen, on the verge of tears. "I can't tell you how sorry I am—to you and the others."

Zeb sighed. "Look, I get it. Your son was sinking fast and needed attention—"

"Which I didn't provide."

"You're doing better with your wife."

"That's kind of you, but I had no right to . . ." The tears flowed, the professor wiping them with the back of his hand. "I just wish there was something I could do to make up for it."

Zeb stroked his chin. "Actually, there might be."

One day later Teresa stood at the edge of the stage as Mayor Hemminger addressed the convocation. Jim and Wylie sat on the front row, alongside Zeb and Kiara, with parents and students occupying the remaining seats. Not surprisingly, Wylie was shrinking into his. What kid wanted their mom to emcee a school event? Kiara's eyes sparkled. Zeb was smiling.

Teresa felt tranquil and excited. Gone was the anxiety of the last decade, displaced by newfound job security. The prospect of showcasing her full potential gave her goose bumps. Best of all, she'd get to do it with Zeb. If she'd been something of an adoring Labrador, well, at least Zeb had earned her love and allegiance. Just as Jim had. Just as she had earned theirs.

Chapel Hill's magic was no longer beyond her grasp. No more being haunted by what might have been. She'd taken a roundabout path, but Blue Heaven was hers to cherish again. She would revel in its splendor, no longer hemmed in by personal failings or the tribulations of International Expeditions.

Teresa took the microphone. "Thank you, Madam Mayor. Please, everyone, give the mayor a hand. Her support was instrumental." As the applause died away, she exhaled deeply. "My name is Teresa Ball. I manage Bright Stars, and on behalf of the institute, I welcome you to our first assembly. I'm truly honored to be here. To our students, let me just say, we can't wait to work with you. You guys are wonderful. My son, Wylie"—she pointed to him—"is part of the incoming class, and he looks forward to making new friends." Wylie was practically on the floor.

"Let me introduce our professionals. Zeb Ackerman—please stand—is one of Bright Stars' cofounders. He'll be tutoring your children according to their individual learning style. Zeb is one year away from completing his master's in education from UNC, where he also received his bachelor's in history. He has eight years of teaching experience."

She pointed to Kiara. "Next is Dr. Kiara Battle, the other cofounder of Bright Stars and a part-time senior advisor to the U.S. Secretary of Education. A psychologist by training, Kiara will assess each student's learning style. She'll also teach study skills, time management, and customized learning strategies. Zeb and Kiara wanted me to mention they both learn differently themselves and can't wait to help you. Assisting them will be volunteer students from UNC."

Teresa waited for the cheers to subside. "Hannah Fletcher is our volunteer physical therapist. She's weeks away from receiving a second degree—this one in occupational therapy. She'll help students with fine motor skills, gross motor skills, and sensory integration.

"Last but not least is Dr. Miles Graham, a former professor of statistics at UNC. He'll be tutoring students in math, after he completes his training in differentiated teaching. We're lucky to have him." More cheers.

"Leo Bello couldn't be here today, but, as our lead philanthropist, he deserves special mention. His donations have matched the state's dollar for dollar!" Boisterous applause.

Teresa smiled. "Remember, we aren't a substitute for your child's primary school. But we'll supplement, reinforce, and fill in the gaps. We're always interested in your feedback . . ."

Wylie hugged his mom, after the invitees had left. "You did great. Thanks for not embarrassing me too much."

"Didn't know I could do more than laundry," Teresa said, winking.

Zeb nudged Wylie. "There's a *lot* your mom is good at—like telling me what to do."

"And heating up frozen dinners," Jim said, snickering. "No, seriously, honey, you're truly a bright star."

Kiara raised her Sprite. "To the person holding this whole thing together!"

"Hear, hear!" the table yelled.

"And to our students!" Kiara said. "For keeping us employed and sane, even if they drive us crazy."

"Hear, hear!"

"Now that we're all toasted out," Kiara said, "I'm off to kick someone's butt in pickleball—with the permission of Czarina?"

Teresa beamed. "Absolutely, my sweet educator!"

74

TRUTH

San Antonio, Texas, August 2018. Leo followed the receptionist into Bill Walsh's swanky office. The attorney was at his desk, huddled with a flunky. They hushed when Leo appeared.

"Look what the cat dragged in—another bad penny," Bill bellowed.

Leo forced himself to smile. "Gotta love that warm Texas welcome."

"Is that any way to suck up?"

Bill was playing hardball, something he'd previously reserved for others. "You used to value truth above sucking up."

"I know the truth," Bill said, frowning.

"Not about what I'm thinking."

"What's the mystery? You're bleeding . . . pissed off."

"It's not that simple, my friend."

Bill leaned back and threw his feet on the desk. "Then enlighten me."

"Simple. The election fiasco I deserved. You blackballing Clara? No one deserves that."

The Texan chortled. "How do you figure that? Sounds like you didn't learn your lesson."

"There was no way I would have leaked information about the REK Cruise Lines merger."

"Why, because I'm a man of the law? Because you are?" Bill motioned to the lackey, who frisked Leo, obviously searching for a wire.

"Come on, Bill. Give me some credit."

"Funny, that's what *I* was wanting."

It was a fair point. Bill was neither saint nor devil. In Canaima he'd set the bar sky-high, a virtual Mother Teresa. But if Bill's generosity had been overestimated, whose fault was that? Was it unreasonable for a mentor to expect reciprocity? Not if he'd been neglected as a child—as Bill had been—and placed a premium on loyalty. "You've got a point," Leo said.

"Leo, without me, your ass would be twenty-five pounds lighter. Or you'd be lying in a mass grave. Ever think of that?"

"All the time. That's one reason why I couldn't give you insider information. I'd have been deported."

Bill snorted. "You'd never have been caught."

"Plus, it's wrong. That shit—everyone taking shortcuts—is what ruined Venezuela. Before you know it, you live in a shit hole."

"Says the saint who molests women and beats up gays."

Leo looked down. "I should've done better."

"You don't say."

"The truth is, with Clara's immigration, I just wasn't thinking. Which I agree is the point. Remembering what you do was the least I could have done."

"Is that it?"

"I also should've shown you the venture-capital deals I came across," Leo said. "You might have passed, but you deserved a look. I dropped the ball there, too."

"Damn right."

Leo removed a folder from his briefcase and handed it to Bill. "Here's the latest VC deal I'm looking at. It's promising. Now, please help with Clara."

75

WE'LL HAVE TO SEE

arrboro, North Carolina, August 2018. Carrboro had always been granola central—even kookier than Chapel Hill—so Kiara wasn't surprised when she and Sarah walked into the Really Really Free Market and were greeted by a Carnival Against Capitalism banner. It was hard not to cackle, but her amusement annoyed her—her armistice with Sarah didn't require cheerfulness.

Kiara followed her friend around the market, collecting pamphlets on binary gender expression, normalized work ethics, and other assorted evils. From the prevalence of unwashed patrons, Kiara figured there was a widely observed leaflet on sustainable personal hygiene. Sarah pointed to a cluster of sharers arrayed under a sign saying, "Liberate yourself from domination and conflict." Conflict indeed. Sarah obviously hoped the hilarity would dissipate the tension.

"I'm so sorry," Sarah said. "I haven't been able to sleep."

"You think I have?"

"I'm not sure what to say."

Kiara rolled her eyes. "Whatever. Blame it on the campaign."

"It wouldn't be true."

They ambled past an arepa stand, stopping in front of piles of clothes, books, and DVDs. Kiara rummaged through a bag of costumes.

"There's nothing there—not on Leo's end, anyway," Sarah continued. "If that's any consolation."

"It isn't," Kiara said crossly. "I hope the sex was worth it."

"I wouldn't know."

"You just apologized!"

"Oh, I tried," Sarah said. "But he's in love with some Venezuelan girl."

Kiara dropped the pirate hat. Clara wasn't news, but hearing the truth spoken so plainly, and having your best friend betray you . . .

Sarah retrieved the hat and placed it in the bin.

"How could you?" Kiara's face was wrinkled in disgust.

"I don't know," Sarah said dolefully. "No excuse."

They strolled along the last row of stands.

"Will you be moving to D.C?" Sarah asked with a hopeful air. "You've got a kick-ass job, senior aide to the Secretary of Education."

"That's only part-time. And remote. I'll never abandon Bright Stars."

"I guess we won't be roomies."

"Nope."

"Hey, we'll always have Polynesia," Sarah said hopefully.

"I don't know. We'll have to see."

76

AGAIN

hapel Hill, North Carolina, September 2018. Rabbi stood smiling on the *bima*, flanked by Zeb and Hannah. His tranquility permeated the sanctuary, overcoming the tension typical of such occasions. But Kiara detected mischievousness in those twinkling eyes.

"And will you, Zebulon Vance Ackerman, take Hannah Lane Fletcher—*again*—to be your lawfully wedded wife, in sickness and in health, for richer or poorer, for better or worse, as long as you both shall live?"

Zeb beamed. "I will."

Rabbi eyeballed the groom, saying with exaggerated sternness, "Don't screw it up this time!"

Zeb shook his head, earning himself a pat on the back. Hannah burst out laughing, as did most of the attendees.

Two hours later Rabbi Norman stepped to the microphone and raised his champagne glass. Up to that point he'd maintained a low profile, not wanting to hamper the celebration. "Zeb, just last week I learned you were named after Zebulon Vance. For the younger ones here tonight, Vance was North Carolina's most renowned statesman, a two-time governor and three-time senator during the Civil War and Reconstruction period. Now, when you were born, Zeb, the late senator was still widely admired for his nobility and achievements. For me personally, as a rabbi living in the South a century later, it meant the world to me that Vance had supported the Jewish people at a time when anti-Semitism was rampant. His speech 'The Scattered Nation' pleaded for religious tolerance. He actually went overboard, claiming the Jews were the most remarkable people of this world, past or present. Vance gave the speech hundreds of times, in every major city in America, over a period of twenty years, until he died. It was an astonishing act of compassion."

Rabbi laid his hand on Zeb's shoulder. "Of course, we know that Vance had a dark side as well. He was too much a man of his times when it came to African Americans, for whom he had no compassion whatsoever. But *you*, Zeb, have always been ahead of your time. You've been compassionate with everyone, a mensch among mensches. You've more than lived up to your name." He gave Zeb a congratulatory pat. "Remember, though, to save more of that goodness for your incredible wife. May you continue to shine, bringing light to our community, and may Bright Stars thrive under your leadership." Rabbi turned to the bride and began, "As for you, my angel." He proceeded to extoll Hannah's loving-kindness, smarts, willingness to forgive, and spunk. He concluded, "You may not be Jewish yourself, but no one is better equipped to keep Zeb on track, Jewishly. May God bless the both of you."

"Next, we call Teresa," the master of ceremony said.

Teresa took the microphone. "Wow, I couldn't be happier for the two of you. Zeb, I just want to say that having been in the trenches with you all these years, I've seen every side of you—from up close. Yes, there are warts, but, like the rabbi said, you ooze character. One incident comes to mind. When it looked like we were about to go bankrupt, I begged you to stop being overly honest with clients and to take better advantage of our selling opportunities. You got mad at me. You said complete honesty was the *only* way to run a business, and that anything else was cheating. That's you, Zeb, in a nutshell."

Teresa tried to swallow the lump in her throat. "My biggest regret is jumping ship before we could prove that uncompromising honesty can drive success. We would have kicked butt if I had just stayed on and kept the back office in order. Bright Stars will be huge, and so worthwhile, but it still hurts.

"It was an honor working with you in travel. You helped me grow"—her voice cracked—"and I'll always love you for it." Teresa exhaled deeply. "But remember, at Bright Stars there's a new sheriff in town—me. If you want a better outcome than last time, you better listen up!"

Kiara stepped up. "Zeb, you know public speaking isn't my thing, but I'm making an exception. Just do me a favor: Don't have a *third* wedding, okay? No, in all seriousness, you changed my life for the better on a number of occasions. Two stand out. First"—she grinned—"when you told me that my math tutoring sucked and that I hadn't taught you in a way that matched how you learned. That piqued my interest, and I ended up quitting medicine for psychology. The second time was after I lost my counseling license. You asked me to join Bright Stars. To this day, you're the one friend who's always been true." She nodded. "Yes, you can be annoying as hell—Lord knows how Hannah puts up with you—but I know, beyond the shadow of a doubt, you'll be with me to the end. Knowing that brings me comfort."

Kiara faced the bride. "And, Hannah: None of this would've happened without you—and I don't just mean the wedding. You got Zeb to understand that getting his PhD in history, or killing it in business, wasn't the be-all and end-all of his life, and that Bright Stars was where his heart was at—the highest and best use of his soul. You bailed Zeb out the way he bailed me out. And now we'll all be helping special-needs kids meet their potential! Bless you for your monumental patience. Finally, Larry and Ruth, I know you did your best with Zeb, but he's still a handful. So, please, keep supporting Hannah so she stays sane." She raised her champagne glass. "To Hannah and Zeb!"

The music commenced, and, right on cue, Zeb led Hannah to the center of the dance floor, where they performed a tango routine that drew wild applause. Teresa grabbed the microphone to read a note from Jackson Duvall's business manager, Moonshine Smith. She relayed Duvall's congratulations to the married couple and his gratitude for Zeb's creation, Fast-Forward Adventures, which his people had reconstituted to good effect. Bright Stars would receive, in perpetuity, 10 percent of Fast-Forward Adventures' profits. Boisterous cheering gave way to "Super Freak," which lured partiers to the dance floor.

Leo once again established his singular lack of rhythm on the dance floor, and Kiara didn't bother suppressing her laughter. Leo was seemingly oblivious, his inhibitions dispelled by the rum and Cokes. When a slow song began, they retired to the table.

"Well, that's one way for Clara to get some comic relief," Kiara said.

"You're a cruel, cruel woman." Leo grinned.

"When does she arrive?"

"Bill says her visa should be approved within weeks."

"Awesome," Kiara said. "I'm glad you patched things up with him."

"Me, too."

"What are your plans, workwise?"

"I'm still with the bank, but I'll be investing in two training academies for aviation mechanics. One in Raleigh, another in Charlotte." Leo smiled. "One day I hope we can attract grads from Bright Stars."

"From your lips to God's ears."

"Oh, you're back to believing?"

Kiara cocked her head. "Considering is more like it. But don't change the subject. Will you ever run for office again?"

"Hey, I'm still licking my wounds!" Leo said, chuckling. "I don't know. I just want to make myself useful."

Dean Acosta, seated at the same table, leaned forward. "You've made yourself very useful. We're grateful for your gift to the Learning Assistance Center."

"You're very welcome, Dean. It doesn't come close to repaying what you and UNC did for me. Bob, why are you smirking?"

"I was trying to fathom how Santa Claus saw fit to prioritize special needs and technical schools over women's soccer. No, seriously, if you do run again, I'd love to help out. I don't usually get involved in politics, but you're a badly needed tonic."

"Thanks, my friend. I'm not there yet, but I appreciate it."

Leo turned toward Kiara so they could converse privately. "So what've you been up to?"

"Things have been crazy—good crazy. Bright Stars is what I was meant to be doing all along. But I'm also working part-time with the Secretary of Education to promote school choice. And this summer, Sarah and I will be heading to Papua New Guinea."

"PNG?"

Kiara sighed. "You remember I worked there with a tiny women's advocacy agency twenty years ago. Well, the founder of it, Alice, was murdered about a decade ago by a bigamist husband. The woman who took over is a former patient I met, Charlize. She needs help. Sarah is joining me as penance."

"Damn, that's unbelievable. Well, if you need reinforcements, let me know. Clara and I will be in Pamplona."

Zeb and Jim walked by. Kiara excused herself and caught up with the groom. "How're you holding up?" she said.

"Fantastic!" Zeb said, clearly buzzed. "It's easier the second time round."

"You and Jim have a nice chat?"

Zeb shook his head. "You're unbelievable."

"Well?"

"He thanked me—for helping him and Teresa stay together."

Kiara nodded. "Remember, you now need to keep your *own* house in order. I'm here if you need me." She kissed Zeb on the cheek and went in search of a dance partner with more rhythm than Leo.

77

HURTLING TURTLES

*E*merald Isle, North Carolina, September 2018. "Not so bad now, is it?" Hannah said, pausing the DVR.

Zeb glanced outside at the sundeck. "It's still pouring."

"I meant hanging out, watching flicks." She lifted her bare feet onto his lap, in anticipation of a massage.

Zeb chuckled. Two days into their getaway, they had yet to venture from the beach house. Hopefully, their "true" honeymoon would see better weather. "I feel like Siskel and Ebert. And *The Book Thief* isn't my idea of light viewing."

"Not to worry. Gotcha covered." She jiggled her foot to initiate the rubbing. "The next one will be a big thumbs-up."

He served himself seconds of General Tso's chicken as she pulled up *Blazing Saddles* on the flat screen.

"I told you," Hannah said.

"Works for me." Her taste was nothing if not eclectic.

Zeb devoured the take-out and, having seen the movie three times, snored through most of it. Sometime later, he was jostled awake. "What?"

"Sit up!"

Hannah had paused the film. She hit resume once he had focused.

The Gene Wilder character spoke, "Mongo, why would Hedley Lamarr care about where the choo-choo goes?"

The so-called half-wit said, "Don't know. Mongo only pawn in game of life."

Zeb smiled, recalling his visit to Key West's Chart Room years ago: the model clipper ship, the chessboard, fiddling with the pawn, and identifying with Mongo and a newborn sea turtle. Hannah had remembered him talking about it. But this had the potential of turning sour because she had never approved of self-denigration.

Hannah flipped off the TV and popped up from the sofa. "What do you say we go outside and bury this sucker?"

"Bury what?"

"Mongo!" she said, pulling a white pawn from her pocket. "Come on, it stopped raining!"

"What in the world are you talking about?" But he knew.

Hannah dashed outside, and he had little choice but to follow. She dropped to the sand and started digging. "Aren't you going to help?"

"This is ridiculous."

Hannah dumped the pawn into the makeshift grave, throwing sand over it. "There. Dead and buried. You're never going to mention Mongo again. No matter what goes wrong."

"What, no 'Taps' on your cell?"

"Don't think I won't."

He kissed her. "You're looney."

"If we weren't all crazy, we'd all go insane."

Nothing like having Buffett lyrics thrown back at him. Zeb took her hand, as they strolled to a dune and plopped in the sand. Waves rolled toward them and only them. A windsurfer zipped past, a momentary intruder. A tranquil feeling enveloped Zeb, and for the first time in so long, he wasn't thinking of what came next.

"Come on," Hannah urged. "Over here!"

Sea turtles were hatching and scrambling to escape their nest. Some hurtled toward the water; others stumbled, their front legs flailing like a faltering rotor blade. At first slow and uncoordinated, the hatchlings gained speed and their sense of direction. They seemed unstoppable upon reaching the ocean, paddling away unimpeded, disappearing from sight.

"Just like you," Hannah said. "The ones in the water, I mean."

"You can't even see them."

"I see the one I care about most."

"Things are going swimmingly?"

She punched him in the arm. "You know, Three would be proud of you."

"You think so?"

"How couldn't he be?"

Zeb gave her a funny look.

"Think about it," she said. "You climbed out of a deep hole. You hurtled, directionless for a while, and then got on track. You lugged your load—your disability and uncompromising honesty—quite a ways. But you stuck your neck out and persevered, until your burden became an asset."

"Did I make it?"

"You know you did. Like Three, you won."

"How's that?" he asked.

"You married me—twice."

"Beats getting gobbled up by a shark."

A sunset wouldn't do—not on an allegorical day—so Hannah whisked him off the beach for an evening of film and passion. Ten hours later they were back on the sand, spooning under blankets. "A beautiful bright star," she murmured as the ball rose over the horizon. *Indeed, you are,* Zeb thought. *And the youngsters, too.*

ACKNOWLEDGMENTS

Burying the Pawn is fiction, but it was inspired by real-life people and events.

First among them are my now-adult children, Nick and Isabelle, whose resilience, courage, and, yes, intelligence in dealing with their learning challenges was so instructive. My wife and I were often moved by the relentless way they pursued their ambitions in the face of repeated setbacks. They never stopped dreaming. But they also received lots of help. My fervent hope is that *all* youths who learn differently will receive the support they need. This is much more likely to happen, I feel, with widespread adoption of school choice and educational savings accounts.

I am endlessly grateful to my wife, Maria, for providing sage advice and encouragement as I plodded along, turtle-like, on this project. Without her heavy lifting on all fronts, I would never have finished. She truly is an angel.

I'm deeply thankful to my mom and dad for offering unwavering love and support and for cultivating my interest in all things foreign: geography, art, music, television dramas, food, and adventure. Their passions permeate the novel.

I am also hugely indebted to former governor Mike Huckabee for believing in my project and for providing crucial support. (Is there a nicer public figure anywhere?) Rabbi Norman Lipson is the reason I returned to the fold, albeit imperfectly. His Torah studies and friendship have enriched my life immeasurably and provided exciting content for my novel.

I could not have been more fortunate than to work with the supremely talented, fun professionals at Greenleaf Book Group: editors Rebecca Logan, Joan Tapper, Amanda Hughes, and Diana Coe; Leah Pierre; Madelyn Myers; Chase Quarterman; and Tiffany Barrientos.

Few things in life matter more to me than the University of North Carolina at Chapel Hill, which does as much as any American university to level the playing field for the disadvantaged. I'm so grateful to the following members of the Carolina community: Daniel Lebold, Dr. Kimberly Abels, the brothers of Pi Kappa Alpha fraternity, Bill Palladino, Wendy Gebauer Palladino, Damon Nahas, Tom Sander, Alessia Russo, Annie Kingman, Julia Ashley, and others who prefer to remain anonymous.

The folks at EdChoice want every child in America to have a good education. Their research is a national treasure on which I relied greatly. Many thanks go to Robert Enlow, Paul Diperna, Mike McShane, and John Kristof.

My brother, Jeff, provided tons of insightful feedback and perspective when I needed it most. He always comes through—in every aspect of my life. Please consider supporting his impressive cancer research organization, Adenoid Cystic Carcinoma Research Foundation (ACCRF.org).

Many thanks go to Aunt Joan, the first person to read the novel and provide discerning feedback. The world would be a much better place if more people learned to *truly* listen to others as she does.

Dr. Monica Dowling provided invaluable help to my children—and to me during the research phase. I am also very grateful to Luis Paz, Brian Harris, and Marcus and Jillian Babb for their creative input.

Nature Expeditions International, Inc., was an extremely rewarding part of my life for eighteen years, and the experience provided grist for the novel. A big hug to Michelle Ostrander, Heidi Perez, Sarah-Jane Laubscher, Helene Glick Landman, Erica Zarchin, and Darren Carboni. Thanks also go to the thousands of loyal NEI clients.

I owe much to Mark Kurlansky, UCLA professor Jared Diamond, and the late Eli Evans, whose books provided bountiful material for my novel. (See the Additional Reading section.)

A special mention goes to Lindsay McCleod and Chris Shearer for their insightful bird's-eye feedback, which greatly improved the book.

Many, many thanks go to the Weston, Florida, librarians: Mary Stephens, Karen Gelover, Connie, Franklin, Bethany, and Sonia.

ADDITIONAL READING

Bridges, Tyler. "Caracas Is as Dangerous for the Dead as It Is for the Living." *McClatchy DC*, May 21, 2009. https://www.mcclatchydc.com/news/nation-world/world/article24539431.html.

Calomiris, Charles W. "'The Myth of American Inequality' Review: Believe Your Eyes, Not the Statistics." *Wall Street Journal*, December 26, 2022. https://www.wsj.com/articles/the-myth-of-american-inequality-review-believe-your-eyes-not-the-statistics-11672095284.

EdChoice. "EdChoice Study Guide: A Review of the Research on Private School Choice." April 2022. https://www.edchoice.org/wp-content/uploads/2022/04/EdChoice-Study-Guide-1.pdf.

Evans, Eli N. *The Provincials: A Personal History of Jews in the South.* Chapel Hill, NC: University of North Carolina Press, 2005.

Kurlansky, Mark. *The Basque History of the World.* New York: Penguin Random House, 2001.

Lavelock, Caroline R., Everett L. Worthington Jr., and Don E. Davis. "The Path to Humility: Six Practical Sections for Becoming a More Humble Person." 2013. https://static1.squarespace.com/

static/518a85e9e4b04323507813b/t/533c6c0de4b047d0e06ba2
68/1396468749812/the-path-to-humility-six-practical-sections
-for-becoming-a-more-humble-person.pdf.

Lueken, Martin. "Fiscal Effects of School Choice: Analyzing
the Costs and Savings of Private School Choice Programs in
America." EdChoice, November 2021. https://www.edchoice.org/
research-library/?report=fiscal-effects-of-school-choice#report.

Lueken, Martin, and William Hughes. "School Choice Research Is Not
a Rorschach Test." *Engage*, October 31, 2019. https://www.edchoice
.org/engage/school-choice-research-not-rorschach-test/.

Organisation for Economic Co-operation and Development
(OECD). "How's Life? 2020." March 2020. https://www.oecd.org/
wise/how-s-life-23089679.htm.

Peterson, Paul E. "Government Should Subsidize, Not Tax, Marriage."
Education Next 15, no. 2 (January 2015). https://www.education
next.org/government-subsidize-not-tax-marriage/.

Vyas, Kejal. "Rationed Bullets, Worthless Money: Tough Times for
Venezuelan Thugs." *Wall Street Journal*, March 15, 2019. https://
www.wsj.com/articles/in-venezuela-some-crime-no-longer-pays
-11552642201.

READING
GROUP GUIDE

1. In the novel, many important things are measured by the "wrong yardstick." As students, Zeb and Kiara's aptitudes are grossly underestimated because they learn differently from their classmates. As young adults, Leo and Zeb's metrics for a successful life evolve greatly from what they had been earlier. As prominent professionals, Kiara and Leo must learn not to overestimate themselves and underestimate others. Having read about their experiences, why do you think it matters to have an appropriate yardstick?

2. What drives each of the three protagonists—Zeb, Leo, and Kiara? What obstacles stand in the way of them achieving what they want? Are their toughest battles internal or external in nature?

3. As Black and Hispanic immigrants to America, what obstacles did Marcus and Leo overcome?

4. How do Marcus and Leo view America? What do you think Americans born in the United States can learn from their perspectives?

5. As a learning-disabled Jew growing up in the South during the seventies and eighties, Zeb never felt comfortable in his own skin. As a young adult, he learns to embrace his heritage, though he still feels out of place at traditional religious services and cannot relate to Torah- or Bible-thumpers. Why does Zeb come to cherish Torah study?

6. Many people with learning disabilities or mental-health challenges have powerful strengths that can more than offset any weaknesses. What special traits and abilities did you observe in Zeb, Kiara, and Leo?

7. When Zeb gets expelled from UNC, his long-held dreams are dashed, and he goes into adventure travel. How does Zeb try to make his work meaningful? Do you think Zeb's quixotic ideas and unorthodox practices are compatible with profitability? Why or why not?

8. After watching the turtle race (Chapter 28), Zeb adopts the winning turtle, Three, as a mascot. What qualities does Zeb admire about Three?

9. In a down moment (Chapter 28), Zeb compares himself to Mongo from *Blazing Saddles*. Why do you think he sometimes feels connected to this character? Does the association affect Zeb positively or negatively? What stories do you tell yourself about how you move through life, and how do those stories affect your goals and aspirations?

10. How might the concepts of destiny and free will figure into the book's title, *Burying the Pawn*?

11. Despite their childhood insecurities, Zeb, Leo, and Kiara occasionally display a lack of humility as adults. How does this

behavior get them into trouble? What do you think makes it possible for them to change?

12. According to Leo, how would Americans—individually and collectively—benefit if humility were more widespread? Do you agree with him? What practical tool does Leo recommend for making this a reality?

13. Kiara explains to Zeb how school-choice programs—particularly those offering educational savings accounts—would benefit special-needs and other disadvantaged students, saying "education savings accounts are often part of school-choice programs. Parents can withdraw their special-needs kid from the public school and have public money deposited into a savings account. That money can be spent on customized learning services," like "specialized therapies, specialized private tutoring, online learning programs, community college." Do you think special-needs families deserve these benefits? Why or why not?

14. In Chapter 70, Leo explains that in Florida, more than 150,000 African American women voted in favor of the school-choice candidate. Do you think expanding educational opportunity has once again become a key civil rights issue? Why or why not?

15. How much of where the protagonists ended up in life was determined by their abilities and disabilities? Luck? Attitude? Obstacles? America's system?

16. In Chapter 72, Leo maintains that, compared with other models, America's free-market system delivered both higher inequality and higher living standards for the poor. He also maintains that America's slightly higher inequality (e.g.,

adjusted Gini coefficient of 0.34 versus 0.29 for Germany) is, in his opinion, offset by America's 32 percent higher income per capita and by the fact that America's net wealth per capita is 250 percent that of Germany. Similar statistical comparisons are made for Japan and Sweden. Do you agree with Leo's conclusions? Why or why not?

ABOUT THE AUTHOR

 **JONATHAN KAUFMAN** is a pickleball- and tango-loving writer whose debut novel, *Burying the Pawn*, reflects his passion for adventure travel and special education. The son of an American diplomat and a Spanish-born artist, Jonathan received his BA in economics and political science and an MBA from the University of North Carolina–Chapel Hill. He ran his own adventure tour company, Nature Expeditions International, Inc., for eighteen years after working as a White House Budget Office economist and corporate banker.

Jonathan married a Venezuelan-born interior designer, Maria, and nothing has mattered more to them than raising their two children with learning disabilities. Jonathan has become an expert on education reform. He divides his time between South Florida and Chapel Hill, and—wherever he happens to be—roots fanatically for the UNC Tar Heels. Read more about him at www.JonathanKaufmanWriter.com.

Made in the USA
Middletown, DE
19 September 2023

38783762R00255